KATIE
MULHOLLAND
VOLUME I

CATHERINE COOKSON

ACKNOWLEDGEMENTS

I would like to offer my grateful thanks to my husband who first suggested that I should write a story with Palmer's shipyard for a background. And to Mr Adrian Palmer, who answered my request for information on his family background by spontaneously lending me books and giving me an unbiased opinion of his great-grandfather, Sir Charles Mark Palmer, who was the founder of Palmer's shipyard in Jarrow.

And to Mr RG Wilson who spent many hours in many northern libraries delving for information covering the past hundred years in the North, and who transferred this information to me in so clear and so precise a manner.

Also to Miss Millie Petersen, who so unselfishly offered for my use material she had gathered over a number of years, together with cuttings and photographs passed on to her by her uncle, one-time photographer on the *Shields Daily Gazette*.

And lastly, but by no means least, to my secretary, Mrs Muriel Johnson, for her hard work and unceasing efforts on my behalf.

However, I must explain that the story, as all my stories are wont to do, decided which line it intended to take, and from the beginning it dictated that this was to be the story of a woman's life, and the shipyard and the mines and the two towns but a backcloth for that theme. Yet without all the information so kindly gathered for me by the aforementioned I could not have written the life of Katie Mulholland.

CATHERINE COOKSON
Loreto, Hastings, March 1966.

CONTENTS

BOOK ONE
KATIE, 1860
page 7

BOOK TWO
ANDRÉE, 1865
page 141

BOOK ONE

KATIE, 1860

CHAPTER ONE

'I DON'T LIKE marriage, Mama.'

'You don't know what you're saying, child.'

'I do, Mama, and I don't want to go back. I'm not going back.'

Agnes Rosier shut out her reflection in the mirror by closing her eyes tightly. She also shut out the face of her seventeen-year-old daughter, her plain, nondescript daughter.

Only three months ago she had sat on this very seat and looked at herself in this mirror and said 'Thank God'. She had said it reverently, as befitted a good churchwoman. She had thanked Him for getting her daughter settled, the daughter she had imagined she was to be saddled with for the rest of her life. But the Almighty, who always answered her prayers, had arranged for Mr Arnold Noble to come visiting in the vicinity. Mr Arnold Noble was a man in his prime, a widower with two children. What caused the gentleman to become enamoured of her daughter, or which part of her had captivated Mr Noble, Agnes Rosier did not question. Had she done so, she would immediately have ruled out her face and her manners, for neither the one nor the other had any claim to charm. There were plain women, she knew, whose features had a certain attractiveness, but not her daughter's. How this had come about was beyond her, for she herself was a handsome woman and the proof of this lay in the fact that she had passed her benefits on to her eldest son, and a portion to her second son. Theresa took after her father, at least outwardly; whom she took after inwardly they had yet to discover, for whoever heard of a mine-owner's daughter going to a Chartist meeting? They had thought they had heard the last of Chartists in 1855 when that madman O'Connor had died; but there was an element trying to revive itself in Newcastle and their own daughter had attended a meeting and dared to voice her views at the dining table. That any girl of seventeen should talk back to her father was unheard of, but that she should bring into the open a matter that was like a gaping wound in his side was so monstrous that she had feared on that particular occasion that Mr Rosier would collapse. And if this wasn't enough, her own brother had espied her, three miles away on the fells, talking to groups of evicted miners from the village, troublemakers, men who were more like savages and brutes than human beings. At the sight of his sister degrading herself Bernard's rage had been almost as great as his father's. To use his own words, he had thrown her into the carriage. Mr Rosier had confined his daughter to her room for a fortnight, and she, her mother, had had to bear the brunt of his tongue. What, he had demanded, had she bred him – a viper? A viper indeed. Then the Lord had provided Mr Noble, to release them from their impossible predicament.

She herself had been in a constant state of nerves until the moment when the ceremony was over, and immediately the couple had left on their honeymoon she had drunk three glasses of champagne, one after the other – a thing she had never done in her life before. Following this, she had proceeded to enjoy the reception and could remember very little after two o'clock in the morning, only that everyone voted the occasion an outstanding success.

And now here was her daughter back home, on a visit presumably to attend the engagement ball of her eldest brother, and daring to tell her that she was not going to return to Mr Noble.

She opened her eyes and looked through the mirror at the face that was staring at her. It was a thin face, thin cheeks, thin lips, thin eyebrows, thin light brown hair pulled so tightly back from her brow that it looked painful. But the main feature of her daughter's face was her thin nose. It poked itself outwards; it was a Rosier nose, a feature that she had always been ashamed of. Her husband bore this affliction, as his father had before him. His father had changed their name from Rosenberg to Rosier, but he could do nothing about this stamp of heritage.

She didn't like her daughter's face; she didn't like any part of her daughter, and the thought of having her in the household again brought her swivelling round to confront her angrily.

'Now listen to me, Theresa. You are a married woman with responsibilities and you must face up to them.'

'I've told you, Mama, I don't like . . . '

Agnes Rosier now held up her hand, and through the narrow aperture of her lips she hissed, 'Would it surprise you to learn that few women do?'

They stared at each other. Then Agnes Rosier, composing herself and moistening her lips, asked, 'Is it the children?'

'No; I like the children.'

'Does . . . does he keep you short of anything? I understood he was of a generous nature?'

'He is.'

Agnes looked down at her hands, lying one on top of the other on her taffeta petticoats. She did not want to ask the question, because she knew the answer; but if she did not ask it her daughter would tell her in any case, and she objected, as much as her husband did, to the free flow of words that emanated without let or hindrance from this child of theirs. It was much better to appear in control of the situation, and so she asked, 'What is it you don't like about marriage?' She lowered her lids again as she waited for the answer. It came brief and terse, startling her, even although she had been aware of its substance.

'Intimacy.'

'Theresa!' Agnes had her eyes wide open now. 'We went into this a month ago. I gave you my advice. I . . . I told you to . . . ' She could not go on and at the same time look at her daughter, so she swivelled round to the dressing table again and began sorting some jewellery on a silver tray as if looking for a particular object, adding as she did so, ' . . . to let Mr Noble have his way, just . . . just be submissive, do nothing whatever. I . . . I told you.' She glanced now through the mirror at the pale face behind her. 'One gets used to it; you . . . you think of other things while it's going on.'

'I'll never get used to it. I hate it, loathe it. I can't think of other things. I'm not putting up with it.'

'Theresa!' Agnes was now on her feet. 'Stop this nonsense once and for all. Where do you think you will go if you leave Mr Noble's house?'

'I . . . I can come back here, I suppose, can't I?'

'No.'

'You mean you wouldn't let me come home?'

'It isn't what I would do, it's your father. Under no consideration would he allow you to leave Mr Noble.'

'What if I leave him without his consideration? What if I just leave him? I've a hundred pounds a year of my own.'

'Don't be ridiculous, child. How could you live on a hundred pounds a year after the life you've been accustomed to? Anyway, you're under age.'

'You seem to forget, Mama, that I'm a married woman; I no longer come under the jurisdiction of Papa.'

Agnes drew herself up to her full height, all of five foot eight. She held her hands stiffly by her sides, the fists clenched. 'Do you want to bring disgrace on us? You'll set the whole county afire if you do this. And at this particular time, this crucial time . . . Theresa.' She took in a long slow breath of air, then, bending slightly towards her daughter, her manner changing, she begged, 'Please . . . please do nothing until after the wedding. Promise me, for if anything should happen to stop Bernard's marriage it will be the end of your father; he's relying on this liaison. In fact our whole future depends on our being joined to the Talfords. I . . . I told you weeks ago how things stood financially. Your father is a very worried man at the moment, so I beg you, if you are set on doing something drastic like this, wait. For my sake, wait.'

For the first time since she entered the room Theresa took her eyes from her mother and, looking down, she said, 'I'll do nothing until after the engagement party, but I can't promise to wait until they are married.'

As Agnes Rosier stared at her daughter's bowed head there came to her a strange thought. Her daughter didn't look like a woman at all, there was nothing feminine in this creature before her. What, as Mr Rosier had said, had she bred him?

With her four flounced petticoats making a sound like retreating waves on sand, she went swiftly towards the clothes closet, saying, 'Leave me and send Stockwell in; I want to finish dressing . . . But, Theresa' – she swung sharply round again – 'you won't leave the grounds, will you? I mean . . . Well, you know what I mean.' Her voice was harsh. 'No going into Jarrow, or Felling . . . Remember.'

To this demand Theresa made no answer; she simply bowed her head and went out of the room.

She kept her head down as she went along the wide corridor that opened out into the gallery, and she did not raise it until she almost bumped into the first chambermaid.

Florrie Green was coming from a side passage that communicated, by a door, with the servants' staircase. She had a big wooden slop bucket in her hand and 'Pardon, mi . . . ma' am,' she exclaimed, accompanying her words with a slight dipping of her buckets. There was no deference in the action; it was merely a habit. Nobody was very deferential to Miss Theresa, or Mrs Noble as she now was. Well, it was as Mr Kennard said, she didn't keep her place. She spoke to you as if she was just like you, and it wasn't right.

Theresa paused on top of the wide oak stairway and looked down into the hall where Mrs Davis, the housekeeper, was bustling about, and Kennard, the butler, was supervising two of the maids, directing how they should move a long oak chest, but never putting his hand on it to assist them. She descended to the middle landing, where the stairs turned at right angles into the hall. She paused a moment looking to the left of her across the hall and into the drawing room. John Swan, the second coachman, and Albert Nash, the under-gardener, crossed her line of vision, one at each end of a long sofa. They were rearranging the furniture in the drawing room, making it and the dining room, adjoining and divided only by a portable partition, into a room large enough for the guests to stroll in and to eat and drink casually from well-laden tables lining the walls. Her mother had brought this idea of eating from London. It was, she said, called a buffet supper. The dancing would take place in the hall, and the musicians would be seated on a raised dais at the back; the gallery wasn't wide enough to accommodate them and allow for the passage of guests. This fact about the construction of the house had always irked her mother, as had these stairs, which she would have had circular . . . One could never sweep down stairs that had a sharp bend; to do justice to a gown and a fine carriage one needed a circular staircase.

This cynical thought seemed to speed Theresa down the remaining stairs and into the hall. Walking quickly across it, and not looking at Kennard, but thanking him merely with a slight movement of her head when he opened the stained-glass door into the vestibule for her, she hurried through this large, tiled and chilly entrance and out into the sunshine. Still hurrying, almost at a tripping run now, she went down the five broad stone steps on to the drive.

The drive was wide and could take three coaches abreast. It was bordered directly in front by an ornamental privet hedge, not high enough to obscure the view of the gardens beyond. Yet the view was chequered by the contorted mass of sculptured trees. To the right of the house was the main drive; to the left, well to the left, was a high, ivy-covered wall, with an arch which led to the walks. Through this she now went. But she did not take any of the paths into the pleasure gardens; she walked by the wall which now became the back of the stables and courtyard. Beyond these the wall continued, covered with a mass of roses and clematis, and the scent of the roses was heavy in the hot morning air. She did not stop and bend towards their fragrance, as her mother would have done; she had no use for flowers. She did not like the garden; you cannot grow to love a prison, no matter how beautiful or sweet-smelling.

The wall ended where a copse began. It stopped abruptly, the sharp ends of the sandstone sticking out here and there from the creeper. It was as if the builders had suddenly run out of material. She continued through the copse and into a green pasture that ran steeply uphill, and not until she reached its summit did she stop. And then she turned and looked over the way she had come. She stared at the scene before her for fully five minutes; then slowly she sat down on the ground.

From where she sat she could see the whole of the back of the house, the stable yard, the courtyard, and the servants' quarters, where the male servants slept; the women had their rooms in the attics in the east wing. The house, like the wall, was made of stone, except for the ornamental pieces at the front which were picked out in red brick. Theresa had always considered it an ugly house; impressive but ugly. It was not large, as country houses went, and from the time she had first become conscious of her home she had never liked it; but now she had the urge to hold out her arms to it and say, 'Take me back. Please, take me back.'

She had looked on her marriage as a way of escape from the narrowness and hypocrisy of her family, and their friends; escape from her plainness and the pain it had caused. She had wondered during the last few weeks if she would have possessed the awareness to gauge her mother's real feelings for her and what went on behind her smiling face, and of those of the women who came to the house accompanied by loud, hearty-voiced men, if it hadn't been for Ainsley. Likely, as she grew older, she would have come to judge for herself, but she doubted whether she would have come to her present way of thinking at her age without the tutoring and guidance of her governess.

Ainsley had been a forcing house, like the one over there near the greenhouses where Mr Wisden, the head gardener, performed miracles on plants with a stove-pipe. Ainsley had been her stove-pipe, and she thanked God for her. Yet, perhaps, without Ainsley she might have suffered this marriage . . . No, no, never. The thing that she couldn't tolerate in this marriage had nothing to do with the mind . . . But hadn't it? 'Think of other things while it's going on,' her mother had said. It seemed to her that without the mind this thing in itself would be nothing, or at least something that was over so quickly it was nothing more than a purge. She plucked at the grass, then raised her head and looked towards the house again and tried to recapture the times she and Ainsley had sat on this very spot, laughing at it and all that went on inside, from the kitchen to the drawing room. The jealousies, the pettiness, the striving for place, the pomp. Ainsley had taught her to see things as they really were.

She had been five years old when Ainsley came into her life. She could remember the day when she first saw the tall, thin woman and realised that Ainsley was plain-looking. That was before she became aware that she herself was saddled with the same complaint. Ainsley was thirty when she came to Greenwall Manor. She was forty-two when she left it, on the day following their secret, exciting visit to the meeting on the Newcastle Town Moor, when the cavalry came and rode into the thousands of people, and they had run with the rest and almost been trampled to death. It was there they had been seen by Mr Careless, a magistrate and friend of her father's.

Ainsley had been turned out in disgrace and without a reference. For who could give a reference to a governess who had corrupted a young mind? That's what her mother had said. Her father had said much more and his language had been much stronger, for had not the woman made him a laughing stock by inveigling his daughter to attend Chartist meetings, and making her an open sympathiser with the rebels and scum in his own pit?

Ainsley had refuted nothing her employer had accused her of, and she had dared to stand up to him and say that she was proud she had enabled one of his family to think for herself, and that he, too, should be proud that he had one intelligent person among the dunderheads in his household.

She had known what it was to die when she saw Ainsley being driven away from the door. She hadn't been allowed any word with her; she was locked in her room, but she had hammered on the window and Ainsley had lifted her joined hands towards her. They said, 'Be strong. Be strong.' She had tried to be strong, but it was difficult without Ainsley's support. She had begun by proposing setting up a weekly class in the village to teach the miners to read and write. When her mother had recovered sufficiently she had said, 'Child, do you think a miner would go down a mine if he could read and write correctly? Do you want your father's business to collapse? Do you want us to starve? Never let such a proposal come to your father's ears, it could cause him to have a seizure.'

Then Mr Noble came on the scene.

Theresa now experienced a sickness in the pit of her stomach; her whole body shrank inwardly, for even sitting on this hilltop she could actually feel his hands on her. He always wanted to touch her; wherever they met, even at the dining table, his hand would come out and touch her. But there was one thing that puzzled, even amazed, her about Mr Noble. It was the fact that he cared for her. Perhaps caring wasn't the right word, but innately she knew she held an attraction for him. Was it just her extreme youth? It certainly wasn't her looks, or her charm, or even her conversation, for she found she couldn't talk to this fat, greasy-looking man, who had stubble all round his face if he didn't shave twice a day, and whose lower lip was soft and moist and whose head was going bald, and whose stomach, without the support of his belt, bulged.

She was on her feet again, looking about her, diverting her thoughts from her husband. There, far away to the left, she could see the headings of her father's mine; and farther away still, where the land fell into the valley, another heading. That was the dead head of the Jarrow mine which had been closed down. To the side of it was the silver thread of the river Don hurrying towards the Tyne – the busy, bustling Tyne.

She had not been along the banks of the Tyne more than half a dozen times in her life, but these brief visits had filled her with excitement. There was so much to see, for what had once been a mining village no bigger than the village attached to her father's mine was fast becoming a town. Already the old salt pans were going, as were the coke ovens that spread along the river bank and whose waste heat had kept the salt pans working. A paper mill was now flourishing on the river bank, as also were three chemical works.

Then there was the main industry on the river, the industry that made her wish at times she had been born a boy. This was Palmer's Shipyard. She knew quite a bit about the Palmer brothers and their shipyard – at least her father's opinion of them, for the Palmer brothers were like a thorn in his flesh, yet a thorn that he wanted to drive deeper, for he wanted, above all things, to be close to the Palmers, to be attached to them in such a way that whatever profits their new and thriving concern would make he would have a share in them. It was primarily because of this that her brother Bernard was marrying Ann Talford.

The Talfords were very rich. They had a house three times the size of Greenwall; also James Talford had his fingers in all kinds of pies, including boat-building, and he was a personal friend of the Palmers. She understood from things that had been let drop, mostly from her brother Rodger, that James Talford didn't like her father and had opposed this match with his only child. But, as Rodger said, Mr Talford had found himself thawed by two weapons, both used against him with effect. The first was he loved his daughter and would do anything to further her happiness; the second was the tenacity of her suitor.

For three years Bernard had wooed Ann, and in so doing had apparently become a reformed character, for once there had been loud whispers about his escapades, and not only with regard to gambling; but now her brother was supposedly a steady, sober man of twenty-six, and James Talford, a strict churchman, could no longer put forward any arguments against the marriage.

Today was Friday and on Tuesday the engagement ball was to be held, and in four months' time, early in October, the wedding would take place. Could she suffer Mr Noble for another four months? Theresa shook her head slowly. Not unless she locked herself away at night. And she couldn't do that either, for there were the servants; and whereas the servants in her old home did not exactly like her, the servants in her new home took no more notice of her than if she was one of her husband's hounds. Were she to ask for a key to a room, they would, she knew, merely refer her to Mr Noble.

Yet it wasn't true that all the servants here didn't like her; there were two who did, three in fact. There was Mrs Davis, the housekeeper; Katie Mulholland, the scullery maid; and Tatman, the head coachman. They liked her, and she liked them. But of the three, she liked Katie Mulholland best. Katie had been the only other young thing in the house that one could look at, and like looking at. It was strange the pleasure she had always got from looking at Katie Mulholland.

As if her thinking had drawn the substance of it from out of the house, she now saw the unmistakably thin figure of Katie Mulholland staggering from the side door of the kitchen with a large wooden bucket in each hand. The door led to the attic stairs down which it was one of Katie's daily chores to carry the maids' slops. She watched the figure crossing the yard. Then she was lost to her sight for a moment until she emerged through the arch in the long wall. She watched her staggering to the bottom of the kitchen garden; then she saw her tipping up her buckets into the trough that led down to the cesspit. Her nose wrinkled and she closed her eyes for a moment. 'The indignities that were heaped upon human beings.' Those were Ainsley's words, but they were her own sentiments.

She now heard, from the far end of the drive, the sound of hooves and she looked away from the small scullery maid to see her father's coach racing up the drive. She wondered what had brought him back at this time in the morning. Trouble at the mine? More than likely; there was always trouble at the mine.

CHAPTER TWO

GEORGE DANIEL ROSIER was a small man, at least two inches shorter than his wife. He had a swarthy dark complexion, thin grizzled hair, round eyes which could be likened to jet beads, and then his main feature, his nose, a large bony protrusion dominating his face. Physically he had no presence, but he made himself felt by his temper and his tongue, and both were feared by every member of his household, except perhaps his eldest son and his only daughter. He leapt straight out of the carriage and up the steps, pushing his butler to one side and crying, 'Get Mr Bernard. And now!'

He stormed across the hall towards the library door, but with the knob in his hand he turned round and cried to Kennard, 'Where is he?'

'I think he's in his room, sir.'

'In his room!' The nose jerked itself upwards in disdain, taking the rest of the face with it, as he thrust open the door.

The library was a long, high room, lined with books from floor to ceiling, and never in the thirty years that George Rosier had lived in this house had he disturbed one of them. At the end of the room were four tall windows which faced the drive, and in front of the middle two was a large bog-oak desk, covered with a disarray of papers and letters. To the right, in the middle of one long wall, was a huge fireplace, and although the day was warm, even hot outside, a wood fire was burning in the iron basket.

George Rosier stood glaring down at the fire for a moment; then he turned his back to it, put his hand under his coat tails and flapped them angrily upwards and, marching to the table, scattered papers here and there until he found what he was looking for. He was reading the letter when the door opened and his son, Bernard, entered.

Bernard Rosier was tall – taller than his mother by five inches. His complexion was dark, as were his eyes; his face and body, like his mother's, were inclined to heaviness, yet his lips and nostrils were thin.

Altogether he looked a handsome man, a gloweringly handsome man.

'Where the hell've you been?'

'In my room.' The reply was cool, and there was no trace of annoyance on Bernard's face at his father's tone.

'At this time in the morning? It's no wonder we're in the devil of a mess.'

'I was at the works until seven o'clock last night.'

'That's no reason to sleep abed till eleven in the morning.'

'I wasn't abed. Nor was I abed at seven o'clock this morning. I've been exercising Falstaff, after which I had a rub-down.'

'You and your rubbing down. This is no time for riding or rubbing down. Rubbing down at eleven in the morning.' He snorted. 'It's a time for action. Those buggers are going on strike again.'

'Well, you knew that yesterday.'

'Don't stand there being so bloody cool – of course I knew that yesterday. At least I expected it. But I thought I'd put a spoke in their wheel and the fear of God into them. I told Brown to set the word around there was a boatload of Irish coming in, but that Fogerty and Ramshaw have started spouting again. If we can't keep to the schedule Palmer'll drop us; he'll just transport our coal when he's slack. He's already too big for his boots. God, if only I was on that board.' He stumped one stubby fist into the palm of his hand, while his son surveyed him calmly for a moment, before saying, 'You should have bought the shares when you had the opportunity.'

'Don't say that. I've warned you, don't you say that to me again.' George Rosier turned a purple countenance upon his son. 'I've told you before. Eight years ago I was in no position to buy shares of any kind. I was just keeping my head above water, literally so, the water in the mine . . . Anyway' – he flung round and glared into the fire – 'who on earth would have thought a hare-brained scheme of iron ships driven by steam would have proved successful? The steam had failed before, the price it entailed was prohibitive; the whole combination seemed fantastic, except as an experiment.'

Bernard Rosier wiped the tiny beads of perspiration from his upper lip as he stared at his father's back. Who would have thought? Now he wanted to say, 'Don't say that to me again.' He was sick of hearing that phrase repeated and repeated over the years. He knew what he would have done if he'd had any say eight years ago; he would have borrowed money and bought shares in the hare-brained scheme; hundreds and hundreds of them, thousands and thousands of them. Even if his common or business sense hadn't told him he was on to a good thing, his gambling instincts, he felt sure, would have guided him.

He was a youth of eighteen, eight years ago, when on a June day in 1852 he had stood with his father in Palmer's yard and watched the launching of the *John Bowes*; and many besides his father thought it was money being thrown to the wind on nothing more than an expensive experiment, for up to this time sailing vessels were the cheapest form of transport. But they were to be proved wrong. On her first voyage the *John Bowes* carried six hundred and fifty tons of coal to London, discharged it and was back on the Tyne in five days. What she had done in five days would have taken two sailing colliers close on a month to accomplish. Palmer was set fair.

Now, eight years and many ships and a great growth of the town later, there was talk of turning Palmer's into a limited liability company, and before that happened Bernard Rosier knew that his father would be in that company or die in the attempt. And he might just do that, for it would not surprise him should his father collapse during one of his spasms of rage and so end it. But he really wasn't concerned about what happened to his father. The old man, as he thought of him, irritated him beyond endurance. But he must bide his time until October, and with his marriage would come money and, what was of equal importance, influence. For had not his future father-in-law been a lifelong friend of Charles Palmer's father, and was he not now mentor to the said Charles Palmer? Oh, give him a year at the outside and the boardroom of Palmer's would be open to him. And not only the boardroom, but all the other concerns that Charles Mark Palmer had an interest in.

At this point in his thinking the door opened and his brother, Rodger, entered. Rodger was a young man of twenty, of medium height, with fair brown hair and eyes to match. His expression was gentle, yet alive. If his sister had been born with his features she would have grown up to be pretty, and if he had taken on hers he would have been dubbed a keen, attractive-looking man. 'I'm sorry,' he said, 'I didn't know you were using the library.'

'Come in, come in. Don't stand there waverin'.'

His father made a wide-sweeping gesture with his hand which held the letter. Then as his younger son came slowly forward he thrust the letter towards Bernard, saying, 'Look at that, an inspection . . . an inspector coming.'

Bernard Rosier read the letter, then handed it back to his father, saying,

'We only wanted this. You can't get into number two working unless you swim, and if they stop work, as they've threatened, it'll be the middle gallery next.'

'It won't, it won't!' George Rosier tugged the ends of his coat to meet in front of his chest. 'I'll see them in hell first; I'll see them gnawing their arms off, as they nearly did two years back, before they get the better of me. I'll do as we all did then; I'll bring in the labour. And this time, if I bring it in, it'll stay . . . every man jack will stay, and my loyal workers can rot watching them feed and sleeping in their houses . . . Thankless lot of scum.' He flung the letter from him, aiming at the desk. It missed and fluttered down to the floor. Rodger picked it up and laid it gently on the top of the pile of papers; then, turning and looking at his father and brother, he said in a quiet, almost apologetic tone, 'Wouldn't it be easier in the long run if you all got your heads together and tried to rectify the damage done by the Percy Main flooding?'

'Don't talk bloody nonsense, Rodger. Why should I pay out hard cash, even if I had it to spare, on helping to keep the water down in other buggers' mines when they never show their nebs outside of London, at least not in this direction. No, they sit tight and enjoy life. I'm about the only bloody fool in this county squatting on my mine shaft, up to my chin in debt, worry, and danger. Yes, an' I say danger, for that mob down there are half maniacs. If I had my way I would chain them up. The Bishop of Durham knew what he was doing when he manacled them to the mangers. Look.' He turned and pointed to Bernard. 'Go down and tell Bunting that he's got to get rid of Ramshaw and Fogerty. I don't care how he does it – I'll leave that to him. He's got to earn his money somehow. It's about time he did . . . ' He stopped abruptly, pressed his hand on the top of his stomach, bent forward, then gave a mighty belch of wind. 'I'm . . . I'm going to Newcastle to see Bullard; I want a draught for this.' He patted his stomach again. 'Nearly driving me mad. Now do as I say.' He thrust his finger towards Bernard; then, turning abruptly from his sons, he marched out of the room.

The brothers looked at each other. Then Bernard, again wiping the moisture from his upper lip, walked to the window and said, 'How would you like it every day?'

'I wouldn't.'

'You're lucky.'

'Yes, I suppose I am. In fact, I know I am.' Rodger's eyes roamed up and down the long rows of books, and again he repeated, 'Yes, I'm lucky,' but to himself this time.

Rodger had just come down on vacation from Oxford. How he had ever got to Oxford was still a surprise to him. When he thought of his father and brother, and he often did, their whole life spent in extracting money from the mine, he wondered how he had escaped. He wondered why they had allowed him to escape from the commercialism, from the degradation of thrusting men and boys into the bowels of the earth, literally to drag out the coal by hand, then to deprive them, by trickery – and this was openly done through the master weighman, such as Mark Bunting – of a portion of their small earnings which at best were not sufficient to support a way of life that it was generally supposed God had willed they should have.

Apparently God had willed that his parents could live no other way but in this house, with its farm and thirty acres of grounds, its twenty servants, not counting the lodgekeeper and farmhands. Yet, with all this, he knew that his parents were not entirely satisfied with their way of life. It wasn't luxurious enough, at least for his mother, nor held enough prestige for his father.

His father had built the miners' cottages in the village, and he ran the grocery shop, and most of the wages that he paid his men came back to him through the shop. You could say he owned the village, but that wasn't enough. His father wanted power and Bernard wanted power. They were social climbers of the first water, and, in a way, that was the reason they had allowed him to go to Oxford. A son, and brother, who could be dubbed a scholar would be an asset in this commerce-ridden district. It would also be something to be scornful about, even though the scorn could be seen merely as a thin cover for the pride of an association with learning. Oh yes, Rodger knew why he had been allowed to go to Oxford. He wasn't a strong-willed young man like his brother, but he was a discerning one, and he knew on which side his bread was buttered.

'I've got a new hunter.'

'What?' Rodger turned, screwing his eyes up against the light to look at his brother.

'I said I've got a new hunter, a chestnut.'

Rodger shook his head slowly and smiled to himself. They hadn't any money, they were up to their eyes, didn't know where to turn, but Bernard had got a new hunter.

'Come and see her?'

Without saying anything more Bernard walked down the long room, and Rodger followed him. They crossed the hall towards a passage that ran to the far right of the stairs, and at the end of it Bernard, going first, stepped through a doorway, straight into the courtyard and Katie Mulholland.

As the girl went sprawling on the rough cobblestones and the two buckets of kitchen slops she was carrying spewed about her, Bernard let out a series of oaths, ending with, 'Blind, blasted fool of a girl!' He glared down at his bespattered breeches and the still figure lying at his feet, the hem of her print skirt around the back of her knees exposing her thin white-hosed calves. One arm was stretched out, the hand still gripping the handle of a bucket; the other hand, pressed against the stones, was cupping her face.

Katie Mulholland remained motionless, not daring to lift her head. It was as if God had rent the heavens and was towering over her. And indeed it could have been, for was it not Mr Bernard who was speaking, and, without looking, she knew that she had messed up his breeches. Anything could befall her for this, anything. It had all happened because she had got such a gliff, for who would think Mr Bernard would come through the side door at this time of day? He had come so fast he had knocked her over . . . Eeh no! She'd better not say he had knocked her over; she had slipped.

'Come along, get up. It's all right.' She was pulled upwards, and through her stretched fingers she peered at Mr Rodger. Mr Rodger was smiling. He looked her up and down and said, 'You are in a mess. Go and get yourself cleaned up. What's your name again?'

'Katie, sir.' She remembered to bob.

'Well, go and have a wash under the pump, Katie, and get that stuff off you.' He wrinkled his nose.

'Yes, sir.' Slowly she drew her hand from her face and glanced to where Bernard was now entering the stables across the yard. Perhaps . . . perhaps she wouldn't get it in the neck if she could get it cleaned up before Cook saw her. She bobbed again and said, 'Thank you, sir,' gave a dive to the left and then to the right, retrieving the buckets, turned and ran across the courtyard and round the corner to the pump, and there, pumping like mad, she filled the buckets with water, brought them back to the yard and sprayed the contents, with a quite expert fling, over the cobbles. This done, she quickly picked up the soggy crusts, bacon skins and bones and other refuse scattered around her, then ran down the length of the courtyard, through the archway in the wall and emptied the depleted contents of the buckets in a pigswill trough. Within seconds she was back at the pump splashing her face and hands and rubbing down the front of her dress. She had taken off her coarse apron – she could put a clean one on and wash this one later. There – she looked down at herself – that wasn't so bad. If only Cook hadn't missed her. The next minute she was in the kitchen pushing the empty buckets under the wooden sink, making sure that one of them was directly under the bung-hole.

Out of the corner of her eye she looked towards Cook who was standing at the far end of the long white table which ran down the centre of the enormous kitchen. Apparently she hadn't heard the commotion. She was in a good temper the day. Katie sighed, then, seating herself on a cracket that was placed opposite a sawn-off wooden barrel filled with potatoes, she began her daily task of peeling them.

Katie had started in the Rosier kitchen when she was eleven. She was now fifteen and the dirtiest, longest and most dreary tasks were still hers. She didn't especially mind, except when Dotty Black, the kitchen maid, got the scraps to take home. After all, she told herself, she was earning a shilling a week and was, moreover, the favourite of Mrs Davis, the housekeeper.

The cook's voice, coming at her now, startled her. 'Haven't you got that lot done yet?'

'Nearly, Cook.'

'You done the turnips?'

'Yes, Cook, an' I cut some with the star cutter and some with the three-cornered one.'

'This'll drive me mad.' Cook now placed a frill around a mayonnaise of turbot done in aspic; then, carrying the dish to a long narrow table that was attached to the length of one wall, she said, 'You'd think they'd pick something easier with all I've got facin' me, and only four days to do it in. You'd think they'd give me extra down here, but no, no, take what little I've got to help upstairs. I'm not standin' it much longer.'

Katie, besides listening attentively to the cook's yammering, slanted her eyes to the colourful array of dishes on the long board. They were having cold upstairs the day, for lunch anyway, but there wouldn't be anything left of that lot, not after it went to the housekeeper's room and Mr Kennard and Miss Stockwell had a go at it. But from the dinner the night there should be some over. The first course was soup, and then there was whitebait, and next there was boiled capon and tongue, and stuffed vegetable marrow and four other vegetables; they would finish up with a choice of three puddings – one was a fruit salad. She felt sure that Mrs

Davis would save her some of the scraps if she could, to take home with her. She remembered suddenly that tomorrow was wage day, and that on Sunday afternoon she could take her month's wages home.

Oh, how she wanted to go home; she wanted to see her ma and da, and her granda and their Joe and Lizzie, and to tell them everything, all about the preparation for Mr Bernard's engagement ball; about the people who had been invited; about the food, the beautiful food; about the chickens, ducks and geese that were hanging up in the cold room; about the pigs that had been killed, and the smoked hams that had been brought in from the wood room; about the gallons of cream being made and the hundreds of eggs that were coming to the kitchen daily; and then there was that great crate of cheeses that had been sent all the way from London. And she wanted to tell them about falling with the slop buckets in the yard and splashing Mr Bernard's breeches. Eeh, she had been scared out of her wits. But now she could laugh at it, and when she was home and she told them how it had happened she would make them all laugh; she could always make them laugh. Her granda would laugh loudest of all because he had no respect for the gentry; her granda was awful in that way.

'Come on, come on. Don't spend all day sittin' there on your backside.'

Katie's head jerked towards the cook as she said, 'Nearly finished, Cook. Just two more.'

'You've taken your time. Now get those pots scoured.' She pointed to the side of the hearth where were standing, one on top of the other, three piles of copper cooking pots. 'And I said scoured, mind – and put more sand in than salt. I want them bright.'

And so for Katie the day went on, a succession of dreary tasks, each one more depressing than the last, until some time after nine she had finished and she took her candle and went to bed.

In the winter they were allowed two candles a week, in the summer one, and although Katie never used all her candles, for she was almost walking in her sleep by the time she reached the attic, there was no chance of taking the ends home because they had to be given in before she could get a new one. She was sorry about this because the ends would have been a great help, especially in the long winter nights and her da wanting to read and teach some of the men their letters the same way as he had been taught by Mr Burns, the preacher.

But, anyway, nothing mattered at the moment but the fact that it was wage day the morrow and on Sunday she was going home. She crossed her two index fingers to placate the gods, and a spurt of joy rushed through her, lighting up her face and giving to her body the urge to leap into the air.

On Saturday morning George Rosier, sitting behind the long desk in the library, looked down at the leather bag that was spewing sovereigns. This monthly occasion always brought on a peculiar pain behind his ribs. The fact that in the course of a year he was doing each member of his staff out of a month's wages did not ease his pain. He considered it was bad enough when he had to pay his miners, although he admitted that some of them, just some of them, earned it. But, in this particular case, to hand out money to people, particularly females, whom he not only housed but clothed and fed, made his bile rise.

He thrust his hand out and pulled on a thick, twisted and tasselled red bell pull. The next moment Kennard opened the door and stood waiting, and when his master said 'Right!' he inclined his head over his shoulder, then entered the room, followed by Mrs Davis, Jane Stockwell, Frank Tatman, the first coachman and James Wisden, the head gardener.

Mary Davis advanced with her sedate walk to the desk. She made a slight dip with her knees, then waited. She watched her master separate a gold sovereign and a half a sovereign from the pile on the table, add to it a florin and push these towards her, saying,

'One pound twelve shillings.' She watched her master sorting money into small piles. And these he began pushing towards her, consulting a list in his hand as he did so, and barking, 'Fanny Croft, sixteen shillings. Daisy Studd, twelve shillings. Florrie Green, fourteen shillings. Mary Ann Hopkins, seven shillings. Delia Miller, one pound. Dorothy Black, eight shillings. Ivy Walker, eight shillings. Betty Taggart, eight shillings. Kate McManus, four shillings. Katie Mulholland, four shillings . . . There.' He pushed the list of names towards her. 'Get their marks. By the way . . . ' His big nose jerked and his face puckered, and now he stabbed his finger towards the last name and, looking at Mrs Davis, said, 'This one, Mulholland. Can she write?'

'Yes, sir.'

'And read?'

'Yes, sir.'

'Who taught her?' He was looking at Mrs Davis under his lids now, and she hesitated for a long moment before saying, 'Her father, I think.'

He considered her while he thought: Big Mulholland, reading and writing. He'd have to remember that. That's how trouble started. He now made an impatient movement with his hand, and Mrs Davis gathered the money on to a salver that was lying ready on the desk, and picking up the paper and making an almost imperceptible bob she turned away and made room for Jane Stockwell.

One at a time, the household staff stepped forward to receive their payment.

When the men had left the room Patrick Kennard stepped up to the desk, and his master pushed towards him two golden sovereigns. It was fitting, at least to Mr Kennard, that he should receive his wages apart from the rest of the staff, and no-one should know what he earned. His master looked at him as he made his mark and he wondered at the incongruity of the situation where the chief member of his staff could only identify himself by two crossed lines whereas the least of his staff could sign her name.

When George Rosier was alone again he looked at the sum total of what he had paid out. It amounted to sixteen pounds eight shillings. Sixteen pounds eight shillings, to which was added their keep, and their clothing. And this wasn't counting the farmhands, or the lodge. Yet it was a mere flea bite to the overall expenses of the house. And where was it all coming from?

And then those blasted savages down there threatening to strike because of unfair treatment by the keeker who had fined them for short corves. Why had he to have this trouble? A few miles away in the Felling pit they had nothing like this. It was true what a magistrate had said recently: the natural place for the Jarrow and Hebburn toughs was underground, and they should be kept there; for most of them were just evolving from the slime. And, by God, he was right.

Chapter Three

KATIE WAS READY to go. She had clean clothes on right to her shift, and at the neck of her best print frock was the brooch that had belonged to her grandmother, and sitting straight on the top of her thick shining hair was the hat with the daisies on that Mrs Davis had given her last year.

She smoothed down the front of her dress that fell to the top of her boots; then her eyes stayed for a moment on her hands. They were red and swollen, the nails worn down to the flesh, but they were as clean as a floor scrubbing brush and hot soda water could get them.

She gave a last look at her corner of the attic to see that she had left everything tidy, in case Mrs Davis had a walk round. Then she went downstairs to the housekeeper's room, knocked on the door, and went in.

The housekeeper was not wearing her cap at this moment, and she looked funny to Katie without it. Her greying hair was drawn back from her forehead, her round face with its high colour had a criss-cross of faint lines covering it, but her body was slim and trim and youngish-looking. She drew Katie to her with an outstretched hand, saying, 'Oh, you look nice and tidy, Katie.' She did not say, 'You look beautiful'; it wouldn't have done. There were times when it pained her to look at this lovely child, especially when she had been younger and she'd seen her dropping with fatigue late at night. She touched the brooch at Katie's neck saying, 'That sets you off, Katie. You look grand.'

Katie smiled at Mrs Davis, the delicate mould of her lips stretching to show her even teeth.

Mrs Davis's fingers moved upwards to Katie's cheek. Its texture was as smooth as satin and its colour was like thick cream with a blush on it. But it was the child's eyes that made the whole face what it was; there was something rare about them. She had never seen another pair of eyes in a human head like them. It wasn't because they were green or heavy-lashed, there was something more. There was a kind of starriness about them, a dewy starriness. And then her hair topping it all, its dark chestnut waves throwing out gold gleams here and there. Her figure, too, was getting to be noticeable. As yet it was too thin, but her bust had developed even in the last month. She put her finger gently in the centre of it, saying, 'You've got your money safe, Katie?'

'Yes, Mrs Davis.' Katie nodded her head. 'I've pinned it in me bag.'

'That's right. Well, now, I've got one or two things here.' She went to a chest of drawers and took out several small flattish packages, and when Katie lifted up her dress and top petticoat Mrs Davis inserted them one after the other in the two side pockets attached to the inside of her under petticoat. 'These,' she said, holding two packages up to Katie, 'are a little tea and sugar. It's my own, out of my allowance.'

'Oh yes, Mrs Davis, I know, I know.' Katie was quick to assure her benefactor that she did not for a moment think the stuff was cribbed from the staff's allowance.

'And this is a little bit of ham and tongue from my supper last night; and this is my pudding from today; and these are some pieces of capons.'

The capons, Katie noticed, was the largest packet of all. Cook had grumbled last night because so little had come out of the housekeeper's room, and here was the reason. Merriment rose in her when she thought that through the ingenuity of Mrs Davis she herself had got one up on the cook.

'There now, you're all ready.' The housekeeper touched Katie's cheek again. 'Give my kind regards to your mother and tell her I said you were doing splendidly and are a very good girl.'

'Oh . . . oh thanks, Mrs Davis. Thanks. I will, I will. An' thank you for all the things.' She whispered the last words.

Mrs Davis jerked her head sideways as one confederate to another. Then, pressing her towards the door, she said, 'And you'll be back by six?'

'Yes, Mrs Davis.'

'That's a good girl. Don't depend upon meeting a trap or any of the carts to give you a lift, mind; set out in time.'

'I will, Mrs Davis. Goodbye and thank you. Thank you very much.'

'Goodbye, child . . . '

The day was hot, the sky blue and high. After she had passed through the wicket gate at the end of the grounds she ran along the rough track until she began to sweat; then for a time she walked, hitching once or twice because she felt happy. Once she laughed out aloud, then clapped her hands over her mouth and shook her head.

The track widened to a rough road and was going steeply uphill now, and when she reached the summit she stopped. She always stopped at this point for a minute because she could see for miles about her, even more than you could from the hill behind the house. To the right and left of her lay wide expanses of grassland and fells, and in the far distance was a dark huddled blur – that was Jarrow. And there was the river. She could just make out the slim outlines of the masts of the ships, and the funnels too, big round chimneys stuck in the middle of the boats.

Now she was running again, and she continued to run, until she caught a glimpse of the first row of whitewashed cottages and she knew that she would be home within three minutes.

There were eight rows of cottages in the village, each containing twenty dwellings of two rooms each. The Mulhollands' house was number twelve in the first row, and the first row faced the moor. There was only a twelve-foot width of powdery roadway, which turned into a quagmire in wet weather, between the doorway and the wide-open grassy slopes.

The situations of the first and last rows of cottages were enviable ones in the summer. In the winter they bore the brunt of the open blast from the fells. And the row where the Mulhollands lived in particular took the full force of the flood water that came down from the hills. But today there was no flood water, there was only sunshine, and dust, and a strong smell from the middens.

Catherine Mulholland was waiting at the door for her daughter. She resisted the urge to run towards her. She didn't want the neighbours to talk. They did enough of that, always showing surprise that Katie should continue to return every other Sunday from the big house where she was living in luxury to a pit cottage. Of course this came from them who had daughters in the rope works, or, worse still, scraping cinders from the pans or tips. And she could understand this. Oh yes, she could understand this envy, for hadn't she felt the same towards the more fortunate at the time when Katie, from the age of seven, had gathered cinders until her fingers ran blood.

'Oh, hello, Ma.'

'Hello, me bairn.' Catherine moved back into the framework of the door; then opened her arms and Katie went into them and hugged her mother round the waist. And after a moment, while they stood still together, she lifted her head and looked at her mother; then turned her eyes and glanced through the half-opened door into the room, to where she could see the outline of men, and hear the buzz of conversation.

Her mother's head came down to her and she whispered, 'It's Mr Ramshaw and Mr Fogerty.'

The smile slipped from Katie's face and, her eyes stretching, she said one word, 'Trouble?' and watched her mother nod once. Then she asked in an apprehensive whisper, 'Are they out?'

'Not yet, but I think they're comin'.' Her voice very low, she explained quickly. 'Your dad was due for thirty shillings and he only got twenty-one, and for a fortnight's work. They said his corves were short. But he's not come off so badly as the others. It's been a bad patch all round. Mr Ramshaw was off two days bad. They said he wasn't bad. That was Bunting again. He couldn't have earned more than four shillings if he'd been there, but they fined him twelve. They've all had it one way or the other this last few weeks. It can't go on.' She shook her head slowly as Katie stared at her. Then she whispered again, 'They won't be long; they're goin' to the chapel in a few minutes. But come on, see your da.'

She drew her daughter around the door and into the room, and there three men and a boy faced her. All were smiling at her. Rodney Mulholland, a tall man of thirty-nine with big, deep-sunken eyes, hollow cheeks and brown hair, stepped towards her, saying, 'Hello, me lass.' He placed his hands tenderly on her shoulders and she looked at him and said, 'Hello, Da.' Katie knew she took after her da. Her da was a fine man; stern, but fine. But today his face looked old, and tired.

'How are you keepin'?'

'Fine, Da.'

'Good. Good.' He took his hands from her shoulders and they gazed at each other for a moment longer. Then she turned to her brother and said, 'Hello, Joe.'

Joe was a year younger than herself, thin like his father and with the same colouring. She noticed that his face was whiter than usual and he too looked tired. Then her father was saying to her, 'You know Mr Fogerty and Mr Ramshaw.'

'Yes.' She nodded at each man in turn, smiling broadly.

'Hello, Katie,' they said, one after the other. Then Mr Fogerty, a small, thickset man, with an Irish lilt to his voice, said, 'You get bonnier every day, Katie.'

Katie did not reply but drooped her head and shook it from side to side.

'You're right there, Dennis,' said Ramshaw, nodding towards his friend.

'Enough of that. Enough of that.' It was her father speaking, his tone jocular yet with a reprimand in it. 'We don't want her head turned.' Then, lifting her chin upwards with his bony fingers, he said, 'I won't be more than half an hour; I want to hear you read.' His look held admiration.

'Yes, Da. All right.'

'We'll away then.' Rodney Mulholland jerked his head towards his two companions, and after making their farewells they left the house.

Immediately the door had closed Katie said, 'I've brought some bits, Ma.'

'Have you, lass?' Catherine stood by the little table looking at her daughter, and Katie, turning her back on her brother, lifted up the front of her skirt and petticoat and brought the little packages from their hiding place. 'There's nearly two ounces of tea, Ma.'

'Oh!' Catherine held the small package on her hand and gazed at it as if looking at gold dust. And at sixpence an ounce at the company's shop – the Tommy-shop, as it was called – it was to her like gold dust.

'And that's sugar; and that's ham; and there's some chicken; and Mrs Davis saved her puddin'. I think she was thinking of Joe and Lizzie.' She turned and smiled warmly at her brother, then said, 'Where's Lizzie and Granda; has he taken her out?'

'No.'

Her mother shook her head. 'Lizzie's in the room,' she said. 'It's better so with company.' She nodded at Katie; then added, 'Your Granda's gone out after larks . . . ' She bowed her head swiftly and pressed her teeth into her bottom lip, saying, 'I'm sorry, lass; I needn't have told you that. But, you see, he's got to do somethin', and it makes him feel a bit independent like. Besides, it helps out in a stew. I'm sorry.' She put her hand on Katie's shoulder now and pressed it sympathetically. She knew that her daughter adored her grandfather but could never understand or get used to him trapping the birds, and she had never eaten them, no kind of bird, not even a sparrow. At that time when her belly had been swollen and rumbling with wind and emptiness she had tried, but had been violently sick, so she had never pressed her again. 'He won't be long,' she said now. 'He thought he'd be back for you comin'. Perhaps he's walked too far; his stump has been playin' him up lately.'

Katie turned from her mother and looked at her brother and asked gently, 'You feeling bad, Joe?'

Joe, seated on a cracket to the side of the hearth, an open fireplace, shook his head, then smiled at her and said, 'No, just tired. I'm at Boldon now.'

Katie's face stretched. 'You mean they sent you there and you've got to walk all that way?'

'Aye.' He nodded. 'It isn't so bad goin', it's comin' back. You're so tired.'

'Will you be there for the winter?'

'I don't know. You've got to go where they send you, it's in the bond.'

Aye, it was in the bond. The words her son had spoken seemed to check Catherine Mulholland's hands as she undid the little packages. Bond, bond, that crucifying bit of paper that her husband and son had to put their name to, that all men had to put their names to before they could get work, before they could eat. Her poor lad had been down the pit from when he was ten years old. She had nightmares, even now, about him sitting in the darkness for ten hours at a stretch. It had been twelve, even longer at times, and for twelve shillings a fortnight.

Joe was the only boy she had reared out of five sons. Her heart had seemed to break with each loss, but now she was glad they were gone, for they were in heaven, and warm, and happy. She had given birth to eight children altogether but had only managed to rear three, and she wished to God she had only reared two. But there, there, she mustn't say that. It was God's will she should have Lizzie.

'Ma.' Katie had come to her side. 'Do you think I should speak to Mrs Davis to speak to Mr Kennard, and for him to see Mr Wisden, the head gardener, you know? He was asking for another boy; I heard Cook on about it.'

Before Catherine could answer Joe said, 'No, I'll not go, so that's it, not for three bob a week. So don't. Next year I'll be gettin' eight shillings and in a couple years' time I'll be up the face with me da. I'll be getting as much as him. I'm not goin' to waste the three years I've done and go and start in a garden for three bob. Besides, I know nowt about gardens, and don't want to.' As Katie lowered her head he said quickly, 'But thanks all the same, Katie.' The brother and sister looked at each other and smiled. They had always been close, never fighting, even when they were small. But this family never fought; they laughed together, and cried together, but they didn't fight. They took their family grievances to God. It might be a different matter outside of the house when the men had to fight for their livelihood, and against the militia, and the police, and the knockers. But inside all was harmony.

'Can I bring Lizzie out now, Ma?'

'Aye, yes.' Catherine nodded, and Katie went across the stone-flagged kitchen to a door which led into the other room.

On a pallet beneath the tiny window sat a woman . . . or a girl. It all depended upon how you appraised her. Lizzie Mulholland was eighteen years old; she was of medium height, and no matter how little she ate she put on weight. To those outside the house she was known as Mulholland's idiot; to her family, she was slightly wrong in the head; but to Katie in particular she was like a crippled bird, and evoked the same tenderness.

Lizzie would sit for hours without moving, and if she wasn't taken to the water closet regularly she would do her business where she sat. Yet she couldn't always be depended upon to sit where she was put, for there were odd times when, as if obeying a beckoning finger, she would rise suddenly and leave the house if not detained, and once outside she would walk and walk. Once she was missing for nearly a day and had been found by a carrier outside Newcastle. He had recognised her and brought her home, and she had not been scolded but welcomed as if she was a member of the family on whom they all depended. But these sudden infrequent spurts of energy made vigilance necessary where she was concerned. Her talk was such as would be expected from a child of two, and now, on the sight of her sister, her flat face stretched into a shapeless smile and she muttered, 'Katie.' And when Katie went and stood by her side and said, 'Hello, Lizzie,' Lizzie placed her big head on the slender breast. It was an action of endearment that she kept for Katie alone; she never did it to her mother, or father, grandfather, or brother.

It was the act of Lizzie leaning on her breast that suddenly reminded Katie of what was secreted there, and, turning her head swiftly towards the open door, while she gave her hand to Lizzie and pulled her to her feet, she cried, 'Ma! Ma! What's come over me. You know what I forgot? . . . Me pay.' She swiftly undid the two buttons of her dress, unloosed the tape that tied her bodice, then thrust her hand inside the neck of her chemise and unpinned the calico bag. Her breath was coming quickly and she gabbled now, 'You wouldn't believe it. That's all I've thought of for days, getting me wages, and I couldn't get home quick enough, but since I come in the door I haven't thought a thing about it. Would you believe it?'

She bent her slender body towards Catherine and pressed the calico bag into her hands, and Catherine slowly shook the four shillings out, looked at them, then swiftly opened her arms and drew her daughter to her, and as swiftly she pushed her away again. Unclenching her fist and holding out her palm with the money in it, she said in a voice that was cracking slightly, 'You must have a shilling back every month.'

'A shilling, Ma! No, no, I don't want a shilling.' Katie's voice was high and she shook her head from side to side. 'The threepence will do. Mrs Davis has got half a crown saved up for me, now; I don't want a shilling.' She pushed her mother's hand away, and so quickly that the money spilled on to the floor, and immediately she was on her hands and knees picking it up. One of the shillings had rolled into a mud-filled crevice between two of the stones, and when she dug her finger in to get the coin she disturbed the earth and a strong obnoxious smell rose to her and filled her nostrils. The smell in the house was always worse in the summer when the water from the middens seeped under the foundations and oozed upwards. In the winter the rain dispersed it more quickly.

When the four coins were retrieved they all laughed. Katie now opening the back door, stood under the lean-to and rinsed her fingers in the wooden tub of water that stood on a bench attached to the wall.

She looked towards the cottage opposite, and over the yard walls she saw the head of Betty Monkton standing at her door. Betty called out to her, 'Oh, hello, Katie,' and she called back, 'Hello, Betty,' before turning indoors again.

At one time she had played with Betty, but it was a long, long time ago, and now she felt different and far removed from Betty, for Betty worked in the rope works and her father drank and her mother was feckless. Besides, they didn't go to chapel or church. Katie knew she was wrong in looking down on Betty Monkton, but she couldn't help it; it was because her own family was respectable and looked up to, even with their Lizzie being wrong in the head. It made her feel different. And then, hadn't she a fine job at the Manor?

She had just seated herself when the clip-clop of her granda's foot and crutch came to her from the yard and she jumped up and ran to the back door in time to see the old man hastily putting a small sack under the bench.

'Aw, there you are, me bonny lass.' With an expertness born of eleven years' practice, he almost jumped over the step, and, pushing his crutch against the wall, he enfolded his granddaughter in his arms.

'Aw, hinny; it seems years. Let me look at you.' Balancing on one leg, he held her away from him now, his hands on her shoulders. 'Eeh, you're growin'; I can see it more every time you come home. But you're not putting much fat on you.' His voice ended on a high inflection, and he tapped his fist gently against her chin. 'With all the grand feeding you tell us you get you've got little to show for it.'

'Aw, Granda.' She smiled widely at him. 'How you keepin'?'

'Fine, fine. Never felt fitter in me life. Come on, let's sit down and hear your crack.' He pulled his crutch to him and moved into the room, and his daughter brought a wooden, high-backed chair from against the wall and placed it in the circle at the other side of Katie.

Now Katie looked from one to the other. Then, resting her eyes on her mother, she asked, 'I won't wait for me da then.'

Before Catherine could reply William Finley put in, 'I wouldn't count on him for the next hour.' He looked over Katie's head towards his daughter. 'There's blokes makin' for the chapel, some comin' over the hills. There'll likely be a lot of talk afore the Sunday school starts.'

Catherine looked away from her father for a moment. She wished they hadn't to use the chapel. Yet if they were seen talking outside, especially to Mr Ramshaw and Fogerty, they'd be suspected of starting trouble. She always had a fear on her of them up top starting the evictions again. They had threatened to pull down the chapel next time; and it wouldn't take much pulling down, being little more than a lean-to against the end of the far block of cottages. The men had had to fight to be allowed to erect it and use it. It was awful; they had to fight for everything. Yet they didn't want to fight, they wanted to discuss and negotiate, but the masters weren't for that. They wanted to keep the men under, stamp them as troublemakers and blame the unions for agitating them . . . But enough of worry; Katie was here, her wonderful little lass, and she was going to hear her news.

'Well,' Katie began, casting her soft gaze from one to the other, 'the house is all upside down; you never saw anything like it. They've cleaned right from the top to the bottom, and all new satin curtains in the drawing room and dining room and gallery windows.'

'What colour?' Catherine put in, leaning towards her.

At this Katie blinked. She had never been in the drawing room or dining room, and only glimpsed the curtains as a distant gleam of colour through the half-open green-baize door when she took the water up to Mary Ann Hopkins. But after a moment's hesitation she said, 'Blue – a bird blue, you know, bright. And they're thick and padded. And they've washed the stair carpet. It was out on the lawn, yards and yards and yards of it. And they've cleaned the hall from top to bottom. And on Friday they moved the furniture out, 'cos that's where they'll dance – you know, to the band.' She now nodded her head to Joe, and Joe, his thin face full of interest, nodded back to her.

'And you should see the food. All kinds. Oh, you should see what's in the storeroom already. And Mrs Davis starts the morrow mornin' making the fancies. She's marvellous at the trifles and fancies. She makes meringues . . . O-o-h!' Katie now worked her jaws and smacked her lips. 'Talk about meltin' in your mouth, Ma, they're wonderful. An' she's arranging all the flowers in between the dishes. She's got a wonderful hand with decorations.' She moved her head slowly to emphasise this statement, and her grandfather asked, 'You seen the tables set afore, Katie?' She stared back at him. If she were to admit she hadn't actually seen a table set the telling of this tale would lose some of its magic. So she told a little lie. She nodded it first, then she added, 'Just a peep . . . once.'

Following this, she went on to give a long description of the cook and her culinary prowess, omitting her pettiness and carping ways. Then she spoke in glowing terms of her mistress – whom she could go months without even glimpsing, her mistress who had been to London to buy a dress for the ball. And she described the dress. It was green and made of taffeta and could stand by itself. Oh, it was beautiful. And it had rosettes and leaves sewn all over it in lovely patterns. Katie's description of the dress was pretty accurate, seeing that it had come through Jane Stockwell discussing it with Mrs Davis, overheard by Daisy Studd, who passed it on to the clientele of the kitchen.

Then she came to Miss Theresa. She described her unobtrusive arrival, saying that nobody would have known she was in the house if Mr Kennard hadn't mentioned it. She described her plain way of dressing, which was even plainer than before she married; and turning to her mother now, she ended, 'She doesn't look happy, Ma, she looks sad like, the way she walks and hangs her head. Afore she was married, when Miss Ainsley was there, I've seen her running and laughin'. They used to go along by the wall a lot up on to the hill, but she's sad now. I like Miss Theresa, Ma.'

'I know you do, Katie,' said Catherine, and she didn't wonder why the seventeen-year-old girl looked sad, married to a man old enough to be her grandfather.

And now Katie came to the incident in the courtyard. She was adept at turning a joke against herself, and when she finished they were all laughing uproariously, even Lizzie, although she didn't know what she was laughing at.

Now Joe asked, 'Was his clothes all messed?'

'Yes, they were splashed round his gaiters.'

'Did you get wrong?' Joe asked.

'No. Nobody saw, thank goodness, only Mr Rodger. He was with him. He picked me up.' She turned her head now and looked at her mother. 'Mr Rodger's nice, Ma. He's like Miss Theresa; kind like, you know.' Catherine nodded, and Katie went on, 'He laughed . . . Eeh! I don't know what would have happened if he hadn't been there. Mr Bernard would likely have raised the yard an' had Cook out, and then . . . oh, dear me.' She drooped her head to one side and closed her eyes for a moment before finishing. 'She would have hung me up on the spit and left me there all night; I'm sure she would.' Again they all laughed.

And so it went on until Rodney Mulholland returned, and then the atmosphere took on a more serious note.

Rodney now sat beside his daughter, as he did every other Sunday, and heard her read passages from the Bible, and during this Grandfather Finley sat nearer to the fire although the day was hot, and Lizzie continued to stare at her sister, and Joe slept.

When his father had come in Joe had given up his cracket and gone to the dim corner of the room where stood his parents' bed, a similar erection to the smaller ones in the other room, and sat on the edge of it; and after a while he had dropped sideways and fallen fast asleep. And his father had not awakened him today and reprimanded him and bid him join in the lesson, but had gently lifted his feet up on to the bed, after placing an old rag between them and the patchwork cover.

Katie's reading was slow and she stumbled on the big words and her father made her repeat them, as when she came to 'atonement'.

'Who shall offer it before the Lord, and make an . . . '

'Split it into three, a-tone-ment, atonement.'

Katie nodded and repeated 'A-tone-ment'; then read, 'Make an a-tone-ment for her; and she shall be cleansed from the issue of her blood. This is the law for her that hath borne a male or a female. And if she be not able to bring a lamb, then she shall bring two . . . '

'Tur-tles.'

'Tur-tles, or two young pigeons; the one for the burnt offering, and the other for a sin offering; and the priest shall make an a-tone-ment for her, and she shall be clean.'

Katie didn't understand a word of what she was reading, but it was nice to read.

She was ready to go. She had, after some protest, allowed her mother to put six pennies into her calico bag; she had stoutly refused to take a shilling, although with a shilling she would have been much nearer to getting the lace collar and the white cotton gloves that she craved for from the pedlar on his next visit to the back door of the house.

The procedure was as always. She kissed Lizzie on the cheek and stood still for a moment while her sister rested her head against her, then she patted her and said, 'Be a good girl, Lizzie; I'll see you in a fortnight's time.' And Lizzie stared at her, and the colour of her eyes changed, indicating that somewhere beyond the dim regions of the stunted brain there was an awareness that understood loss.

Next Katie stood in front of Joe. She put out her hand and touched his shoulder, and he did the same to her. 'Try to get more sleep,' she said.

'Aye,' he said, 'Ta-ra, Katie.'

'Ta-ra, Joe,' she said. Then lifting her arms she put them round her father's neck and kissed him on the cheek, and he held her tightly for a moment. Then it was her mother's turn. Her mother did not embrace her until she was actually at the door, and then she, too, held her tightly; after which she traced her fingers gently around her face, straightened her hat, then said, 'Be a good lass, and please Mrs Davis.'

'I will, Ma. Yes, I will. Ta-ra.'

'Ta-ra,' they all said, all except her granda, for he always accompanied her on the first mile of her return journey.

At the end of the row of cottages she turned and waved, and they waved back, and when she and her granda were on the moor making for the road, just before they dropped from sight, she turned again and waved vigorously; then she and her granda were alone.

For William Finley this was the peak of his granddaughter's visit, when, side by side, they walked together over the fells. Rain, snow, or shine he had set her on her journey every other Sunday since she had been at the house. Down the shallow valley he hobbled, and up the other side to the high ground, where she would leave him and from where he could watch her progress for almost a mile.

William was not a God-fearing man like his son-in-law; he did not hold with chapel, or church, but there was scarcely a day went by that he didn't thank God for giving him his granddaughter; he thanked Him for the light and joy she had brought into the fast-fleeing years of his life, years that would have been corroded with bitterness, because of his infirmity, had she not been there to prove to him that God tempered the wind to the shorn lamb. He had lost his leg in an accident at the Hebburn pit. It was just after they had started to use the Davy safety lamp. Instead of an asset to their work the men of the pit had viewed this new and much-praised acquisition with the same feeling they viewed the men who had introduced it into their working life, for the owners looked upon the safety lamp as if it was Aladdin's very own, and after its inception they took even less safety precautions in the mine than they had done before.

The very necessary ventilation shafts were not sunk; why go to such expense when they had this wonderful lamp? And so the danger of bad air that was ever present, the increasing invasions of water, resulted in explosions. Thirty-one men had died in the accident where William had lost his leg. And from that time he had suffered from nightmares, nightmares in which he was suffocating among mangled bodies and blood. He never saw the mangled bodies or blood, he only felt them, for the nightmare always placed him in total and absolute blackness . . . But in the daytime there had always been the child, his only daughter's laughing, gay, talkative, lovely child.

They were now approaching the top of the hill, where she would leave her granda. He was puffing a bit and she said to him, 'You shouldn't come this far.'

'You get me a pair of eyes that can see through the hill and I won't.' He jerked his head at her.

'But it's all right now, not like in the winter in the dark.' She always ran like a hare the last mile or so of her journey in the winter.

On top of the hill the old man lowered himself down on to the grass, and she sat down beside him, then she undid the front of her bodice, took out her bag again, and, taking three pennies from it, she pushed them in his hand, only to have him say, 'No, no, I'll not. I'll not.'

'Go on, Granda; get some baccy.'

'No, lass, no.' He thrust her hand away. 'Workin' for a month for threepence.'

'I don't, I don't.' Her voice was high and indignant. 'I get four shillings.'

'Aye.' Now his face looked stern. 'You get four shillings and it goes to support me.'

Her eyes stretched, her mouth fell open; then her lips came together and she swallowed as if in indignation and said loudly, 'Don't be a silly billy, Granda. What put that into your head? I'd always given me ma me money.'

'Aye, aye.' His head was moving slowly now. 'I suppose so.' Then, turning towards her, he ended, 'But I'm not takin' it.'

'You are so. There it is.' She put the coppers on the ground. 'And if you don't pick them up they'll stay there till they take root.' She was smiling gently at him and he was looking at her from under his eyebrows. It was at this point they both became aware of the approach of footsteps. They turned simultaneously and looked down the hill, staring for a moment into the distance, where a man was approaching. Then William, screwing his body around, looked directly ahead and said under his breath, 'It's Buntin'.'

Katie looking ahead now said, 'I'll get off, Granda.'

'No, sit tight till he's passed; let him get his distance.'

Mark Bunting, the master weighman for the owners, or the keeker as he was called by the men, was the man who checked the corves of coal hewed by the miners; he was the man who had the power to cut a man's wages by as much as half if the seven-hundredweight basket the miner sent up from the black bowels of the earth should show a deficiency of two or three pounds. Often when this happened all the coal in that basket was made free to the owner.

The same procedure was followed when there was a small quantity of stone among the coal. No account was taken for the men having to get the coal out, even by the light of a candle. The keekers worked on a commission basis; the more corves they found faulty and could pass as free to the owners the more money they themselves made.

Mark Bunting was a man of medium height, thickset with dark bushy brows over deep-set eyes. His face was full and his lips thin. Like most keekers he was a lonely man, working between the devil and the deep sea, between the men who hated him and the owners who despised him. Bunting lived half a mile from the village, not in a stinking two-roomed cottage but in a good solid house with two rooms up and two down. It was provided by the Rosiers and it had a garden in which a dog was chained. Mark Bunting needed protection; he needed warning of approaching visitors. There was a blue mark running from the rim of his cap down to the top of his left cheekbone, which was proof what he had not always been on his guard. It was not an uncommon thing for keekers to be found in ditches with their heads split open.

'Fine day.' He came to a stop about a yard from where William sat.

It was some seconds before the old man, without glancing at him, said, 'It'll do.'

Katie, lifting her eyes slowly upwards and over her granda's head, looked at this man about whom she had heard so much yet had never seen. She saw that he was very well put-on, and he looked entirely apart from the men in the village in that he was wearing a cravat and a fancy waistcoat. There was a pattern about him that reminded her of her master, and his sons, but she did not include his voice in that pattern, for it was rough-sounding. In the brief space of time that she looked at the man there came over her a feeling that she couldn't understand, only that it was in a way a betrayal of her own kind, for why should she feel sorry for a keeker?

Bunting's eyes were covering her face when William lifted his head sharply and glared up at him, and the man, turning abruptly, walked away from them.

William didn't speak until Bunting was well out of hearing, then he said under his breath, 'Bide your time; you don't want to come up with that 'un.'

No, she didn't. The way he had looked at her had frightened her a bit. Perhaps he frightened the men in the same way, by just looking at them, because although he was thick he wasn't very big.

Silently now they watched the figure become smaller, and when the head disappeared from view William pulled himself up, tucked his crutch under his arm and said, 'Well now, you'd better be away.'

'Yes, Granda.' She dusted some dry grass from her skirt; then raising her face to his she kissed him, while putting one arm around his neck and the other hand in his pocket and dropping in the three pennies, and before he could protest further she was running down the slope. At the bottom she turned and called, 'Ta-ra, Granda,' and he called back, 'Ta-ra, me bairn.'

At intervals along the road she turned and waved; and then came the bend and after one last wave she could see him no longer.

It had been a lovely day, a wonderful day. She felt so happy she could sing. Suddenly she whirled around, and her scraping feet sent up a cloud of dust from the road, while the skirt of her print dress swirled into a balloon about her legs. Then she was running and laughing. She was daft, daft, but she was happy, and the ball was on Tuesday. The excitement of the event brought a fluttering in her chest. Perhaps she would see them dancing. Mrs Davis had let her and Dotty peep through the landing door once, but they hadn't seen much from there, just the occasional figure floating past the bottom of the stairs. But even that had been wonderful. Oh, on her next day off she would have something to tell them at home, wouldn't she?

She began to run again. Then suddenly she stopped and her step became sedate, while her eyes stared to the far end of the road and the approaching figure. Even at this long distance she knew it was the keeker coming back from his walk. As the distance lessened between them her limbs began to tremble. Dotty had told her that she had once seen the devil and that she got such a fright her face came out in spots and she hadn't been able to get rid of them since. And it was true; her face was covered in spots.

Mark Bunting now took on all the appearance of the devil, and when he stopped dead in front of her she thought her knees were going to give way, and she put her hand to her face.

'Where are you off to?'

'The . . . the house.'

'Rosier's?'

She nodded.

'What do you do there?'

'I'm scullery maid.'

He stared at her, wondering the while why he had stopped; he didn't like women. Fortunately for him they were not a necessity in his life. 'What's your name?' he said.

'Katie . . . Katie Mulholland.'

Big Mulholland's girl. 'That your grandfather back there?'

'Aye. Yes.'

He hadn't taken his unblinking stare from her face. He saw that she was frightened of him and this fact gave him a sense of pleasure and he prolonged the interview.

'What do they pay you?'

'A shilling a week.'

'Huh!' His head went up and he made a sound like a laugh, yet it wasn't a laugh. 'You get off every Sunday?'

'No.' She shook her head and backed a step from him as she said, 'Every other.' Then she added quickly, 'I'm due in; I'll be late.' She took another two steps back.

Her fear amused him; he had the desire to pretend to spring on her. He was further amused by the thought that she would do it in her bloomers if he did. It came to him, as he watched her turn swiftly round and move from him at the point of a run, that she hadn't addressed him as 'Sir'. A girl of her standing should have; he wasn't a man of the village. He felt piqued that even her fear hadn't prompted her to use the term 'Sir'. He watched her for a full minute before going on his way.

When Katie left the track and entered the grounds by the wicket gate she was still running, but once inside the grounds she came to a halt and pressed her two hands to her chest as she gasped for breath. Eeh, he had frightened her; the way he had looked at her . . . Yet it was funny she couldn't help feeling sorry for him. But she'd better not let her da or granda hear her say that.

She was still panting when she reached the rise that overlooked the house and saw Miss Theresa sitting there. She had a book in her hand but she wasn't reading.

Katie gave a slight bob and went to pass her, when Miss Theresa spoke. 'You've been home, Katie?'

'Yes, Miss . . . Miss Theresa.' Somehow she couldn't call her ma'am.

'How are your folks?'

'Oh, they're fine, Miss Theresa.'

'And you enjoyed yourself?'

'Oh yes.' The smile reached to Katie's ears. 'It's been lovely.'

'Come and sit down a moment and tell me all about it.' She moved on the grass as if making room for her, and Katie looked down on her, her mouth falling into a gape, and she said, 'What, miss?' as if she hadn't heard. But she had heard all right. Miss Theresa was funny. Just imagine what they would say back at the house if they saw her sitting there. It was as the others said, she didn't really act like a lady. But that didn't stop her from liking Miss Theresa the best of the lot.

'Thank you, Miss Theresa, but . . . but I'm due in and Mrs Davis will be waitin'.'

'Yes, yes.' Theresa looked up at her and moved her head slowly. 'But I'm glad you've had an enjoyable day, Katie,' she said.

'Thank you, Miss Theresa.'

Katie turned and walked slowly away now, down towards the copse. She wished she could have done what Miss Theresa had asked because she sounded lonely. But there, Miss Theresa couldn't be lonely. She was with her family, and in this lovely house and garden, besides which she had a great big house of her own – better than this one, they said.

It was odd, Katie thought, as she neared the yard, but in the last half an hour she had met two people and she had thought they were lonely. Likely they weren't at all; it was just her and her fancies. She was daft.

Back on the grassy slope, Theresa sat, her legs straight out before her, her hands lying limply in her lap. She was thinking of Katie, and Katie would have been surprised, even amazed, had she known of the times since she had come into the household that Miss Theresa had thought about her. From the first Theresa had been fascinated by the young girl's face. She thought the feeling was an artistic quality she possessed that could appraise beauty, that could be stirred and excited by it. Once, when they had been talking about money, Miss Ainsley had said, 'Now take a child like Katie Mulholland, educate her, clothe her and what would you have? Someone who would doubtless be acclaimed from here to Rome. Yet what will happen to her? She will marry a miner, have two or three children before she's twenty, and by the time she's thirty there'll be no semblance left of the beautiful girl. Whereas if she had money she could cosset and pamper that beauty and at thirty she would just be in her prime. Never despise money, Theresa,' Miss Ainsley had ended.

Oh, if she could only go to Ainsley, but Ainsley was now in London, instilling wisdom into two young ladies.

What was she to do following Tuesday? Write to her husband and tell him she wasn't coming back, or do what her mother asked and put up with it until after the wedding? She closed her eyes and saw vividly what it was she would have to put up with, and it came to her with clarity that never, as long as she should live, could she bear to be a partner in this with any man. Turning her body slowly round, she lay on the grass and buried her face in the crook of her arm.

CHAPTER FOUR

THE BALL WAS well under way, and there was a pause in the running, rushing and scurrying. All the guests had arrived, all had eaten and some were now dancing, and the house was filled with the echo of the music.

This side of the façade of the flower-bedecked rooms the staff were breathing more easily, some even daring to relax; and Cook was one of the latter. She was sitting in the rocking chair to the side of the open spit fire, fortifying herself with a strong cup of tea laced with gin. She was extremely tired but was experiencing a sense of deep satisfaction, for, as she had just remarked to Dotty: say it, as she herself would, for nobody else was likely to, she had done more than her duty this past week. More had been asked of her than should have been asked of any human being. But had she faltered? Not a step. And now her legs were killing her.

Katie's legs too were very tired and every other part of her body, especially her arms. She had been on her feet from half-past five, and now all she wanted to do was to drop her head forward on to the table and go to sleep. She slid off the end of the wooden form, lifted her plate and said to Dotty, 'I think I'll swill me face under the pump, that'll bring me to.'

'Before you do any swillin' you see to them boilers.'

'Yes, Cook, I'll do them right away.' And she did them right away.

The last of the twilight was fading and it was very warm when she went outside, but cooler than in the kitchen, and she breathed deeply for a few moments before walking across the yard to the pump. The aspect of the courtyard was changed tonight, for the wide entrance was blocked with carriages. She would have loved to squeeze in between them and look towards the drive and the front door where all the lights were hanging, but she was afraid of running into the grooms. At present the grooms and coachmen were all in Mr Tatman's harness room where beer and food was set for them, but if one of them should come out and catch you on your own they would rumple you, so Dotty said.

46

She pumped the water, then quickly held her face towards it, being careful that she didn't get her cap wet or the front of her dress . . . There, that felt better. She looked up into the sky. It would soon be black dark and then the house would look lovely. She wished she could go along the wall and up the hill and look at it from there. But she would never dare, not only because she would be frightened of the dark, but because some of the guests went into the garden, and things went on, Dotty said. But Dotty told lies; her mother had told her to take everything Dotty said with a pinch of salt.

She finished drying her face on the underside of her coarse apron; then she walked back to the kitchen.

Florrie Green, the head chambermaid, was in the kitchen now and she had apparently caught Cook's interest enough to cause her to put her feet down and sit up straight. 'Frumpish the mother is,' Florrie was saying. 'Little and dumpy, and no style at all. Well, I was surprised. An' you know what? She's an honourable, and Mr Kennard says she's one sister who's a lady, and another who's a countess. Well! To look at her' – she bent down now and put her face close to Cook's – 'you would think a pedlar had dressed her.'

'No!'

'Aye, you would.'

'How's the daughter dressed – Miss Ann?' Cook asked now.

'Not bad.' Florrie adjusted the bib of her fancy apron. 'Pink she's in; it suits her complexion. She's pretty in a way, but she's the kind that'll fade early.' She accompanied her pronouncement with a telling movement of her head. Then she went on quickly, 'But the father now, he looks somethin'. He's tall and thin, and his hair's dead white. He's got a sort of . . . a presence. You know what I mean, Cook?'

The cook now wagged her head slowly, signifying her complete understanding of class; then, bringing it close to Florrie's, she said in a low voice, 'It's funny them not staying in the house, isn't it? All going back to Shields.'

'You're not the only one who thinks that, Cook.'

'Who they staying with?' Cook asked now, and Florrie replied, 'The Palmers; old family friends. They're here; husband and wife. Uppish lookin' . . . I bet Miss Ann's disappointed.' She pushed the cook in her flabby chest with the flat of her hand. 'She's right over the hoop for him; you should see her lookin' at him.'

'You've seen them together then?'

'Uh-huh! I was taking the dishes from Fanny at the side door and they were dancin'.'

As the chambermaid went to leave the kitchen Cook screwed her body round in the chair and called to her, 'You never said what the missus looks like?'

Florrie turned, saying, 'Outshines the lot of 'em, if you ask me. Her frock looks wonderful, an' you can see she's pleased as punch; everythin' goin' smoothly an' that. But there's one damper on the proceedin's.' She flapped her hand towards the cook. 'Miss Theresa. Coo, she looks as if she's lost a sixpence and found a threepenny bit. She was never very pleasant at any time, was she, but her face the night, Lordy me! I saw her dancin' round with Mr Rodger; I don't suppose anybody else would ask her. An' she's got a frock on . . . well.' She closed her eyes and made a deep sweep with her head. 'I'm tellin' you, I wouldn't swap it for me Sunday one.'

'No!'

'It's a fact, Cook. And it isn't like as if she mightn't be able to buy one, for the old fellow was potty over her, wasn't he? An' her with a face'd turn milk sour. But God, there's no countin' for taste, I say that every day in the week – there's no countin' for taste.'

'You're right there, Florrie. You're right there.'

The final word had been said on the matter, and Florrie went out and Cook settled herself again, only to turn her gimlet eyes on the girls seated at the table and shout, 'An' don't you two sit there as if you're finished. You, Dotty, can clear up the dishes and get the pans ready for the porridge; an' you, Katie, get on with your floor.'

Katie stared through her tired eyes at the cook. She had somehow thought that the floor would have a miss the night, seeing that people would be tramping back and forward on it until the small hours of the morning. Her thoughts must have shown in her face, for the cook, her voice even higher now, cried, 'An' don't you look at me like that unless you want your ears boxed.'

Katie immediately sidled from the form and went and got her bucket, and she had just started on the floor in the corner next to the ovens when Mrs Davis came hurrying into the kitchen. Seeing the cook sitting with her feet up she said, 'It's all right, it's all right, take a minute when you can; I just wanted to tell you how pleased everybody seemed with the dishes. I've heard a number of favourable remarks.'

To this the cook inclined her head and gave Mrs Davis a tight smile, then said, 'Well, I did me best as always. Nobody can say I don't do me best.'

'Yes, you always do your best, Delia.' Now Mrs Davis turned her head to the dim corner to where Katie was kneeling, and without stopping to think she said, 'Oh, that's going to be a waste of time, Katie, with all the tramping back and . . . ' Her voice trailed away as she realised that in a way she was infringing on Cook's domain, and so, looking at Cook again, she added in a pleasant, and apologetic, tone, 'It'll be dirty again by two o'clock, Delia.'

'Well, you would have somethin' to say if I made her scrub it after that hour, wouldn't you?' Cook had put her feet down and was sitting bolt upright in her chair.

'Yes, I think I would, Delia. But this being a special occasion I should have thought the floor could have been left for one night.'

'And have you find fault the morrow?'

Mrs Davis immediately became the dignified housekeeper. 'If I gave an order that a thing wasn't to be done, Cook, I wouldn't be so foolish as to find fault the following day because my order had been carried out; besides, you'll need Katie in a very short while to see to the side dishes and the big plate that will be coming from the tables. Mr Kennard and I will see to the sets and the silver in the pantry, but the rest can be washed here.'

The cook and the housekeeper looked at each other squarely in the eye. Then Mrs Davis turned slowly about and left the kitchen, and the cook repeated to herself, 'Mr Kennard and I will see to the plate in the pantry.' There was no doubt but they would. She glanced towards Katie, who had moved to a fresh patch of stone floor, but she didn't countermand her order. If the dishes were to be washed, then she would wash them when she had finished the floor.

It was now two o'clock. The music from the orchestra could still be heard in the kitchen. Cook held her candle in one hand while she supported herself against the table with the other. She was dead on her feet, she told herself. 'You two ready?' She spoke over her shoulder, and Dotty was the first to say, 'Aye, Cook.' She, too, held a candlestick in her hand.

'Katie.'

Katie came running out of the pot room, saying, 'Yes, Cook, I'm comin'. I've just banked the fires down. I'll just wash me hands.'

'Come on this minute, girl. Don't try me any more, I've had enough for one day.'

Katie grabbed up her candle from the mantelpiece, lit it from the glowing embers of the fire, then followed Dotty, who followed the cook.

In procession, they went out of the kitchen, along the long corridor that led to the butler's pantry and the housekeeper's room, and through the door that led to the back staircase.

They had just reached the first landing when the green-baize door connecting with the gallery was pushed open and Mrs Davis came through, and with her a loud swell of music. Closing the door behind her, she said in a thick whisper, 'Oh, I was just coming down . . . Would you like to have a peep?'

This was the moment Katie had been waiting for, but the work of a long day and a longer night had swamped her interest; all she wanted to do now was to reach the attic and throw herself down on her bed; she doubted if she would be able to take her things off. She knew a sense of relief when she heard Cook say in a stilted tone, 'Thank you all the same, Mrs Davis, but I'm done up. All I want is me bed.'

As she finished speaking she raised her candle just the slightest and peered at the housekeeper, at her flushed face and bright eyes, which told her that Mrs Davis had drained a number of not quite empty bottles already and would doubtless drain a few more before she went to sleep.

She was about to move on when Mrs Davis said, 'But you would, wouldn't you?' She was bending towards the two girls.

Dotty Black stared at Mrs Davis dully. She knew on which side her bread was buttered. The housekeeper might have power in the house, but she was in the kitchen under Cook, and she didn't intend to get on the wrong side of her and have a life like Katie Mulholland, so she said, 'I'm tired, Mrs Davis.'

Mrs Davis straightened her back and her lips took on a set line, and her eyes stayed on Dotty some seconds before she looked towards Katie and asked, 'Well, you, Katie; you would love to have a peep, wouldn't you?'

Katie peered up at her benefactress in the dim light. She always wanted to please Mrs Davis – she had promised her mother she would – and she knew now that if she refused her invitation she wouldn't please her. Mrs Davis seemed bent on showing off the scene in the hall as if it was a personal triumph of her own. Katie sensed this, as the housekeeper's wine-laden breath wafted over her; and so, while knowing that tomorrow in the kitchen she would suffer the consequences of her choice, she said, 'Thank you, Mrs Davis, I'd like to.'

'I knew you would.' Mrs Davis, not quite herself, put out her hand and caught at Katie's, saying, 'Put your candle down and nip it.'

Katie did as she was bidden, and as she was taken through the green-baize door she was aware that Cook and Dotty were standing still, their faces dark with disapproval, watching her.

Mrs Davis now led her along the short passage to where it opened out into a corner of the gallery, and there she brought her to a halt, whispering, 'We'll wait here a minute until they start dancin' again.'

Katie stood blinking in the light from the chandelier hanging over the hall and from the four lamps hanging along the length of the gallery. After the dimness of the kitchen, and latterly the stairs, the light was dazzling. And then there was the smell – scenty, warm, like the smell from the flower garden late at night.

'There, they've started.' Mrs Davis glanced about her, then, saying to Katie 'Stay still,' she went along the gallery until she came to the last of the big windows and there she stopped, looked around her again, then beckoned Katie towards her.

Slightly more awake now with the excitement, Katie scurried across the strange ground of soft carpet, past the wide passage that led to the bedrooms; then, hugging the wall, she went swiftly past the four long windows and came to where Mrs Davis was standing pointing.

There was an open balustrade edging the gallery, and through it, from where they were standing, Katie could only see a quarter of the hall below and the odd dancing couples. One, two, three steps forward, one, two, three steps back, then the men bowing and the ladies dipping; then twirling round and again one, two, three steps forward, and one, two, three steps back. She glanced up at Mrs Davis and found that Mrs Davis was looking at her.

'Aren't they lovely, Katie?'

'Oh yes, Mrs Davis. Oh yes.' She was gazing down on the dancers again before she finished speaking. Oh, if only her ma and da and their Joe could see them. But somewhere at the back of her mind, even as she thought this, she got the impression that her da and Joe might not have viewed the scene through hers, or her mother's, eyes.

How long she stood entranced she didn't know, but she almost jumped from the ground when Mrs Davis caught her arm tightly and pulled her backwards, then stood looking in the direction of the main passage as she whispered low, 'Someone's coming.'

The next minute Katie found herself gripped by the collar of her frock and thrust between the long curtains of the gallery window.

'Sit on the sill,' Mrs Davis hissed at her, and Katie, always quick in emergencies, hoisted herself up on to the broad, padded window sill, and there she knelt stiffly, waiting.

It seemed dark in here after the light of the landing; yet, glancing through the window without moving her head, she saw that a moon was riding high behind fluffed clouds. She was also aware that Mrs Davis was still standing in front of the curtains. Then she heard a voice, which she recognised instantly as belonging to Mr Rodger. She heard him say, 'Oh, there you are, Mrs Davis; I was just going to look for you. It's Miss Theresa; she's feeling upset. It must have been something she ate that has disagreed with her. I wonder if you've got a minute to look in on her.'

When Mrs Davis' voice came to her she knew that she was no longer outside the curtain but along the gallery. She heard her make some answer but she couldn't make out what was said. Following this there was just the music again, soft now, muted.

After waiting for some minutes she sat back on her heels, careful not to touch the curtains. She wished Mrs Davis would hurry and get her out of this. The tiredness was overpowering her again, and sitting on her haunches was a strain, yet she was afraid to alter her position in case she touched the curtains. She knew if she had been one of the parlourmaids, or a chambermaid, she could have walked across the gallery to the green-baize door and it wouldn't have mattered very much if she had met one of the guests, or even a member of the household, because she would have been dressed for inside the house. But the way she was, with her dirty frock and apron, and crumpled cap, she knew she was no fit person to be in this part of the house at any time, but especially tonight.

Minutes passed, which seemed like hours, and Mrs Davis did not return. Daringly now, she inserted a finger between the curtains and squinted along the gallery. It was empty, and they were still dancing down below . . . Slowly she let herself down from the sill and, creeping close to the panelled wall between the windows, she had almost reached the last one when the music stopped. At the same moment she heard a door open along the corridor and from the direction of the stairs came voices, and she must cross in front of the stairs to get to the passage that led to the green-baize door. For just one second she pressed herself against the panelling, and then, with the quickness of a lizard, she was behind the curtain and on to the sill of the last window.

On her hands and knees now, she remained motionless, and her breathing almost stopped when she heard her master's voice. He must have been only a foot or two away from the curtains; it was as if he was shouting in her ear. He was talking in a hearty, laughing way to someone. Then came other voices, ladies' voices and a lot of rustling sounds as they walked up and down the gallery. After an eternity when she found she couldn't remain on her hands and knees any longer she held her breath as she slowly let herself down on to her side; and there she lay with her head on her arm not daring to move.

The sill was not long enough to take her stretched-out length, but it was broad enough to allow her to bend her knees without them touching the curtains. She told herself that when the music started again they would all go downstairs, then she would fly out and get away. But when the music did start there remained the sound of voices, and the one on which she concentrated her attention was the loud boisterous voice of her master. It went on and on until it became mixed up with the music. The music was slow now and lovely, and soothing; becoming softer and softer, it gradually faded away altogether and she was asleep . . .

It was about ten minutes later that the gallery emptied and Mrs Davis hurried to the end window, only to find that Katie wasn't on the sill. She drew a deep breath of relief. Katie was quick, bright; she had taken the opportunity to slip away when all was quiet.

Half an hour later the ball came to an end and the guests came upstairs for their cloaks and the hall rang to the sound of goodbyes and congratulations to the happy couple, not forgetting the master and mistress of the house who had put on such a splendid show for them. The last of the guests to leave were the Talfords. James Talford shook George Rosier's hand, saying courteously, 'I only hope I do them as much justice at our little affair next month as you have done them tonight.'

'Oh, I have no doubt but that you will excel anything that I have attempted, no doubt at all,' said George Rosier heartily, beaming up at the tall man. And he hadn't any doubt.

Agnes Rosier was now embracing Mrs Talford as if they were devoted sisters, and when she came to say goodbye to her future daughter-in-law she hovered over the blushing girl as if she was finding it hard to restrain her affection for her, and then with a gracious gesture of her hand she passed her over to her son, and Bernard accompanied his future wife down the steps to the carriage. Once there, however, he was quick to turn aside to assist her mother into her seat and bow gravely to her father before bending over his fiancée's hand and raising it to his lips.

Not until the carriage had disappeared round the curve in the drive did he enter the house again. He walked slowly through the vestibule, crossed the hall and looked to where his father and Rodger were standing talking. Then he turned his gaze to his mother where she was standing in the doorway of the small parlour, and as he went towards her his father and brother joined him.

Once inside the room, and the door closed, they all stood looking at each other. It was Agnes who spoke first. 'Well,' she said, looking directly at Bernard, 'what do you think?'

'You mean, how it went?'

She inclined her head impatiently.

'Oh, excellently.'

'You think they were impressed?'

'Who can tell? He's as close as a clam.'

'You're right there.' George Rosier walked to the mantelpiece and rested his hand on it, and, looking down into the almost dead fire, said, 'You never can tell with types like him, the holy Joes, but I think he was impressed all right. Nothing was too ostentatious, everything just as it should be. Don't you think so?' He had now turned his head sharply and addressed his younger son.

Rodger undid the second pearl button of his waistcoat as he replied, 'I thought everything went marvellously, and the food was superb.' He would have never dared say what he was thinking; that if tonight's show hadn't been ostentatious he wondered to what extreme they would go to put on something they did consider ostentatious.

'Good; good.' George Rosier returned his gaze to the fire, and Agnes said, 'I must remember to tell Mrs Davis to congratulate the cook tomorrow . . . Ah, well!' She heaved a deep sigh. 'We can do no more at present, so if you'll excuse me I'll retire.'

Her husband made no comment on this, not even casting his glance towards her, but her sons went to her and, one after the other, kissed her on the cheek; then Rodger opened the door for her. But before she had actually passed through it George Rosier turned from the fireplace and asked, 'What happened to Theresa? Where did she get to half the night? And she wasn't there at the end.'

Agnes turned her head and, looking over her shoulder towards him, said, 'I don't know what happened to her'; her tone implying, 'Nor do I care.'

'She felt sick and had to go to her room,' Rodger put in. And now both his parents turned and looked at him, and, glancing from one to the other, he said, 'It must have been something she ate, the lobster perhaps; it never did agree with her.'

Agnes continued to look at Rodger for a moment, but she made no comment, and when she turned away he watched her walking across the hall to the stairs, her dress spreading like a peacock's tail behind her.

'Well, I'm off too. Goodnight, Father. Goodnight, Bernard.' Rodger nodded to each in turn, and they both answered, 'Goodnight.'

The father and son left together now, there was silence between them until Bernard, stroking the hair on his cheekbones with his spread finger and thumb, said, 'He was more affable than I expected.'

'Yes, I suppose you could say that; in fact I found him surprisingly civil. But don't you take anything for granted. Be wary. And mind—' George Rosier now turned fully around and faced his son, and wagging his finger at him he said darkly, 'Keep your nose clean. You understand?'

Bernard moved slowly away. His father's expression was distasteful and it angered him, for he understood its implication only too well.

'God, I'm tired, and that's putting it mildly. You coming?'

'In a moment or so.'

George Rosier turned to go, then stopped and asked, 'What do you make of Palmer?'

'I don't really know except that he's playing the father figure already and he's too young for it.'

'He's too young for nothing. He's as wily as a cartload of monkeys. Did you notice they went off early? You would have thought they'd have waited for Ann and her people, seeing they're friends of theirs and are giving them hospitality for the night. You didn't talk big to him, did you?' When Bernard looked at him he added, 'Well, I wouldn't put it past you, even sober.' And on this show of confidence he marched out and into the hall, where he stood for a short while watching the men quenching the candelabra, and putting out the lamps.

Back in the parlour, Bernard brought his staring gaze from the door; then, dragging a chair towards the hearth, he dropped into it and, bending forward, poked the fire and threw on a log. As he sat back he shivered. He'd had very little inside him since yesterday to keep him warm; for having been cautioned by his father to take his wine in moderation when in the company of the Talfords, he had gone even further and hardly drunk anything at all. But now the time for moderation had passed. He leant towards the bell rope, but, remembering that there would be no-one in the kitchen at this hour, he rose from his chair, went to the door, pulled it open and called softly across the hall to Kennard.

The butler left his two assistants and came to the door, saying, 'Yes, sir?'

'Bring me a tray and bottle.'

'A wine, sir?'

'No, brandy.'

'Very well, sir.'

A few minutes later Kennard returned to the room and, placing a small table near Bernard's side, he put down the tray holding a bottle of brandy and a glass.

'Pull them off.' Bernard nodded to his feet, and Kennard, standing in front of him, lifted one foot after the other on to his bent knees and gently eased off the soft leather boots.

Bernard now said, 'You needn't wait up, I may be some time. I'll put out the lamp.'

'Thank you, sir.' Kennard walked with his stately step towards the door, giving no sign, at least in his posture, of his utter weariness.

Bernard poured himself a large measure of brandy, placed his feet on the top of a tapestry stool and lay back with the glass in his hand. He swirled the liquid around the glass once or twice before putting it to his lips; then he contemplated the now glowing log on the hearth as he let his mind travel into the future.

She'd be like clay in his hands, and through her he'd win the approval of her father; he had no doubt in his mind but that he could achieve this. Yet he was aware that he would have to be cautious; all the while he would have to be cautious. He did not really know what she would prove to be like behind the four-poster curtains, and he doubted very much if she'd be entertaining in that way, for already she was much too pliable. He knew that he would soon sicken of her adoration, in fact it tired him already, but the price he would have to pay for what she would bring to him would be in proving to her that his ardour was sincere. He did not minimise the fact to himself that this pose would be hard to sustain.

He favoured two kinds of women; one that could turn lovemaking into a wrestling match, and, at the other end of the scale, the clever, intelligent woman who could spar with her tongue. His future wife belonged to neither of these categories. His mind now dwelling on a lady of the first kind that attracted him, his body moved restlessly in the chair. He hadn't visited her for over a month, but, by God, he would rectify that within the next twelve hours, come what may.

He refilled his glass and set to wondering how long James Talford had before him. He was much older than his wife – nearing seventy, he would say; he had married late. He hoped he would not leave his demise too late. The bulk of his money would be left to his wife. Well, that wouldn't matter; she was just an older edition of her daughter. He would enjoy managing them both. She was attracted to him too. He knew this; he had always appealed to older women.

When the clock struck four he was finishing his fifth glass of brandy. Slowly now he rose from the chair and, taking from the mantelpiece a candlestick that held a new waxen candle, he lit it from the embers of the fire, blew out the lamp and went from the room.

His gait was not unsteady; except once when his stockinged feet slipped on the highly polished surface of the hall floor, and he laughed to himself as his hand went out and gripped the huge round knob of the balustrade. Slowly now he mounted the stairs and, having reached the gallery, he was about to cross it when he was brought to a dead stop by the sight of a leg being thrust out between the folds of the window curtains. Another leg followed. They were white-stockinged right up above the knees. Then the curtains parted and he saw a pale face peering out. It was there for a second; then both the face and the legs disappeared as quick as a flash of lightning.

Slowly now he approached the window; slowly he parted the curtains and, raising the candle high, looked down on to the crouched figure and staring face of a young girl. The buttons of her dress were open and showing the top of her calico shift, and this was rising and falling rapidly over her sweating flesh.

As he continued to stare down into her face that was now without movement, her body odour came to him. It was neither an unpleasant smell nor a pleasant scent; it was what some women gave off more than others. He had always been sharp to detect this odour, and it had in the past played tricks with him. He put his hand out and, placing it on her shoulder, brought her from the sill, and as she stood on her feet staring up at him through the candlelight the tremors from her body passed through his own.

Slowly, and still staring down at her, he turned her about and pressed her along the gallery. Almost opposite the stairs was a table with a lamp on it. This lamp was kept burning at low ebb all during the night. It augmented the solitary candlelight and showed the way more clearly down the broad passage to the bedrooms.

When Katie realised that she wasn't being pushed towards the far passage that held the green-baize door her body stiffened, and at this the pressure on her shoulder tightened and she was pushed rapidly forward. The next minute she was standing in a big bedroom. As yet there was no power in her to protest; she was dazed with sleep and petrified with fear. All the muscles of her body felt stiff and out of her control; even when she watched, out of the corner of her eye, Mr Bernard place the candle on the table near the four-poster bed, it was as if her eyes were stuck in her head and she could only move them with an effort.

Then as her terror heightened to an intensity that brought her muscles into play and her mouth open to scream Bernard's hand came tightly over her stretched face; his other hand, gripping a handful of her clothes about her chest, heaved her, with one lift, into the centre of the big feather bed.

For a moment he held her there with only one hand, and that across her mouth. It kept her head and shoulders deep in the bed, but her limbs flayed wildly, until a weight dropped on her body and hell opened and engulfed her. The hell she had read about in the Bible, the hell Mr Burns talked about in the chapel, the hell into which sinners were thrust for their everlasting life. Her body was being rent in two; she was screaming but could make no sound. Then for some seconds she was aware of nothing, nothing at all, no pain, no fear, no terror. But all too quickly this passed and she was crying through every pore in her body. Her eyes were gushing water, her pores oozing her tears through sweat. The weight rolled off her and she lay sunk deep in the centre of the soft downy coverlet, limp and drained of life, her crying soundless.

After a time, and of a sudden, his hand came on her again, this time giving her a great push that thrust her to the edge of the bed. But before she could fall to the floor he had stayed her; he remembered just in time that she might even yet cry out and rouse Rodger next door. He raised himself up and looked at her sprawling, part-naked limbs with distaste. Then his eyes travelled to her hand which was clutching the bedclothes; it was red and smeared, the nails broken and the cuticles encased with dirt, black dirt. He heaved himself up and away from her and on to the floor. Gripping her shoulders again, he pulled her to her feet; then, jerking her head up, he stared down into her twisted, wet, terrified face and, lifting his forefinger, he wagged it at her.

He had taken her without the slightest endearment, not even bothering to caress her limbs, which courtesy he bestowed on the meanest of his women. He had taken her with less feeling than a dog would a bitch, and he hadn't deigned to open his mouth to her from beginning to end. But the wagging finger spoke volumes and she understood his meaning.

Now he was again pushing her towards the door, but before he opened it he once more wagged his finger cautioningly before her face; quietly he turned the knob and glanced into the corridor, then pulled her forward and thrust her from him.

Her hand pressed tightly over her mouth, her feet dragging, but soundless, on the thick carpet, she stumbled along the passage towards the gallery. Once there she turned to the left and groped her way to the dimmer passage until she felt the green-baize door.

When she had been pushed from the room Katie's head had been bent, and she had kept it so; yet even if she had raised her head her terror was blinding her so much it is doubtful whether she would have noticed the woman standing in the gallery near the head of the stairs.

Theresa had been sick again and had gone to the toilet room for a potion and she was returning, a bottle in her hand, when she heard a door click open and saw a head come poking out, which she recognised as Bernard's; then before her amazed gaze she watched Katie Mulholland come stumbling down the corridor, her body crumpled, her hand across her mouth, and apparently in great distress.

The only reason her brother hadn't seen her, she concluded, was that she was standing in the shadow of the pedestal that held the bust of her grandfather. She had also, from the moment she heard the door open, remained still. Now she was still no longer. A rage that was deaf to reason and decorum, even the decorum required of a sister to a brother, flooded her, and on its wave she was swept to Bernard's door, and without even knocking she thrust it open and entered the room, taking him unawares and catching him in a very undignified position as he completed his undressing.

'What the hell!' He turned towards her, not bothering to cover his nakedness, at least not for a moment. Then, pulling a dressing gown towards him, he strode towards her where she stood with her back to the door and hissed at her, 'What the hell do you want coming in like that!'

'You're a fiend.'

'What!' All the muscles in his face moved upwards, almost closing his eyes as he peered at her in the dimness. For a moment he was unable to understand her rage. It didn't dawn on him that she was here on behalf of his late visitor; sisters minded their own business, that was part of a woman's duty. But Theresa, although still his sister, was no part of the household now; she had nothing whatever to do with what went on inside it. Never having had any affection for her, he had always considered her utterly lacking in feminine appeal. He had even voiced the opinion to Rodger that the best place for her would be a convent. He had at one time likened Ainsley to a jocular Mother Superior and Theresa as her doting novice . . . He bent towards her now and whispered hoarsely, 'What's the matter with you? What are you talking about?'

'You know what I'm talking about.' She thrust her face so close to his that their noses were almost touching. 'You're a fiend. That child . . . Katie Mulholland, she'll be another Maggie Pratt, I suppose, pushed out and into the poorhouse, and someone else blamed.'

'Shut your mouth!' He was glaring at her now, his rage equal to her own. 'You mind your own business.'

'Yes, I'll mind my own business. I'll make Katie Mulholland my business. I'm warning you, if anything happens to her she'll be my business.'

He gripped her by the shoulder, his fingernails digging into her flesh, and she growled at him, 'Take your hands off me at once!'

'You'll mind your own business, do you hear? Promise me. Promise me.' His breath was on her face.

With a twist of her body and thrusting at him with her two hands, she freed herself and, grabbing the door handle, she said under her breath, 'I'll promise you nothing; I'll just warn you, and also at the same time remind you that that child has parents, and menfolk, which Maggie Pratt hadn't.'

His hand came out to make a grab at her again and she said quickly, 'You put a finger on me and I'll raise the house. One last word. I'm leaving tomorrow, or today rather, but I'll be back.' With this she pulled open the door and went out. Her body was still shivering with her anger.

Back in her own room she sat down on the side of the high bed, her feet resting on a footstool, and rocked herself. That poor child, that poor child. Yet in this particular moment she was not seeing Katie Mulholland under the hands of her brother but herself on her wedding night.

Then Katie, in all her utter dejection, was before her eyes once more, as Maggie Pratt had been three years ago. She was supposed to know nothing about Maggie Pratt. Maggie had been second chambermaid. She was an orphan, plump and pretty. She was sixteen, she became pregnant, and she had named the man as Bernard. Bernard had denied it indignantly, and Maggie was sent packing. With no home to go to, no reference, she ended up in the poorhouse, and there she was yet, and there she would remain until her child was of an age when it could work and earn its own living.

But that it should happen to Katie Mulholland, that beautiful, beautiful girl . . . child. How old was she? Fourteen, fifteen at the most. How had this come about? What was Mrs Davis up to? She suddenly stopped the rocking movement. She had an impelling urge to go to the housekeeper's room and demand to know what she was doing, not to see that the junior staff were safely in their rooms before she retired; that was part of her duty, an essential part which had been emphasised by her mother since the Maggie Pratt affair. But what good would that do now? It was done, and only time would show if there were to be consequences.

Katie, sitting on the edge of her pallet, was also thinking about Mrs Davis. She had not been to bed, and she hadn't taken off any of her clothes. She had a fear on her; it was new, different. She didn't know much about fear, except of the dark, and Cook going for her, but this fear was strange, making her sick, for all of a sudden she was afraid of her body. She wished she could throw it off, get outside it and take on the body that was hers yesterday, but the strange fear told her that that body would never be hers again. She wanted to fly home to her ma and get rid of the fear by telling her what had happened; but she couldn't tell her ma without her da knowing, and her da mustn't know about this. Her da was quiet and even-tempered, except at times, and at these times, which she had witnessed only twice in her life, he forgot himself and shouted and threw things. The last time she had seen him like that was when the cavalry charged the men in the village and the police and mine officials turned the Monktons and the Hepburns and a lot more families into the road, and threw their furniture after them, breaking it in the process. It was on that day that her da had attacked two policemen and one had hit him on the head and left him senseless in the ditch. The other attackers weren't so fortunate; they had been taken and locked up and brought before the magistrates. Five of the men had been banned from the pit and had taken to the road with their families . . . So, if she told her ma about this and her da got to know he . . . he could do things that would make him lose his job . . . but she'd have to tell somebody; she'd have to tell somebody . . . Mrs Davis? Yes, she would tell Mrs Davis, because if he came after her again she would scream this time; she would even scream at the sight of him.

As she rose from her bed Dotty turned over in her sleep and her loud snores were checked by a succession of snorts. In the faint light of the dawn she looked awful with her spotty face, wide gaping mouth, and tangled hair, but Katie envied her.

Her body was shaking and the tears were raining from her chin as she groped her way down the dark stairs and along the short passage and down the three steps and through the door that led to the landing and Mrs Davis' room, and she had her hand actually raised to knock when she heard a voice. It came from within the room and it was a man's voice, and although it was speaking very low she recognised it. Then there was a movement on the other side of the door. One minute she was gaping at the door, the next she was flying up the steps again, and she just reached the foot of the attic stairs when she heard the passage door being opened gently. Halfway up the stairs she stopped and, pressing herself against the wall, she stood rigid, looking downwards to where a man had paused on the landing below and now stood buttoning up his trousers. He was wearing only his undervest and carried his coat over his arm. With a quick movement he swung the coat behind his back and thrust his arms into it; then, taking a few noiseless steps forward, he dropped from her view.

Katie was now experiencing another feeling, shame mixed with revulsion, and added to it was a strong element of surprise. The surprise kept her lips apart. Her Mrs Davis, the woman whom her mother said was a natural lady and as good as any she served, was up to things with Mr Kennard. In this moment it was made clear to her why Cook dared to sit in her presence, why she dared to speak as she did; why Mr Kennard rarely came into the kitchen and, when he did, never spoke to the cook.

She could never tell Mrs Davis now. She could never tell anybody, but she was resolved that if Mr Bernard came near her again she would scream, and fight, and kick. She would know what it was all about next time. She would never let it happen again. She stopped crying and, lifting up her dress and taking the rag pinned to her petticoat, she rubbed it round her face, then softly blew her nose. She'd better get washed. She wouldn't go to the pump because somebody might see her, and it was still very early. No, she'd go down into the boiler room and lock the door and wash herself. Yes, she'd wash herself all over with hot, hot water. Scrub herself all over until she got rid of the feeling.

CHAPTER FIVE

'WHAT IS IT, lass?'

'Nothing, Ma.'

'But, child, you've been like this on your last few days off.'

Catherine had brought Katie into the bedroom and they were sitting on the side of the low bed looking at each other. Catherine put out her hand and stroked the soft hair from Katie's brow. 'And you're so white and peaked lookin'.'

'It's the cold, Ma. I couldn't get rid of it; me eyes and nose were runnin' all the time.'

'But that's weeks ago, child, as far back as the ball. Is . . . is the other all right?'

Now Catherine bent towards her, and Katie, lowering her lids, said under her breath, 'It hasn't come yet, Ma.' She didn't say it hadn't come the last two months either.

'Aw, that's it.' Catherine straightened herself up and pulled her chin into her neck, saying knowingly, 'There's nothin' that makes you feel more off colour than that. And you were never really regular; that's it. Oh, I've been worried about you, but I never gave that a thought. But that's it,' she repeated. 'An' we've all missed your chatter. Meself, I just live for your Sunday.' Again she was leaning forward, and gathering Katie's hands between her own she shook them gently, saying, 'Once that gets goin' you'll be your old self. And you know' – she dropped her voice – 'I forget you're growing up, you're no longer a child. You're just on sixteen. I can't believe it; it seems but yesterday since I had you on me knee.'

Katie's head drooped over her swelling throat. In another minute she would be on her mother's knee again, her head buried in her neck while she poured out this dreadful fear that was filling her and told her of the sickness that was always assailing her, and her absolute horror of the future. She pulled herself from the bed, saying, 'It's nearly time, Ma; I'd better be going.'

'Yes, lass.' As Catherine followed her to the bedroom door her brow puckered, and her face showing once more a look of bewilderment, she said, 'The wedding will soon be on you, an' you've never told us anything about it.'

'I've been so busy, Ma, and Cook keeps at me.'

In the kitchen she picked up her cloak and put on her straw hat, then tied a band round it and under her chin, for the day was windy and wet; then she stood watching her da put on his coat and tie his muffler. And when he was ready she went to the side of the fireplace, to her granda. William's face looked yellow and drawn; the hollow cheeks were sucked in, as were his lips. He put his arms about her, saying, 'I'm sorry, me bairn. This is the first time I've never set you along the road.' There were tears in his eyes and she kissed his stubbly chin. Then, patting his hands, she whispered brokenly, 'Get better soon, Granda . . . Soon.' She stood looking at him, nodding her head, while his eyes held her face as if drawing each feature into himself.

And now she was kissing Lizzie, and Lizzie, as always, laid her head against her. But she did not speak to Lizzie, telling her to be a good girl, as she usually did. Then she turned to where Joe sat, and as usual they touched shoulders, but today he did not immediately relinquish his hold but mumbled under his breath, 'Watch that cold, Katie.'

'Aye, Joe, I will.'

At the door, as she bent to kiss her daughter, Catherine thought, She looks like Jimmy did afore the fever got him – all her other children had died with the fever. She pressed her tightly to her; then, again looking down into her face, she said, 'Now if you feel bad you go and tell Mrs Davis. Promise me?'

Katie did not look at her mother as she said, 'Yes, Ma.'

Now putting his hand on his wife's shoulder and pulling her back into the room, Rodney said, 'Keep in, woman; you'll get soaked.' And Catherine, looking at the tall spare figure of her man, at his threadbare coat, said softly, 'Put a sack over your shoulders,' to which he replied, 'I can do without a sack on a Sunday, lass.'

Pressing Katie before him, they moved out into the road, and immediately the mud came over the uppers of their boots. But once clear of the road and on the fells the ground, though slippery in parts, was hard. They hurried, their heads down against the driving rain, and now and again, when a heavy gust met them, Rodney's hand would go around her shoulders and support her, and, apart from the question 'All right, lass?'

and her nodded reply, they had nothing to say until after they reached the top of the hill, where on that glorious Sunday many lifetimes ago she had sat with her granda and the sun had shone, and the sky was high, and her heart was light. On her half-days since, the sun had never shone.

Both breathing hard, they stood for a moment squinting through the rain that was falling like a great sloping curtain across the land below them. Then, bending towards her, his eyes blinking, his face streaming, Rodney said, quietly, 'What is it, lass? I feel somethin's troublin' you.'

She forced herself to look back into his eyes. She loved her da, but in some corner of her mind she was a little afraid of him. She had been brought up under her mother's idea of her father's moral code, with sayings such as 'Your da wouldn't stand for that', 'Your da's not afraid of the truth', 'Tell the truth and shame the devil', 'Straight as a die, your da is'. But she could at least answer part in truth and say, 'I'm tired, Da.'

'Aw, lass.' He passed a wet hand over her streaking face; then, cupping her chin, he said, 'If it's too much, leave. You'd be better in another job. There's piles of things openin' up in Jarrow, chemical works and such; there might be work of some sort in them for you. Leave, lass.'

'I'll think about it, Da.'

'Before you come home again I'll prepare your ma so she won't be disappointed. She lays so much stock on Mrs Davis.'

'I know, Da. Thanks, Da.'

'Now go on, on your way.'

'You go home, Da, don't wait.'

'Just for a little while.'

'No, please. You're soakin', and you can't see far anyway. Go on, Da.'

'I will when you get to the bottom of the hill. Go on.'

She turned away from him and went on her way.

She made herself hurry as much as she could against the wind until she knew she was out of her father's sight, and then her step became slow and dragging. Already her cloak was soaked through and she could feel the water seeping through her dress on to her back, but she didn't mind; she wouldn't mind about anything if only the jollop had worked. She had taken so much senna and salts that she felt she had no inside left, but it hadn't helped. What was she going to do? Oh, dear God, what was she going to do? Dotty was noticing things about her being sick in the mornings. There'd come a time when she'd have to tell Mrs Davis, and then her mother must know. But she wasn't now really afraid of telling Mrs Davis, or her mother; it was her father she was afraid of knowing, not because of what he would do to her but of him coming up to the house. She was terrified of him coming up to the house. If he were to hurt anybody . . . if he were to hurt HIM he would be put in the house of correction. Then what would her ma do, and her granda, and Lizzie? They would be turned out of the cottage, and nobody would dare take them in. She had seen people thrown out on to the fells for much less than what her da would do to Mr Bernard. She couldn't bear to think what would happen to her family if her da did anything, and all through her; she would die first.

The dark figure loomed in front of her before she was aware of his approach. It was Mr Bunting. She had met him every time on her day off since that sunny Sunday. She wasn't afraid of him any longer, because, with the exception of one thing, she wasn't afraid of anything any longer.

Mark Bunting had his dog with him. It was a big dog, a cross between a collie and a labrador. It came to her feet and sniffed round her ankles; it had done that twice before. Bunting, looking down at her, his eyes moving round her face, did not give her any greeting but said, 'He's taken with you. That doesn't often happen with him.' Then, his gaze narrowing, he said, 'You all right? You look under the weather.'

'I've had a cold.'

'The same one as you had last time?' He ended this on the sound like a laugh, and she nodded at him, saying, 'It hangs on.'

He now let his eyes roam over her, but her cloak told him nothing. One thing he was certain of, she wasn't the same girl he had met some weeks ago. The sparkle had gone out of her face. In an odd kind of way he was interested in her. Nor, apparently, was he the only one who had an interest in the Mulhollands. He was still wondering why young Rosier had called him into the office and pumped him about Big Mulholland. It looked, by what he said, as if he was wanting something on him to get rid of him. Yet Rosier hadn't known until he told him that Mulholland was thick with Fogerty and Ramshaw, the troublemakers, and so, in the first place, it couldn't have been about that. But once he did know it he had harped on about it . . . Now why would he want to get rid of Big Mulholland, for Mulholland was an excellent worker. He himself had put the manacles on him once or twice by docking his corves, but that was a different kettle of fish. He wouldn't want to get rid of him. There were many others he would like to see go before Mulholland. He could send up half as much coal again as most of them.

He said now, 'Is it hard work up there?'

'Yes.'

'Do you still like it?'

She paused before saying, 'Yes.' And now she added, 'I've got to go; I'm wet through.'

As he had given her no greeting he gave her no farewell, but he smiled his queer smile as she turned away, and he stood watching her for a moment before hitting out with his stick at a bramble, then striding on again . . .

When Katie entered the kitchen, Cook was sitting at the table drinking from a mug of steaming tea. She turned her head and looked at Katie for a long moment before saying, and not unkindly, 'I'd get them things off, you must be wringin'.'

'Yes, I am, Cook.'

'Hang them in the boiler room.'

Katie went into the warm steamy room and took off her dripping straw hat and her cloak; and when she re-entered the kitchen, Cook, still in kindly tones, said, 'You must be wet to the skin; I'd go up and put your other frock on. But first fetch the teapot.'

Katie went to the hob and, lifting the big earthenware teapot, brought it to the table; and there Cook, looking at her with a slanting gaze, said, 'Pour yourself a cup out.'

'Oh ta, Cook, ta.'

'Sit yourself down while you're drinkin' it.' She nodded to the form and Katie sat down. But Cook's unusual kindness and the hot tea began to undermine her, and slowly great tears whirled from her eyes and rolled down her face and dropped off the end of her chin.

Cook, turning fully round to her now said, 'What's the matter?'

'I don't feel very well, Cook.'

It was a full minute before Cook, nodding towards her, said, 'Well, you wouldn't, would you?'

Without looking at what she was doing Katie pushed the mug to the corner of the table while her eyes remained fixed on the cook's face. Cook knew. She knew!

She jumped up from the form, ran out of the kitchen, along the corridor, through the door, up the back stairs, past the green-baize door and up the rest of the stairs to her room, and there, flinging herself on her bed, she sobbed unrestrainedly.

It was fully a quarter of an hour later when Dotty came into the room, and, shaking her by the shoulder, said, 'Come on, you're wanted.'

Katie turned on her side and looked at Dotty, and she saw that Dotty also knew. She felt that Dotty had known for some time. She looked at Dotty's spotty plain face. She had always been sorry about Dotty's spots and the way she looked, but she wished now from the bottom of her heart that she could change places with her, be her altogether, although she wouldn't wash her face in the chamber pot every morning like Dotty did because the cook had told her it was good for the complexion. But at this moment she would have willingly been her in every other way.

When Katie sat up, Dotty, giving a hitch to her skirt, placed herself on the mattress beside her and, putting her face close to hers, whispered, 'Who was it?'

Not a muscle of Katie's face moved as she stared back like a petrified rabbit into the kitchen maid's face, until Dotty said, 'Was it Billy? He's always pokin' me; he's tried it on more than once. He caught me one night and I knocked him into the midden. You should have heard him swear.'

Katie sprang up from the pallet now, tore off her dress, pulled the dry one from the hook, and she was buttoning it up before Dotty spoke again. And then quite patiently she said, 'Aw, well, if you won't tell, you won't; but it's one of 'em isn't it? There'll be high jinks when Mr Kennard gets goin' . . . You'd better come on, Mrs Davis is in no good mood.'

When Dotty left the room Katie's head sank on to her chest. This was only the beginning. Would she be able to stand what was to come, or should she do what she thought of doing last week, jump into the water-filled quarry on the road to the mine?

She had been standing before Mrs Davis for ten minutes and Mrs Davis had been talking all the while, quietly if somewhat stiffly; and now, seeming to lose patience, she said harshly, 'Katie! You've got to answer me. I'm asking you again, are you sick every morning?'

Katie drew a great long breath into her body, and as she let it out there went with it her resistance. She would have to tell, at least some part of it, and so she said, 'Yes, Mrs Davis.'

Mrs Davis now closed her eyes, bowed her head for a moment and wiped her mouth with a small white handkerchief; then, looking at Katie again, she said, 'How long is it since you saw anything?'

'Over two months, nearly three, Mrs Davis.'

'Are you going to have a baby, Katie?'

It was some time before she could bring herself to answer this, and then she could only do it by bowing her head.

'Oh, Katie, Katie!' There was utter despair in the housekeeper's voice. 'How could you let this come about, you above all people? I trusted you more than anyone else in the house. Do you hear me, Katie? Before anyone else. Who is it, Katie?'

A full minute elapsed and Mrs Davis said again, 'Come along, Katie; you know you'll have to tell me in the end, so you might as well do it now, because I'll find out. Who is it? Is it Billy?'

'No, no,' she answered Mrs Davis, emphatically now. Billy, the garden boy, with his great loose lip and grinning face – she would hardly speak to him, let alone allow him to touch her. She had never let anyone touch her, and when she came to think about it there was only Billy who had tried. No other man attempted to lay a hand on her until . . .

Mrs Davis stared at the young, slim, pathetic figure before her. Dear, dear Lord, how had this come about? Who? Who? She felt responsible for the child. Hadn't she been the means of getting her the position? Her mind asking when this had taken place, she was presented with a picture of Katie the day following the ball. She had not been herself. Her face was red and swollen and Cook had reported that she had been sick twice, doubtless with stuffing herself. But it was from that morning that she had noticed the difference in her . . . It must have happened the night of the ball, and it must have been the first time, for whoever had done this to her it hadn't been to her liking. Poor, poor child. But who? Who? Mrs Davis tried to recall the events of the night of the ball, but they were hazy in her mind, she had been very tired. Moreover, although she drew a veil over it, she knew that she had taken more wine than she should have done. But, as she told herself the following morning when she was suffering from a bad headache and an irritable temper, so had everyone else.

Vaguely she remembered taking Katie to the gallery. She also had a vague memory of hiding her behind the curtain, then returning to see if she was still there. She wondered now if, in her bemused state, she had gone to the wrong curtain. Anyway, there had only been three male servants in the house that night, and she couldn't for a moment suspect Frank Tapman, the father of two daughters of Katie's own age, and certainly not John Swan, a God-fearing good man. That only left Patrick. Her whole being rejected the idea that Kennard would perpetrate such an act with a young girl, little more than a child. No, she knew Patrick. Who better? Then someone in the house? . . . Oh no. No. She must never think that. But it had happened before, hadn't it? Yes, but this had been his engagement ball; she would not think that of Mr Bernard. She had no liking for him, but after all he was a gentleman and had his code and . . . and he would certainly have done nothing like that with his fiancée hardly out of his sight . . . Mr Rodger?

Again, no. Mr Rodger was a gentleman. There was no doubt in her mind about that. Well, it only left the master. Nonsense. The word was loud in her head. The master, be what he may, rough-mouthed, uncouth at times, he was a man of honour . . . Billy Denison. It must be him – unless, that is, it was someone from her village. She had been home on the Sunday and the ball was on the Tuesday. Yet she had seen her in the intervening time, and if she had looked like she had done on the morning following the ball she would have remarked on it to herself. No, it was Billy Denison. And that was why the child was so vehement in her answer when Billy's name was mentioned.

'I'll have Billy brought in and then we'll see, Katie.'

'Oh no, Mrs Davis.' Katie was daring to grip Mrs Davis' arm. 'It wasn't him, it wasn't him. I wouldn't . . . I mean, I wouldn't let him touch me; I don't like Billy, he's dirty.' She squared her lips from her teeth and the action alone fully convinced Mrs Davis, in spite of her reasoning, that whoever the man was it wasn't Billy Denison.

Mrs Davis bowed her head. She felt utterly deflated, terribly sad, and not a little afraid. The mistress would have to be told. She remembered what happened the last time on an occasion like this. But that time was different. Then there had been accusations against the son of the house. Her voice now flat, she said, 'The mistress will have to be told, Katie.'

'Oh no, please, Mrs Davis.' Katie's head was back and bobbing as if on a string. 'I can just leave. Nobody else need know. I can just leave.'

'Your mother or father will be bound to come to the house, Katie. More likely it will be your father.'

On this thought Mrs Davis realised that she was more afraid of Rodney Mulholland visiting the house than she was of imparting this obnoxious news to her mistress. Rodney Mulholland was a righteous man, and righteous men could be terrible in their anger.

She had been brought up by a righteous man; she knew all about righteous men. Her life would be different today if it hadn't been for the fear of that particular righteous man.

But, apart from whatever action Rodney Mulholland would take, there was Catherine. She would have another mouth to feed, two shortly . . . and on the pittance that Rodney worked for . . . She could let the child stay on for another few weeks, say until after the wedding. But then there was more than a possibility that Catherine would become aware of what was wrong with her daughter. She was surprised that she hadn't already done so. But would she ever dream that her Katie, her beautiful, good little

Katie, was in this predicament? And the term remained as it had been, for the child was good; this thing had surely happened to her against her will. But the point she must consider at the moment was that if either of her parents should come to the house and demand to see the master or mistress then she herself would be in the soup, for the mistress would demand to know why she hadn't been told about this before . . . There was nothing for it but she must tell Madam, and it was a foregone conclusion what the result would be. Katie would be sent packing.

Katie was sent packing. Two days later she left the house carrying her belongings in a bundle that was no bigger than the one she had arrived with five years earlier. But she didn't go home alone. It was Mrs Davis' half-day and she took her in the carrier's cart.

They arrived at two-thirty in the afternoon, and Mrs Davis left the house an hour later, and she had to let herself out because Catherine was too stunned to move.

Catherine sat looking at Katie, who was sitting on the cracket by the fire, her body almost doubled in two, and by her side with his arm around her shoulder sat William. He, too, had been stunned, but now a feeling of rage was ousting the stupor. It boiled in him, stiffening his muscles and pushing his jawbones outwards. He took his arm from about her, but not before he had patted her. Then, pulling himself from his seat, he grabbed at his crutch and stamped across the room to the door.

Only now did Catherine rouse herself, saying, 'Da! Don't . . . don't go out; you're not fit. Stay where you are . . . please.' But William paid no heed and the door banged behind him.

And now Catherine stood looking at her daughter, and all the while she shook her head; then, moving slowly towards her and seating herself in the chair her father had just vacated, she pulled Katie round to face her, and she had to press her body upwards before she could look into her face. It was no longer beautiful, and in this moment it was so contorted with sorrow that she couldn't find it in her even to harshen her tone as she asked, 'But why, lass?' Not 'Who was it?' but 'Why?'

Katie, looking into her mother's face for the first time, shook her head and muttered, 'It wasn't me, Ma.'

'Not you? What do you mean?'

'I . . . I didn't want . . . I mean, I would never have. He . . . ' She dropped her head and could go no further, but Catherine finished for her. 'He forced you?' And to this Katie gave a small nod.

And now Catherine asked, 'Who, child?'

For answer she received silence, and no matter how she talked, or how she coaxed, she couldn't get her daughter to say who had done this thing.

Then Rodney came in at half-past six. He came in with William, who had walked all the way to the pithead to meet him and to try, in his own thoughtful way, to lighten the shock. But by the look on Rodney's face he hadn't succeeded.

He came in the back way, as he always did when coming from the pit, but tonight he did not take his black, damp, coal-impregnated coat off and bang it against the wall underneath the lean-to. He did not even drop his can on to the shelf outside the back door, but he entered the kitchen as he had left the pit, and inside the door he stopped and looked at his daughter.

Katie was sitting at the far side of the table, not eating, just sitting, and she no longer needed to wonder how her ma would go about telling him, for she knew immediately that he knew. He looked taller than usual, older, terrible. His eyes were no longer the nice grey colour but seemed to be shining red out of his black face. He approached the table slowly, the can still in his hand.

Catherine, at the stove where she was stirring a stew in a black pot, did not turn round. After the first sight of her husband's face she could not bear to look at him, and as her father came in and sat slowly in his chair she thanked him in her heart for taking this burden from her. She went on stirring the pot, and all the while Rodney stood at the table staring down into his daughter's face.

All along the road he just wouldn't believe it. He had wanted to strike William when he told him this thing about his beloved child, whom at times he had thought he would never rear because she was so good, so beautiful. Never a Sunday went past that he didn't kneel in the chapel and thank his God for the gift of her; for her gaiety, her joy, her kindly nature, her beauty. And now she had come to this. He stared at her until her head drooped deep into her chest, but he didn't speak to her. His feelings were beyond words. Slowly, he turned away and walked into the bedroom, and William, quickly putting out his hand, touched Catherine and indicated the door with a jerk of his head.

Catherine took the pot off the fire and placed it on the hob. Then, rubbing her hands on her coarse apron, she went into the bedroom and closed the door. And there they stood looking at each other until he said simply, 'Who?'

'I don't know.'

'You've asked her?'

Catherine lowered her head on to her breast and swung it from side to side as she said, 'Until I'm tired. All afternoon I've been at her. She wouldn't tell Mrs Davis – Mrs Davis brought her home.'

Rodney looked away from Catherine towards the little window. He could see the sun going down behind the roofs of the cottages opposite. It was a calm, quiet, October night, a night when after a wash and a bite to eat he would have taken a walk in the long twilight and become refreshed in mind and spirit. But now the darkness had enveloped his spirit. It was a darkness blacker than the bowels of the mine when a man was entombed behind a fall. He said slowly, 'That's what has been wrong with her all these weeks.' He turned his eyes back to her. 'She didn't mention anything to you?' The words came from between his gritted teeth.

'No. No.' Her voice became high for a moment; then it dropped to a whisper again as she added, 'How could I have kept it from you?'

Thrusting his body round as if pressing it against a force, he turned his back on her and demanded, 'Why am I pestered like this? Four of them taken, Lizzie as she is, and now this. A shame before God. Brought down to the level of the middens.'

'Rodney!' She went to him and put her hand gently on his shoulder, and she gazed at his stiff black profile as she said, 'She must have been taken against her will. Mrs Davis said as much. She came in here and had a word with me. She said she had grieved since the day following the ball; she had grieved long before there were any consequences.'

Rodney did not look at her as he asked, 'Hadn't she any idea at all?'

'Only the gardener's boy, Billy Denison, but she said that Katie had denied flatly that it was him, and she's denied it to me an' all.'

Turning now, his step heavy but unhurried, Rodney went into the kitchen and, facing Katie again, he said to her, 'Will you give me his name, or have I to go up to the house?'

She looked up into his face, her eyes wide and dry. They were burning as if they had been sprayed with hot sand. If she said Mr Bernard he would stalk up to the house, but he would never get inside. They wouldn't let him into the real part of the house. And should he wait for Mr Bernard and waylay him and hit him, what then? He would, as she had known all along, be sent to prison. If she could only be silent and keep on being silent . . . She could as long as they didn't blame Billy Denison. Although she didn't like Billy, she wouldn't want to get him into trouble through her. They might send him packing too, and he was from the orphanage.

'Very well.' Rodney answered her silence. Then, still with the unhurried step that spoke more clearly of his anger than any bustle could have done, he stripped himself to his small clothes, washed himself in the tub of water that Catherine had got ready to the side of the fireplace, changed into the only pair of decent trousers and coat that he possessed, and without bite or sup after his twelve-hour shift, and without speaking another word to anyone, he left the house.

He must have reached the road leading off the fells by the time the lie came into Katie's mind, the lie that, with her agile, imaginative brain, she should have thought of much earlier if she hadn't been half demented with worry about the very thing that was taking place now, what her da would do when he found out. She sprang from her seat, making both Catherine and William start; then she was out of the front door, rushing by the cottages, past Mrs Weir and Mrs Bailey, who were talking at their front doors about the trouble that had come on young Katie and the Mulhollands; for anybody with half an eye could see the way the wind blew with the housekeeper bringing her home, then big Rodney going along there looking like that. And they didn't need two guesses as to where he was making for. She ran unheeding past three girls coming home from the rope factory who knew nothing yet about the scandal, and who half paused and greeted her almost in a voice, saying, 'Why, hello, Katie. What's fetched you hyem?' and she flew past the men who were playing quoits at the top of the end cottages.

She caught sight of Rodney as he dropped on to the road from the heathered bank, and she cried, 'Da! Da! Wait, Da.'

Rodney turned and waited, and when she was standing before him, gasping for breath, unsteady on her feet, he put a hand to her shoulder and stayed her.

Her words interspersed with gasps, she looked up at him and cried, 'Don't go, Da. Don't go. I'll tell you. ''Cos . . . 'cos it wouldn't be any use you goin'.'

She bowed her head; then after a moment, during which he waited without speaking, she went on, 'It was the night of the ball. It was dark, late. I . . . I was tired. I . . . I went into the yard to get the air so's I wouldn't feel so sleepy. It was warm and I went through the arch and along the path by the wall for a little way, and . . . ' The lie now stuck in her throat, but her da's voice eased it out as he said, 'Aye, go on.'

'Well. Well, somebody caught hold of me. They put their hand over me mouth.' That was true enough, anyway. 'And . . . and I couldn't do anything. It . . . it was then . . . ' Her voice trailed away, and after a space he said, 'You didn't see him, his face?'

'No, Da. No.'

As he stared down on her bent head he remembered the moon had been shining on the night of the ball because Catherine had remarked it would be lovely up there. The moon shining and it being nice and warm, the guests would likely be strolling in the garden. He said, now, 'The moon was shining, Katie, remember?'

Her head jerked, and she looked up at him under her eyelids, staring at him for a moment before saying, 'It was dark, where . . . where he pulled me into the bushes.'

'Tell me one thing, and tell me truly, for you're bound to know. Was it one of the staff?'

'No. No, Da.' She could tell the truth about this, and she was wise to the fact that her da would know that she knew the difference between the clothes of a servant and those of the gentry. Moreover, as she had found, there was a distinct smell about all gentry – not only a soap-and-water smell but the smell of pomades on their hair and such.

Rodney turned his gaze from her and looked into the blue misted night light falling over the fells. There had been a hundred guests at the ball; half of them would have been men. If he went up to the house now he would have to say, 'My daughter was taken by one of your guests,' and they would laugh at this. 'Send round the three counties,' they would say, 'to find out which man had had a tussle with a maid behind a bush in the garden, a place where she didn't ought to be on that particular night. What was she doing in the garden, anyway, if she didn't want trouble?'

The hopelessness of the situation pressed his anger down and there came into its place a feeling of compassion. When his arms went out and drew her gently to him, the dam of terror inside her was released, and there, in the growing dusk on the fell, her crying reached a height of hysteria, until Rodney, lifting her, carried her up the bank and sat down on the heather and cradled her as he hadn't done since she was a child, and rocked her until he brought a measure of comfort to her.

CHAPTER SIX

GEORGE ROSIER PULLED himself up straight as the carriage entered the drive. He tugged at his green satin waistcoat, patted his protruding stomach and smiled to himself. It had been a very good day. He'd had a fine lunch with James Talford, but, what was more important, there had been present at that lunch Mr Charles Palmer. It had been stimulating just to be in Palmer's company . . . There was enthusiasm, drive and the Midas touch if ever he saw it. Palmer was no age yet, only thirty-eight, and the yard had only been going nine years, but he was coining money, making it hand over fist; not only was he building ships but he was making the materials on the spot to build the ships. Jarrow was booming. He had turned it from a village into a literal iron and steel gold mine. The thought that thrilled his breast now was that he, too, would soon have access to this particular mine. He had prepared the way over the last few years. Young Palmer knew what was in his mind, but he was no fool. If, as was likely to happen, the concern which was growing too fast for Palmer and his brother to handle was turned into a limited company, then he intended to be of that company, and young Palmer could make the going easier and would do so if he got his finger in another mine. He had already more fingers down mines in the county and about than he had on both of his hands, but he wouldn't mind having another down the Rosier mine. Oh, he was no fool was Charles Palmer, this fast-rising star, who was cunningly making a name as a philanthropist. We could all be philanthropists if we could dig gold out of steel.

But in the end it all boiled down to the number of shares one could buy, and this was where Talford came in. Talford himself was too old to take an active part in a company like Palmer's, but he had the wherewithal to make it possible for both him and Bernard to accomplish this – an active part. He had the vision of himself running the shipyard. And why not?

So buoyant did he feel that his small body almost bounced out of the carriage and up the steps to the house. Kennard was waiting at the open door, and although the lamps were burning at each side of the door he held another at head height to illuminate the steps; then he ushered his master through the lobby and into the hall and there relieved him of his hat and coat, before saying, 'The family are in the library, sir.'

George Rosier glanced at his butler, at the man who had valeted him for the last twenty years. There was little they didn't know about each other, and the inflection in Kennard's voice told him that his words meant more than they said.

'Mrs Noble arrived this morning, sir.' Kennard did not make the mistake of still calling his master's daughter Miss Theresa.

'Yes. Well?' He stared at Kennard. He was surprised to learn that Theresa had arrived; she wasn't due until next week. If . . . if there were any more bees in her bonnet about leaving Noble and coming home he would soon scatter them for her.

'Mr Bernard is also in the library, sir. They have been closeted for some time.' Kennard's voice dropped to a discreet whisper as he added, 'I went to attend to the fire, sir; I found the door locked.'

George Rosier's face puckered, his eyes narrowed to slits, and he gazed at Kennard for a moment longer before turning briskly away and marching towards the library door. The bees in her bonnet must be working, and Agnes and Bernard must be trying to cope.

He turned the handle of the door, and when it didn't respond to his touch he said loudly, 'What's this?'

The next moment the door was opened and there stood Agnes, her face under its coating of powder and rouge looking like dirty dough. He glanced beyond her to his son and daughter, then in his usual bustling manner he charged into the room.

Bernard was standing with his back to the middle window and Theresa was sitting to the side of the fireplace. His son's face, he noticed immediately, was not pale but almost purple. Of the three, his daughter looked most composed. He hadn't seen her for some weeks; she looked different, older, a woman, and yet that was not the proper description for his daughter. Always being devoid of womanly attraction, he did not imagine her marriage to old Noble would have improved matters in that direction. But there was a change in her.

'What's this?' He stalked to the centre of the room and cast his eyes from one to the other; then when he received no answer he bellowed, 'What's this, I say? Locked doors in my own house. What next!'

'George.' Agnes Rosier moved slowly towards her husband, and when she was close to him she said in a strangely quiet voice, 'Sit down, George.'

'What the hell's this? I'm not sitting down. Come on, spit it out. What's the matter? You're acting like a lot of bloody amateur players.'

Her husband's swearing and obscenities no longer affected Agnes Rosier. The first time he had levelled a mouthful at her, shortly after their marriage, she had swooned, and immediately he had made sure she wouldn't do it again by swearing even more roundly as he slapped her face on both sides. But she did close her eyes before she said, 'Theresa is determined to make trouble.'

'Trouble! What about?' He looked towards his daughter, and Theresa, rising to her feet, looked towards Bernard and said, 'You'd better ask him, Papa.'

Now George Rosier turned towards his son and demanded, 'Well?' Whereupon Bernard, taking one step from the window and bending his body in the direction of his sister, growled through his teeth, 'She's mad. She should be locked up, certified.'

'And I have no doubt but that you'd try it. You'd try anything, wouldn't you, to shut me up. Well, you won't.' Now she swung round to her father and went on, 'Do you know that the Mulhollands have been turned out of their house under the pretext that Mr Mulholland is an agitator.'

'What the hell has that got to do with you, girl?' George Rosier moved towards the back of a chair and, gripping the knobs at the top, bent his head over it and peered at her.

'Did you give the order that put them out, Papa?'

Slowly he straightened up and looked towards Bernard. No, he hadn't given the order. He didn't know what this was all about, but he'd damned soon find out. Returning his attention to Theresa again, he said, 'That's neither here nor there. Anyway, what have the Mulhollands to do with you?'

'Nothing, Papa, except that Katie Mulholland was your scullery maid, and she was dismissed last week because she was going to have a baby. But she hasn't, up till now, said who gave her that baby because it's likely she was frightened of the very thing that has just happened – of her father being dismissed from the mine and the family turned out to live on the fells.'

George Rosier was experiencing a feeling as if a cold hand had been pushed inside his shirt and was gripping his flesh. He wanted to look towards his son but kept his eyes on his daughter and said grimly, 'Go on.'

And Theresa went on. Her voice sounding thin and cold and coming through lips that scarcely moved, she said, 'It was on the night of the ball, the ball that was celebrating his engagement to Ann Talford, that he took Katie Mulholland into his room . . . I . . . I was crossing the landing turned four in the morning; I was feeling unwell and had been for a draught, when I saw him pushing the child out into the corridor. She was crying and in great distress. I immediately went into his room and told him that if anything should happen to that child he wouldn't get away with it this time, it wouldn't be another case of . . . of Maggie Pratt.'

Now George Rosier was looking at his son, and Bernard, his whole body quivering visibly with his rage, cried, 'I tell you she's mad. Her mind's gone.' But before his father could make any reply to this Theresa put in, 'As I've said already, you'll have to prove that, but I wonder what the Talford's will make of my state of my mind when I tell them the pretty story . . . '

'What did you say?' George Rosier sprang round to her, and again he cried, 'What did I hear you say?' This was followed by a silence that trembled on the outburst of terrible rage.

At one time Theresa would have been intimidated by her father's voice alone, but now neither his voice nor his ferocious attitude had the slightest effect on her. It was as her father had recognised, she had changed. Six months of marriage had brought her slumbering, shrewd, unfeminine, dominant personality to the surface. She had just passed her eighteenth birthday and she was as mature as she would ever be, and more so than many a woman four times her age. She knew she would never like men – perhaps with one exception, her brother Rodger. The knowledge that she preferred women's company and that their figures and faces gave her pleasure did not frighten her. She knew now why she had always been attracted by Katie Mulholland, why she liked looking down on the kitchen quarters from the hill.

She said, in a clear, unswerving tone, 'If something isn't done for Katie Mulholland in way of reparation, and good reparation, then I intend to inform the Talfords.'

'You devil! You bloody little devil!' As George Rosier's hand went out to grab his daughter, Agnes cried, 'George! George!' And now he turned on his wife, crying, 'You think I'm going to be defied by a slip of a girl just because she's got a wedding ring on her finger? Do you know what this could mean?'

'I know well enough, George.' Agnes' voice was low and trembling, and she added, 'And unless you want the whole household to be aware of the situation I would speak a little quieter. And it will be less tiring in the end. You've just come into the fray; we've been battling for hours.' She cast a quick glance towards Bernard, then went on, 'And we can't make her see sense.'

'See sense!' George Rosier was glaring at his daughter. 'I'll make you see sense, madam, if I've got to take a horsewhip to you. Now get to your room and I'll see you stay there until your husband comes to fetch you, and I'll see that he does that double quick.'

Theresa rose to her feet. Her face was flushed but her voice was still cool. 'I'm not afraid of your threats, Papa. If you'd look at things calmly you'd see the solution doesn't lie in locking me up . . . even if you could. I could write a letter to the Talfords any time within the next fortnight, and even if I was prevented from doing it during that time I could do it later . . . after the wedding.' She now turned her eyes towards her brother and the hate between them seemed to vibrate in the tense atmosphere. Then, turning to her father again, she said, 'The damage is done, but I'm going to see that you supply the means whereby Katie Mulholland doesn't suffer by your son's action for the rest of her life. I will keep my tongue quiet if you'll agree to settle a thousand pounds on her and see that her child, whether male or female, is educated.'

George Rosier stared at the girl as if she was indeed mad. He stared at her for fully a minute in absolute silence; then with the palm of his hand he beat his brow in a slow, regular motion. A thousand pounds, she said. A thousand pounds! And to educate the child, and by doing so own up to the fact it was a Rosier. Why was he standing here doing nothing? Why didn't he pick up the long steel ruler from the desk and beat her with it? His hand dropped to his side and he stared at the grey-clad figure before him. She wasn't even dressed as a young woman should be dressed. You could almost see the shape of her limbs through her straight skirt. It was indecently short, well above her ankles. She hadn't the figure of a woman, she was more like a youth . . . a man. Yes, she had the character and disposition of a man. As if he was attacking a man, he gripped her fiercely by the shoulders and dragged her towards the door. But there Agnes' hands pulled him to a halt, and, her voice hoarse, she whispered, 'You don't want the household to know about this; have sense. Not even Kennard; not a whisper, it would be fatal. Go up with her; lock her in but don't mishandle her. They can imagine it's because she's left Mr Noble.'

Agnes was speaking as if Theresa was no longer present, or at best as if she was someone who didn't matter; yet she did matter, and nobody was more aware of this than herself.

Reluctantly George Rosier released his daughter. His stomach was moving up and down as if worked by bellows. He drew in a succession of short, sharp breaths; then, bending forward, he opened the door, waited until she had passed him, then followed her closely up the stairs.

Back in the library, Agnes Rosier covered her face with her hands; then, drawing them slowly down her cheeks she looked at her son, who was now standing rigidly gripping the high mantelshelf, and she muttered tensely, 'Bernard! Bernard! You must have been mad.'

'Shut up, Mother.' He turned his body half towards her. 'What do you know about it? There'll be enough when he comes in . . . Look, go on, leave me alone; I can fight this out with him in a way I can't when you're here.'

He watched her turn her stately, overdressed figure around like a ship on still waters and walk out of the room. When the door closed on her he began to beat his fist on the sharp edge of the marble mantelpiece, and he was still beating when his father re-entered the room.

George Rosier didn't demand of his son, 'Is this true?' but going up to him and clamping his hand on his arm he pulled him round and, facing him squarely, growled, 'You know what you are? You're a bloody, stupid maniac, nothing more, nothing less. You couldn't wait to go into town to ease yourself, you had to revert to the kitchen again. Your tastes favour the kitchen, don't they?' His grip tightened and he shook the arm he held. 'And it's a hell of a pickle this time, a hell of a pickle. You bloody fool! Do you realise that this could put the kibosh on everything? It just could, it just could, me boy. Just think of old Talford being confronted with a story like this and coming to find proof, and it here to his hand, with your own sister being able to substantiate all she says through the Mulholland slut . . . Well, should that happen – get this into that big head of yours – you're on your own; for, as you well know, the mine, working under the present conditions, is not even paying its way, and it's no longer able to support you and your gaming debts . . . and your women. I'm hard put to it to keep this place and all its commitments going . . . so if you've never bothered thinking before start now. But don't start thinking in lump sums of a thousand pounds. As for signing a paper to the effect that you'll educate the brat, you might as well go straight away and tell Talford the lot. Another thing I've just thought of.' He stabbed his finger into Bernard's chest. 'It's a certainty that Mulholland's got no inkling yet as to who interfered with his daughter. It's as that mad bitch said.' He jerked his head towards the ceiling. 'The girl's kept mum to keep him in his job, but I'd be wary. I've known Mulholland since he was a boy. He's the quiet type and they're the most dangerous sort when they're aroused . . . By the way' – he narrowed his eyes now – 'who gave him the push?'

His lips stiff, Bernard said, 'I did. He was agitating; he's been seen with Ramshaw's lot.'

'You were very high-handed, weren't you? He's been seen with Ramshaw's lot for years, but you didn't give him the push and turn him out of his cottage before . . . You did it because you thought that he would move on, take the whole family with him, didn't you?'

Bernard returned his father's stare without blinking, and when his father said again, 'You bloody fool!' his teeth grated against each other, and the muscles of his stomach tensed.

Of a sudden George Rosier dropped into a deep leather chair near the fire and, resting his elbow on the arm, supported his head with his hand. After a moment, and in a more moderate tone, he said, 'Well, what are you going to do?'

Bernard Rosier walked to the window and stood staring out into the darkness. Then after a time he returned to the fire and, looking down into it, asked, 'Can I have a hundred pounds?'

'What are you going to do?'

'I'll . . . I'll tell you later if I bring it off. Can I have a hundred? At least fifty tonight and fifty ready to hand.'

'I hope you know what you're doing this time.'

'I know what I'm doing.'

'Who's it with?'

'I'll tell you later. I'll be back in a couple of hours. If it works, everything will be settled, as will that cow up there.' He threw his head back and gazed towards the ceiling for a moment.

George Rosier now rose from his chair, and unlocking a section of a panel near the fireplace, disclosing behind it a cupboard, he took a leather bag from a number lying there, and, carrying it to the desk, emptied the contents on to the table, counted out fifty sovereigns and pushed them to one side.

When Bernard had picked up the money and placed it in his wallet he walked down the length of the room and would have left without further words had not his father stopped him, saying, 'Whatever it is, make it foolproof; it's your future.' And to this Bernard answered bitterly, 'Do you think I need to be reminded?' He then collected his hat and cloak from the vestibule, together with a walking stick, and went out into the night. He did not call for the coachman, nor yet take the trap, nor yet his horse.

There was a shortcut over the fells to Bunting's house, which was only half a mile from the mine, and the more unobtrusive his visit the better.

At half-past nine the same evening Agnes Rosier visited her daughter to tell her that Katie Mulholland was going to be married to Mr Bunting, the master weighman at the mine, and she was a lucky girl to get a four-roomed house with a garden, together with a man like Mr Bunting who could earn a lot of money if he tried.

The fact that Bunting had agreed to Bernard Rosier's plan was sufficient for Agnes Rosier to consider the matter closed. Pregnant girls with the alternative of the workhouse or sleeping in the open on the fells had very little choice.

CHAPTER SEVEN

MARK BUNTING WALKED through the village on his way to the lower fell. He could have avoided it, but he didn't choose to do so. He was dressed in knee-breeches and leggings and wore a dark green cloth coat that reached to below his hips. He was also wearing a white neckerchief tied in the form of a cravat. On his head was a hard high bowler, and in his hand a thick hawthorn stick.

It was early dusk and there were children playing in the roadway and women at the doors. Some of the children stopped their play and stared at him; all the women stared at him, and with hate in their eyes. One of them even spat in his direction; another, on his approach, went in and banged her door just as he was passing it.

Women were fools, he thought; they endangered their own and their men's livelihoods by showing their spleen. But their attitude had little or no effect on him – in fact he relished it in a way; it gave him a further sense of power. When one woman said in a loud voice, apparently speaking to her neighbour, 'We does like copyin' our betters, doesn't we?' he knew she was referring to his mode of dress, and he felt complimented.

Although he hadn't been the means of Mulholland being stood off – Brown, the under-manager, had seen to that – he knew he was being blamed for it, but it didn't trouble him. He had been blamed for so much that he now set out to earn as much blame as possible. Blame usually meant money in his pocket.

When he left the road and took to the fells he saw the shanty, or what looked like a shanty, when he was some distance away. When he got nearer he saw it was an erection made with two tables, one standing on blocks of wood with a chest of drawers for one wall and a cupboard affair for another. The third wall consisted of the backs of two chairs and the top of one table; two sides of the shelter were draped with bracken and pieces of material.

To the side of the erection a fire was burning in a square of stones; and he saw a woman bending over the fire, a pan in her hand. To her side there was a jumble of pots and pans and crockery. He saw Mulholland kneeling in front of the shelter bending over someone lying on a pallet, and beyond him more figures were huddled.

When Mulholland twisted round on his approach and sprang to his feet Bunting stopped. He knew it was always well to keep a distance between himself and men who had been evicted. He spoke immediately, saying in a conciliatory tone, 'This wasn't my doing, Mulholland. I'll have you know that right away.'

'What do you want here?'

'I want a word with you.'

It was on the point of Rodney's tongue to say, 'Get yourself away,' when Catherine spoke. She just said his name, but it was so full of pleading that he remained silent. Straightening his shoulders, he walked a few yards from the shelter and Bunting followed him. When he stopped, Bunting came closer to him, but still not within arm's reach. He said again, 'You mustn't hold it against me for this; I had nothing to do with it, it was Brown. And even if I'd had anything on you I wouldn't have used it under the circumstances.'

'What do you mean?' Rodney's voice was a growl.

'Well' – Bunting dropped his head to the side and looked towards the ground – 'your daughter's condition; not to speak of the other handicaps you have in your family.'

Rodney forced himself to remain silent. His teeth clamped tight together, he waited. He couldn't imagine this man's actions being motivated by anything but greed, and so when his proposal came he was stunned into absolute silence.

'I wonder . . . I wonder if you'd consider me marrying your girl?'

The shock on Rodney lasted for some seconds; and then it was thrust aside by the thought, It was him. It was him. William had said he had seen him on the road Sunday after Sunday when she was going back to the house. He could have been sneaking around the night of the ball, keeking at the gentry. The voice that erupted from him was a cross between a roar and a yell. 'You! You!' He would have been on Bunting within the next second had not Catherine's voice again checked him; and not only her voice but Katie's too. Katie's cry was even higher than her mother's. 'No, Da, no! Not him. It wasn't him. Never.'

It was something that Katie put into the word never that brought Rodney back to himself.

Bunting lowered his hawthorn stick. You see, it was as he had always told himself; they would be on you whether you were guilty or not. In an offended tone, he said, 'I have never been near your girl, Mulholland. I have passed the time of day with her on the road on an occasional Sunday, that's all. I made the proposal out of good faith. I need a woman in the house; my mother has been dead for years. I'm offering her a home that even you should see is necessary at the present time. Moreover, I can promise that you'll be reinstated.'

They all stood in silence for a moment; then Rodney, after moving one lip tightly over the other said, 'Thank you . . . Mr Bunting' – he laid stress on the mister – 'but I can see to me daughter.'

For answer Bunting slanted his eyes towards the shelter and said, 'I'll leave you to think it over. I'll come tomorrow night.'

As he went to turn away Rodney said, 'I wouldn't trouble; the answer'll be the same.'

Bunting now turned and looked to where Katie was standing close to her mother's side, but he did not allow his eyes to rest on her, his gaze was directed fully at Catherine and it said, 'You'll suffer this too.'

Catherine watched him walk away. If it had been anyone else but him she would have gone down on her knees to him, but not to Bunting. She couldn't bear the thought of her daughter being under the protection of this hated man, as great as her need was. Anyone who attached himself to Bunting was shunned by the whole village. But at the same time Catherine wondered how long they could last out living like this. They were all right as regards to food, for the neighbours had been kindness itself. Each day they collected enough to feed them, but it was more than their livelihood was worth to offer them shelter. Anyone in the village found harbouring those who had been evicted as troublemakers at the mine shared the same fate as those they were endeavouring to help. But her Rodney hadn't been a troublemaker; this was all some plot which she couldn't fathom. She put out her hand and pushed Katie towards the shelter, then went to her husband and, looking into his face, whispered, her voice laden with regret, 'If it had been anybody else but him.'

He bowed his head before her gaze, and in his heart he repeated her words, 'If it had been anyone else but him.' His daughter needed shelter, and his father-in-law needed shelter because the old man was in a bad way. If it hadn't been for William he would have moved to a fresh town; travelling the road couldn't be any worse than up here on the windswept fells and the bad weather on them. But he wouldn't put William in the poorhouse; the old man had a horror of dying in the poorhouse.

From under his lowered gaze he saw Catherine's joined hands trembling, and he put his own out to steady them, saying, 'There's always a chance I'll get set on at Palmer's. I'm going in the morrow again; they're setting men on all the time.' He didn't add that it was hard for a blacklisted man to get a job anywhere, for she knew that, but he went on, 'The place is like a gigantic hive now, you wouldn't believe it. They've got four blast furnaces goin' an' rolling mills, and boiler shops, and engine shops. You wouldn't recognise it now. You'll see, I'll get a start in one or the other of the shops.'

'But they'd want experienced men, wouldn't they?' Her voice was very small.

'No, no; there's a thousand and one jobs that doesn't need experience. I've as much experience as the Irish, I'd say, and the place is alive with them.'

'But . . . but would there be any chance of gettin' shelter? You said last week they were sleeping twelve to a room in some of the tenements. It wouldn't be any use getting a job if you couldn't get shelter.'

He closed his eyes and bowed his head and said helplessly, 'One thing at a time, Catherine, one thing at a time. Let me get a start first.'

Her mind overwhelmed with despair, her body shivering with the cold, Katie lay curled up between her mother and Lizzie. All night she had lain like this, listening to the breathing of the others, to the hard cutting cough of her granda, to the moaning of her father. She knew when they were awake and when they were asleep; only Lizzie slept undisturbed. Even Joe, who could sleep on his feet, told her at intervals, by the small sound he made in his throat, that he was awake. Now that he had the chance to sleep – he had been dismissed three days ago – he couldn't take advantage of it.

Sometime, long before the dawn broke, she heard her da get up; then her ma moved from her side. The day had begun, the endless day of just lying or sitting. No-one talked much any more.

It was early in the evening of this day that Katie put on her cloak and said to Catherine, 'I'm goin' over to see Betty.'

Catherine stared at her. The Monktons, knowing the risk, had offered to give shelter to her father and Katie, but both had steadfastly refused to go. Now she imagined that Katie, feeling frozen to the bone as they all were, was about to seek the warmth of four walls for a short while before the night set in.

'All right, lass. Stay as long as you like,' she said, after which she added quickly, 'You'd better get back afore dark though, hadn't you.' Then as she stared into the white peaked face the real reason for Katie seeking shelter at the Monktons came to her. She didn't want to be here if Bunting kept his word and came back tonight. That was it . . .

But Bunting didn't keep his word and come to the shanty that evening, nor did he come the next night; nor yet the next; nor the one after that, on which particular night Katie again went to visit Betty Monkton.

It was the eighth morning after Bunting's visit, when things had reached the point of desperation for them all, with the exception of Lizzie, that Rodney rose just after four o'clock and made his way to Jarrow, to be at Palmer's Shipyard when the gates opened at six o'clock. A man had said that was the time to be there when there was a likelihood of jumping into someone's boots, a sick man's boots, because no man stayed away from work unless he was sick, and desperately so.

And it was later the same morning when the wind was driving the rain into the shelter that Katie, having taken off the dress in which she had slept, put on the only other one she had; then, washing her face and hands in the dead-cold water from the stream, she pulled on her cloak and set her straw hat straight on her head.

William, watching her from his pallet, asked feebly, 'Where you goin', lass? Have . . . have you heard of a job?'

She was kneeling, searching in her bundle for a handkerchief, a new handkerchief, the one Mrs Davis had given her on her sixteenth birthday, which was only a few days before she was sent home, and, still on her knees, she moved towards him and, bending down and kissing his sunken cheek, she said, 'Yes, Grandpa, I'm going after a job.'

Catherine, coming to the opening of the shelter, stared down at her, then exclaimed, 'What did you say? Where you goin', lass?' She pushed Lizzie under cover as she spoke; she had just returned from making her clean. She took her some distance from the dwelling each morning for this purpose.

Katie moved past her mother and a few steps away from the shelter, and Catherine went with her, and again she asked, 'Where are you goin', lass?' Then added, as her father had done, 'You've heard of something? A job or something?'

'You could look at it that way, Ma.' Katie's lips were trembling, and now she clutched at Catherine's hand and stared beseechingly into her face as she muttered, 'Don't be upset, don't, but I . . . I'm going to marry Mr Bunting.'

Catherine drew in a sharp breath that cut off her words; then she gulped twice before crying, 'No, lass! No! It would drive your da mad. No! No!'

'I promised; it's all arranged. That's where I went the other night, an' the night he was to come here . . . I told him then.'

'But . . . but it's only a week ago, lass.'

'I know, I know. They can do these things quick by a licence, he said . . . He said leave it to him and . . . and he's promised you'll have a house by the morrow.'

'Aw, lass.' Catherine moved her head in slow wide sweeps, never taking her eyes from Katie's face.

'I've . . . I've got to do this, Ma, 'cos . . . 'cos Granda'll die if he's out here much longer, an' you an' all and . . . and then the baby comin'.'

'But your da, child.'

Katie now hung her head and said softly, 'It was because of me he was stood off and you were turned out. They did it because . . . ' She stopped and bit on her lip and Catherine said quickly, 'No, lass, no. It was nothing to do with you; it was because he had been holding meetings with Fred Ramshaw and Mr Fogerty, and they're known to be strong union men going from pit to pit stirring up – at least Fogerty does.'

'No, Ma, no. It wasn't because of that; it was because of me.'

Catherine stood contemplating her daughter. For a space of time, during which her mind took in and rapidly sorted what Katie had said, she continued to stare at her, and then, putting her fingers tentatively to her lips, she whispered, 'They know up at the house, the master and them, who it was?'

Katie lowered her head as Catherine exclaimed, 'Oh, dear God! And you, you know who it was?'

Katie's chin jerked up and she whispered rapidly, 'Yes, Ma, yes: Mr Bernard. But don't tell me da ever. He would make trouble. You saw him at Mr Bunting; he . . . he would kill somebody.'

'Aye, yes.' Catherine knew that her daughter spoke the truth. Her God-fearing, quiet husband was quite capable of killing the man who had brought his daughter to this pass. But she need have no fear; he wouldn't get to know anything from her.

'So you see, Ma' – Katie's lips were trembling so hard the words spurted unevenly out of her mouth – 'by . . . doing this . . . me da, me da an' all of you will be all right. He'll . . . have his job, for good.'

'Oh, Katie! Oh, child!'

'Bye-bye, Ma. Tell me da not to come. Don't let him come, Ma. Stop him; 'cos once it's done, it's done. An' . . . an' tell him I want to have the baby properly; tell him that.'

As her hand trailed away, Catherine grabbed at it, saying, 'But the village. Nobody will speak to you any more, lass.'

Now Catherine saw her daughter straightening her stooped shoulders, she watched her head go up, and it wasn't her Katie but someone much older who said, 'It doesn't matter to me now what anybody says and who speaks to me and who doesn't; all that matters is that you and them' – she inclined her head slightly towards the shelter – 'are all right. Bye-bye, Ma.' Bending swiftly forward, she kissed Catherine, and Catherine clutched her tightly, crying, 'No, lass, no,' until Katie, tearing herself away, ran from her, her hands covering her mouth to stop the moaning sounds.

It was in great trepidation that Catherine waited for Rodney to return. But it wasn't until half-past six, when the last vestige of light was going, that she saw the dim outline of him hurrying over the fells towards her. And when he came up close to her she saw that his face was dirty, and bright and happy; more so than she had seen it for years. His hand came on to her shoulder as he said, 'I've got a start, lass. I've been at it all day. An' we've got a place . . . of sorts. It's not what I would want, but in this case beggars can't be choosers. An' we'll soon get out of it; it'll just be for the meantime.'

His words were gabbled; the excitement was filling him so much that he did not for the moment take in her pitiful expression, but, turning his head to the side, he shouted towards the shelter, 'I've got set on, William, in the rolling mills.' He expected an answer to come back immediately to him saying something like, 'Thanks be to God, lad!' But William didn't answer him, nor yet did Joe make his appearance. He brought his eyes back to Catherine, and, putting his face close to hers, asked, 'What is it? Something's happened.' Then, looking wildly round him, he added, 'Katie!'

'She's gone, Rod.'

'Gone? Where's she gone? What do you mean, woman?'

She now took hold of his arms and she felt the hard knots of the muscles as she gripped them and said slowly, 'What she's done she's done for us, remember that. Do you hear? Remember, what she's done she's done for us.' Her voice had risen. It was loud, like a cry echoing across the fells, and he pulled himself away quickly from her, saying, 'What's she's done? Where is she?'

She kept her eyes tight on him as she said, quickly now, 'She married Bunting this mornin'.'

She had feared his reaction. All day she had steeled herself against this moment, imagining herself hanging on to him, trying to hold him down to keep him away from Bunting until he saw reason, but she hadn't prepared herself for what was happening now. Her man seemed to be shrinking before her eyes. She watched his body slump; she watched him turn from her and cover his face with his hands, much as her father had done when he had heard the news. He was acting like a man from whom the spirit had been whipped. He had got work; he had got them shelter; but the light had gone out of his life.

CHAPTER EIGHT

If KATIE COULD have been sustained by the fact that her marrying Mark Bunting had provided her family with food, warmth and shelter, she might have felt that there was a purpose in her suffering. But the morning after a surprising night – surprising because this man, who was now her husband and whom she already feared, had not touched her – Joe came to the door and, gazing at her as if she was an utter stranger, told her that they were going into Jarrow to live. In a kind of cottage, was the way he described their new home, off Walter Street, No. 3, The Row. Their da, he said, had got started in Palmer's Shipyard.

On this news she'd had the childish desire to take Joe by the hand and fly with him to this new home in Jarrow. It was only the sure knowledge that Bunting . . . her husband . . . would come and bring her back that stopped her.

She did not ask Joe into the house, for already she'd had her orders on that score – no visitors. Bunting had sat most of last evening opposite to her at the other side of the blazing fire and given her her instructions. He wasn't having her family here or her going there, and it wasn't likely they'd have any visitors from the village. He'd buy the food, as he had always done, and dish it out to her every day. And she'd have to be careful; if there was any waste she'd have him to reckon with. Moreover, there was to be no saving of bits and pieces to be sneaked out.

If the cooking was done properly the food would be eaten and nothing left over. Did she understand? She had moved her head, and on this he had taken his hawthorn stick, which was never far from his side, and poked it, not too gently, in the middle of her stomach, saying, 'You've got a tongue in your head.'

Later, shaking like a leaf in a gale, she had preceded him up the steep stairs, and on the tiny landing he had pushed one of the two doors open and, thumbing inwards, had said, 'You're in there, until I need you.'

By the light of a stub of tallow candle she saw a little room holding a single bed and a chest of drawers. Her relief at finding herself alone was so great that her shivering increased until her whole body appeared to be affected by ague.

And so the pattern went on for three weeks. She would rise early in the morning, make up the fire, heat his water to wash in the big black kail pot, make his breakfast of porridge and potato cakes fried in dripping; then when he was gone she would start her business of cleaning the house. She would have loved this task under other circumstances, for to her it was a lovely house, with a big kitchen holding two tables: one for eating off, one for cooking on. At one side of the fire was a small wooden settle, at the other a straight-back wooden chair with a padded seat. There was a long delf rack in the kitchen with good crockery on it. In the parlour there was a horsehair couch and two chairs, all worn but comfortable still. There was a round table in the middle of the room on a spindle leg, and under the good-sized window was an oak blanket chest. The stone floor was almost covered with hand-made clippy rugs.

The first time she saw the parlour she imagined a roaring fire in the grate and her ma and da sitting in the armchairs, and her granda on the couch, and their Joe and Lizzie and herself on the mat in front of the fire.

At the end of the first week the longing to see her people was so intense that she got as far as putting her cloak on and going to the door, but there she stopped. He had come in early last night, around five. It was now nearly two o'clock; she wouldn't be able to walk there and back before five o'clock. If she had known where Walter Street was she might have taken a chance. As it was, she thought better of it and contented herself with sitting mending his clothes.

It was on this day that she made the further acquaintance of Roy.

The dog had shown an interest in her from the beginning; it hadn't growled when she took its food down to the kennel. Bunting had said nothing to her about what attitude she should take to his dog, so as soon as the thought came to her she ran down the garden and undid the chain, and holding on to his collar brought him into the house. He acted in such a queer, mad way at first, tearing round and round the room, sniffing here and there, that if she could have laughed she would have. After a while, his curiosity satisfied, he came to her where she sat and put his front paws on her knee, and she put her arms around him and cried.

But then came the day when Mark Bunting hastily swallowed his dinner and was out of the house around half-past twelve instead of one o'clock. The yearning to see her people had been almost unbearable for days, and so, donning her cloak and tying her straw hat on with the band of ribbon, she locked the door, put the key underneath the wash-house table, patted the dog, telling him she was sorry he would have to remain on his chain all day, then she set off at a good pace to walk the three and a half miles into Jarrow.

It was years since she had been in Jarrow and she remembered it as a busy place with rows of white cottages and streets branching off containing bigger houses, two-storey houses. Now it was a bewildering place. The cottages were still there but grimy-looking; and there was a maze of streets and houses all around. The main road was packed with carts: dray carts with barrels piled high on them, coal carts, coke carts, fruit carts.

Going up one of the streets she saw two women filling buckets from a tap in the middle of the road and she asked them the way to Walter Street, and they told her.

When she found Walter Street and the row of cottages behind it she was appalled by the dirt and the stench. She had to go down a bank to get to the little row of cottages, and she slithered in mud right to the very door.

When she knocked on No. 3 it was opened by her mother. They looked at each other for a moment; then fell into each other's arms, Catherine crying, 'Oh, me bairn, me bairn!' and Katie repeating brokenly, 'Oh, Ma, Ma!' Then Catherine, pressing her daughter from her, turned her head into the dim depths of the room behind and cried, 'Da! She's come.'

Katie, guided by Catherine, stepped down into the room. Then in the dim light she saw her granda lying on a raised wooden platform to the side of the fire, and she rushed to him and was enfolded in his arms, and his tears wet her face, but he said not a word.

When he had lain himself back on the bed Katie looked at him and her heart sank. He wasn't better. Having shelter hadn't helped him. He looked bad, so bad. She touched his cheek and said, 'Oh, Granda,' and still he didn't speak, only held tightly on to her hand.

Now of her own accord Lizzie came to her side and she spoke Katie's name, saying it softly, and when Katie got up from the bed she put her arms around her and brought her head down to Katie's shoulder and laid it there.

After a moment Catherine gently drew Lizzie from Katie's arms, and, taking her to a chair, said, 'There now. There now.' She was touched and slightly amazed that this daughter had the sense in her to feel Katie's absence.

Going to the fire in the back wall, she said between her catching breath,

'I'll . . . I'll make a pot of tea,' and, turning and looking at Katie again, she added, 'Get your things off, hinny, and sit down.'

'I . . . I can't stay long, Ma. Perhaps half an hour; I've got to be back afore five.'

'Oh!' Catherine turned to the fire again. Then William spoke for the first time. 'How are you, child?' he said.

'All right, Granda.'

And now quite bluntly he asked, 'And how does he treat you?'

She paused before answering. How did he treat her? How he treated his dog, giving her orders and expecting them to be obeyed without question. Only he didn't sit staring at his dog as he sat staring at her for hour after hour until she felt she would scream. Once she got up and said she was going to bed and he had ordered her to sit down again. She always made sure now that she had something to occupy her hands in the evening so she wouldn't look at him looking at her. Yet he had never touched her. She was still sleeping in the little room by herself. She couldn't understand it. Although she was petrified of the moment when he would come near her, she still couldn't understand why, as yet, he hadn't.

Catherine now asked, 'Is the house comfortable?'

'Oh yes, Ma.' There was even a touch of enthusiasm in her voice. 'It's a nice house, and warm . . . ' She wished she hadn't said that because this place wasn't warm, it was chilling to the bone. She now glanced about the room. It was dreadful. The walls were running with water; the bricks of the floor were oozing water. It was dark and damp and terrible.

As if Catherine read her thoughts, she said, 'Houses here are impossible to get. This is bad, but we're on our own. You should see them up the streets; they're packed closer than hens in a cree. And the beds are never aired; as one gets out another gets in. The night shifts sleep through the day and there are strange men and women in one room. It's awful. And the middens – they've got to be seen to be believed. The smell would knock you down. You might think this is bad, lass' – she shook her head – 'but it's nothin'. And they're asking three shilling a week for a room; they can get any price now. We were lucky to get this. It was a Mr Hetherington who got it for us; he's the one who got your da set on. He knew your Granda Mulholland years ago. As a lad he worked under him. It was a stroke of luck in a thousand your da meetin' him. He knows your da; he knows he's no troublemaker at the pit or anywhere else.'

Katie watched her mother moving around the dim, smelly room, talking as if to herself most of the time. The smell that pervaded the room was a filthy smell like sitting in the closet. She wanted to get into the air and breathe deeply. Oh, if she could only take them all back to the house; if only Mr Bunting – she thought of him as either Mr Bunting or he – if only he was different, a bit kind; if only she could talk to him . . . She missed talking, although she hadn't wanted to talk very much since the night of the ball. Somehow now she felt inclined to talk, but not about the things she used to talk about, such as the Rosier family and Mrs Davis, and the staff, and food. She didn't know what she wanted to talk about now; she only knew that she needed to speak to someone and hear them reply.

She had a cup of tea but would eat nothing, and then it was time to go, and she felt she'd hardly got in. She kissed and hugged her granda to her; she kissed and held Lizzie; and when she was at the door she mentioned Joe for the first time. 'Where is he, Ma?' she said. 'Our Joe.'

'Oh!' Catherine smiled weakly. 'Didn't I tell you? He's been set on; he's in the boiler shop. And the way he describes it, it's marvellous. And he's tickled to death working in the daylight. He'll never go down below again, never. He's a runner to one of the men with hot rivets and things, you know. Oh, he likes it. So you see, lass' – she spread her hands – 'we're all right if only we could get out of this.

'Will you come again, lass?' Catherine asked tentatively now, and Katie nodded her head. Then she put her arms around her mother and they kissed and held tight for a moment; but when it was over she didn't immediately walk away, for there was a question she wanted to ask. She looked down as she said, 'How's me da?'

'Not bad, lass. He was upset, but he's getting over it. I know one thing; he's dying to see you. You . . . you couldn't come one night?'

Katie turned her eyes towards the bank again and said, 'No, Ma, I couldn't come at night.'

'He'd walk you nearly all the way back.'

'I couldn't, Ma.'

'All right, lass.' Catherine patted her arm, and again she kissed her; then she watched her mount the slimy bank. And when she turned at the end of the street she waved to her.

It wasn't four o'clock yet the winter twilight was already beginning, and the effect of night coming fast was helped by the smoke belching from the great chimneys of the steelworks. When Katie reached the main road she found it blocked with stationary traffic. Men sat high on their carts or stood at their horses' heads and shouted to each other. She walked quickly up the uneven pavement, past a row of shops all showing, to her mind, wonderful things: food, clothes, boots, butcher's meats, pig meat. She would have liked to stand and gaze in one window after the other, but she knew she mustn't waste a minute. Further along the pavement she came to the reason for the blockade. Two drunken women were sprawled in the middle of the road, fighting. Their hair was hanging down their backs, their clothes were rent and muddy, and as they tore at each other they were encouraged by a large group of onlookers, while a policeman tried to disentangle them, getting no assistance from any bystanders.

The sight of the fighting disgusted her – not that she hadn't seen drunken women before. But her mother never touched beer or gin, nor did her father. Her granda did, but only when there was a copper to spare.

The whole town seemed crowded with people, and it was not four o'clock. What it would be like when the shipyard and the chemical works let the men out she couldn't imagine.

When she reached the outskirts of the town and the open land stretched for miles before her, with the river winding through it, she breathed deeply and told herself she would die if she had to live in Jarrow and that hovel; she needed fresh country air.

The thought brought her to a stop and she clutched the neck of her cloak; she didn't need fresh country air. Given the choice she would run back to that evil-smelling room this minute.

As she skirted the village she was confronted on the narrow trail by a number of men coming off the second shift. She knew most of them; they all knew her. Some of their glances were scornful, some pitying, but no man spoke to her.

It was dark when she reached the house. She had run most of the last part of the journey. She was still running when she reached the wash-house, but when her hand went to pick up the key her fingers remained stiff and bent; it was gone. Her eyes moved wildly about. If he were in the candle would be lit. She went slowly towards the house door and turned the handle, and when she entered the room she saw him in the light from the fire, sitting on the settle just as he had come from the pit. His eyes were waiting for her, and the look in them caused her whole body to go cold. She walked slowly forward, taking off her cape as she did so, and she passed him and was pulling off her hat and going towards the scullery to bring in the wooden tub for him to bathe in when he barked at her, saying, 'You did it then?'

She turned and peered at him outlined against the firelight, and she gulped twice before she dared to protest, 'I had to go; they're my folks.'

'Are they, begod!' He was on his feet now, coming towards her. 'Well, I'll tell you something which you seem to have forgotten, Mrs Bunting.' He stressed his name. 'You happen to be a married woman now.' He put four stiff fingers out and pushed her in the chest, causing her to stumble backwards. 'You think because he's got work away from the pit you can take a high hand now, don't you? Well, let me tell you, Mr Rosier's arm is long and it's linked with Palmer's and a word from me and your da'll be out in the gutter again. Now remember that, the next time you want to take a walk . . . Get goin'; I'm waiting for the water. I've been waiting for the last half-hour.'

While she scurried back and forward filling the bath, first with cold water, then adding the boiling water from the kail pot, he stripped himself of his clothes. He stripped himself naked as he had done since the first day she got the bath ready for him, not leaving his small clothes on as her father did, and other miners, when there were women and bairns about. While he washed she always kept her eyes lowered from him. She couldn't understand this attitude of his any more than she could understand him letting her sleep alone. She would have understood it better if he hadn't let her sleep alone.

When he sat down in the bath, his knees level with his chin and the water barely covering his thighs, she went forward and, stooping low, picked up the flannel out of the water, keeping her gaze fixed tightly on it the while; then, going behind him, she washed his back. Following this, she scooped some hot water from the pot into the wooden bucket; then going to the back door, where stood a barrel that caught the rainwater from the roof, she half filled another bucket, returned to the kitchen, and with it she cooled the hot water in the other bucket. Then, lifting it up, she stood waiting.

And Mark Bunting kept her waiting. His movements were slower now, leisurely. After a time he got to his knees and, bending forward slightly, held on to the sides of the tub while Katie poured the warm water over him. It was a refinement to his toilette that he had thought of only recently.

He always changed his clothes after the bath, and Katie now took his pit suit and underwear into the yard and banged them against the wall, getting rid of as much dust as possible. When she returned to the kitchen he was almost dressed and he barked at her again, 'You could have left that till after, couldn't you? Where's the meal?'

The small protesting voice within her was quite silent now, and, scurrying still, she set the table. It was cold meat left over from dinner time. He measured out for her three slices of bread, a small two-inch square of meat, a dob of dripping, and a mug of tea. He put no sugar in her tea but some in his own.

When the meal was over and she had washed the dishes she took her seat by the fireside and began to sew. She was turning in the frayed ends of his working trousers. She could hardly see what she was doing, for there was only one candle alight, and if she moved nearer to it it would mean moving nearer to him.

Mark Bunting now lit a spill from the candle and applied it to his wooden pipe – he did not smoke a clay pipe as the ordinary men did – and when the pipe was going well he lay back in his chair, his stockinged feet resting on the raised stone hearth, and surveyed his wife.

If Bunting had been other than he was, this scene could have held happiness for him, even having married Katie for a price, as he had done. She would have repaid the smallest kindnesses shown to her a thousandfold if he could have found it in his heart to be kind. If he had been kind she would have liked him, because he wasn't an unattractive-looking man. Being Katie, with a bountiful amount of sympathy and affection in her nature, she would have stood up for him in spite of what was said about him, if he had only been kind. And who knew but that the kindness would have grown into love, for kindness, like witchcraft, caused things to happen.

But there was a strong unnatural twist in Mark Bunting's make-up. How else could he have stood for years the scorn of his fellow men and found pleasure in their suffering, especially when the suffering was instigated by himself? With workmen, however, he knew exactly where he stood, what the result of his actions towards them would be, but in the present situation his position wasn't at all clear and he was in a quandary. He pulled hard on his pipe now as he looked at Katie: at the mass of gleaming hair, the tendrils hanging across her pale face; at her big eyes – the eyes that told him all her feelings – lowered over the sewing; at the small swelling bulge of her stomach; and he wondered where he stood. He didn't know but that young Rosier wasn't finished with her; he had been vague the night he called here, asking simply if he wanted to earn a hundred pounds. When he had replied with a laugh, 'Show me the man who doesn't, sir,' he had been told, 'If you'll marry the Mulholland girl there'll be fifty when you ask her and fifty when it's done . . . she's to have a child.' He had stared into the lean, handsome face which he hated more than that of any other man in the mine, and he had considered the proposal for a full moment, during which his thinking hadn't been concerned with the Mulholland girl but with the fact that this business could mean an assured income for years ahead. And even when he had given his answer he had not allowed himself to appear eager, but had said, slowly, 'All right, sir; it's a deal,' and all Rosier had said after that was, 'Go to the Reverend Pinkerton. Tell him you want a special licence. Explain the situation, without my name of course; make it urgent. I'll see to the cost.'

And that was all. It might be that when the child was born he would see to its upbringing if it was a boy. As for her – well, if you fancied women she was a one to fancy. Rosier likely wasn't done with her. He had only seen him once since his marriage into the Talford family and then he had looked straight through him. But that was part of the game; he didn't mind being treated like scum as long as he was paid for it; he was treated like scum most of the time and not paid for it.

As he stared at her he wondered why he had no desire to take her to bed. She was his wife, he could, and Rosier couldn't do much about it, could he? It would be like eating your cake and having it. He had often thought if he had a woman in the house he would feel different, but he didn't. The thought of having her in bed stirred him not at all, but there were other ways in which she could afford him satisfaction, only he'd have to hold his hand about them until the child came and he knew Master Rosier's reactions. It wouldn't do to get on the wrong side of him; because it wasn't only the source of revenue for years ahead that could be jeopardised, there was also his job, and this house, of which he was very proud, that went with it. He would hold his hand. There was no hurry; he was a patient man.

He startled her by saying, 'Have you seen about a midwife?'

Her eyes wide, she said, 'No.'

'Then you'd better, hadn't you? They get full up. A very busy time the spring is . . . for babies. Mrs Morgan in the village, she's one, isn't she?'

She dropped her head before saying, 'She wouldn't come.'

He was sitting bolt upright in his chair now. 'Who said she wouldn't come? You've asked her?'

'No . . . but a village woman wouldn't come to the house; you know she wouldn't.' She felt a certain strength flow into her after having dared to say that to him, and something of this seemed to get across to him, for he got to his feet and, standing over her and digging his thick finger into the hollow of her shoulder, he said, 'Go the morrow and ask her. She'll come. If she's sensible she'll come.'

Again, in spite of his prodding finger, she forced herself to speak what was in her mind. Although her voice was little more than a whisper, she said, 'I'd rather have me Ma.'

She was nearly knocked from the chair with the flat of his hand on the back of her head. 'You're not havin' your mother here. I'm not having any of your scum inside these four walls, get that! At no time. Do you hear me?'

She snapped off the thread from the trousers with trembling fingers; then she folded them up and laid them by the side of the fireplace where he always left his clothes so that they would be warm to put on. Following this, she proceeded to set the table for his supper, and when this was done she stood between the kitchen and the scullery door and said, 'I'm going to bed, I'm tired.'

'Like hell you are! If you go on walks that make you tired that's your look-out. Sit yourself down there.' He pointed to a chair. 'You'll go when I'm ready and not afore.'

So she sat until nearly ten o'clock, and only the thought of having to light one more candle drew him up the stairs, and she followed him, thinking all the while that tonight he would push her into his room. But he didn't.

CHAPTER NINE

KATIE'S BABY WAS born towards the end of April, in the first minutes of a Thursday morning, and it was a girl.

She lay exhausted after the long fifteen hours of labour while Mrs Morgan cleaned her up and washed her and saw to the child. Then the midwife, sitting on a chair by the bedside, dozed until the dawn should break and she could see her way home.

The sun was shining in through the little window when she stood, her shawl over her head, ready to go. She looked down on Katie with the child in her arms and said, 'You can be proud of your bairn; she's a beauty, lass. What you goner call it?'

'Sarah,' said Katie.

Hearing the door bang downstairs, Mrs Morgan went and looked out of the window and, coming back, she said, 'He's gone.' Then after a pause, during which her head drooped to one side, she asked, 'Why in the name of God did you marry that one?'

Looking all eyes, Katie said quietly, 'Because of them, Mrs Morgan, me ma an' da and them. I couldn't stand to see them freezing to death out there. And he said he'd get me da set on straightaway and give them a house.'

'And then your da went and got set on in Jarrow. Aw, lass, all for nowt. . . . Is it hisen?'

'Oh no, Mrs Morgan, no.'

'Well, you can say thank God for that, an' all.'

'Mrs Morgan.' Katie eased herself upwards on the straw pillow. 'Could . . . could you get word to me ma and tell her I've had it, and tell her not to come afore Tuesday. That's the best day. It's No. 3, The Row . . . '

'Oh, I know where she lives, lass, an' I'll get our Micky to go as soon as I get back . . . But don't you think she'd better come up and see you ordinary like?'

'No, Mrs Morgan. It's no use asking, an' I'm afraid for me da's new job.'

'Aw, to hell's flames with him, he can't do anything in Palmer's; he's got no say there. Did he say he could get your da the push if your ma came?'

Katie closed her eyes, then said, 'As much.'

'The stinking bugger! Somebody'll do for him one of these days, an' I hope it'll be soon. And you won't be the only one that's relieved, lass. But there you are; don't worry your head at the moment.' She patted her kindly. 'I'll be back in a little while; you're all right for the time being.'

'Thanks, Mrs Morgan, thanks.' She put out her hand and touched the thick rough hand of the old woman, but she withheld her tears until Mrs Morgan had gone down the stairs. Then they flowed so fast that they dropped on to the child's face and rolled down its cheeks like dewdrops.

The child was nearly a month old before Mark Bunting got the chance of a private word with its father.

Bernard Rosier wasn't seen so much at the mine now, and for two reasons. First, because he was living in Newcastle, in a house that had been a wedding present to his bride from her father; the second was because his interests had apparently widened. It was said that his father-in-law had a slice in Palmer's Shipyard and Mr Bernard was moving in that direction to take a bite.

On this particular morning Bunting saw him going into the works office apparently looking for Brown, the under-manager. The office was separate from the one where the clerks were housed, and Bunting, knowing that Brown was below ground, saw this as a good opportunity to speak of the matter that was foremost in his mind.

Bernard Rosier turned, on his entry, and stared at him; then when Bunting took off his cap but made no effort to speak he said in a cutting tone, 'Well?'

Bunting moistened his thin lips and, his hands remaining stationary on the rim of his cap, muttered in an undertone, 'I was thinking, sir, perhaps you'd like to know, the baby came nearly four week ago. It's a girl. I – I just thought as you'd like to know.'

As Bunting watched the blood flood up into Bernard Rosier's face he knew immediately he was on the wrong track. His eyes were unblinking as Rosier came and stood close to him and he watched him sift the words through his teeth as he said, 'Now look here, my man; you were paid for what you did, and well paid, and that's the end as far as I'm concerned. If you think you're going to bleed me over this matter you'd better stop and consider . . . Get it into your head you've had all you're going to get

. . . And don't say that you can talk; you can do all the damn well talking you like and who'll believe you? And even if they did, it's no longer of any importance.' He paused here for a number of seconds before adding, 'If you want to find another job just bring up this subject again. Do you understand me?' His head moved just the slightest bit towards the keeker, and after a moment of silence he picked his hat up from the desk, then gave Bunting one last long, hard look and walked out.

There was a cold black fury in Bunting as he hurried towards his home at the end of the day. He saw himself in a situation that he had been over and over again during the hours since he had met Rosier. He was saddled for life with a woman in the house, and a squawking kid – Rosier's squawking kid. And for what? A hundred pounds. If he had stood out he would have paid him five hundred. Aye, he would, five hundred. He saw now that Rosier had that night been in the tightest corner of his life. What the real reason was for wanting her married off he didn't know and he couldn't guess at it. Certain, it wasn't the fact that that little loose bitch would give him away, because if that had been her intention she could have done it afore, or she could have got money out of him to keep her family. But he'd know the ins and outs before he'd finished with her. But here he was, saddled with the pair of them. He would have to feed and clothe them for the rest of their lives. At least her he would. The thought brought the sweat pouring out of him. He didn't take into account that she washed and cooked and cleaned for him; he had done that for himself for years and found it no hardship.

By God, he had been taken for a monkey, hadn't he? All these months he had held his hand because he didn't know where she stood with Rosier, but now he knew all right, and he need hold his hand no longer. No, by Christ alive, he needn't!

He almost put his foot through the door as he entered the house, and Katie turned a startled face on him from the fireplace. He stood for a moment glaring at her, and then towards the child lying in a basket near the window which was open from the bottom. The window gave him something to start on. 'Close that blasted window. What's the good of having a fire on and letting the heat out, you bloody fool?'

He had never sworn at her before; and now he didn't only swear but from him flowed a torrent of obscene abuse. As she filled the bath and poured the clean water over him every action of hers brought a vile stream from him. She was at first stunned by it; then as it continued without ceasing, through the meal and after, it came to her that something had happened, something that had released the real Mark Bunting, for the objectionable, hard, unfeeling man she had lived with since she had married was a nice person compared with this fiendish individual.

To every filthy word he threw at her she said nothing; nor did she retaliate when he almost pushed her on her back as she carried the tub from the kitchen; but when his foot came out to kick at the child's basket she checked it with a scream that startled herself. 'Don't you dare do that!'

He turned round and stared at her. Then a twisted smile spread over his face as he said, 'I'm glad you've got some spunk; it'll give me all the more pleasure to knock it out of you.'

Not waiting now for him to give her the order when she could go to bed, she lifted the basket with the child in it and carried it up the stairs, and she had just taken off her things and put on her coarse calico nightdress when the door burst open.

'Come on,' he said.

'Wh-at!' She stammered on the word.

'You heard what I said. Come on.'

When she made no move he thrust out his hand to grab her, but she crouched against the wall. Then slowly, her eyes riveted on his face, she sidled past him. On the landing she stood transfixed for a moment; then, like someone in a trance, she moved before him into his bedroom.

After banging the door behind him he advanced on her and, grabbing the collar of her nightdress, wrenched it from top to bottom with a twist of his hand and, saying 'You won't be needing this any more,' tore it from her back.

And this was only the beginning of Mark Bunting showing his hand.

It was fourteen nights later. Katie thought of them as nights, for so she had totalled them up. Each evening, like a prisoner approaching the rack, she wondered if she would be able to suffer what was before her. Not the least of her feelings was humiliation. The indignities he heaped upon her crushed her spirit so low that in the agonising, wakeful stillness of the night, when she was afraid to move in case of waking him again, she would tell herself that in the morning she would take the child and go to her mother, but in the light of day she was always deterred by the thought of him following her and what would happen when her father and him came face to face. But she knew that when her ma came on one of her secret visits she would tell her; at least she would tell her that she would have to get away from here, if not all the reasons why. Then she would think that were she to go he could put the police on to her and claim the child. Perhaps it didn't matter that it wasn't his; he had taken on the responsibility of it, so he could claim it. There were so many things that seemed to block her way of escape. If only her ma would come. She hadn't been for the past fortnight; afore that she had been every week.

Then came the beautiful June evening. If she had stood at the door she would have heard the birds singing, she would have seen the rabbits scampering on the moors and a hare sitting in startled surprise at finding himself only a few yards from the gate; but she was busy preparing the meal, and making it as tasty as possible so as to give him no loophole to find fault.

He came in as he had done over the last fortnight, his brows meeting, his mouth tight. Then followed the usual procedure. He tore off his clothes, he got into the bath, he washed his front and she washed his back.

Came the moment when she was about to get the water to rinse him. He had been spitting obscenities at her, just single words, and it was at the precise second when she had filled the bucket half full of boiling water from the kail pot that the child began to cry. It let out a sharp wail, a hungry wail. Katie turned from the stove, the bucket in her hand, to hear Bunting curse and to see him scooping up a ladle full of black-scummed water with the evident intent of throwing it on the child who lay in the corner only a couple of arms-lengths from him; and as she had stopped him from using his foot on the basket with a scream, now she screamed again, 'Don't! Don't do that!' At the same time, without pausing to think, she threw the water over him.

His scream ascended high above hers; it rent the house. She was knocked flying backwards, and, the settle breaking her fall, she cowered trembling in the corner of it, utterly petrified at what she had done, and done unintentionally.

She watched him dancing like a mad dervish, screaming all the while. Then to the screams were added deep groans, while the fingers of his hands, like those of a blind man, hovered over his neck and shoulders. After a time his screaming stopped and there was only his moaning filling the strange silence. He turned towards her, staring at her; his face looked inhuman, twisted, like a stone gargoyle. The next minute the silence was broken by his loud screaming curses. She was still crouched on the settle and her breathing almost stopped as she watched him scattering his clothes and riving his leather belt from out of the loops of his trousers. Before the buckled end of the belt came down on her she screamed, and she continued to scream as he flayed her round the room. Her own warm sticky blood ran from her fingers, and she thrust them into her wide open mouth as she screamed. When she felt the clothes being torn from her back she clung on to the end of the settle, and when he dragged her forward the settle came with her. And then he was belabouring her again, but she wasn't screaming so hard now. She had almost stopped screaming when the hammering came on the door. Before she fainted she imagined she saw Joe and heard his voice shouting.

When she slowly came to her senses she actually saw Joe's face above hers; it was streaming with tears and he was moaning as if he, too, had been almost beaten to death. She tried to speak but found she couldn't. Her body seemed to be torn in all directions with pain, and then she thought of the child and pushed at Joe and rolled on her side, looking towards the basket. When, after a moment, she pointed, Joe whispered, 'It's all right; it's all right.' He now helped her to prop herself up against the overturned settle; and there she sat, her eyes glazed and her breath coming in painful jerks.

Slowly her wits returned to her, and now she muttered faintly, 'Where . . . where's he?'

Joe pointed upwards, then whispered, 'His back is all scalded. He said you did it.'

'Joe.'

'Aye, Katie.'

'Get . . . get me cloak. It's on the door . . . in the scullery.' She lifted one trembling red hand and pointed.

When Joe returned with her cloak she was on her hands and knees pulling herself upwards. Her clothes were hanging in blood-soaked ribbons from her back, and when she stood on her feet the room swam about her and she had to clutch at Joe to steady herself. Her vision clearing, she now whispered urgently, 'Can . . . can you carry her?'

He nodded; and quickly gathering the child up and supporting it on one arm only, he put the other around her waist and led her through the open door.

The main bedroom window faced east and their road from the house lay westwards. As they stumbled on they heard no voice behind them, but before they approached the village Katie could go no farther and she dropped down by the side of the road, and it was only Joe saying 'Come on, Katie, try and carry on a bit farther; he could catch us up yet' that got her to her feet again.

When they came in sight of the village there were the men playing quoits, and one turned and looked at the young boy carrying a baby and leading the stumbling girl, and when he made an exclamation in a loud voice the men, almost as one, hurried towards them.

It was Jimmie Morgan, the husband of the midwife, who reached them first, and softly he said, 'Why lass, what's happened thee?' Yet he had no need to ask. Her face and hair were blood-spattered, her neck was bare and a gash along her shoulder-blade was oozing blood still. Through her open cloak they could see her torn, blood-stained clothes.

'Come, lass,' said Jimmie Morgan, 'the wife'll attend thee,' and with the help of another man he carried her the rest of the distance.

It was Jimmy Morgan himself who went into Jarrow and brought Rodney. Catherine couldn't leave William who was dying, and there was Lizzie to see to. It was the message that William wanted to see Katie before he went that had brought Joe to the house.

It was close on nine o'clock when Rodney entered the room. When, in the light of the tallow candle, Katie saw the tall, commanding figure of her da she wanted to throw out her arms to him, but she could move neither hand nor foot. Rodney, kneeling down by the bed and touching her cheek gently, said pityingly, 'Lass,' and she whimpered, 'Oh, Da.' He did not ask her any questions; he just continued to stare at her, his eyes moving over her face. It was nearly eight months since he had seen her, and she had changed almost beyond recognition. Her eyes were still the same shape, still the same colour, but they were no longer his Katie's eyes. Her mouth was still the same shape, but it was a trembling, pathetic mouth he was looking at; and the cheeks that had been round were now hollow.

He was aroused from his scrutiny by Mrs Morgan saying, 'Take a look.' With this, she pulled down the single blanket, and Rodney, leaning over, saw the distorted mess of open wounds, weals, and discoloured, darkening flesh.

Mrs Morgan's voice now came to him as if from the far end of a pit drive, saying, 'I've done the best I can, but she should see a doctor.'

'Aye.' He got to his feet, his eyes still held by the sight of his daughter's back, and he said, 'I'll get her there. In a little while I'll get her there.' Then, turning abruptly, he left the room. And his departure brought Katie to life, and against the pain that racked her she forced out her arms towards him, crying, 'Da! Da, don't. Take me home, Da . . . Da!'

Through the open door she heard Mr Morgan say, 'I'll come along of you,' and her da replying, 'No, no. I'll do this on me own. Thanks, Jimmie, but I'll do this on me own.' His voice dropped on the last words and they seemed like weights pressing her back on to the bed.

Mrs Morgan pushed the damp hair from her face, saying soothingly, 'There lass, don't fret yourself; it's got to be done. He wouldn't be your da if he let this pass, an' if he didn't do it there's others who would. The place is up in arms. They've been waitin' for something like this for a long time.'

Although it was impossible for her to think clearly, there was in the back of her mind a deep sense of futility for all she had done over the past months to avoid this moment when her da and Bunting should meet. It wouldn't, she felt now, have been half as bad as if he had met . . . the other one, because he wasn't hated like Bunting was.

It was an hour later when Rodney returned. Katie heard his voice in the other room and she pulled herself up on her elbow and waited for the door to open. When he came in her eyes searched him for evidence of what he had done, but his clothes looked tidy. It wasn't until her eyes dropped to his hands, with the knuckles broken and running blood, that she whimpered, 'Oh, Da! Da!'

'There now.' He did not touch her but dropped on to his hunkers before her and repeated, 'There now. Everything's all right. Don't worry any more. You're going home.'

Mr Morgan's voice came from the doorway, saying, 'We'll rig up a sling and the lads will give a hand.'

Rodney turned and looked at Jimmie Morgan, then moved his hand in acceptance, and looking at Katie again, he said, 'Don't worry any more. I'm telling you, you'll never go back. Don't worry any more.'

Half an hour later they lifted Katie into the canvas sling, a replica of those they used to get injured men from the pit bottom, and, Rodney and Mr Morgan at the front and Mr Morgan's two sons at the back, they carried her into Jarrow. And they broke their journey to take her to a doctor in the town, because doctors didn't come out in the night for people who lived in places like No. 3, The Row, and when he had seen to her and asked a number of questions they took her home.

It was about five o'clock the following day that the police came to the house. There were three of them, two dressed in uniform and a man in a black cloth coat and hard hat. Catherine opened the door to them, and her heart almost stopped at the sight of the uniformed men. 'Is your husband in?' the man in the ordinary clothes asked.

'No, he's at work.'

The police knew that Rodney was at work, but they had no intention of arresting him among a crowd of workmen. They didn't look for trouble – not the kind of trouble the Jarrow shipyard men could stir up; they experienced enough of that during the strikes. 'We'll come in and wait,' the man said, and the three of them walked into the room.

Katie raised herself on the pallet which was lying near the fireplace. She pressed her joined hands into her breast and stared at the men, her mouth wide open. And she looked from them to her mother as Catherine, her voice trembling, said, 'What do you want him for?'

There was a long pause before the man in the ordinary clothes said, 'He's wanted for the murder of the keeker at the Rosier pit, a man called Bunting. He was found in the ditch this morning with his head split open. He'd also been beaten up and scalded. Nice sight,' he said bitterly.

'What! What!' Catherine held her face between her two hands. 'My . . . my husband never did that, not him. He hit him, yes; he hit him because . . . look.' She flung her arm wide in the direction of Katie. 'If you saw what he did to my lass – she's his wife – any father would do the same. But kill him? No! No!'

'Well, he'll have the chance to prove that he didn't do it. But nevertheless the man is dead.'

'But who said my man did it? There are others who want rid of him, and my man would never use an implement to anybody. His hands, aye, but nothing else. There's the whole village lives near to him; it could have been any one of them.'

'But as things stand the evidence points to your man, missis. You see, the doctor who attended to your girl last night took her name down as Mrs Bunting, and it so happened that he's the colliery doctor an' all, and it didn't take much to put two and two together when he saw the body this mornin'.'

At this point Katie gave a moan and lost consciousness and she didn't regain it until she heard her father's voice raised high, crying, 'I didn't kill the man. I wanted to but I didn't. Look, I hit him with me fists – look at me knuckles; but I used no bar on him, an' I left him glaring at me. He was alive, more alive when I left him than he left my lass. I didn't kill him, I tell you.'

And then he went out with the men and there was no sound in the kitchen until Catherine let out a shuddering cry, and, flinging herself on the floor, beat the bricks with her fists.

CHAPTER TEN

IT WAS A week later and Rodney was awaiting trial in Durham Prison. Bunting had been buried. A clerk from the mine had come and asked Katie if she had any wishes concerning the funeral, and when she had turned her head to one side he had apologised and said he had been sent; it was a matter of form. Then another man had come, a Mr Brown, and asked her if she had any money to pay the funeral expenses, and she had rounded on him and cried, 'No, no. Where would I get money?' He had then said that it was known that her husband hadn't been without money; he had been a careful man. Did she know where he kept his money? Again she had said no, except that he carried it around with him. 'You can get into trouble for withholding it,' he had said darkly, 'for although you are his widow I doubt whether you would be entitled to it under the circumstances.

It was following this man's visit that Katie's mind was forced to move along practical lines. As she said to herself, somebody would have to do something, and soon, because her mother was so overwrought at what had come upon her that she seemed incapable of thinking for herself, let alone for the family. There she had sat, as she was doing now, day after day and far into the night, staring at the wall, rousing herself only when a strange voice was heard at the door. Her mother couldn't cope any more.

Joe was earning six shillings a week, but that only paid the rent and bought firing; there was nothing left to live on. She herself was in no fit state as yet to look for work, and even if she had been her mother was quite incapable at the moment of seeing to her granda, who was still lingering on, and the child, and Lizzie.

Besides all this, her mind was numbed with agony concerning her father, and to the pain was added the weight of her conscience, for was not his plight due entirely to her? If she had never married Bunting he wouldn't be in jail at this moment. She was to blame for it all. But no, no, not all. The child was not her blame; she would never take that blame on herself. She looked towards it now lying on a blanket in a low wooden tub, and a separate part of her, untouched by the misery of the moment, seemed to leap towards it and enfold it. She had never imagined she would feel like this about the child. She had hated it all the time she was carrying it, but now her love for it seemed to swell her body every time she looked at it.

But Sarah was now whimpering; she was hungry because Katie was hungry, she wasn't making enough milk to feed it. There was no food in the house for any of them, and Joe would be coming in at six, and Joe must eat. If he was to work he must eat. And then there was her granda. As she now washed the old man's face with a flannel and made him tidy and answered the thanks in his eyes by gently patting his cheek because his speech had gone, she thought that soon there'd be another funeral, but this one would be a workhouse one. Her poor granda; he had always dreaded the workhouse. But he wouldn't know anything about it; he'd be dead before they took him there.

As she went into the kitchen with the dish of water there came back to her the man's query, 'Have you any money for the funeral?' and immediately following it three words flashed through her mind. They seemed to come out of nowhere; they had no real connection with anything she had been thinking. The words were . . . a hundred pounds, and what brought a tremor to her body was that it didn't seem to be herself who was saying them, but . . . him. A hundred pounds. A hundred pounds. The sum went over and over again in her mind and she was hearing it said in Bunting's voice. Vaguely, very vaguely, she remembered hearing him say this. But the more she groped in her mind to bring the memory to the fore the more vague it became. If he had said anything about a hundred pounds to her she would have remembered, as she did everything he had done to her up to the night of the beating. Things that she considered worse than the beating she remembered.

It was as she threw the water on to the spare ground outside that a door opened in her mind and she heard his voice coming through it, clearer now, and accompanied by the swishing of the buckled belt, 'A hundred pounds,' it was saying. But now there were two more words added. 'For you,' the voice said. 'A hundred pounds for you!'

And so it went on all that day, the words kept coming and going in her mind, and that night as she lay awake thinking of her da shut away in prison, perhaps never to come out again, they broke through again, loud now, yelling, 'A hundred pounds for you! A hundred pounds for you!'

At one point she thought she was going mad, or funny like Lizzie, because she couldn't stop the words from repeating and repeating themselves. And then as she lay wide-eyed and hungry she began to think about what the man had said about it being known that Bunting had money, and Mrs Morgan too had said he should have money. Everybody in the village knew he had money hoarded away, she said, and all out of his cheating the men . . . Well, if he had, where had he hoarded it? She had cleaned every inch of the house and she had never come across anything that looked like a hidey-hole. Yet if he had money he must have hidden it somewhere . . .

It wasn't until the next day when she climbed the six-foot ladder that gave entry to the roof space where Joe had his bed that light dawned on her.

Every Saturday afternoon Bunting had sent her to Batley's farm two miles away for half a dozen eggs and some vegetables. Immediately dinner was over he would hand her the money and tell her to get going; whether it was rain, hail or shine he would order her out. Even when she had to carry the baby all that way – she would never have left it with him. Why did he want her out of the way like that every week if not to have a space of time in which to hide his money? And what better place to hide it than in the roof? She had never thought of going up there because the hatch was eight feet above the landing . . .

The following day was Sunday, and early in the morning she said to Joe, 'I'm goin' out for an hour or so. Will you see to them?'

'Where you goin'?' Joe whispered, and she whispered back, 'I'm goin' to the house to get some of me things.'

'But you won't be able to get in; it'll be locked up.'

'There's a way. I know how to open the scullery window.'

'Won't you get wrong if you're caught?'

'I can't see how. Me things are there; I'm goin' for them.'

When she was about to leave the house he came to the front with her, and, his voice very low, he said, 'Why don't you have a look round and see if there's anything about. You know what I mean?'

She nodded at him and they looked at each other in full understanding. And then he said, 'But you're not fit, you're not up to that trek; you shouldn't try.' To which she answered, 'The air'll do me good.'

But even before she left Jarrow she didn't see how she was going to complete the journey. For the past week she had just moved slowly around the room, but now she was finding the movement of her muscles, particularly her back muscles, excruciating. Moreover, as she put it to herself, she felt bad right through.

The morning was bright and warm; the larks were soaring like winged notes from their ground cover into the heavens. She had always loved the larks and was horrified at their destruction. But this morning she did not even look upwards, for out here in the open the enormity of the trouble that had come upon them seemed enlarged. It seemed to spread away from her on all sides, filling space, filling her life right down to the end; she could see no easing from the feeling that was in her now.

When she saw the village away to her left she was surprised that she had got this far. She kept well clear of the village, for she didn't want to meet any of them in case she would say, 'Why don't you get them to own up – the ones who did it, Mr Morgan's sons and the rest?' But the Morgans had been kind to her and she had no proof, only another jumbled memory of men talking in the Morgans' kitchen, and later, after her da had gone to Bunting, of men and women, silent men and women, coming and looking at her back.

As she approached the house a fear settled on her, a fear of entering it, of him still being there. It was no use telling herself he was dead and buried.

She entered the back garden by sitting on the low stone wall and lifting her legs over, one after the other. Then she was standing outside the wash-house door. She stood quietly listening for a moment. Who knew but someone might be about; a house that had had a murder always attracted sightseers. She went into the wash-house and looked for the key. Perhaps it had been put back in its hiding place; but no, it wasn't there.

She sat down for a moment on an upturned tub; then, realising that it was the tub in which he had bathed, she sprang up and, pulling her skirts about her, leaned against the half-open door, looking at it. If contact with the tub frightened her, how would the inside of the house affect her? Before her thinking would drive her down the road again she went round to the scullery widow, and, lifting her skirt and taking from the pocket in her petticoat an old knife, she inserted the blade between the window and the latch.

The process of climbing through the little window racked her body, and as there was no support on the other side she had to fall to the floor on her hands and pull her legs after her. When she was through she lay panting for a moment, looking round at the familiar scene. Then, rising slowly, she closed the window and made towards the kitchen door. It took a great effort of will to open the door, and having done so her body jerked and her eyes closed simultaneously before she looked into the room. It was no longer familiar. The settle was pushed against the wall and in front of it stood three broken chairs. On the delf rack, piled together as if someone had swept them up, was the crockery; all smashed, and the mantelpiece was stripped of its pewter mugs and brass candlesticks. But they were nowhere to be seen; someone had likely taken them. As she looked at the devastation she whimpered, 'Oh, Da! Da!' Slowly she crossed the room to the stairs. But at the foot of them she remained standing; she couldn't go up there, she couldn't. The sweat was pouring down her face now, and she glanced behind her. She could feel him; he was still here. Only the thought of No. 3, The Row full of hungry bellies impelled her forward.

When she stood on the landing she had to open the bedroom door to be able to see the hatch, and immediately she knew she could never reach it from a chair. The only thing to do was to bring the chest of drawers out of the little room and climb upon them.

After taking out the three drawers from the chest she pulled it through the doorway; then with trembling limbs she mounted it and, putting both hands up, she pressed against the hatchway and, to her surprise, it moved easily. With her head through the aperture she looked around her. The roof space was lit by a tiny window, but little light came through because of the grime on it.

It took something of an effort to pull herself up and on to the floor, and when she was standing upright she gazed about her. The floor was boarded and there was nothing on it except a wicker basket and a wooden box lying close to the sloping roof.

When she pulled up the close-fitting lid of the basket she saw it held clothes, women's clothes – his mother's clothes likely. They were all tumbled together as if someone had already been sorting them. She forced herself to pull the garments out one after the other. They smelt musty and dirty, but there was no money lying among them. In the long wooden box there was a gun and two boxes of small shot, but no money.

Where? Where? If he'd hidden it anywhere it would be up here; it must be up here. The chimney breast ran up through the floor, then through the roof. She examined every brick but couldn't feel a loose one. That left only the floor. On her hands and knees now she tried each board to see if it was loose. But no; they were all firmly held by nails. Wearily she sat down on the long black box, her back bent because of the roof. She had looked everywhere, searched every corner; there was nothing more she could do. If he'd had money he had hidden it well, and it would lie hidden until in the far future the house would be pulled down, and then somebody would find it; somebody who didn't need it like she did the day.

When she got wearily to her feet she stood shaking her head, her eyes cast down, and like this there came over her a strange feeling, an excited feeling, a sort of nice feeling that had no connection with the horror she had experienced during the past weeks. She felt for a moment as if she was back, up there, in the house, going happily about her work, eating well, sleeping well, with the knowledge of the forthcoming pleasure of going home on her day off always looming before her. The feeling made her grab the iron handle of the box and drag it aside. Before she came to laugh at the existence of a God, she thought that He must have instructed one of His angels to reveal Bunting's secret by way of repayment for what she had endured; but she never really could work out what made her suddenly heave the box aside.

Now she was looking at a floorboard with a gap in it, just a little gap that wouldn't have been noticed unless someone was looking for it. Inserting her little fingernail she lifted up the loose board, and there below her, on a piece of wood supported between the beams, lay four bags and a little black, leather-bound book.

Like someone mesmerised, she picked up one of the bags and, undoing the loop of string that tied its neck, she looked down on to the gleaming gold coins, sovereigns. The same in the next bag, and the other two: all full of sovereigns. And the little black book. She opened it, but the writing was so small and the light so bad that she couldn't read it.

She stood up, her hands holding each side of her face. All that money, all that gold. She was overcome by a panic feeling. What if someone came? It would be no use saying she was just after her clothes if they saw the chest on the landing. Like lightning now she swooped up one bag after the other and, putting two in each side of her petticoat to balance her, together with the little book, she replaced the board, left the box as she had found it, then went to the hole and let herself down to the top of the chest, pulled the hatch into place, and dropped to the floor. Five minutes later, the chest back in the bedroom, she went stealthily down the stairs.

Now, as if the devil was after her, and he could have been from the feeling that filled the house, she let herself out of the back door – there was no time to make the difficult journey through the narrow window. Running now, she got over the low wall, and not until she was well away from the house did she slow to a walk. And it was just as well, for, in the distance, around a rise in the fells she saw coming towards her, from the direction of the road, three girls. They were Haggie's rope-work girls, from Wallsend. Haggie's Angels they were called. You could always tell them by their clogs and thick serge skirts and woollen shawls. Their fearlessness of man or beast was personified by their coarse prattle. They were laughing and larking on as they walked, one of them pushing at another while she gripped her own waist to ease the ache of her mirth. Catching sight of Katie, they came in a straight line towards her, their faces still broad with their laughter, and when they were abreast one of them said, 'Can we get to the hoose where the morder was done this way?'

Katie stared at them. Her instinct was to fly from them, but that would make them think she was wrong in the head, perhaps even suspicious of her, and they might talk. One thing led to another; it always started that way. She made herself say as calmly as possible, 'It's about five minutes' walk. That's the straight way.' She pointed back towards the road they had left, and, their faces still laughing, they said one after the other, 'Ta.' She could still hear them laughing when she was a good distance from them, and as she hurried on she thought, The dog'll go for them . . . Roy. She stopped. She hadn't thought of Roy. Poor Roy. One thing was sure: he hadn't been there else he would have raised the place. Somebody must have taken him. It came to her that she must have been in a bad way altogether these past days not to have thought of the poor beast.

When she entered the town again she forced herself not to scurry. With every step she took she was conscious of the bags knocking against her legs. It being Sunday, the town was quiet. The good God-fearing people were returning from church, the men in their broad cloth and tight-fitting trousers and shining boots, the women in their best dresses of grey, dark blue or black. You could almost tell which church they had been to from their dress. The women going to the Church of England nearly always were bonneted; the women who went to the Catholic church nearly always wore shawls. But then what could you expect, for the Catholics were mostly drunken Irish. In her own chapel just some of the women managed a bonnet, and then it was nothing as elaborate as those worn by the Church of England women. Her mother had pointed all this out to her, yet she had told her that farther away up in Newcastle, and farther still in the Midlands, the Methodists had fine chapels and the women nearly all wore bonnets.

But there were those in this town who didn't go near a church or a chapel. The men were now filling the public houses, and the women were making the Sunday dinner, and between times standing on their front steps talking to their neighbours while their children scampered in the muck and running filth of the road.

It was among most of this latter type that she had to pass before she came to The Row, and there was many an eye turned on her and many a whisper that came to her ears, such as 'You don't get a hammerin' for nowt, not if he doesn't booze, you don't. He must've twigged summat.' When she pushed open the door and entered the dim room she was on the point of collapse.

Catherine was sitting at the table. There was no sign of a dinner of any sort in preparation. Lizzie was sitting on the pallet that was Katie's bed, and Joe was walking the narrow distance between the walls shaking the child up and down to try to stop its crying.

They all looked towards her. Then Catherine, for the first time in days, showed interest in what was going on around her. She got to her feet and asked dully, 'Where've you been, lass? Why did you leave us?'

Katie didn't answer, but, going to Joe, she took the child from him and, sitting down, bared her breast to it. Then after drawing in a number of quick deep breaths she looked up at Joe, whose eyes were waiting full of enquiry, and she said softly, 'Put the bolt in the door, will you, Joe, and pull the curtain.'

She hitched the cracket on which she was sitting nearer the table, and, supporting the child with one arm, she pulled the four bags and the book from her petticoat and laid them in front of her. Then she said to Joe, 'Open them.'

Joe spilled a bag on to the table, then stood gaping at the sovereigns. And Catherine stood staring at them. Then, looking at her daughter, she whispered, 'In the name of God, lass, what have you done now?'

It was the word 'now' that pierced Katie, telling her that deep in her heart her mother held her responsible for all that had happened. She swallowed in her throat, then said, 'He had money hidden up in the roof. I went and got it.'

'You shouldn't have done that, lass. It's bad money, evil money. Any money he had would be evil money.'

'But, Ma, listen. Listen.' It was Joe now tugging at her arm, bringing her round to face him. 'We need it, an' Katie's got a right to it. Who better after what she's been through? Don't be daft, Ma.'

'No matter what way you look at it, it's bad money.'

'It'll help me da, Ma.' Katie was looking up at Catherine. 'We . . . we can buy a man to speak for him like they do for the miners.'

'Aye. Aye.' Joe was excited. 'That's it, Katie.' He put his two hands on the table and leant towards her. 'The miners have got one – solicitor he's called. Aye, yes! How much is there?'

'I don't know,' she said. 'Count it.'

Joe counted the coins from the four bags, and when he was finished he looked at Katie and said, in awe-filled tones, 'Two hundred and twenty-seven pounds.' And again, 'Two hundred and twenty-seven pounds.' Then, gazing at his mother, he added, 'We'll never be hungry again, Ma.'

'Be quiet!' said Catherine harshly. 'Can you only think of your stomach.'

Joe bowed his head and murmured, 'I know, Ma, I know.'

Catherine, now looking down at Katie, said, 'Where are you going to keep it? And when you start spendin' people will twig, an' you'll be had up.'

That was a point. Katie stroked the soft hair from her daughter's brow. Sovereigns were few and far between among the poor. If she went round here breaking into sovereigns and no man in the house to bring even half a one in, of course people would twig. She would have to go farther afield to do her spending, and be careful at that. As to where she would hide the money, she had already thought of that on her way home. 'I've figured that out,' she said now. 'I'm going to sew them all on to me shift.'

'Sew them on to your shift? Carry them round with you?' said Catherine. 'But the weight, lass.'

'It'll be spread over. I'll make a sort of little pocket for each one and just take them out as we need them. I can wear me other shift near me skin for washin'.'

'Aye. Yes.' Catherine was nodding now, and it brought a little lightness to Katie's mind to see that her mother had come out of her trance-like state.

All afternoon they sat, the three of them, Joe cutting out inch squares from pieces of old calico, and Katie and Catherine sewing three sides of them to the garment, slipping in a coin, then securing it with a stitch or two.

They had come to the last twenty sovereigns when Joe said, 'If you're going to see a solicitor hadn't you better keep some money out, Katie – say ten pounds or so. They cost a lot.'

Just as she was about to answer Catherine said, 'Where will you say you got the money from . . . golden sovereigns?'

The question stumped Katie. Then after a moment she said, 'I – I could say I got it from a friend.'

'Lass, folks like us don't have friends who throw golden sovereigns around.'

'Well' – Katie shook her head impatiently now – 'I'll think of something, Ma, when the time comes.'

'What'll I do with the bags and the book?' asked Joe, holding them out in his hands.

'Burn them,' said Katie. 'But wait a minute . . . Here, let me see the book.'

She now opened the book, and going and standing near the window she drew the curtain just the slightest and looked at the column of figures which filled the first page. The entries always followed the same pattern, and the dates went back for years. They started on a January day in 1850, and opposite this date was the sum of three pounds. The second entry was in June 1850, and the amount stated was four pounds. As she turned the pages she saw that as the years came more up-to-date the entries followed closer together, there being frequently two in the same month. Then an entry made last year brought her attention fixedly on it. The date of this entry was the day following that on which she had gone to him and said she would marry him. The entry was for fifty pounds; and something else was added to this entry, two letters, B.R. The next entry in the book was also for fifty pounds, and it was made on the same day on which she married Mark Bunting, and again this entry was followed by the letters B.R.

'A hundred pounds for you' . . . B.R. He must have given him a hundred pounds to marry her. She lifted her eyes and looked at her mother, and then at Joe. She wanted to say to them, 'But why? Why?' If she hadn't let on up till then, wasn't it pretty plain to him that she was going to keep her mouth shut? So why had he paid Mark Bunting a hundred pounds to marry her?

'What is it?' said Catherine.

'Nothing,' said Katie. Going to the fire and pushing the book into the dull embers, she moved it about until it caught fire, then motioned to Joe to follow suit with the bags.

It was the following day that Katie learned why Bernard Rosier had paid Bunting to marry her. At the same time it was made possible for her to spend a sovereign when she liked, and these two things were brought about through a visitor to the house.

The visitor was Miss Theresa, and she came to the door surrounded by a horde of children. When Katie heard the noise outside she opened the door and a girl said, 'She was lookin' for you, missis.'

There stood Miss Theresa, surrounded by barefooted, ragged, dirty children. An ordinary woman coming to this quarter would have aroused no curiosity, but even children could recognise gentry when on the rare occasions they happened to meet.

'May I come in, Katie?'

Katie turned her head round and looked into the awful room. Her shame was deep. She would like to have said, 'No, Miss Theresa,' but what could she do but pull the door wider and allow the quietly dressed, tall young woman to enter. Then she closed the door and pushed the bolt in in case the children might be curious and open it.

'Ma.' Katie looked towards the seat where her mother sat and said, 'This is Miss Theresa from the House.'

Catherine got slowly to her feet. She did not bob or curtsy, she merely inclined her head. This was a member of the household that had brought disgrace on her girl; she owed them nothing, only hate, and she had been taught not to hate.

Theresa willed herself not to look round the room, at the shocking conditions under which this family was living, but one thing she couldn't do was close her nostrils to the smell that pervaded the whole place. She moved towards Catherine and, looking her straight in the face, she said softly, 'I'm deeply sorry, Mrs Mulholland, for what has come upon you. I . . . I wonder if I could be of any help?'

'I would welcome help from any direction, ma'am,' said Catherine quietly. Following this, an embarrassing silence fell on them, until it was broken by a noise from the corner of the room, a noise which startled Theresa. Lizzie had pumped. She looked in the direction and saw sitting in the dimness a great fat lump of a girl.

'That's . . . that's Lizzie,' said Katie apologetically under her breath. 'She's . . . she's not quite right in the head.'

There was pain in Theresa's eyes as she brought them back to Katie.

'Won't you sit down?' said Katie now, pulling a stool forward, and Theresa, thanking her, sat down. But she was no sooner seated than she was startled again by another noise coming from beyond a door facing her, and as Catherine turned away without excusing herself and went through the door Katie again explained, 'That's me granda; he's . . . he's had a stroke.'

'Oh, Katie.' Theresa began to twist her hands together. 'I feel that all this has come upon you through me. I've suffered agonies of mind since I heard about this happening, because I feel that . . . that I'm to blame; not because of . . . of that.' She pointed to the child lying in the tub. 'That began it all, but if . . . if I had only left it there and let you work out things for yourself, as I'm sure you would have done with the help of your parents, you wouldn't have been in this terrible trouble today. But I did what I thought was the best. Believe me, believe me, Katie.'

Katie looked back into the thin, troubled, pale face and said, 'I don't quite understand what you are on about, Miss Theresa. I don't see how you had anything to do with it.'

'I had, Katie, and you'll hate me for it when I tell you. You see, it was me who forced Bernard's hand. I told him and my parents that if reparation wasn't made to you I would tell his fiancée. It was then, and then only, he thought up the scheme of getting Mr Bunting to marry you. . . . You see?'

Yes. Although bewildered by this information, Katie saw in part; what she didn't see was how Miss Theresa knew it was Mr Bernard, and she said so.

'How did you find out, Miss Theresa, about . . . ?' She moved her hand towards the child, which did away with the necessity of using Bernard Rosier's name.

'I . . . I saw him push you from the room the night of the ball, and witnessed your great distress.'

'Oh!' Katie bowed her head and Theresa went on, 'I was greatly concerned for you.'

'Thank you, Miss Theresa.'

The silence fell on them again, and in it the smell seemed to have become intensified, and Theresa, taking a handkerchief from her beaded bag, dabbed gently at her nose, and then said softly, 'I'm in much the same position as you yourself are, Katie, in that I'm poor.' God forgive her. The same position as this child, for she still looked a child, in spite of her swollen, milk-filled breasts. There were grades of poverty, and she was in the presence of the lowest.

'What do you mean, Miss Theresa?' Katie's face held concern now for her visitor.

'Well, I have left my husband, Katie. You know I should never have married him; it was my parents' doing. I . . . I was to have a baby but I lost it.'

'Oh, Miss Theresa, I'm sorry.'

'Don't be sorry for me, Katie; I didn't want the baby. I'm really very fortunate. I see that now. I . . . I have a small income and it's been accumulating over the years; it's been enough to buy me a little house on the outskirts of Westoe village in Shields. And Miss Ainsley's going to join me at the end of the year. We're to start a little school.'

Miss Theresa a school marm! Brought up in that big house with everything she wanted, and now she was going to be a school marm, and seemed to relish the idea. Life was funny, very funny.

Theresa was now bending towards her, her hands joined on her knees as she said, 'I wonder, Katie, when . . . when your trouble is over, whether you will come and live with us. You . . . you can bring the child.' She wanted to add 'Not as a servant'; she wanted to go further and say, 'I will teach you all I know. There is time yet for you to be not only a beautiful woman but a cultured one.' She had a picture of a life that appeared to her like paradise spent in the company of Ainsley and Katie, but the figure of Katie loomed much larger than Ainsley within the frame.

'Oh, thank you, Miss Theresa, but . . . but I don't know how things are goin', an' I'll have to see because me mother isn't well at all now. She can't manage like she used to. And there's Lizzie.' She motioned her head towards the corner. 'But it's very kind of you, Miss Theresa, very kind of you. I'll . . . I'll think of it.'

Although Katie said she would think about the offer, which if it had been made a year ago she would have considered came straight from God, she now had no intention of accepting it. Already she knew what she was going to do. Whatever happened to her father – and the thought of what might happen to him made her shudder – she had plans for the family, plans that would take them out of this hovel. She went on quickly now, 'It all depends on what happens to me . . . me da. Miss Theresa . . . ' She bent forward. 'Do you know of a solicitor man that would speak for him? I . . . I've got a little money, I could pay him.'

Theresa knew of many solicitors; her husband's solicitors, her father's solicitors, solicitors who were friends of the family, but would they be impartial and speak for such a man as this girl's father who had murdered a keeker at the mine? Anyway, it would need a barrister to defend him. She thought for a moment, then said, 'There's a firm in Shields by the name of Chapel and Hewitt; I remember my father mentioning them. You could try them. I think their business is in King Street.'

'Thanks, Miss Theresa, I will. I'll go down straight away.' As if she had appeared rude she added, 'Well, I mean later.'

'I hired a trap to fetch me here, Katie; would you care to drive back with me? I could take you right to the door.'

'Oh, thanks, Miss Theresa, yes. Yes. Would you wait till I put me other frock on?'

'Certainly, Katie, certainly.'

In the room, as she changed her dress, Katie whispered to her mother, who was sitting on the foot of William's bed, what she was about to do. 'This'll solve it,' she whispered. 'If they see me drivin' up in the trap with her they'll think she's given me the money. If anybody asks where I got it, I can say I got it from a friend, and they'll think it's her.'

Catherine nodded her head. 'Yes. Aye,' she said. 'You'll see to the child, Ma?' asked Katie, anxiously now.

'Yes, don't worry. But . . . but I'm not comin' out there again; tell her anythin', but I'm not comin' out there again.'

'It's all right, Ma.' Katie put her hand on her mother's head and stroked her hair for a moment; then bending over William she patted his cheek and smiled into his dim eyes. 'Everything's going to be all right, Granda,' she said. 'Everything's going to be all right; Miss Theresa's come an' she's going to help us. She's takin' me down now to get a solicitor man to speak for me da. Everything's going to be all right, Granda, don't you fret.' And she believed what she said; since she had found the money she had found hope.

CHAPTER ELEVEN

THEY SAT IN the court like reluctant visitors to a strange world, and just as fearful. Katie sat on one side of Catherine and Joe on the other, and each gripped one of her hands.

Rodney was sitting between two policemen. He looked grey, thin and gaunt. His eyes had sunk deep into his head and it seemed to Katie that she hadn't seen him for twenty years, so changed was he; yet he held himself straight. In contrast, his guards looked thick and solid; their bodies seemed to be pressing out of their uniforms. They represented to her the impregnable wall of the law, a wall at which the barrister who had talked, and talked, and talked, seemed to be beating his head in vain. She had felt the inevitableness of the whole proceedings from the beginning, although he had done his utmost – and she felt sure he had done his utmost, but mainly because he thought she was under the patronage of Miss Theresa. Miss Theresa was a Rosier, and the name told. She had let it be known to the solicitor the first time she had seen him that Miss Theresa had recommended him to her, had even brought her along. She knew that this recommendation would make a difference to his fee, that he would sting her because he thought Miss Theresa was paying, but that didn't matter; nothing mattered except that the man up there would convince the judge of her da's innocence. And he had tried – oh yes, he had tried – but he hadn't touched the old man in the wig sitting on the high bench, and now the old man was about to speak to the jury.

Mr Justice Dowry was tired; added to this, his gout was troubling him, and he was hungry. He had no patience with the case in hand and had been further irritated by the defending counsel, talking the way he did. A valuable man had been lost to the industry, and so he began to speak pointedly to the jury. Passing lightly over the facts presented by the defence counsel, he dwelt on that of the prosecution.

'As you have heard,' he continued, nodding three times slowly towards the jury, 'the deceased made an offer of marriage to the daughter of the accused who was with child, and not to him. Let that point be remembered, gentlemen. The daughter of the accused bears this out: the child was not the deceased's, yet this man married her and gave her a home.'

'On the night of the events which you are considering the deceased comes back from his work; tired, no doubt, as all men connected with mines are tired at the end of the day. He takes his bath. What followed, we are given to understand, is that he splashed some water from the bath towards the child, probably in play; but we are told the action was not in play. However, this is a point that can't be proved. His wife evidently thought that the action was malicious and she retaliated with something equally, if not more malicious. Repeating her own words, she tipped the hot water over him. From the condition of the deceased's back when examined by the doctor we have his assurance that the water must have been more than just hot, it must have been boiling . . . What happens when a man gets scalded? He is almost demented with pain. Isn't it understandable that when the deceased was suffering the agony of his bare neck and bare back being scalded he should be beside himself, and the reflex action would be to grab the first thing that came to hand and belabour the person who had scalded him?

'It is not for the moment to be thought that if the deceased had been in his right senses he would have used his belt on his wife to the extent he did. We are not disputing the fact that she was beaten cruelly. Dr Bullard, who examined her, has been emphatic about this. But I would stress the point here that, given the opportunity when once again in his right mind, I have no doubt but that the deceased would have been extremely sorry for his actions, but he wasn't given the opportunity. What followed you have already heard. The deceased's wife made her way to the village with her brother who had called at the house. A man, James Morgan, goes into Jarrow and brings her father. From there we take up the accused's account. He saw the condition his daughter was in and he was filled with rage. He went to the deceased's house and fought with him. He said he fought with him. You must remember that the deceased had been badly scalded and would still be suffering from shock; would he be in any condition to fight? But we have the accused's word that he made a stand. We also have the accused's word that he beat him round the room with his fists, then left him lying on the floor . . . Alive, he said. You know the rest, gentlemen of the jury. The deceased was found not far from his house, lying in a ditch; his head was split open and near him lay an iron poker. Remember there was no poker of any kind to be found on the deceased's hearth when the police searched, so we can but understand he was beaten to death with his own poker. That is the case, gentlemen. It is up to you to bring in a verdict.'

Among the jury were the managers of three mines; they were out for five hours. When they returned, their spokesman gave a verdict of guilty and Rodney bowed his head deep into his chest. Catherine, after one look at him, collapsed, and Joe put his arms about her, crying, 'Ma! Ma!' But Katie looked at her da. Her da was going to die . . . her da was going to die, and it was all her fault. 'Oh no, you can't! You can't!' She had turned and was screaming at the judge. 'He's good; he reads the Bible, he does. You can't! He didn't do it, he didn't! It's wicked, it is. Don't do it! Don't do it!'

Before Mr Justice Dowry passed sentence the man's family had to be removed from the court.

Chapter Twelve

I⟨T WAS ON⟩ a beautiful soft day in early August that the cart came to the little village of Hilton, lying between Bishop Auckland and Barnard Castle. It was a four-wheeled flat cart driven by an old shaggy-haired horse.

The cart was covered by a canvas canopy supported by four poles. It had the appearance of a square covered wagon. The cart passed through the village and stopped on the outskirts; it wasn't always wise to come too near the houses. Some people got nasty and turned their dogs loose; they always thought you wanted something for nothing, but Katie was always quick to hold her hand out with money in it before she asked for anything. They had taken three weeks over the journey from Jarrow. They had travelled by the coast road to Sunderland, then on to Seaham Harbour; from there they had cut inland, bypassing Durham and coming to Bishop Auckland. And now Joe was restless, wondering when Katie was going to stop.

Between blowing on the fire and wafting the sticks with his cap he whispered, 'When are we going to settle, Katie? We're getting farther away from the towns; I'll never find work around here, 'cos it's wilder than any part we've come across yet.'

'There's no hurry for you to find work, you know that,' Katie whispered back. Then, leaning nearer to him, she said, 'Did you notice the stone cottage standin' back from the road about a mile before we came to the village?'

'Where the blacksmith's shop had been? Aye, I did; but it was tumbled down.'

'The main thing is it was empty. We could repair it. It might be let cheap. I've been thinkin' I'll take a walk back in the mornin' and have a look round.'

Joe screwed his face up as he looked at her and asked, 'You'd be content to stay out here in the wilds?'

'Yes, yes. Wouldn't you? Isn't it different from Jarrow and the filth and the smell?'

'There's new houses going up there all the time; we could have got a better one . . . '

'Don't be silly!' Katie's voice sounded harsh, adult. 'What would have happened if I'd rented a new house and us not supposed to have any money, and after the under-manager comin' again and asking how I'd been left, and him saying he was sure there was money somewhere? He said they had searched the house; you know he did.'

'Aye, I know. I'm sorry, but . . . but Katie, I wouldn't like to settle out here.'

'We'll settle where we can, Joe. She wants peace; she'll never find it back there.' Katie rose from her knees and went to the cart, to where her mother was sitting with the child in her lap. 'Come on, Ma; give her to me and get down and stretch your legs.'

Obediently Catherine handed Katie the child, and as obediently she stepped down on to the grass and began to walk slowly about.

Katie, the child in her arms, said to Lizzie, 'Come on, now, and you'll soon have a drink,' and Lizzie sidled off the tail end of the cart, smiled widely at Katie and rolled towards the fire.

Joe unharnessed the horse and staked him by a long rope to allow him to feed – not that the animal would have strayed far, he was too old and tired; also, he was content with his new owners.

Katie sat on the grass feeding the child, while with her free hand she fed the fire with bits of dry twig from a sack which they kept slung under the cart to be used when they couldn't find wood or when it was raining; and like this she waited for the kettle to boil, every now and again glancing round to see that her mother was still with them.

She had thought that once she had got Catherine away from Jarrow and the quay corner she would recover her balance, but as yet there was no sign of it. For days after her da had been hanged her mother would walk through Jarrow without a covering to her head or a coat and would stand at the quay corner in front of the little white cottages at the point where the River Don ran into the Tyne. She would stand looking across the expanse of the Jarrow Slacks, the great mudflat that twice a day was covered by the tide flowing in from the North Sea and swelling the river.

Dotted here and there on the mudflat high black posts were standing. So many enterprising people, like Simon Templer, had had ideas of what could be done with the Jarrow Slacks, and the posts had been the beginning of one idea that never reached fruition. Over a foot square and ranging from eight feet high above the mud line, they looked ominous;

and they were, for on one of them about thirty years earlier a man had been gibbeted. His name was William Jobling; he was a miner and on strike, and when out for a walk with a mate he stopped for a drink at an inn on the South Shields road, and it should transpire that a magistrate named Mr Fairless happened to be passing by on his pony. The two men dared to argue with the magistrate and Jobling's friend hit out at him, giving him a blow from which he later died. Jobling's friend Armstrong disappeared from the scene, but the authorities had Jobling and they hanged him for the murder of the magistrate. The execution took place in public, and later the man's body was covered with pitch and gibbeted on one of the posts in Jarrow Slacks. This event had taken place during Catherine's lifetime. She was a child at the time, but she well remembered seeing the dangling, putrefying body, which the soldiers guarded until the stench became too much for them. The penalty for removing the body was death, but it was eventually removed, supposedly by Jobling's mates. And it was to that place where she had stood as a young girl, looking towards the horror, that Catherine returned daily. It was as if she could see Rodney, who had no burial place, hanging from the black post out there.

At first Katie didn't know where her mother went. It was a woman from the white cottages overlooking the Slacks who came and told her. From then onwards part of Katie's daily routine was to try to keep Catherine away from the scene, and if she should escape her vigilance to go and fetch her back.

The life had gone out of Catherine. She was a being now without a will, except the will to die. Even this mustn't have been strong enough, else she would have taken measures to end her life.

And so Katie had thought up the idea of the cart to get them all away. But there was more than one reason why she wanted to leave Jarrow. There was Miss Theresa. Miss Theresa was wanting to help her, but somehow she didn't want her help. She wanted no help from the Rosiers, no one of them, for it was they who had put her where she was today; put them all where they were, even her da. Moreover, she was embarrassed by Miss Theresa, for she treated her as if she were the same as herself. So she had bought the cart and horse in Gateshead, and one morning at four o'clock she had loaded them all with household goods, even Lizzie, and set off to walk the four miles to the cart and horse. And now it had brought them this far.

The following morning Katie, taking the child with her and leaving Joe with whispered orders to watch her mother, made her way back to the village and there enquired as to who owned the stone cottage with the broken roof farther down the road.

'Oh,' said a little fat woman who was feeding her hens at the bottom of a garden, 'that belongs to the Misses Chapman. Never been lived in for years, gone to rack and ruin.' And on Katie asking her where she could find the Misses Chapman she was told, 'In the Dower House. Not in the big house, that was their cousin's, Mr Arnold Chapman; the ladies preferred the smaller house.' She pointed across the open moorland to where in the distance stood a pair of iron gates. 'Go inside them,' said the little woman, 'and to the right of the lodge. You won't find anyone in the lodge because Alice Worsley sees to the Misses Chapman and her man does the garden and such, but if you go right up to the house they will see you. They are nice ladies, the Misses Chapman; they've done a lot for the village in their time, and their father and grandfather afore them.'

After thanking the woman Katie hitched the child up in her arms and went towards the gates, then through them to the house.

The pleasure the sight of the long, low, white creeper-covered house gave her brought something like a smile to her, but it was only an inward feeling, she showed no expression of it on her face; the face that had smiled and laughed so readily now looked like a piece of alabaster, and, in repose, just as set. As she neared the house, out of the open door came a tall, middle-aged lady with a garden basket on her arm. She paused for a moment and stared across the terrace down at Katie and the child, then called cheerfully, 'Are you looking for Alice?'

'No, ma'am; I'm . . . I'm looking for Miss Chapman.'

'Oh.' The lady came forward to the top of the steps. 'I'm Miss Chapman.'

'Good morning, ma'am.' Katie dipped her knee.

'Good morning.'

'I've . . . I've come to see if you would think of letting me your cottage?'

'Our cottage? But the lodge is taken. I have . . . '

'I mean the one down the road.'

'Oh, that! But it isn't habitable, the roof's rotting and no-one has lived in it for years.'

'I'd be very much obliged, ma'am, if you'd rent it us.'

'Is your husband with you?'

Katie lowered her lids for a moment, then said, 'No, ma'am; he's . . . he's dead. It's my family I have with me, my . . . my mother, who is sick, and my sister and my brother.'

'How . . . how did you get this far? Have you come from the town by trap?'

'No, ma'am; we've come from Tyneside, from Jarrow. We've got a cart.'

Ann Chapman stared at the thin young girl with the beautiful, sad face and remarkable eyes. Then she came slowly down the shallow steps and stood within a yard of Katie, and on closer inspection she remarked to herself, Dear, dear, such an unusual face, and come all this way from the coast on a cart. She said now, 'I don't think you'd be able to live in the cottage, it'll need so much repair.'

'We could do that, ma'am. My brother is very handy; he's very good with wood. He can make stools, and chairs, and things.'

As Miss Chapman stood considering, there came round the side of the house another lady, not so tall as this one but younger and prettier. Miss Chapman turned to her and said, 'Rose, dear, this young woman, who is a widow, is wanting us to let her and her family have Putman's cottage, but I'm saying it isn't habitable. Yet she thinks they could do the repairs themselves.'

Miss Rose Chapman came and stood near her sister, and she looked at Katie for a moment, then at the baby in her arms, but she didn't speak and Miss Ann went on, 'They came from the coast, the Tyne. They've come by cart. It's a long journey, don't you think, Rose, to come by cart?'

'Yes. Yes.' Rose's voice was low and unemotional. She turned her eyes to her sister then back to Katie and said, 'How old is your baby?'

'Just over five months, ma'am.'

'May I look at it?'

'Yes, yes, of course, ma'am.' Katie pulled the shawl back from the child's head and showed its sleeping face to the two women. Miss Rose now moved two steps nearer to Katie, and she stared down at the child for a full minute without speaking; then, looking over her shoulder towards her sister, she said, 'It's a beautiful child, isn't it, Ann?'

'Yes, yes, Rose; it's a beautiful child. You take great care of it.' Miss Ann nodded towards Katie. 'It's so very clean.'

'Thank you, ma'am.'

'What do you call it?' Miss Rose addressed Katie stiffly.

'Sarah, ma'am.'

Now Miss Rose turned round, her back towards Katie, and looking at her sister she said quietly, 'I think they might be able to repair the cottage, Ann. Perhaps Worsley could give them a hand.'

Miss Ann looked hard at Miss Rose, then she inclined her head forward and smiled and said, 'Yes, dear, perhaps that could be arranged.'

Katie closed her eyes, swallowed and said with deep gratitude, 'Thank you, ma'am. Thank you, indeed. An' we'll be able to pay the rent. You needn't fear about the rent, we'll be able to pay it.'

'Oh, the rent.' Miss Ann's head went up. 'We couldn't charge you very much rent for it, not in the state it is in at present . . . You said you had a brother; how old is he?'

'Just turned fifteen, ma'am.'

'Well, then, perhaps we could come to an arrangement. Perhaps he could help Worsley, our gardener and handyman. We had a boy from the village but he has gone into the town. The town is attracting so many of them these days. Yes, I think we could come to some arrangement.'

Katie now bent her knee, first towards Miss Ann, then to Miss Rose, but as she turned to go she hesitated and said, 'Will the key be there, ma'am?'

'Oh, the key.' Miss Ann laughed, a high amused laugh. 'I'm afraid there's no key; you'll find it open. My cousin's coachman used to live there, but my cousin is away so much abroad that he doesn't keep many staff now. I think there are bits of furniture in the house too. I've never been near it for years.'

'Thank you, ma'am. Thank you ever so.' Again Katie bent her knee to each, then hurried away, her heart lighter than it had been for many a long day. They would have a house; Joe would have a job. They might be able to keep a few hens and have a garden, and when her mother got better, which she would do in this peaceful atmosphere, she would be able to look after the child and Lizzie, and then she herself would find work at one of the big houses round about.

The black curtain that shrouded their existence was lifting. She could see their life moving into quiet, peaceful lanes. There would always be a sadness on them, for no life would be long enough to make them forget what had happened, but through time they wouldn't feel it as acutely as they did now.

The very air of this place was like a balm, and those two ladies were like angels. Katie looked down at her child and whispered aloud to it, 'Yes, like angels they are.'

As the days turned into weeks and the weeks into months Katie became filled with a sense of security. There was now some colour in her cheeks, and twice recently she had laughed at the antics of the child as she crawled about the floor.

The cottage was a daily source of wonder to her. She couldn't understand how such beautiful furniture had been left to rot. There were two chests of drawers, a carved settle, a black oak chest, and a corresponding refectory table, two real beds and many other smaller items, among which were two sets of heavy brass candlesticks. All the pieces, Katie realised from their quality, must have come from the big house, for she had glimpsed similar ones in the Rosier place.

Joe had mended the roof carefully, plastering the broken tiles, then fixing them back into place. Together they had whitewashed the stone walls inside and out, scrubbed the mould off the furniture, then polished it with wax. When all was complete they had laid the three bright rugs that Miss Ann had given them in the living room, and it was home – a home that Katie had never imagined possessing.

But as time went on she shut her mind to the fact that of the three thinking people in the household she was the only one that was finding any form of satisfaction in their new surroundings. During the day Joe went up to the house and worked in the garden and did odd jobs, for which he received three shillings a week and the cottage free; added to this he brought vegetables home daily. In his spare time he whittled at things. He made a cradle on rockers for Sarah. He cut and hand-polished pieces of oak and made rough platters with them, and all the while he worked he sat quietly, as if he were brooding.

Then there was her mother. Catherine occasionally helped with the chores, but for most of her time she sat staring ahead, staring straight back into the past. She didn't speak more than half a dozen words a day.

Katie told herself she was better, much better, since they had settled here; but she wished she would talk more, move about more, for then there might be a chance of getting out to work. There were several big houses within walking distance of the cottage, and she was sure she could get daily work if she tried. Miss Ann would recommend her; she knew she would. Her shift was very much lighter than it had been when they first sewed the sovereigns on to it; she had a little over a hundred pounds left. The solicitor's bill had been seventy five guineas, and there had been her granda's funeral to pay. She had seen that he was put away decently, and she had bought the horse and cart. Besides which they had all to be fed for weeks. The way they were living now she reckoned the money would last them just over three years, but what then? What if her mother didn't improve? It would be years before she could leave the child on her own . . . Added to this there was the ever-present burden of Lizzie.

But then, she kept telling herself, three years was a long time, and before then something nice would happen. In this place only nice things could happen. She supposed it was because of Miss Ann and Miss Rose; she still thought of them as angels, Miss Rose particularly. There was hardly a day went by that Miss Rose didn't call in on them; at least not on them, but on the child. She had a great liking for Sarah, and Sarah for her. Sarah always gurgled happily when held in Miss Rose's arms. She had said to Miss Rose only yesterday, 'She's taken a great fancy to you, ma'am.' And Miss Rose had looked at her and smiled that half-shy, half-sad smile of hers as she asked, 'You really think so?' And Katie had answered, 'I do indeed, ma'am.'

Katie found she always wanted to be nice to Miss Rose, because Miss Rose, like herself, had known sorrow, only a different kind of sorrow. She had heard her story from Alice. Miss Rose's affianced husband had been killed in the Crimean War and she had never been the same since. She had been very gay at one time, Miss Rose had, so Alice said, but now, to use Alice's own words, Miss Rose's heart was buried with Mr Francis and she would die an old maid, like Miss Ann. But then Miss Ann had never been bespoken, and, as they said, what you never had you never miss. But it was different for Miss Rose.

On Sarah's first birthday Miss Rose and Miss Ann came to the cottage. They carried between them a large hamper, and Miss Rose carried a long cardboard box in the crook of one arm. In the box was a beautifully dressed doll and in the hamper was a great quantity of baby clothes which, explained Miss Ann, had been packed away in the attic, and only yesterday Miss Rose had remembered them, and did Katie think she'd be able to alter them to fit Sarah?

The tears came into Katie's eyes at the kindness of these two ladies.

There were such good people in the world. There were bad, oh yes, yes; but, on the other hand, there were many more good people. She looked at Miss Rose clasping Sarah, and Sarah clasping the doll, and she sent a prayer of thanksgiving to God for guiding her to the Misses Chapman.

This took place in the morning. When Joe came in at six o'clock he started on his tea; then, pushing his plate away before he had finished, he walked to the door and from there beckoned Katie outside. The evening was soft, the air was filled with the smell of wallflowers and lilac, the birds were singing, and Joe said, 'Katie, I want to go back.'

She looked down at him – for Joe hadn't grown much – into this thin face, into his kindly eyes, and she shook her head at him before saying, 'Oh no, Joe.'

'I can't stand it here, Katie; it's getting on me nerves. I was rude to Mr Worsley the day.'

Again she said, 'Oh no, Joe.' But now she had her hand to her face.

Joe bowed his head. 'I couldn't help it, Katie, 'cos I keep thinkin' all the time of Jarrow and the shipyard. I was happy there. I wouldn't go back to the pits, but I felt I'd found me place like in the shipyard. Those few weeks in the boiler shop were the happiest I've known in me life . . . Look, Katie, I'll go back on me own an' find lodgin's. I'll go to Mr Hetherington. He'll get me lodgin's; I know he will. He was sorry I left; he said everybody didn't take to it like I did, they just work 'cos they had to. He'll set me on if he can.' He now looked up at Katie and added, 'It isn't as if you hadn't anything to get by on – I wouldn't go if you hadn't; but I can't stick it here.' He flung one arm out indicating the open land and the abundant greenery. 'It drives me mad all this, it's so quiet.'

'Aw, Joe.' She bit hard on her lip but she couldn't stop the tears running down her cheeks. 'I thought we were settled. It won't be the same if you go. Me ma . . . well, you know what she's like now, hardly a word. I haven't a soul to say a word to me all day, except when the ladies come along. Oh, Joe, it'll be awful without you, and I won't be able to get a place because of Lizzie and the child.'

'I'm sorry, Katie.' He caught hold of her hand. 'I don't want to leave you, honest I don't, but I'll go daft here, I will.'

There was a movement behind them and they both turned to see Catherine standing in the doorway. She was looking straight at Joe, and speaking directly to him she said, 'Did you say you were goin' back, Joe?'

He made a small movement with his head, 'Aye, Ma.'

'Well, I'm goin' with you; this is no place for me.'

'Ma, Ma, you can't. What'll we go back to? The Row?' Katie's voice was harsh now. She had taken control of the household; she had done her best; she had got them this lovely little house amid peace and quiet; they ate well, and slept soundly; when they awoke in the morning it was to fresh air, not to a filthy stench; and yet her mother wanted to go back, and Joe wanted to go back. Suddenly all words of protest dried up in her and, bowing her head and pushing past her mother, she went indoors and into her little room, and there she threw herself on to her bed and sobbed.

The Misses Chapman appeared in a state of great distress when Katie told them of their coming departure, but she made it plain that she didn't want to leave, but her mother and brother did, so she must go with them. While she was speaking she had watched the colour drain from Miss Rose's face; then she watched Miss Ann go to her sister and put her arms about her and say, 'There, there, Rose. There, there, we'll see to it.' That had been yesterday, and now here were the two sisters sitting in the cottage making a startling proposal to her.

They wanted to adopt Sarah.

Katie stared at them dumbfounded for a moment. Then, stooping instinctively and gathering up the child from the cradle as if to protect it from an onslaught, she shook her head vigorously, saying, 'No! No! Oh no, I couldn't ever. Thank you all the same, but no.'

Miss Ann was speaking now, gently. 'Have you a home to take her to, Katie?'

'No, but we'll soon find one; if not in Jarrow, in Shields. There's plenty of houses in Shields.'

'I know this has come in the form of a shock to you, but I think on reflection you might reconsider. You see, we can offer Sarah great advantages. She would be well educated; she'll never know want of any kind; moreover, she'll be loved. It isn't as if you will be letting her go to someone who didn't really want her. Miss Rose, as you have seen, loves the child, Katie, and you have said yourself that the child is greatly attached to her. We'll . . . we'll go now and leave you time to think it over, and please, please think carefully, Katie.'

The two ladies turned towards the door. Then Miss Rose, coming back, put out her hand and touched Katie's arm, saying softly, 'I know what I'm asking of you, but I . . . I love her so. I've . . . I've seen other babies, but not one that has touched me as she has done, and I promise you I'll spend my life seeing to her needs.'

Katie said nothing. The chill had already settled on her heart, and it grew colder when the door had closed on the visitors and she looked from Joe to her mother. It was a long time before either of them spoke; then Joe said, 'You've got to think what's best for her, Katie; you'll never get a chance like this again. And . . . and when you get back and you want to go to work you'll have to put her out to be minded.' As he finished speaking he glanced quickly at his mother with an apologetic look in his eyes. Katie, too, looked at her mother. She knew what would happen once they got back to Jarrow. There would be journeys to the quay corner; there'd be Lizzie to see to . . . besides the child. There'd be no chance of her going out to work, and when the money was gone from the shift they'd have to depend on Joe. She knew it wasn't fair to Joe, but she couldn't give up her child, she couldn't. If she had been asked when she was carrying it would she give it away she would have said, without hesitation, yes, but not now . . . 'It'll have a fine education and want for nothing; moreover, it will be loved.' That's what Miss Rose had said. Well, it would never have more love than she could give it. But there was no hope in her to give it an education of any sort, or to promise it would never want for food or warmth. She could only promise it it would be brought up in the smoke, dirt and grime of Jarrow or Shields.

Joe said now, very quietly, 'You might get married again, Katie, and have another one. She . . . Miss Rose, I mean . . . there's no chance for her; she's thirty, if she's a day.'

For the first time in her life Katie rounded on her brother, crying, 'Shut up! Shut up! You know nothing about it, an' I won't marry again.' On this she turned from her mother's staring eyes and Joe's bent head and Lizzie's laughing, gaping face and went into the bedroom, and there, sitting on the edge of her bed, she held the child closely to her, rocking it backwards and forwards. Then, stopping the movement abruptly, she looked down into the child's face and Sarah laughed up at her with eyes just like her own.

Almost daily since the child was born she had searched its face for some feature that might identify it as a Rosier. Although it had looked like herself from the first day, she knew that children had a habit of changing; but Sarah resembled herself more closely as time went on, at least the self she once was. This had comforted her, except at times when she thought that perhaps her daughter would grow up to be a Rosier inside, a particular Rosier. Yet the nature of her child, seen so far, showed only a reflection of her own inward character – again as it had once been, laughing, free . . . She couldn't let her go, she couldn't. She was rocking the child once more when the door opened and Catherine came in.

Katie stared at her mother and saw that the dazed look had lifted almost entirely from her face. She kept her eyes on her while she seated herself on the other side of the bed, and when she started to speak she thought, with not a little resentment, she can talk all right when she likes. She's likely been all right inside all the time; she just doesn't want to bother any more, for now Catherine was saying in a quiet, persuasive tone, 'It's the best thing, lass. What chance is she going to have back there? And remember, many of them never see five. Get a bout of fever, typhoid an' such, an' they're gone, if they've not already been took with whooping cough or diphtheria. Don't I know. There's little chance for youngsters back there. But with them' – she gave a lift of her head – 'she'd have every chance.

She'd have all the things I dreamed about givin' you.'

'Would you have let me go, Ma?' There was a deep note of bitterness in Katie's voice, and Catherine looked away for a moment before she replied, 'Aye, I would. It wouldn't have been easy, but I would. Given a chance like you have, I would.'

Although she sounded sincere, Katie couldn't believe her mother, yet it was at this moment, she knew, that the decision was made; the child had already gone from her. She knew that should she take it back to what Jarrow had to offer and anything should happen to it, what she had suffered through Bernard Rosier, Mark Bunting, and the death of her father would be a pinprick compared to the mountain of remorse that would weigh on her for being the cause of depriving her child of a better chance in life, perhaps of life itself, for, as her mother said, many of them died before five.

Suddenly she began to cry, loud uncontrolled crying, unlike any crying she had done before; not even when the hour came for her da to be hanged had she cried like this. It was like an avalanche of sorrow pouring from her body, getting stronger with its flow.

Joe came into the room and took the child from her, and Catherine held her in her arms, but her mother's affection now brought her no comfort, only a strange, growing resentment; for no matter how the Misses Chapman had pleaded, and no matter how Joe had backed them up, it would have made no difference if her mother had, as she had done for months past, kept quiet. But it was as if she was saying to her, you owe me something. I'd have your da here the day but for you. You've caused all this, so do this one thing that is not only good for the bairn but will simplify matters back there, and ease our plight.

And it was in this moment, too, that she realised that her mother had never liked the child. She had never touched it unless she'd had to. It was a child of sin, unintentional, but nevertheless sin.

The thing was settled; she had lost her Sarah.

BOOK TWO

ANDRÉE, 1865

CHAPTER ONE

AT TEN MINUTES to five on a January morning in 1865 Joe closed the door
of No. 14, Crane Street behind him and walked up through Temple Town
in South Shields. The air cut at his throat like a knife; the black darkness
seemed filled with ice and all pressing on him. He could feel it on his skin;
it was as if he wasn't wearing two coats, a shirt and a singlet; and he might
not have hobnailed boots on, for his feet were already stiff with the cold.
But he had the comfort of knowing that before an hour was out he would
be sweating.

As he neared the corner of a street, a few yards from the low wall that
bordered the river, two small hopping figures came out of the darkness
and joined him, saying, 'You, Joe?' and got for a reply, 'Who else, you think
– the devil?'

'Coo! Joe, it's a freezer, ain't it?'

'Aye, Ted, 'snifter all right . . . You awake yet, kidder?'

The twelve-year-old boy, towards whom Joe had turned his head, gave
a shudder and through chattering teeth replied, 'I'm gonna try for the docks
next week; this mornin' march is too much of a bloody good thing.'

'Oh you get used to it, man; you've only been on it a few months. An'
I'm tellin' you, Bob, there's no chance in the docks, else I'd be there
meself . . . But no, I wouldn't.' Joe pushed out his chin. 'It's Palmer's for
me, even with the trek. Not that I like it, mind, but I'd rather do it in the
mornin' than at night, comin' home dead beat. Aw, man, I could fall asleep
on me feet.'

'Me an' all,' said Ted.

'It would be all right if they would pick us up or summat an' take us
there,' said Bob.

Joe put his head back and let out a bellow of a laugh. It was a deep,
manly laugh, and at nineteen Joe was a man. Although he was still small,
below medium height, he was broadly made and his voice was deep and
pleasant. He said now, 'Let's do a sprint,' and began to run up the long

road by the new Tyne Dock wall, past the stables where they heard the horses champing at their bits, and past the dock gates, without much bustle yet. The bustle here wouldn't start for another hour; at about the same time it would start in Palmer's Shipyard three miles away. After a while they stopped for want of breath and Joe asked, 'Is that better?'

'Aye,' said Ted.

'How about you, Bob?'

'I'm warmer,' said Bob, 'but I wish I was there.'

'Now don't keep yarpin' on.' As a man of years, Joe admonished the young boy. 'You'll have somethin' to grumble about if you're out shortly. Then you'll have plenty of time to lie in an' all; but remember, it's better to walk on a full belly than sleep on an empty one.'

'Do you think there'll be a strike, Joe?'

'It's lookin' like it. If Andrew Gourlay doesn't get his way there will be. It's a nine-hour day or nowt. The only thing we've all got to do is to stand together.' He addressed the boys as if they were staple men of industry.

'Me da says when men stop spittin' we'll get a nine-hour day,' said Bob now.

'Your da's wrong then,' said Joe. 'It'll come. It could be here now if they'd all hang together and not have so many bloomin' little craftsmen's unions, all going at each other's throats.' Following this piece of wisdom there was silence between the three of them, until Joe said, 'Come on; let's do another sprint.'

'But we'll only have to stand and wait for the gates to open if we get there too soon.'

With a gentle cuff along the ear, together with a 'Come on, Dismal Dan', Joe urged the boys forward, and again they were running. They passed the Jarrow Slacks and made across the fields, cutting off the quay corner, and so entered Jarrow.

Joe never went round by the quay corner if he could help it; it reminded him too much of his mother and the times he had to go and fetch her home. From the very week they had come back she had started going to the quay corner again and standing staring out at the gibbet pole. Katie had become worn out with trailing after her, and so it had been part of his day's work to take the road to the quay corner when he left the shipyard, and there nearly always, and in all weathers, he would find her, just standing staring.

It was on a black day such as this one tended to be that she had caught pneumonia, and within a fortnight she was gone. At times he was weighed with a sense of guilt concerning her – he had been very fond of his mother – but he couldn't help but admit to himself that life was much easier without her. There was only Lizzie now, she was a problem all right, but Katie saw to her. But here again his conscience worked overtime when he wondered how long Lizzie was likely to last. She was so fat and swollen up she could hardly walk now, and she had taken to crying out aloud and making weird wailing sounds. He didn't envy Katie stuck with her all day.

When they came on to the main road the half-past-five buzzer sounded. It was like a trumpet in their ears, and Joe remarked, 'We've made good time this mornin'.'

A flat cart trundled by them, its presence made visible by a swinging lamp near the driver. On the cart itself sat a number of men, their legs dangling over the side, their bodies making a darker pattern of blackness. When Ted suggested they should hang on the back Joe answered quickly, 'Don't be daft; you'll get the whip or a kick in the teeth.'

'I wish I could take the cart,' said Bob now; 'but I'm not payin' fourpence a day. It's robbery. A third of me wages for a ride there and back to Shields!'

'Well, from where he comes it's a good four miles, and he's got to get back there.'

'He takes night-shift chaps back,' said Bob. 'He's coinin' money.'

'I went in the steamer to Tynemouth on Saturda',' said Ted; 'there and back for fourpence, half-price. Eeh, it were grand.'

'You're barmy,' said Bob. 'Wait till Blaydon time comes, an' you won't have a penny put by for the races, like last year.'

'Aw, give over, man, an' shut your clapper. By that time I'll have a rise. Mr Palmer hissel told me t'other day that he was goin' to double me wages 'cos I'm a good lad. "Ted," he said, pattin' me on the heid, "they don't come like you every day. Without men like you the *Defence* would never have been finished. Nor would the last troopship's keel've been laid. It takes men like you, lad, to build a battleship in three months."'

At this point Ted found himself flying into the roadway from a push of Joe's big hand; then they were all laughing.

A little farther on and they were just three small dots in a mass of moving blackness, men coming from all districts of the town converging on the shipyard. The clatter of their boots was like the sound of an army marching out of step.

Joe and the boys took up their position some yards from the gates in the middle of the dense mass. They stamped their feet and blew on their hands, and the ten minutes they had to wait before the gates were opened seemed longer than the whole journey from Shields.

Then the great iron gates were pulled back and the black human mass surged in and spread itself. Like streams of tar running over a great surface they flowed in all directions: to the boiler shops, the engine shops, the puddling mills, the blast furnaces, the carpenters' shops, the fitting-out shops, the dry dock.

Presently, Joe bade goodbye to the two small boys, who were making for the dry dock; he himself, in the midst of a smaller flow of men, crossed over a railway siding where stood wagons filled with stone which had been brought there by the company's own boats from the Yorkshire mines. This stone held the ore which would eventually be known as Cleveland iron. They passed the great blast furnaces. Here was the heart of the concern; here was where the stone, after being roasted, gave up its ore. It was here that it was fed into the blast furnace, together with coke and limestone, two essential additions, necessary to complete the manufacture of the iron, or pigs, as the iron bars were called. There was a special ore imported from Spain and Africa, again in the company's own boats. This was a sulphur and phosphorus-free ore which did not need to be roasted as did the Cleveland ore.

The knowledge of the making of iron was known to every man in the yard. They were iron men, steel men; they talked of hardly anything else, for only by iron and steel could they eat. Once a man had worked in Palmer's for some years he felt he would be no good for anything else; nor did he want to be. There were men who had started with the yard in its infancy and who spoke of its creator with the respect that men give to a general. As they said, 'the old man' not only conceived the ships, he gave them ribs, bones and guts; then dressed them fully and fine ready for the water. Anything that left Palmer's, they said, could sail to the limits of the globe. But this was the talk of the older men. The younger ones didn't eulogise so. They were more apt to ask questions.

Along their way now, near the rolling mills, there lay great lengths of iron. They lay on bogies and would finally find their way to the boiler shop.

Joe had been working for three years in the boiler shop under Mr Hetherington, and he knew he was fortunate, for he could not have found a better man to serve his time with; for Mr Hetherington not only supervised the making of boilers – hearts for ships, he called them – but he talked, ate, and slept boilers, and was said to be able to tell with his eyes shut whether he was touching Cleveland iron of number one, two, or three quality, or simply number four forge, the stuff that was made into wrought iron. Nor did he have to see the brand of Jarrow or Tyneside stamped on the pigs to distinguish between the grades.

Apart from feeling himself lucky he was working under Mr Hetherington, Joe also felt proud that he held a special place in Mr Hetherington's esteem. He had been to Mr Hetherington's house a number of times, and only yesterday, when Mr and Mrs Hetherington were passing through Shields to get the steamer across the water for a Sunday jaunt with their daughter Mary, they had called in.

Joe now entered the great boiler shop that would, to an outsider, have appeared like a large enclosed space which had experienced an earthquake. It looked a place of utter disorder, a place of contorted iron, jibs, cranes, cylinders, all seeming to be mixed up together. Joe made his way to the far end of the shop, took off his outer coat, pulled off his muffler and stuffed it in his pocket. Then, picking up his black tea can from his bench, he prised off the lid, sniffed at the stale grouts, and wrinkled his nose. Then, reaching out to his coat, he put his hand in the pocket to make sure he had brought his tea – he had forgotten it one day last week. He pulled out the small twisted piece of paper that held a spoonful of tea, jerked his head at it as a man might do who knew himself to be the possessor of something special, then pushed it back into the pocket. As he did so a voice came to him above the din that was already filling the shop, saying, 'Hello there, lad.'

'Oh, hello, Mr Hetherington.' Joe smiled broadly at the prematurely aged man facing him.

'Nippy this mornin'?'

'Aye, it is, Mr Hetherington.'

'Well, let's get started; standin' jabberin' won't get anything off the stocks.'

'No, it won't, Mr Hetherington.' Joe was moving forward to pick up his hammer when Mr Hetherington, coming to his side, said quietly, 'Joe, at break I'd like a word with you.'

Joe narrowed his eyes at Mr Hetherington, and there was a note of apprehension in his voice as he said, 'Aye, Mr Hetherington. Have I done owt wrong?'

'Oh no, lad, no.' Mr Hetherington put his hand on his shoulder. 'It's a private word I want with you, just a private word.'

'Oh aye, Mr Hetherington, all right.' Joe still felt a young lad when talking to Mr Hetherington.

From then until eight o'clock, when the shop stopped for a short while to enable the men to have a drink and a snack, which came under the heading of breakfast, Joe kept on thinking about what private word Mr Hetherington could want to say to him.

He was seated with his can lid full of tea on his knee and a shive of thick bread in his hand when Mr Hetherington came and seated himself by his side, and looking straight at him he said, 'I'm comin' to the point, lad, without goin' round the houses. You see, it's like this. After callin' on you yesterday the missus and I got talkin'; in fact she's never stopped talkin' about it since. It's about your sister.'

'Katie?'

'Aye, it concerns her; but it's about the other one an' all. Have you ever thought of putting her away, Joe?'

Joe looked down into the lidful of tea, and it was a moment before he spoke. 'I've thought about it a lot, Mr Hetherington. But . . . but Katie won't. You see, she promised me ma. Me ma went on terrible at the last about Lizzie, and she made Katie promise . . . '

'Aw.' Mr Hetherington threw his head from one side to the other. 'These deathbed promises make me sick. The people who are crippled for life through deathbed promises . . . Look, lad.' He brought his face close to Joe's. 'Your sister Katie is wastin' her life. She's a bonny lass, I've never seen bonnier. The wife's never stopped, I tell you, since yesterday. She says it's a sin afore God to have that lovely lass cooped up there at the top of that awful house with that lass. It would be no company for an old 'un but a young fine lass like that . . . '

'I know, Mr Hetherington.' Joe still had his head down. 'I've been at her time and time again, but she won't.'

'How long has she been lookin' after her?'

'Oh, since me mother died last year. And afore that. You see, she would get a place – she's had three in Westoe – but then me mother would take to her roaming, you know, and it was then Lizzie would start to howl and the woman below started to complain; mind you, aye, they're very good, the rest – oh aye, they're very good. An' that's why we stay there. I could get a little place farther into the town, away from the waterfront, more respectable like, but the neighbours might kick up, whereas the present ones . . . well, they understand.'

'How many families are livin' in the house?'

'Three aside us.'

'Sup your tea up; time's getting on.' Mr Hetherington watched Joe empty the can lid then fill it again before he said, 'It isn't fair on either of you. Say you wanted to get married, what's going to happen to the pair of them then?'

'Aw, Mr Hetherington,' Joe smiled. 'It'll be a long time afore that happens to me; I'll always look after them.'

'You're talkin' through the fat of your neck, lad. It'll hit you one of these days an' you'll want to marry afore you know where you are. And there's no lass in her right senses . . . I'm not meanin' to be nasty, I'm just using common sense, Joe, but I maintain there's no lass in her right senses who'll take you on if you have to support the two of them. Anyway, you'd never make enough because afore you knew where you were you'd have a family of your own . . . Aw' – he raised his hand palm outwards towards Joe – 'don't contradict me on that; you're a man and you'll want to marry.'

'I don't want to contradict you, Mr Hetherington; only if it came to the push I know the road I'd have to take.'

'Well, as you say, it'll be up to you, lad. An' I hope you don't think I'm interferin'. But the wife kept on talkin' . . . By the way, has Katie got a lad of any sort?'

'No.' Joe shook his head. 'She wouldn't have a lad from round there, not among those sorts, foreigners, sailors, an' the like.'

'But they're not all foreigners and sailors; there's decent fellows about, an' some good fishin' families down there, an' I can't see them closin' their eyes to one that looks like her.'

'Oh, they haven't. She used to be followed time and again, but you know, Mr Hetherington . . . ' Joe cast his eyes towards his boots. 'She's not taken with men of any kind; she had a bellyful for the short time she was married. I told you.'

'Aye, aye, lad, I suppose she had. But nature has a way of covering things up. It's some years gone now an' it isn't natural for a lass like her, a woman – for that's what she is – to be on her own and without friends.'

'Oh, she isn't entirely without friends, Mr Hetherington. Miss Theresa – you know, the daughter of the house where she used to work – she's always popping in. She's got a little school in Westoe. She lends Katie books; Katie's a great reader.'

'Aye, she might be. And it's a great thing in itself to be able to read, but that's not goin' to satisfy her all her life.'

They remained silent for some minutes until Joe, trying to turn the conversation, said, 'What do you think about the movement, Mr Hetherington?'

'What do I think about it?' Mr Hetherington took a bite out of a meat sandwich. 'I think it's comin' to a head, lad.'

'You think there'll be a strike?'

'It's as near as damn it, but none of us wants it.'

'Have they put the petition to the old man?'

'Aye, but things are different now.' Mr Hetherington put his head back and looked up at the tangle of gear attached to the grimy roof. 'They've changed; the whole place has changed since it went over into a company. I've seen the day when you could go to the old man an' talk to him. Aye, even me. Many's the time he's stopped by me side an' said, "What do you think, John? Is it an improvement?" He was always out for improvement, makin' things better and better.'

'Well, he still is, isn't he?'

'Aye, yes, but at a price. He hasn't got the hundred per cent backin' of the men he used to have in the old days. You can't get at him, or any of them up top for that matter; they're workin' from London now instead of inside the works here, although the bloody place is so full of offices and staff now we'll soon have to move the blast furnaces.'

Joe laughed at this but continued to look at Mr Hetherington – he liked to listen to the older man talking – and Mr Hetherington went on, 'See what they've done to the puddlers. Given them a ten per cent cut, and the whole country has accepted it like sheep – that is, all but North Staffordshire. They're standin' firm and they've come out.'

'Do you think more puddlers'll support them, Mr Hetherington?'

'No, lad, I don't. There's too many unions, too many heads of unions, too many bosses, too many under-bosses. It's every man jack for himself, or his own little band, instead of them all joining up together. After all, we're all steel men. But God knows we don't want any strikes; I've seen enough of them in me time.' On this Mr Hetherington rose to his feet, saying, 'Well now, here we go, lad. Let's see those rivets flyin'.'

And all day Joe helped the rivets to fly until the buzzer went at half-past five. He had entered the boiler shop in the dark and he left it in the dark. But that didn't trouble him; he had seen the daylight through the grimed windows of the shop, and at dinner time he had sat on the river bank where the skeleton ribs of a ship were rising from the keel, and with his mates he had talked ships, talked 'Palmer's' with as much pride in the firm as if he was one of the shareholders getting his ten per cent.

Palmer's men might fight, and argue, and talk against the bosses, even against the old man himself, but they were Palmer's men, and, underneath it all, proud of the title.

CHAPTER TWO

IT WAS MARCH and the strike had come about. The steelmasters of the country were determined to break trade unionism, and so on March 11, 1865, seventy thousand men all over the country were locked out. Palmer's men were particularly bitter about this because earlier they had been presented with an ultimatum. There would be no lock-out in the yard, they were told, if they did not support the Staffordshire men by contributions in any form. The leaders of the various unions had reluctantly agreed to this, because the struggle for a livelihood was hard enough as it was now, but in a lock-out there were the wives and bairns to think about. Moreover, scab labour could be imported from other parts of the country, but mostly from Ireland, and when that started hell was let loose. It had been let loose before through the same cause. The Jarrow men became a fierce, battling, frightening horde when treated unjustly. They were aware of this; they knew themselves, and it wasn't only the low drunken types among them who gave scope to their battling tendencies. Quite a good percentage of the workmen were property owners under Charles Mark Palmer's factory building society scheme. When in work, even for as little as twenty shillings a week, they felt responsible men; they and the town were going places. The overall general feeling had been that old man Palmer was not only pushing the ships out of the yards, he was also pushing the town on. Wasn't the building society proof of this? And also the Mechanics Institute he had built for them last year? The town was growing. Subsidiary firms were prospering, streets and streets of houses were springing up like mushrooms. They had actually brought the mains water into the town from Shields, and some of the new houses had their own taps in the yard. Moreover, the sewage was being seen to; the gutters were no longer running with filth. Things were moving in Jarrow; they didn't want a lock-out.

But the lock-out had come; their earthly God, whose name was Charles Mark Palmer, who had promised them that if they played square with him he would play square with them, had joined up with the other steelmasters. Many excuses were given for his action, one being similar to that which had brought the Staffordshire men out: a depression in trade. This only made the men angry, for the yard was full of work, with a troopship for the Admiralty in the stocks.

But anyway they were out, and such was the fibre of the men that within a fortnight, when Mr Palmer would have restarted them again, they became stubborn and refused to go back, and now because of Andrew Gourlay and his demand for a nine-hour day. Only one or two unions could afford to pay the men strike pay, for the rest there was nothing. This meant families living, or existing, on tick, or help from their more fortunate neighbours, who might be in work at one or other of the new factories.

For the first week of the strike things had been normal for Katie and Joe. Katie had Joe's pay to work on and she made it spread out into the middle of the second week, at least with regard to food. But the rent hadn't been paid.

She sat now looking at Joe across the small refectory table that had once graced the little cottage in the country. She drummed her fingers on the edge of the polished wood and watched their movement as she said, 'Well, there's nothing for it. I'll just have to break into it.'

Joe ran his hand through his sandy-coloured hair and, twisting round in his chair, looked out of the window on to the jumble of rooftops and chimneys. The roofs were grey slate, and the chimneys, though made of red brick, were black. Nearly all of them were spouting forth smoke, and this moved upwards to form a cloud under the already lowering sky. The wind had dropped and within a few minutes it would likely rain. He was glad he had got in before he got wet; you always seemed much more hungry when you were wet. He had just finished a meal that Katie had ready for him; it had been tasty enough, for she was a grand cook, but there hadn't been enough of it. Now they were really on their beam ends and she was saying she would have to break into the last sovereign. Times had been hard before, but they had never touched the sovereign; they were both of the opinion that if they kept that one sovereign intact they were all right. But now they had to face up to the fact that whereas they could economise on food and pull their belts well in they could do nothing about the rent man. Owe two weeks around this quarter and you were put on the street. It was anything but a savoury neighbourhood, but the rooms and houses were always snapped up, and for a purpose Joe's mind wouldn't allow him to go into. Although Joe no longer went regularly to chapel, his early training under his father was still with him, and there was only stern condemnation in him for the dirty, low-living bitches who changed their rooms frequently to keep one jump ahead of the police. He had his strong suspicions about the two occupants on the ground floor of this actual house, but they had made no advances to him, and they didn't complain about Lizzie, so he did not question how they made their living. He said now, 'It'll likely be over next week, and then we can put it together again.'

'What if it isn't, Joe?'

'We haven't got to think like that.'

'Look, I could get a daily place the morrow, you know I could, if you'd stay in and look after her.'

He got abruptly to his feet and walked to the fireplace, where some salt-soaked damp wood was smouldering, and he took the poker and turned it over before saying, 'Aw, Katie, don't let's go into it again. I can't, lass. I've told you. I'd go stark starin' mad being stuck up here with her all day.' The poker still in his hand, he turned round and faced her. 'I don't know how you stick it, I don't really. You know, some time ago, in fact the day after they first called here, Mr Hetherington said . . . Well . . . ' He made an impatient movement with the poker. 'He said she should be put away.'

Katie slowly put her elbow on the table and supported her face on her hand before she said in a tired way, 'She's not going into the workhouse, Joe.'

'But as I said' – he was moving towards her now – 'she won't know; she doesn't know where she is.'

Katie's face jerked from her hand and she stared at him, her tone low and harsh now. 'Get it into your head, Joe,' she said, 'she does know; she's not just a lump of puddin'. She might look like it, and act like it, but she's not. I can tell by the look in her eyes when I go near her she's not. After she's been left alone for hours an' I come back her face changes.'

'You just think that.'

'I don't, I don't, I know.' Her voice had risen to a shout; but now she clapped her hand over her mouth and, bowing her head, finished quietly, 'I'm not puttin' her away, Joe.'

'Well, where's it going to end?' Joe's voice was rough now. 'You could give your whole life to her; it could go on and on. It isn't fair.'

'No, no, I know it isn't; it isn't fair to you.'

They were looking at each other, and he said quickly, 'I wasn't talkin' about meself. I haven't got her all day.'

'Well, don't worry about me, Joe, I'm all right. As long as you're all right.' There was a pause, and then she smiled, and it was a replica of the smile that he remembered was hers as a young girl, and he thought, Mr Hetherington's right; she's a beautiful lass . . . a beautiful woman.

'Where did you get to this mornin'? Nothing doing?' she said now as if to change the subject.

'No, not a thing. You know' – he turned from her and walked to the fireplace again – 'you wouldn't believe it, but they treat you like mad dogs. I mean in the docks here. You go in just to ask if there's any chance, and it must be something about you that shows the fellows you're after a job, 'cos they're givin' you the full of their mouths an' tellin' you to bugger off or what they'll do to you. I . . . I felt like hittin' one at the mill dam this mornin', an Irish bloke he was. I did say to him, "If you were back in your tatie fields there'd be more jobs for them that have a right to them." I thought him an' his pals was goin' to brain me, but a ganger came up. Then I went along the pier. Coo, that's a walk! They're still mucking about at the end, an' you know what one chap said to me? I'd better clear off if I didn't want to go down with the ballast. I tell you, when there's a strike on anywhere t'others are like tigers.'

He now went to the window, and from there he said, 'Charlie Roche is talkin' of walkin' to Seaham Harbour. He's got a cousin there who's set up on his own. Blacksmith shop and carpentry next door; the whole family are in it. They make chairs an' things. He said they can always do with a hand or two, an' they'd likely be able to stretch a point when it's only for a short time. He wants me to go along of him. He said he wouldn't go on his own, not walkin' all that way; he wants company. He said one thing is certain, we'd come back with as much grub as we could carry. They've got pigs and things, and there's always umpteen hams hangin' up.' He smiled at her. 'Me mouth's waterin' already.'

'How long would it take you?' she asked.

'Aw well, going at it hard we could do it in a day there and a day back, an' if we could put in a few days' work we'd get a few shillings; enough to pay the week's rent. An' I could bring enough back to feed us. It would help things along, don't you reckin'?'

'Yes.' She nodded.

'You wouldn't be afraid to stay here on your own?'

She closed her eyes and smiled derisively. 'Don't be silly,' she said.

'Do you think I should go?'

'Yes, yes, of course. An' there's a chance you might strike something on your way.' And as she looked at him she added to herself, 'And it will take you away from here, away from her for a time.'

She had never fully understood Joe's antipathy towards Lizzie. Unlike herself, he had no compassion for his sister; she had only to look at the misshapen form and her heart became moved with pity. Yet there were times when she wished her dead. Yet she didn't really want her to die, for when Lizzie went there'd be no-one to mother. Lizzie was her child now, the baby she still cried about at night.

She said to Joe, 'Go and tell him you'll go along with him. And look . . .' She went to the mantelpiece and taking the last of Mark Bunting's hoard from a little box she handed it to Joe, saying, 'Get it changed and take five shillings with you.'

'No! No, I'll do no such thing.' He waved her hand aside.

'Well, look' – her voice was harsh again – 'you're not goin' on the road with nothin' in your pocket; you don't know what happens; you might have to come straight back if there's nothing doin'. An' you'll want a bite to eat. Anyway, if you don't spend it you can bring it back . . . Now you're not going unless you take it.'

'Aye, well.' He nodded briskly at her as if she was forcing him to do something mean and underhand. 'You can take it from me, you'll get it back whole. I'm not going on a trip.'

She was smiling as she said now, 'Make it a trip; you might as well be killed for a sheep as a lamb. An' don't worry about us. Everything at this end'll be all right; I'll see to that.'

He dropped his head shyly before her. Then, going out of the room, he took his hat and coat off a nail on the wall on the tiny landing where there was just room enough to turn round between the two walls, that held two doors, and the little table, on which stood a wooden bucket and a wash bowl. Then he went down the steep dark stairs that led to a similar landing; down another flight that opened into a small dark square hall with doors at either side, and into the greasy street, where, through the steady falling rain, there loomed the river and the masts of ships lying at the buoys.

Upstairs, Katie went into the bedroom where Lizzie was sitting propped up in a low bed, and, pulling the bedclothes aside, she took her two hands and tugged her to her feet, then wrapped the patched quilt around her. Katie herself was now five feet six inches tall with a finely shaped figure, but without the bulbous hips seen on so many women, yet compared with Lizzie's bulk she looked a thin slip of a girl, for Lizzie's glandular disease had made her into a living balloon. Katie guided her waddling form into the kitchen and sat her down on a broad cracket with her back against the wall near the fire – there wasn't a chair big enough to hold her – and she patted her bulging cheek with her fingers and said, 'All right?' And Lizzie looked at her and blinked and moved the muscles of her face into greater contortion.

Katie always kept Lizzie in bed when Joe was about, but she reckoned that once he got talking about the journey to Charlie Roche it would be an hour or so before he was back, and she sensed that the only pleasure her sister could experience was to be in her presence, so whenever she could she brought her into the kitchen.

She now went to the chest of drawers and her eyes moved over a number of books lying there. She had read them all many times over – that was, all except *The Stones of Venice*; she had only read it once. She couldn't get interested in painters and buildings. But Miss Theresa said you had to read such a book again and again before you could appreciate it. She knew she was very lucky to possess this book, where under the name of John Ruskin was that of Rodger Philip Rosier. Miss Theresa had given it to her after Mr Rodger had died, and she treasured it because it had belonged to Mr Rodger, but as a book she couldn't like it. She wondered again why Mr Rodger had to die; why couldn't it have been the other one, why couldn't he have got smallpox? That any gentry should die of smallpox had been a surprise in itself.

She picked up another book; it was *Vanity Fayre*. She liked Mr Thackeray's books, they had a story in them.

Going to the fireplace, she pulled her chair as close to it as possible and, in a position such that the light would fall on the paper, began to read. But she only read for a short time, and then, as she had done often of late, she allowed the book to drop into her lap and she turned and looked about her as if expecting to see something different, something that might surprise her about this room that had become an enclosed world to her. She knew that she should consider herself fortunate that it was decently furnished. THEY – she always thought of the Misses Chapman as THEY – had insisted that she take the entire contents of the cottage with her when she left. THEY had also wanted to pay her for the transaction of signing her daughter to them. She knew they had been amazed when she refused to take their money. But she was glad now she had brought the furniture – all except the beds – for she would never have bought the like of it round here, even if she'd had the money, for they were craftsmen's pieces and she kept them shining. Miss Theresa always remarked on this.

Miss Theresa. Katie now brought her eyes to the window and to the blue velvet curtains that hung there. Miss Theresa had brought them the last time she had called. She had apologised for them being faded at the edge but had pointed out they could be cut down. Miss Theresa was kind. She was always bringing little things, but she wished she wouldn't; more and more she wished she wouldn't. She couldn't forget she was a Rosier, although she'd said openly that she hated her brother. But there was something more, somehow she didn't like her the way she used to do; she didn't really know why, except that she thought Miss Theresa was a bit dominating, always telling her what to do, and how to do it, yet at the same time treating her as if there was no difference between them. It was odd, disturbing.

Joe left the house at eight o'clock the next morning. His face wearing an expression of excitement, he looked as if he were actually going on a holiday. Yet again he asked Katie if she would be all right, and in answer he received a push from her. Then self-consciously he kissed her on the cheek and, turning hastily away, ran down the stairs, the sound of his hobnailed boots reverberating through the house.

Katie stood in the middle of the kitchen for a moment looking about her. She was going to miss Joe. No matter what she said, she was going to miss him. But there, she told herself, she must get on if she wanted to get to the market this morning.

Her 'getting on' took the same pattern it did every day: getting Lizzie up, changing her, washing her, then draping her in a gigantic napkin. This done, she tackled the bed. It was always wet, and she was lucky if this was all she had to cope with. After making the bed up with rough dry pieces of twill she took the dirty pieces in the wooden bucket down the two flights of stairs to the yard and there, in the communal wash-house, she washed them, without soap, in cold water and hung them on the line. She was always thankful for a fine day when she hadn't to try to dry them completely indoors. She next filled the bucket with cold water and humped it back upstairs. This done, she did Joe's room, which was on the other side of the landing. It was only large enough to hold a six-foot pallet bed and a wooden box. Next, she tackled the kitchen, first of all stripping her own bed, which, just being a raised wooden platform, acted as a settee during the day; then once more she polished the furniture, after which she scooped the drips of tallow from one of the brass candlesticks, trimmed the wick of the small piece of candle left in the socket, then carefully gathering up the nodules of tallow she put them in an iron pan together with other tallow scrapings and small ends of candle to be melted down for further use.

The room put to rights, she now got herself ready to go to the market. She took off her coarse apron and rough working skirt and put on a grey serge one. It was of fine quality and edged with a dust fringe at the bottom. This, together with her three-quarter-length coat, had also come from Miss Theresa; the coat was a plum colour and heavily braided, and if anything more was needed to bring out the beauty of her complexion it was this. Her bonnet had been given to her by her last mistress. According to the present fashion it was now out of date; the trimmings were mostly on the brim, the crown being quite plain. When she was ready she took a bass bag from the cupboard and her purse from the top drawer of the smaller chest. She opened it and after looking at the money within she decided against leaving any of it in the house. You never knew; anybody could break in. Meggie Proctor from down below had stopped her last week and told her there had been a robbery only three doors down; they had got over the roof and through the attic window.

She now went to Lizzie, who was sitting on the cracket, and, bending her knees, she brought her face level with her sister's and slowly she said, 'I'm going to the market, Lizzie, for the groceries. You'll be a good girl?'

Lizzie's hand came out and touched her, and from her shapeless mouth came a sound that only Katie could interpret as 'Yes, Katie'.

Although there was no longer any necessity to tie Lizzie up she always did this, just in case the old urge should revive itself and set her on the move; not that she would get far, but once out on the landing she might fall down the stairs. And so taking a piece of rope she put it round her waist, then tied it firm to the table leg.

When she reached the foot of the second flight of stairs she saw the tenants from the bottom rooms standing on the step talking. One was Meggie Proctor, whom Katie always addressed as Miss Proctor, the other was a Mrs Wilson. Katie had never seen Mr Wilson, nor had anyone else. Both women were in their early thirties and looked dirty and unkempt, but they were warm-heartedly pleasant to Katie. 'You're out shoppin'?' said Meggie Proctor.

'Yes, Miss Proctor. Goin' to the market.'

'Aw, lass, I wish you wouldn't call me Miss Proctor.' Meggie's mouth stretched wide and she laughed. 'You're the only one that does; it makes me feel funny . . . She's always called me Miss Proctor since she come here.'

Meggie addressed her neighbour, and Jinny Wilson, laughing too, said, 'Aye, weel, she was brought up proper; you get that way o' talkin' when you're in good service. Me mother was in good service for years.'

'By, she looks grand, doesn't she?' Meggie stood back and surveyed Katie. 'I wish I could go out shoppin' in clothes like them. You're lucky to have a friend like that Mrs Noble.'

'Yes, yes, I am.' Katie squeezed between them. You could keep nothing hidden living in a house like this, living in a district like this; everybody knew everything about you. They all knew, for instance, that she had been married to a keeker, and her father had murdered him and got himself hanged for it, that it had turned her mother's brain, and also that her sister was barmy.

Perhaps it was this knowledge, together with Katie's own reserved manner, that set her apart from her neighbours. Then there was her looks, those big, misty, sad-looking eyes. Meggie had once said to her, 'If I had your peepers they wouldn't look sad on me, an' I'd be livin' in clover.'

She knew the two women were watching her as she went down the street. And not only them; there were others at their doors. There was a high wind blowing and she had to hold on to her bonnet as she turned into Thames Street and cut up by Comical Corner, and she paused for a moment by the steps leading down to the river. There was a sculler boat tied to a ring in the wall and some small children were jumping from the bottom slime-covered step on to one of its two plank seats. She wondered that they didn't slip and drown themselves. But then they were used to the water; they lived as close to it as the rats that infested the houses round about. She went on past the Cut, or the Mill Dam as it was now known, then on down the hill into the market place. The market place was a large open square, grassy in parts, with the town hall, supported on its arched columns, dominating it. It wasn't full market day and there weren't many people about – some women sitting by their high skips of taties, some pedlars with tapes and ribbons and such, and at the far side a number of stalls. It was towards these she made her way.

She knew exactly what she was going to buy: a quarter-stone of potatoes, some pot stuff to make broth, a scrag end of mutton, a quarter-stone of oatmeal, a half-stone of flour and some yeast, some pigs' fat, two ounces of tea, some bacon ends, half a pound of black treacle if it was still tuppence, and a quarter-stone of salt, also at tuppence if they wouldn't split it and let her have a pennorth. She could get everything but the flour and yeast in the market, and these she would collect from Tennants on her way home.

To save her arms she got the lightest things first. The tea was the cheapest brand and the two ounces cost her sixpence, but the stall hawker was yelling its merits. She opened her purse and handed him a shilling, and when he had given her the tea and a sixpence change she placed it in her purse and put it back in the bass bag. She next went to the bacon stall, and, her searching eyes coming to rest on some scraps, she pointed to them and asked for a pound.

'That lot throopence ha'penny, lass,' the man said.

'Thank you.' She nodded and put her hand into the bag for her purse. Then, her two hands tearing the bag open, she let out a yell that made the stallholder jump and those nearby turn and gape at her.

'Me purse! Me purse! It's gone. Oh, my God, it's gone!' She looked wildly around her, her arm outstretched, the bass bag dangling from her hand. 'It's all I've got, every penny,' she appealed to two women and a man who were standing staring at her.

'You should have kept it in your hand.' The stallholder came round to her. 'A daft place to leave a purse, in your bag.'

'It's all I've got.' She stared at him, her eyes stretched wide; her voice was still high but it held a choking sound now. She brought her clenched fist to her mouth, and one of the men said, 'How much was in it, lass?'

'Fifteen shillings. No, fourteen and six. I've just bought the tea.' She held out the small package in her hand.

'Let's see if you've dropped it on the way. Walk back to the tea stall,' said one of them.

Like somebody drunk, and accompanied by the two women and the man, Katie walked back to the tea stall, searching the litter-strewn grass as they went. But there was no sign of the black purse. Back at the bacon stall once more, Katie looked at the man. Her bacon pieces were all wrapped and lying on a board, and he looked at them and said, 'I'm sorry, lass, but you should've been on the lookout for your money; it's happenin' every day. Transport the buggers, that's what I say, not just send them along the line. Transport them when they're copped . . . Here!' He pushed the package of scraps towards her, and she took it and muttered, 'Ta. Thank you.'

The two women and the man moved away muttering; people were going about their business, the little incident was over; there were many such in a day. The stallholder said, 'You go and tell the police, hinny. They might catch him some time later and he might have yours on him. On the other hand, it could be a woman who snipped it. Some of the bitches' fingers work like greased lightnin'.'

Like someone in a deep trance Katie slowly moved away. She knew there was a policeman standing outside the town hall but she didn't go towards him; she was afraid of policemen, the pollis always meant trouble. She was still walking slowly when she reached the house.

Meggie opened her door as she was passing and said, 'I brought your sheets in, Katie; it was startin' to drizzle.' Then, bending forward, she said, 'You taken bad?'

Katie shook her head. 'Me purse was stolen in the market.'

'God Almighty! Much in it?'

'All I had, and the rent.'

'Christ! The buggers want crucifyin'. Why don't they go up Westoe and do their pickin' there? It's like the other night. One of my . . . ' She blinked. 'A friend of mine, he was fleeced, pulled up an alley near the Anchor and every ha'penny cleared off him; an' got a bashin' in the bargain. Oh, if I could only lay me hands on the sods at it . . . But I'm sorry, lass . . . You stranded?'

Katie moved her head slowly downwards, then said, 'I'll have to go out and get some work. You won't mind if she cries?' She jerked her head upwards, and Meggie said, 'Not me. She could scream the hoose doon for all I care, and the same goes for Jinny. But Ma Robson up above she'll open her mouth. But don't you worry, lass.' She pushed Katie gently. 'If she opens it too far I'll stick me foot in it for you.' Katie made no reply to this, but turning blindly away she went up the stairs.

Lizzie's eyes were waiting for her as she opened the door, but on this occasion she took no notice of her. Letting the bass bag fall to the floor, she pulled off her bonnet and, sitting down at the table, dropped her head on to her arms and gave way to a paroxysm of weeping.

Three days later Katie had reached the end of her tether and was in a state of panic. Between them Meggie Proctor and Jinny Wilson had lent her half a crown with which to meet the rent, and yesterday Meggie Proctor had lent her another shilling, out of which she had got a quarter-stone of flour and yeast, and a bucket of coal to bake the bread. But now the fire was dead and they had just eaten the last of the bread – at least Lizzie had. Lizzie's appetite was insatiable, and when she was hungry she cried. She was crying now. All she herself had had to eat over the past three days was a third of the bacon scraps and a small amount of bread and weak tea. She looked at Lizzie looking at her, the tears lying in puddles on her puffed cheeks. Joe was right; she should have let her go to the guardians. At least she would have been fed, and warm. But if she were to go now to the guardians and ask for them both to be taken in, even temporarily, they would come and take the furniture, and then there'd be no home any more, for Joe or any of them.

If only Joe would come. But it wasn't likely he'd be back; a day each way and two or three days there, was what he said, and this was only the fourth day. If only Mrs Robson hadn't complained about Lizzie's crying and threatened to bring the pollis she could have got a job. Lizzie would just have had to put up with being left all day; there were worse things that could happen to her that she didn't know about. She wondered if she knew what was happening to her now, except that she was hungry. Joe was likely right in all he said.

She could have got set on in four different places today, but not part-time. Two of the places were cookhouses, and each wanted her there at six in the morning till six at night. She would have got six shillings a week and her food. Either would have been splendid if only she could have taken it. But she was terrified at coming back home and finding that Mrs Robson had carried out her threat and brought the authorities in. The next step from this would be they'd contact the landlord, and then she and Lizzie would find themselves in the street, with the furniture around them. She had seen so many people in the street sitting helplessly amid their furniture that she had a horror of it happening to them.

There came a tap at the door and when she opened it there stood Meggie Proctor. She was dressed ready for outdoors; she looked different to what she did in the mornings. She had on a bright skirt and blouse, and a blue woollen shawl over her head. She said to Katie, 'I don't know if it'd be up your street, but the *Anchor*'s wantin' help in the evenin'. I was talkin' to a . . . a friend of mine, and he said the barmaid's gone down with the fever and Jimmy Wild is looking for help. He'll set you on in the evenin' 'cos that's when they're busiest. That . . . that's if you fancy it.'

'It doesn't matter what I fancy, Meggie,' said Katie frankly. 'I'll take anything. I'm at me wits' end.'

'I wish I could help you more, lass.'

'You've done all you can and I'm grateful. Believe me, I don't know where I'd have been if it hadn't been for you and Mrs Wilson.'

Now Meggie leaned forward and, peering closely into Katie's face and her voice very low, she said, 'I'm surprised you haven't got a friend.'

'A friend?' Katie narrowed her eyes as she repeated the word.

'Aye.' Meggie pushed her now in the breast with her forefinger. 'With your looks it would be as easy as slippin' off the docks. Lass, I'd never have an empty belly if I had your face.'

Katie felt her stomach puffing itself tight, as if away from physical contact, but she showed no offence and said simply, 'I couldn't, Meggie.'

'Aw well, you know your own know best, lass, but hunger's a long whip. Anyway, you go along to Bullard. He'll likely snap you up, 'cos you'll thicken his custom if anything will. I must be off now. Ta-ra.'

'Ta-ra, Meggie. And thanks.'

Katie stood with her back to the closed door. The *Anchor* was only a few streets away. It was a notorious public house, notorious for many things. One of its activities had gained it the name of the 'whore market'.

If only Joe was here. But he wasn't here, and there wasn't a bite or sup in the house, and no warmth, and she was down to her last half-candle. She came from the door as if released by a spring, pulled Lizzie to her feet, guided her into the room and got her into bed, and again she tied her by the waist, this time attaching the end of the rope to the leg of the bed. Then, going back into the kitchen, she took the iron shelf out of the oven – it still retained some heat – and taking it into the bedroom she pushed it under the clothes beneath Lizzie's feet, hoping that the warmth would send her to sleep and ease her crying. She could hardly see her face in the dim light of the room, but, bending close to her, she said, 'I won't be long, Lizzie. Be a good girl.' For a minute longer she stood and stroked the lank hair back from the bulging brow; then, going into the kitchen, she rapidly donned her outdoor things and went out of the house.

She hated to be out on the streets after dark. Although some streets were lit by the new gas lamps there were alleys and dark corners where things were known to happen.

The noise from the *Anchor* greeted her long before she reached it, and she paused outside the double doors before pushing one open and half stepping inside. And then she could go no further. Through the light of the oil lamps she saw a seething mass of people, mostly men, and mostly sailors. Two faces turned towards her with lifting eyebrows and drooling lips, and when two pair of arms came out to her she sprang back, pulling the door with her, and, dashing to the end of the building, she hid round the corner. Here she stood panting. She couldn't go in there . . . Yet, perhaps her duties might keep her behind the counter. She could ask him. She'd have to ask him.

She moved along the wall to where there was a side door, and from behind this, too, there issued the sound of men's laughter. This was still the bar, likely the best end. She must find a door to the house. But there was no light farther on. She was about to grope her way along the wall beyond the door when it opened and a huge figure stepped into the yard. The next moment a hand was placed on her shoulder and she was swung round, and in the light from the doorway she looked up into an enormous bearded face. The eyes looking out of it were moving over her, the expression in them like that of the two men in the bar. She watched the red lips in the fair beard part, and a deep voice, which she knew immediately was not English, said, 'Ah-haa!'

She stammered, 'Please . . . I . . . I want to see the barman. I'm after a job . . . Please.' She tried to pull herself away from the man, but his hold on her tightened and, bringing his face down to hers, he said in precise clipped English, 'A job is it? Oh, *min skjoun*, I could give you a job. Ah yes.' His head went back and he laughed.

'Look, give over, you. Let me go.'

Still peering at her, he said, 'Stop trembling. You frightened? Why do you come here if you're frightened?'

'Please, I . . . I just want to go. I want to go home.'

'You want to go home?' He was laughing at her again, his face seeming to expand to twice its size. 'All right, *min skjoun*, we will go home. Ah yes, how pleased I'll be to go home with you.'

'No, no!'

'Aha! Yes. Yes.'

At this moment the door was pulled wide open and another man appeared. He, too, was a sailor and spoke in a foreign tongue, and the bearded man answered in the same tongue, and when the second man emerged into the yard Katie found herself pulled from the wall and pushed forward. And now the bearded man called over his shoulder to the other man, who shouted back apparently in reply. Then they were in the street.

'Which way?' He still had his arm about her, gripping her firmly and forcing her to walk, but when they reached the flare lights outside the pie and pea shop he stopped and peered at her again, saying now, 'Why do you tremble all the time? Why go to the *Anchor* if you tremble?'

'I . . . I went for work; they . . . I heard they wanted a barmaid.'

Again his head went back and the street rang with his laughter, of which the passers-by took no notice. A drunken Swede laughing with a woman in the streets at night was nothing new. 'You a barmaid in the *Anchor*! Ah!'

He grabbed her face in his big hand and pressed her jaws in as he said, 'You'd be eaten alive. Do you want to be eaten alive. . . ? No, no.' He answered himself. 'You're frightened of being eaten alive. Why did you want to be barmaid in the *Anchor*? There are other works you could do.'

'My . . . my sister is sick. I've got to look after her; I can't go out durin' the day.'

'No-one else to look after your sister? No parents?'

She shook her head.

'You married?'

Again she shook her head.

'You live by yourself?'

'With . . . with my brother.'

'Why does your brother not work for you then?'

'He's on strike. He's away lookin' for work . . . ' Before she had closed her mouth on her words she knew she had made a mistake, and he lost not a minute in making use of it. With a nod of his head he said, 'So. So he's away. Well, we go home then?'

'No!' Her voice was harsh now. 'No, no, I tell you. No!'

He did not seem to take any heed of her protest but went on, 'What do you want money so badly for you go to the *Anchor*?'

When she didn't answer he brought his face down close to hers and said on a surprised note, 'You *sulten* . . . hungry?'

She closed her eyes for a moment but still didn't speak; and when she opened them she did not look into his face but at the top brass button of his uniform, and some section of her mind registered the fact that he was a captain. This seemed to explain the way he talked, for although a foreigner he used his words like the gentry did.

'My God! That's right, isn't it? You're hungry. Come, come.' He now took her by the hand as if she was a child and pulled her through the doorway of the pie and pea shop, and there, in a voice that seemed to shake the ramshackle place, he cried, 'Pies! Half a dozen. Hot. No, one dozen; I could eat half a dozen myself. And peas, two pints.'

'Where's your can?' said the man.

'Can?'

'Aye, sir, yer can't carry peas in a bit paper.'

'That one there, I'll buy it.'

'It'll cost you fowerpence, sir.'

'Fourpence it is. And fill it to the brim.'

The man behind the counter now wrapped up the pork pies in a piece of newspaper, and when he pushed the parcel across the counter the captain, picking it up, thrust it into Katie's arms.

As she held it against her breast she could feel the heat of the pies through the paper and she had a desire to grab one out and thrust it into her mouth. She also had the desire to take to her heels and fly; and she saw her chance as he was paying the man. Once outside the door she could be away up one of the dark alleys and safe, and the pies with her.

She was backing to the door when he turned round, and like someone chastising a child about to do a mischief he turned his chin to the side, while his eyes remained on her and gave that telling exclamation of 'Ah-haa!' Then, thrusting his hand back towards the counter and the man, he received his change and without looking at it thrust it in his pocket. Then his hand groped towards the can; he picked it up and came towards her, and after looking at her hand for a second said, from deep in his throat, 'We go home now, eh?'

He held her with one hand and carried the can of peas with the other, and like this they went through the warren of dimly lit streets and past the black alleyways until they reached the end of Crane Street, and here, pulling him to a halt and her voice full of pleading, she said, 'Please, please don't come any farther.'

'You don't want me to come to your home?'

'No.'

'You're lying. You want me to come.'

'I don't, I don't, I tell you.' She was hissing at him now. 'I just want you to leave me alone. Don't you understand? Just leave me alone. You can have the pies . . . here.' She thrust them at him. But he ignored her action and said, 'I don't believe you. But, look, we're on the waterfront and near the Middle Gates. There'll be one of your pollis men there. Shout. Go on, shout, and they'll come and order me off . . . Go on.'

She stood breathing deeply and peering at him. She had thought of that herself. She had thought, if I shout the pollis'll come. But as afraid as she was of this great, bearded man, she was more afraid of the pollis. It was when she thought of being afraid of him that she realised she was only afraid of him because of what they would say in the house, her taking a man up there, and what Joe would say if he found out.

She said lamely, 'We . . . we could walk and eat these as we went.' She patted the bundle of pies.

'But I don't want to walk, I want to go to your home. I want to know where you live . . . Besides, it would be very uncomfortable eating pies while we walked.' He gave a small laugh now. 'Come,' he said. 'This is your street?'

When she didn't answer he took her arm again, and like someone under escort she walked up the street with her head bowed.

There were people about, but they took no notice of her or her companion. Again, what was unusual about a sea captain walking this street with a woman?

Before she opened the door softly she paused and was about to say to him, 'Be quiet,' but she felt that if she did he would let out his big laugh and raise the house.

As soon as they entered the hall Lizzie's wailing came to her, and she hurried forward up the dark stairs; and when he stumbled after her she put her hand out to steady him, and he gripped it and held it until they came to the top landing. And there she whispered, 'Stand still; you . . . you might knock the bucket over.' As she groped for her key in her coat pocket he said, 'What is that noise?' She didn't answer but unlocked the door, and when she opened it it came to her that here was another chance of escape, she could bolt the door in his face. Yes, and have him bellow the house down. From the little she knew of him she could well imagine him doing just that.

She groped her way towards the table, put the pies on it, then moved cautiously towards the mantelpiece and instinctively her hand found the candlestick. There was no glimmer left in the fire to light the candle, so, going back to the landing, she whispered, 'I haven't a light.'

Without a word he handed her a bulky box, and taking a match from it she struck it on the rough underside of the candlestick; then she lit the candle, shielding its flame for a moment with her hand. Now, turning abruptly, she walked back into the room.

He was standing in the centre of the room near the table when, looking towards the door from where the noise came, he said, 'Your sister, is she a baby?'

'No. You . . . you can sit down; I'll . . . I'll have to see to her for a moment.'

'You do. Do that; the night's young.' He turned from her and looked slowly around the room.

'I'll have to take the candle,' she said.

He was looking at her again. 'That's the only candle you have?'

'Yes.'

'Go ahead.'

She picked up the candle. Then, pointing towards the pies that had now spread themselves out of the paper, she said, 'I'll . . . I'll take her one of these.' Under his penetrating gaze she picked up a pie and went into the bedroom.

'There, there,' she said to Lizzie. 'Don't cry. Aw, don't cry any more. Eat this, it's a pie.'

Lizzie's face moved into a smile; she opened her mouth and in two bites the pie had disappeared, and her eyes, looking into Katie's, said she wanted more.

'Later. You'll have another later.'

As she straightened up from over the bed she was aware that the door had opened, and half turning her head she saw him standing looking at them. She wanted to place herself in front of Lizzie to shield her from his sight, but it was too late. Lizzie didn't see him, or if she did she took no notice, and Katie, pushing the pillows into position behind her back and putting the patched quilt over the enormous bulging stomach, said, 'There now. Be a good girl. I'll be back in a moment.' She walked past the man and into the room, and it was a full minute before he came and joined her.

'Is she a mongol?'

'A what?'

'A mongol?'

Katie did not know what he meant by a mongol. She said, 'She was born like that; she's always been like a child.'

'And you, you look after her?' He was standing straight now, his face unsmiling. 'Since when?'

'Since my mother died. And before that. The past few years or so.' She looked down at the pies now, and, his gaze following hers, he said breezily, 'Well, let us eat.'

She brought two plates and some cutlery from the cupboard, and she had just started to eat when he said, 'Bread. I like bread with peas.'

She had her mouth full of pie and she had to swallow three times before she could say, 'There's no bread.' There was a rough defiant note in her voice, and her expression was bitter as she stared at him through the candlelight and added, 'I wouldn't have gone to the *Anchor* for the job if . . . if I'd had bread to spare.'

He put down the spoon that was hovering over his plate, and leant against the chair rails. Pushing his elbows well back until his hands were resting on his stomach, he slowly drew in his bearded chin tight against the high collar of his jacket, and like this he surveyed her from across the table. He was looking into a face the like he had never seen before in any port, and he was not even seeing her clearly, for the illumination from the tallow candle was limited. Her eyes were the largest, the strangest, most arresting he had ever beheld. He had come upon something here he couldn't as yet understand. Why wasn't there any man about the place . . . about her? What were they up to in this land of frozen faces, faces which didn't know how to laugh; this land of mean, calculating minds? He didn't like the English. He had never liked the English. All brothers under the skin, so the saying went; but how did you know you were an Englishman's brother? You could never get under the Englishman's skin. But this woman, this woman without a man, this woman with the face of . . . what? Not an angel. No. No. What kind of a face was it? A strange face, a beautiful face. Yes, yes, but something more. A good face. Yes, a good face. A lonely lost face. Why hadn't it brought a man to her? There must be a man; somewhere there must be a man who owned her. It was against all nature that, looking as she did, she should be alone. He slowly brought himself from the back of the chair, and leaning forward, his elbows one each side of his plate, he asked quietly, 'You have a man? The truth now. You have a man?'

She raised her eyes from the plate and said with a calmness that puzzled him, 'I have no man. Nor do I want one.'

'No!' There was that jocular, cynical tone in his voice again, but hers was hard as she replied briefly, 'No.'

Not moving his position, he said, 'Pity, great pity, you feel like that, because . . . I have a surprise for you . . . you've got one.' He now dug his thumb into the middle of his waistcoat. 'I am your MAN.'

She had been chewing on a mouthful of peas and one stuck in her throat and brought on a spasm of coughing. She rose from the table and stood aside, her head bent, one hand pressing against her chest. She had her back to him, and when she heard his chair scraping on the wooden floor she turned swiftly, still coughing, and the next minute she found herself pressed against him. One big hand on her buttocks, the other under her armpit, he arched her stiff body into his. Her eyes staring into the face within an inch of hers, at the full red mouth through the mass of fair hair, she watched the lips move and say again, 'I'm your man . . . yes?'

She was trembling from head to foot, more than she had done when he first grabbed her. There was no pore in her body that wasn't open, pouring sweat. Yet it wasn't with fear – at least not the kind of fear she had previously experienced; the fear that Bernard Rosier had brought into her body; the cold, cold fear that Mark Bunting had filled every hour of her waking days with, and most of her nights. Nor was the fear that was possessing her now created by this great, blond man, this utter stranger. The fear was of herself, her feelings, of the very fact that she wasn't afraid of him.

When he kissed her her whole face seemed lost in a tangle of hair. The kiss lasted a long time, and the strange fear in her mounted again. After the first moment of it she no longer resisted it; she did not return it, but she did not resist it. When he withdrew his face from hers he did not look at her, but his eyes flashed around the room and alighted on the raised pallet in the dim corner. Still with his arms about her, he now drew her towards it, circling the dark bulk of a chair in the progress. When they were standing near the bed her body became stiff again and unyielding. He felt the change in her immediately and, one hand going swiftly around the back of her knees, he lifted her upwards as if she was a child and the next minute she was lying on her back on the bed and he was beside her, and when his arms went about her the trembling of her body increased. He became still against her for a moment, silent and still, and then he said, 'Don't tremble; I won't hurt you.'

And he didn't.

She was actually laughing. She couldn't remember the last time she had laughed like this. As a child she had felt full of joy and laughter, but she imagined that that was a natural part of childhood; all children could laugh and feel joy until life got at them. But now, with her arms laden with packages of food, more food than she had ever seen in her life at one time, except up at the House, she was walking beside the burly captain, who had a sack of coal perched on his shoulder which he supported with one hand, while under the other arm he carried a bundle of candles, and she was laughing.

Just over an hour ago she had wanted to go to sleep, drop into a soft beautiful sleep, but he had pulled her to her feet and said one word 'Food.' And she had repeated dazedly, 'Food.' And then shaking her by the shoulder, he had laughed and cried, 'Wake up, wake up, *min elskling*. Yes, food and coal; I'm going to warm you inside and out.' He had gripped her face in his hands, pressing her mouth outwards. She had explained that it was too late, at least for coal; the shops were open till ten, some after, but not the coal depots.

But he had opened the coal depot. Knocking on the man's door, he had demanded him to fill the sack with coal. And now here she was, like an excited child, hurrying by his side. What had come over her? For a moment she thought of Joe, then dismissed him. Joe wouldn't be back the night. Something had happened to her, something strange and beautiful, and she wanted to hang on to it. She would have to face Joe, likely tell Joe, but that was tomorrow; there was still tonight . . .

The fire was blazing, the cupboard was full, she had eaten the best meal she'd had for many a long day. She'd had a piece of steak half an inch thick, a lump of black pudding and two fried eggs. Between them they had finished a crusty loaf and half a pound of butter, and now they were sitting on her bed which he had pulled right up to the fire, drinking cups of steaming tea, with whisky in his. Lizzie was asleep on a full stomach; the grate was full of burning coal; and she felt at rest within herself as she had never done in her life before.

She was pressed close to him, held there by his arm, and every time she turned her face towards him his eyes were waiting for her. She liked his eyes. She could see them clearly now in the light of the six candles he had lit all at once. She had wanted to stop him lighting more than two, but she didn't; this was a night apart, a strange night, a night that would never happen to her again. She knew she was doing what the bad women did, and she knew that her mother and father, and her granda, would be turning in their graves, but she didn't feel any great sense of sin because God and sin and chapel-going had fled her life the day they put a rope around her father's neck.

Her head now resting against his shoulder, she asked softly, 'What do they call your ship?'

'The *Orn*. It means "eagle" in your language.'

'Is it a big ship?'

'So so, big enough to carry timber . . . and odds and ends.' He raised his eyebrows.

'Do you come into the dock often?'

A deep rumbling chuckle went through his body and into hers, and, putting his head down to try and see into her face, he said, 'Do you want me to come into the dock often?'

'No, no.' She tried to pull away from him now, but he held her tight and she muttered, 'I didn't mean I . . . '

'There. There. It's all right. I understand you to mean whatever you didn't mean.' He chuckled quietly as he pressed her hard against him, then said, 'Half the year we come to the Tyne, from April to October. Some of our men come over on the last ship and stay here all winter. They get ships plying along the coast.' He laughed heartily as if at a joke; then, stroking his beard with his hand, he asked, 'How old are you?'

'Nearly twenty-one,' she said softly. Then, glancing up at him, she said, 'And you, how old are you?'

'Ah!' He closed his eyes and moved his big head from side to side. 'Too old. Too old.'

'Thirty?' She knew she was being kind to him.

'Huh!' His head jerked backwards. 'You think I look thirty? That is good. Ah, good.' After a space of time, during which he held her face turned upwards to him and staring into her eyes, he said, 'I am thirty-seven years old. But tonight I am twenty-seven. No, twenty-three, and life is just beginning.' There followed another silence before he said, 'We have been together three hours – no, three hours and a half, and I don't know how they call you.'

'Katie Mulholland.' She never called herself by her married name.

'Kaa-tee Mulholland. It is a full mouth of a name. Kaa-tee Mulholland.'

'And your name?'

'Andrée Fraenkel.'

'Ann-drée. It's like Andrew in English.' She laughed and said, 'I'll call you Andy.'

'Andy!' He put his head on one side. 'That is like what my . . . ' He broke off, swung her around until she was resting with her back against his chest, then said, 'Andy it is.' After this he remained quiet for a time, his arms tight about her, his bearded chin resting on the top of her head.

In the strange warm silence, as she lay staring into the fire like someone entranced, there were forced into her mind thoughts of tomorrow, of who might see him leave; Meggie Proctor, Jinny Wilson, or Mrs Robson. She was afraid of Mrs Robson seeing him go. Perhaps he would go early before anybody was up; he'd have to get back to his ship. She brought the niggling worry to the surface by asking, 'When do you sail?'

'Sail?' He seemed to drag his thoughts from some distant place. 'Ah, not for some three days. She is having repairs and her bottom is needing a scrape. Three whole days, Kaa-tee.'

She hadn't time now to feel fright or apprehension at the thought of him being around the place for three days, because his hands were loosening the buttons of her bodice and she did not stay them.

It was when her breast was exposed above the line of her shift that his eyes came to rest on the zig-zag red weal standing out from the warm cream flesh. His eyes now asked her a question, but she did not speak.

Then slowly he moved his finger from the end of the weal and following its course, his hand mounting to her shoulder. Now, half hitching himself up, he swivelled her round towards the candlelight. She felt his hands undoing the hook of her skirt; then, with a quick jerking movement, her shift was tugged up from within the bands of her petticoat and thrust forward over her head. Following this, there was silence again.

Slowly now she turned towards him and she saw the red gap of his mouth open and his tongue waver in it before he asked in an undertone, 'Who did this?'

'Oh.' She drooped her head and swung it back and forward before saying, 'Oh, it's a long story.'

'Who did it?' His voice was louder now and roughly his hand jerked her chin up.

'My . . . my husband.'

'Your husband?'

She moved her head once, then said, 'My father killed him for it . . . No, no.' Again her head was shaking. 'He didn't, it was the others; but he beat him and he was found dead later and they hanged him, my father.'

He was staring at her, his eyes wide, his mouth open, his cheeks pushed upwards with incredulity. He began to speak rapidly now, in his own language, but when he finished it was in her own tongue and he said, 'Almighty God, you have been flayed.'

Turning her slowly round again, he once more examined the network of red ridges, some pronounced, some faint, that covered her back. When he turned her to face him he said simply, 'Tell me. From the beginning. Tell me.' Then he pulled up the coverlet and put it gently round her shoulders and pressed her towards him again.

So, sitting cradled in the arms of this strange man, a man whom a few hours ago she hadn't known was alive but whom she felt she knew better than anyone in her life before, even her parents, her grandfather, or Joe, she talked, and as she did so she unwound herself back to the time before the night of the ball.

She told him everything, right from the beginning; from the day she had started as scullery maid to the Rosiers right up to the day when they hanged her father. And she finished with meeting the Misses Chapman and giving them her child. The only thing she didn't tell him was the name of the man who had given her the child.

And as he listened Andrée Fraenkel realised, with disquieting certainty, that he had reached a crossroad in his life. He had felt the pull of her when he had grabbed at her and looked into her face for the first time. But with the telling of her story he knew that a woman had been washed up to him the like he had dreamed of from when he was a boy. For good or bad he was ensnared – possibly for bad, for to keep and hold her would mean the eventual breaking up of his home in his own country, if not the end of his career; at least with the big ships.

Chapter Three

FOR TWO AND a half days Katie lived between a joy that she likened to heaven on earth and an apprehensive feeling that she likened to all hell being let loose as she waited Joe's return. For three nights the captain had stayed with her, and most of the two days, leaving her only to look over his ship. But today he was sailing. He had to be aboard before eleven o'clock tonight and she was praying earnestly within herself that he'd be gone before Joe got back.

It was to happen that he and Joe were to meet; but before he met Joe he was to meet Miss Theresa.

He was sitting in the armchair; his big feet, encased in a pair of bright red soft leather slippers, were sticking upwards on the fender. He had his two hands joined behind his head, which swivelled slowly back and forwards as his eyes followed Katie about the room.

'Kaa-tee.'

'Yes, Andy?'

'You happy?'

For answer she came to his side and stood looking down at him; she did not touch him, nor he her, but she said, 'If I'm not it doesn't matter, because I want to remain in this state all me life.'

'It's not three days, do you realise that, not three days since we met?'

'Well, as I told you, I think I knew within the first three minutes. That's why I couldn't stop shaking.'

His fingers now snapped apart, his head and body came up like a released spring and he was on his feet with his arms about her, holding her close. His face above hers, he stared down at her as he asked, 'What are you going to do with yourself all the time?'

'Oh, the usual. Lookin' after the house, and Joe and Lizzie. But it won't be the same . . . ' She smiled softly at him. 'Nothing in me life will ever be the same again.'

'It'll be a full two weeks before I'm back.' He didn't say, 'You won't have anybody else in the meantime?' He would not insult her; he hadn't linked himself with any waterside trollop.

'I'll be here,' she said softly. 'I'll always be here, and waitin' . . . What time are you leaving? I mean . . . I mean from here.'

'I should be aboard by five to see things under way; but if I can slip ashore for a while later, I'll be back.'

Their lips were pressed close when there came the sound of footsteps on the wooden stairs, and Katie, pulling herself away from his arms, turned and stared towards the door. Then she took in a deep breath of relief when there came a tap on it. After glancing at him she went and opened the door, but slightly, and there stood Miss Theresa.

'Good afternoon, Katie.'

'Oh! Good afternoon, Miss Theresa.'

When she didn't stand aside and allow her visitor to enter the room, Miss Theresa looked at her for a moment in silence, then said, 'I've brought you some books . . . and this.' She held out a parcel towards Katie, and as she did so her eyes lifted from her face, over her shoulder, and to a great bearded man standing with his back to the fireplace. Her eyes darting back to Katie, she looked at her with her mouth slightly agape. Then, when Katie, her head erect but her eyes cast downwards now, moved aside, she went slowly into the room and stood near the table.

'This . . . this is a friend of mine, Miss Theresa, Captain Fraenkel.' Katie pronounced it Frenkall.

Then, looking at Andrée, she said softly, 'This is Mrs Noble.'

Andrée, his hands now hanging by his sides, bowed slightly from the shoulders. It was a courtly gesture and Theresa recognised it as such; she recognised it as the action of a gentleman. After staring into the big vivid blue eyes for a moment her own dropped sharply away, but not before they had traversed his broad chest, only partly covered by a white shirt, his belted trousers and slippered feet. The awful truth deprived her of speech.

From shaking fingers Theresa dropped the books on to the table, then the parcel, and turning her back slowly on the man she confronted Katie, her eyes wide and accusing. Through her thin lips she now said, 'I would like a word with you in private, Katie.' And on this she went towards the door, and Katie, after casting a glance at Andrée, a helpless one this time, followed her on to the landing and to the head of the stairs, where Theresa had taken her stand.

'Katie! What . . . what have you done?' Theresa's words were accusing, bitter, and they came through her clenched teeth. She was trembling as if consumed with rage.

'He's a friend, Miss Theresa.' Katie's chin was up.

'A friend? How long has he been a friend? Answer me.'

Katie blinked her eyes, then brought her head forward as if to see Miss Theresa better, and in a voice that was almost calm and held a touch of dignity she said, 'I'm a woman, Miss Theresa, I'm no longer a child; and I'm me own mistress, I can do what I like.'

'And with whom you like, I suppose.'

Again Katie screwed up her face as she looked at the woman opposite. She had been prepared for Miss Theresa being shocked, but she couldn't understand her anger. It was like, like . . . She couldn't find words to translate Miss Theresa's attitude so that she could understand it.

'Joe. What has he to say about this?'

'It's not Joe's business, it's mine, Miss Theresa. I . . . I don't want to seem ungrateful. I've always been grateful because you've been so kind to me, but . . . but what I do with me life is, as I said, my business.' Now she bent towards Theresa again and, her voice dropping to a soft whisper, she said, 'And, I'm happy. I'm happier than I've been in me life afore. He's a good man.'

'A good man!' Miss Theresa's lips moved away from her teeth as if she had tasted something vile. 'A sailor from the docks – because that's what he is, isn't he? And a foreigner, and twice your age, I would say.' Now, her voice and face matching each other in viciousness, she cried, 'Don't you know that they have women in every port they touch, filthy women, diseased women?'

Following this, they stared at each other in the gloom; then Theresa, her voice filled with pleading, her manner changing utterly, beseeched, 'Send him away, Katie. Go on in now and send him away. Please, please. I . . . I can't bear to think of you with him. I've . . . I've always been kind to you – you said yourself I have – well, do this for me. Go on and send him away . . . now.'

Katie moved back from Theresa. The funny feeling that she'd had a number of times when Miss Theresa had come near her was emphasised in her now, and she said to her, 'No, I won't, not now or at any time. And although I thank you for your kindness in the past, I'd . . . I'd thank you now to leave me alone.'

To her amazement Katie now saw Miss Theresa's face crumpling and the tears stream from her eyes. The next minute she was watching her running down the stairs. Slowly she turned towards the door, and when she opened it there was Andrée standing not a foot away. As she looked at him he nodded at her and said, 'Come, come.' He put his arm gently round her shoulders and led her towards the fire where, seating her in the chair, he dropped down on his hunkers before her and, taking her hand in his, said, 'I've done you a service; you're well rid of that one.'

'But she's been so kind to me.'

'Kind? Huh! Unnatural women are always kind to women.'

'Unnatural women?'

'Yes, yes, she's no woman, she's a man under the skin. I recognised it, even before she looked at you. I have a cousin who's the same. It is a trick of nature.'

'Miss Theresa? No!' Katie shuddered, and he drew her hands to his breast, saying, 'Not that I blame her for loving you; no-one could help loving you, and it will remain a mystery to me to the end of my days that I found you alone.'

'Aw, Andy.' She leant her face forward and rubbed her cheek against his beard, and he fondled her and kissed her and spoke long sentences to her in his own tongue, but when he wanted to make love to her she protested softly, saying, 'No, no, our Joe might come in. He might come in; you never know.'

'Do you think he will come today?'

'I don't know. He might.'

'I hope he does; I would like to meet him.'

She closed her eyes and said to herself, God forbid . . .

They were sitting having a meal when Joe made his appearance. Andrée was laughing loudly about something she had said. In the last few days it seemed she had recaptured her art of telling a tale, and so she didn't hear the footsteps until they reached the landing. By the time the door opened she had screwed round in her chair and was facing him.

In the framework of the door Joe stood, one elbow bent, his fist gripping the end of a small canvas sack that was hanging over his shoulder. He looked dusty and tired, and in this moment his face had a mild, childlike look of bewilderment on it.

Katie sidled up from her seat that was set close to Andrée's. He, too, rose with her and stood looking at the short young fellow in the doorway, and he waited for him to speak.

And Joe spoke. With a sudden twist of his wrist he flung the canvas bag to the corner of the room where it hit the wall with a soft plop, and, moving towards them, but looking only at the man and taking in, as Theresa had done, his attire, right down to the red slippers – mostly the red slippers, for they indicated something that shot the words from him – he said, 'What in hell's name are you doin' here?'

Katie, pushing herself in between them now and with her face close to Joe's, said, 'I can explain, Joe, I can explain. Now look. Don't lose your temper, just listen an' hear me out. This is Captain Fraenkel.'

'What's he doin' here?' Joe, his body as stiff as a ramrod, his fists clenched by his side, was glaring up over her head towards the big bearded fellow.

'I'm a friend of your sister's. I am pleased to meet you.' Andrée took a step to the side.

'Friend be buggered. Now get yourself to hell out of this. She wants no friends among Swedes; she can pick her friends from among English blokes, and not from the riff-raff of the boats, either.'

'Joe, listen to me.' She clutched at his arm, only to have him pull it away from her grasp. But she went on, 'You're mistaken; just listen. Andy, he's a captain, a captain of a big ship . . . '

'It wouldn't matter to me if he was captain of the *Terror*, he's a foreigner, and no good at that, else he wouldn't have taken you down.'

'Joe, Joe, he didn't! It wasn't like that at all. I lost me purse an' . . . an' he helped me.'

Joe turned his eyes from her and his gaze dropped to the red slippers again, and he looked at them for a time before he moved across the floor towards her bed, and there he looked at Andrée's boots standing at the foot of it, and at his coat lying across it. Swinging round now, he barked, 'Get out? Do you hear? Get out!'

'What if I don't go?' Andrée's voice was calm-sounding.

'Then I'll bloody well make you, as big as you are.' Joe seemed to spring from where he stood to the centre of the hearth, and in a split second he had picked up the poker and had raised it in his hand, and as Katie let out a scream she saw Andrée's arm flash upwards and the next minute the poker dropped like a matchstick to the floor, and so hard was Andrée gripping Joe's wrist, and so high was he pulling it upwards, that Joe was almost standing on his toes. Then, as if flicking off a speck of dust, Andrée flung him aside. It was a disdainful action. He now went to the bed, and, sitting down on it, pulled on his boots, then stood up and got into his jacket, following which he went to the chiffonier and took his cap from it. This done, he came slowly to Katie where she was standing, her head bowed, and her joined hands pressed into her neck, and said grimly, 'I'll be back before I sail. Talk to him, tell him how things are . . . I'll be back.' He put his hand out and lifted her head up to him, and they looked deeply at each other. Then he turned and went towards the door, but before he reached it Joe shouted at him, 'This is my house, I pay the rent, an' if you show your nose on these stairs again I'll put the pollis on to you. Get that?'

'*Det er det samme for meg*,' said Andrée. 'Do that. But I'll be back.'

The door had hardly closed on him before Joe, picking up the red slippers, pelted them towards it. Then, with his fists and teeth clenched, he glared at her and she looked at him sadly, pityingly, until, his hands suddenly coming out, gripped the front of her dress. And at this action her whole manner changed. With a swift movement she thrust him from her, crying, 'Don't you start that, our Joe! You're not dealing with a child, an' you remember that. There's nobody gonna knock me about again. No, by God!'

From a distance now he glared at her. Then, his voice bitter, he said, 'No, you're not a child. I've learned that all right in the last few minutes. It's a whore I've got to deal with now.'

'Joe! I'm not, I'm not!' Her protest was loud.

'He slept here, didn't he? Don't deny it. Didn't he?'

'Yes, he did.' She reared herself up. 'An' he'll sleep here again.'

'By God, he won't, not while I'm payin' the rent. Now look here . . . ' He came towards her, his forefinger thrust out stiffly. 'You can make your choice; it's either him or me. I'm not runnin' any house for whoring. Now you've got it. You give him the go-by, and right now, an' we'll try to live this down; if not, you're on your own.'

'Joe, Joe, listen to me.' She put out her joined hands towards him. 'I'll tell you how it happened; just listen to me, will you? I went down to the market an' I lost me purse . . . '

Joe interrupted her with a harsh mirthless laugh. 'You lost your purse. You who could look after two hundred and forty-seven pounds. You lost your purse.'

'I did, Joe, I did. You can ask Meggie Proctor an' Jinny Wilson downstairs; they lent me the money atween them to pay the rent. I was at me wits' end. I went to the *Anchor* to get a job and it was there I met him.'

'The *Anchor*!' His head was back now, and again he made the mirthless sound. 'Well, you went to the right place to start, didn't you? You mean to tell me you didn't know what goes on in the *Anchor*? It's not called the whore market for nothing. You mean to say you didn't know?'

'I only knew I was hungry,' she said bitterly, 'an' Lizzie was cryin' because she was hungry. I had no heat an' only half a candle. Besides, I'd had nothin' for nearly three days but a drink of tea and a bit bread.'

'You could have gone to Miss Theresa.'

Now her voice was loud and harsh. 'Well, I didn't go to Miss Theresa. An' I wouldn't go to Miss Theresa. An' I'm glad I didn't.'

He stared at her in silence for a long while, and then his voice, quieter now, but his words terrible-sounding to her, said, 'You're bad, our Katie. Right at bottom you're bad. There was the bairn, an' then off your own bat you go to Buntin'. Nobody made you go to him, an' because you went me da was hanged and me mother went out of her mind, an' now you're gone on the streets. You're bad . . . you're bad.' He repeated the last two words in a dazed fashion as if he had just become aware of the truth of his assertion, and she cried at him, 'Joe, don't say that. I'm not, I'm not bad. What happened to me years gone I couldn't help.'

Again they were staring at each other in silence. And then he answered her last remark, saying, 'Perhaps not, perhaps not all the other things, but this one you can. This is your test piece. Send him packin', an' I'll believe you.'

Another silence. And Katie, closing the gap between them, came to a stop quite close to him and said, 'No, Joe, I'll never send him out of me life. He's in it for as long as he wants.'

'That's it then. Aye, well, that's it then. Now we know where we stand . . . An' her?' He nodded towards the bedroom. 'He's goin' to take on her an 'all?'

'I'll see to her.'

'By God, an' you'll have to. You'll have to work overtime. Bloody well double time.' He now let out a spate of obscenities.

She had never heard him talk like this before in her life. She knew he likely did in the shipyard, but he had never used bad language in the house. Neither of them had been brought up to it, but now he was acting like any man out of the docks. And yet, to his mind, wasn't she acting like any low woman from the docks? Yes, she could see that his attitude was justified, but she could do nothing about it.

Clutching at anything that might act as a stumbling block, he now said, 'This is me furniture in here.'

'Your furniture?' She wagged her head, then said quickly, 'Aw, no, Joe. No, it isn't yours. Miss Chapman gave it me in exchange for the child. They'd have given me the moon to carry away, but you'll remember I wouldn't take anythin' except the furniture because I knew we would want it when we got this end . . . No, Joe, the furniture isn't yours, an' don't you try to take it from me, Joe, I'm warnin' you. It's all I've got.'

He stepped back from her now, his jaws champing, and, groping at the handle of the door, he said, 'Well, you think you've made your choice, but I'll let you sleep on it. I'll come back the morrow and see if you've come to your senses.'

When the door banged she stood staring at it, her heart beating fast and aching painfully; then slowly she dropped into a chair and, burying her face in her hands, she cried, 'Aw, Joe! Joe!' Over and over again she repeated his name, 'Joe . . . Joe.' What would she do with her days? Without Joe to look after, what would she do? There'd be nobody coming nobody to get meals for, except Lizzie and herself . . . Except when Andy was here . . . Oh, Andy, Andy.

Her body rocked now back and forward. What had come over her that within three days she could leave Joe without a home because of this man, this strange man? But she couldn't help herself, she couldn't. Nor did she want to; there was no question of choice between him and Joe. If Andy went out of her life now the pain of his loss would be unbearable. All that she had gone through before would be as nothing compared with it. She would give up or sacrifice anything to keep this strange man.

She had waited through the long twilight and now the darkness had set in and he hadn't come, and she was sick to the soul. She had gone to the head of the stairs countless times. She had wanted to go down to the street door and wait there, but she couldn't face the look in Meggie Proctor's and Jinny Wilson's eyes. As yet she had not encountered Mrs Robson from the first floor.

On that first day after Andy had left the house she had gone down to the yard to empty the slops and they had been waiting for her, Meggie and Jinny.

They had come out of their doors together and they had looked at her and smiled. It would have been less disturbing if they had ignored her, or been scornful of her, but their smiles had said, 'We're all lasses together. Fishgate whores or Dock Dollies, we're all lasses together.' It was Jinny Wilson who had jerked her head at her and said, 'Yer started off well, lass. Keep it up. No need to borrow any more now.' She had wanted to defend herself against the insinuation, but she couldn't. What defence had she?

When she heard the quick heavy tread on the lower flight of stairs she went to the door and leant against it for a second, faint with relief. Then she was in his arms, and he was leading her back into the room. And there she clung to him and he pressed her close, and after a moment he said, 'He's gone, then?'

She moved her cheek against his and he said, 'I'm sorry . . . Would he have stayed if you had promised . . . ?'

Again she moved her head; and now he raised her face to his and, with great solemnity, said, 'You have not made a mistake, Kaa-tee, I'm for you. We have talked over all this. We know, so you go on knowing you haven't made a mistake. And now' – he drew in a deep breath – 'I have not more than five minutes; I must get back, and quick. I would have been here sooner but I was held up with the dock authorities, so what I must say will be terse, short. We sail to Stavanger, unload our coal there, and if there is a cargo ready for us we should be back under three weeks. However, if I've got to take her to Bergen it could be another week or more before I return; it all depends on the weather and the charters. Now, in the meanwhile you must live, so here is five pounds, and if for any reason I should be delayed beyond a month I will get money to you. Never fear, I will get money to you . . . Take it, take it.' He closed her fingers over the sovereigns.

Up to this very moment she hadn't felt a whore, or a bad woman, because all she had taken from him was something to eat, and coal, and candles; but now the exchange had been made, the price had been paid, and it was as Meggie Proctor had said, Fishgate whores or Dock Dollies. No, no, she wasn't one of them, she wasn't. She flung herself against him and her crying shuddered his body, and he began to talk rapidly to her in his own tongue. After a moment his mouth sought hers and he kissed her with a hard, intense passion which she returned. Then, pressing her from him, he looked at her. His blue eyes, seeming to have darkened, now searched her face, moving from one feature to another, before they came to rest on her hair, and his hands moved up and touched it for a moment. Pulling a strand loose from the coil on the back of her head, he whipped out a knife from his coat pocket and, bending the strand into a loop, he cut off about three inches from it. Then he rolled it around his finger before putting it into his top pocket. And now, taking her face between his hands, he muttered thickly, 'Know I will be back, Kaa-tee. Know that.' Then again touching her lips, but softly, he said, 'Don't come. Just stay there.'

It was some time before she moved. It was Lizzie's whimpering that stirred her, and as she looked wearily towards the bedroom door her gaze

184

was caught by the hessian sack that Joe had brought in. It was lying between the wall and the chiffonier. She hadn't noticed it before, she had forgotten that he had thrown it there. Now she moved slowly across the room and picked it up, and when mechanically she toppled its contents on to the table she saw a hand of smoked bacon and a ring of black pudding.

Odd, the things that happened, and when they happened. She had a cupboard full of food now and here was a hand of smoked bacon and a black pudding, and if Joe had brought them three days ago she would never have met Andy . . . A hand of smoked bacon and a black pudding.

At twelve o'clock the next day Joe walked down the stairs and into the street. He looked white and was shaking inwardly. He had got his answer from Katie. As he walked to Tyne Dock and through it, and up the long road past East Jarrow, he told himself over and over that he just couldn't believe it. He was hurt and shaken to the core, but his most intense feeling was that of being slighted. He kept muttering to himself, 'She's mucky, filthy, putrid. She is. She is.'

He went up the bank that led into Jarrow, along past the rows of whitewashed cottages with the women sitting on the steps and the men standing idly at the corners. The whole town was dead; it looked as if everybody was waiting for a hearse to pass. Some of the shops were closed, and those that were open looked empty; only the pubs had customers, and these were from the factories that cluttered round the feet of Palmer's and managed to thrive independently.

But he wasn't bothered about the strike at this minute; he had nobody to care for but himself now and he felt lost, thrown off, tossed aside. Aye, that's what she had done, tossed him aside. And he'd worked for years to keep the house going, giving up every penny to her. He couldn't have done more. And just because she was hungry she had gone and done that. But what staggered him most of all was that she was brazen with it, for she said she wouldn't give him up. She couldn't see she was making a mug of herself; these kinds of chaps didn't wait to be given up, they just went and never came back. Well, it would be no use her coming crawling to him when her eyes were opened. No, by God! He would give her his answer, that he would.

He felt the urge to cry, and he cut down a side street where they were building houses. The builders were still working; the houses were popping up as quick as corks from bottles on New Year's Eve, because the contractors knew that Palmer's would flourish again; whoever sank, Palmer's would swim.

He passed a patch of open ground where a gang of men were playing quoits, and another were surrounding a couple of cocks; then into a district that looked clean and superior compared to the part of the town through which he had just passed. He went up a back lane where every few feet of yard wall had two wooden hatches let in; one denoting a coalhouse beyond, the other indicating the new innovation of the dry midden. When he came to the eighth door he lifted the latch and walked up the narrow yard and knocked on the kitchen door.

Mrs Hetherington answered his knock and said cheerily, 'Oh, there you are, Joe. You've got back.'

'Yes, Mrs Hetherington.'

'Come in; come in, lad.'

Joe went into the kitchen, and there looked at Mr Hetherington where he sat cobbling a pair of boots on an iron last which he held between his knees.

'Hello, lad,' said Mr Hetherington. 'How did it go? You made it up?'

Joe stood rubbing his hand hard across his mouth. Then, looking from the dumpy little woman to her tall, thin husband, he bowed his head and said, 'It wasn't quite right what I told you about me an' her just havin' words, Mr Hetherington. It's worse than that. I . . . I can't go back 'cos she's gone on the streets.'

Chapter Four

ALMOST A MONTH to the day Andrée returned to the Tyne. Katie knew of his coming before he docked; she heard of it through Meggie. Meggie had come knocking at the door late last night and woken her up. She said that a friend who was on one of Palmer's colliers plying between Peterhead and Sunderland had sighted the *Orn* when they were about thirty miles offshore from Aberdeen. She was making good headway and had the wind with her, and if she was lucky she should come in on the tide, which was around five in the morning. But if she couldn't make it owing to the weather, she should surely be in later in the day. Then Meggie had added, 'Do you think he'll turn up?'

Katie had swallowed and said, 'I think so, Meggie. ' And when she was alone she stood with her back to the door, her hands pressed against it. She would as soon have doubted the dawn breaking as him not turning up.

And now it was morning. Half-past seven and she was ready and waiting. She had made the fire up high and it was burning brightly, the table was set, and she had on her new dress – at least new to her. And as she looked down at it she thought that if Miss Theresa knew to what use her last gift was being put she would burst into flames. The thought had the power to make her laugh inside. She had never laughed outright since Andrée had gone.

During the first terrible week of loneliness she had cried most of the time. At one period she nearly went looking for Joe; she knew she would find him with the Hetheringtons. She hadn't intended to ask him to come and live in the house again, only to come and see her now and then, not to cut himself right off from her; but remembering Joe's face when they had parted she knew it would be useless, because Joe had a great deal of her da in him; he might not go to church but he was still a church man inside.

The second week she had taken to talking to Lizzie, talking as if she was getting answers. But she had stopped that; you could lose your mind that way . . .

She had to make the fire up three times more before Andrée arrived, and when she heard his tread mounting to the landing she could not leave the centre of the room and go to the door.

He did not knock but turned the handle and pushed the door wide and stood there. He had a big canvas bag hanging from one hand and he dropped it to the floor, then moved forward slowly, like she had seen him moving towards her in her dreams. His eyes spraying their blue light over her, he came now, and she couldn't move a muscle to welcome him until she was in his arms.

Not only her mouth but the whole of her body became lost in his, and when the first moment of swaying, rough, painful ecstasy was over he pressed her from him and looked at her and whispered, 'Ah, Kaa-tee, Kaa-tee.' Then, moving his head slowly, he said, 'I didn't dream it, but my memory wasn't vivid enough. You are more beautiful than I remember.' She fell against him again, crying, 'Oh, Andy, Andy. Oh, I've missed you. Oh, how I've missed you. I've worried every day. And when the wind was high last night I was terrified lest it took you on to the Black Middens.'

He stroked her hair gently and leant his cheek on it and said quietly, 'Never be afraid of the wind. As long as it blows it'll blow me to you . . . '

It was an hour later and they had loved and talked and loved again, and now, dishevelled but still unable to lose contact with each other, they were standing close at the table and Andrée was undoing the canvas bag.

She had never seen so many beautiful things all at once in her life – at least things that were beautiful to her – and not least of them was a seven-pound jar of strawberry jam. Food to her came under the heading of beauty; anything as necessary as food was beautiful. He spilled on to the table now a whole ham, a pickled tongue, a box of ginger encased in lumps of sugar, another box filled with strange-looking candy. Then there was the cloth. Two rolls of cloth, one of fine green gaberdine and the other of cream silk. She held a length of this latter in her hand and the rough skin of her fingers caught at its fineness. She gazed up at him and said, 'Oh, it's beautiful, Andy. Beautiful, real silk.'

'For your nightgown and shift.'

Her eyes stretched wide and her mouth gaped open before she said, 'Use this for a nightgown and shift?'

'Of course.'

'It's too good.'

'Too good for you?' He pulled her to him. 'Spun gold wouldn't be too good for your nightgown and shift.'

'Aw, Andy . . . '

Two hours farther on, when they were sitting on the mattress that was now spread before the fire, she said, 'How long this time?'

'Two days, perhaps three.'

'Oh, no. Only two days. Oh, Andy.' She lowered her head slowly on to his shoulder and he asked, 'Are you very lonely by yourself with just . . . ?' He motioned his head towards the bedroom door, and she said, 'I'm lonely all the time you're not here.'

'I've got a plan.' He put his finger beneath her chin and tilted her face towards him. 'I'm thinking about leaving my company . . . This – this Palmer company in Jarrow, they have steam boiler ships that don't have to wait for wind and weather; they just fly ahead. They can do the crossing in half the time. This company get a lot of their ore from Bilbao in Spain. It is a long way off, but it will be quicker in their steamships although the distance is twice as far. I have been talking to a friend of mine. He knows the owner, this Mr Palmer, and he is going to place a word for me.'

'Oh, Andy.' She smiled softly at him. 'That would mean you always docking here; you wouldn't have to go back to Sweden every time.'

He traced his finger around every feature of her face before he said softly, 'There is something I have to tell you, but it will keep.' Then he added quickly, 'Don't look worried; there's nothing to worry about. I just want to tell you about my home. It isn't in Sweden, it's in Norway. Although I'm Swedish by birth, I've always lived in Norway.'

'Tell me now – please, Andy, tell me now.' Her request was urgent, fear traced, and she held his hand to her breast.

During the weeks that had separated them she had thought about his home and dreaded the ties she imagined were there, a mother and father, a wife and family? No! No! He mustn't have a wife and family. Sisters and brothers, mother and father, but not a wife and family. 'Tell me, Andy,' she said again.

Andrée now turned from her and, pulling his knees up, he leaned his elbows on them, and his forearms and joined hands made a bridge between his legs, and over this he bent his broad chest and stared into the fire. And he remained silent for so long that Katie, putting out a tentative finger, touched his shoulder and said softly, 'I'm sorry. It doesn't matter.'

'Yes, it matters.' He turned to her again. 'It matters, Kaa-tee, and I think perhaps now is the time to tell it . . . but I'll do it in my own way, it'll make it easier.' He gave her cheek a gentle tap, then said, 'Look.

My coat, hand it,' and she turned from him and, getting to her knees, reached towards the back of the chair and, lifting his coat down, gave it to him.

Andrée now proceeded to empty the inside of three pockets. Out of one he took a bulky wallet; from another a fine leather case; and from the third a small book with a brass lock on it. Taking a key from the same pocket, he undid the lock and opened the book and, tapping it with his finger, he said, 'Diary.'

'Diary?'

'Yes, what I write personal in.'

'Yes, yes, I know.'

He smiled now and patted her cheek again, saying, 'I forget. I forget you know these things, that you can read.'

She moved her head slightly as she smiled softly at him. She noticed something about him at this moment that she had encountered once before; his English became more precise, more stilted when he was upset or agitated. That time with Joe he had talked clipped like he was doing now. The thought that what he was about to tell her was agitating him strengthened the apprehension in her and the smile slid from her face, and she waited.

'Look first.' He was pointing to a small map in the back of the book. 'Can you see? The print is very faint, but there, that tiny dot there, it is called Karlstad. There I was born. My father was Norwegian and my mother was Swedish. Sweden and Norway, you see, are close like your Scotland and England, you understand?' She nodded, and he went on, 'My father's father was English, my mother's father was Norwegian. My English grandfather lived in Norway from he was a young man, and from the age of seven I lived with him. That's why I speak English so well.' He stated this seriously. Then he went on, 'You see, we are a large family, eleven – eleven brothers and sisters – so my parents let my brother Jon and me go and live with my grandparents, and life was wonderful.' He smiled broadly now and pulled at his beard. 'They lived in a little house between Bergen and the top end of Hardanger Fjord, and all around us was water. Water, water everywhere you looked. And great mountains of rock with their feet in the water; and in the spring, blossom. Water, rock and blossom . . . Ahh!' He sighed and closed his eyes. 'I went to sea when I was fourteen. I sailed out of Bergen on a spring night with the moon and the wind filling the sails, and that was my first marriage. That night the sea and I were joined for life.'

First marriage. A chill came on her, and not even the hard pressure of his fingers could warm her now.

'Seven years later I was first mate on that same ship, and there came the day when we returned to Bergen and almost the whole town was on the quay, for we had been away for two years. We had been right across the North Atlantic Ocean, south to the West Indies, then right round to Montevideo in Uruguay. And here we were, safely back. We hadn't lost a man and we had a rich cargo. There was a ball given that night in the *Radhus* . . . town hall, you know.' He nodded at her, and she nodded back. 'And there I met a young lady. I had never seen a woman for many months, and this young lady had a fair skin and pretty hair and she seemed to like to dance with me. I did not know then who she was, she was only a pretty girl, but next day I found out when my brother Jon, who also went to sea, and whose boat happened to be in, teased me for being the choice of Miss Petersen at the ball.

'My grandparents were all oohs and ahs and laughter, for was not Petersen Papa one big hell of a man, as you say. Why, he owned great slabs of the town. Well, that, thought I, was the last I would see of Miss Petersen. But no, I was invited to her home and – well . . . ' He lifted his big shoulders and spread his hands before Katie. 'I was young, I was very flattered, and yes, yes, I was in love . . . In love. It is a strange thing to be in love. You don't love when you are in love. You can't because you are in a state of madness. Youth and those two long years at sea, and flattery, and the man-urges that were burning me up, took me to the church as if I had all my sails trimmed to a following wind.'

He now stopped and brought his face close to hers and, tracing his fingers under her eyes, said softly, 'Don't look like that, Kaa-tee. There is nothing to worry about, I tell you, nothing.'

He straightened up again, and, his voice taking on a louder note, he went on, 'Within months I was a captain and had my own ship. Oh, Kaa-tee, it was a very good thing to be married to the daughter of an influential man.' He nodded his head slowly at her. 'I was at sea when my first child was born; it was a girl-child, and I did not see her until she was seven months old. I was at home for five weeks with her, and, of course, she did not know me. She cried when I lifted her up . . . screamed. I was always a big hairy thing. I was at sea when my second child was born; I saw her when she was a month old. My first child still screamed when I lifted her up. When I had been married for four years I became master of a bigger vessel – oh, a fine vessel. My father-in-law had a large thumb in the shipping pie, you understand.' She nodded again, her eyes fixed, unblinking, on him. 'On my first trip in the new ship I was gone for two years. When I returned I had a sixteen-month-old son, and my eldest child still screamed at the sight of me.' He smiled widely now. 'I think it was this, my child not knowing me, that made me express the wish to change ships yet again, to trade back and forward to England say, in order to be home more often and get to know my children. Strangely, my wish met with opposition, and mostly from my wife. She, it appeared, was perfectly satisfied with the situation as it was. She . . . she lived for her children, whom she spoilt, and her house, which her father had bought her.' Again he shrugged. 'A master's money is not small, but it is not big – not big enough to provide for ten rooms and a family. Yet, as big as this house was, it was no place for a great clumsy sailor who walked on the floors with his feet.' He thumbed towards his waggling toes, then laughed, and said, 'I mean with his boots on. Well, away I went again, but this time I returned two days before my fourth child was born. It was another girl. When I held her in my arms I caused a great upheaval in the family because I said I was finished with the big sail. I was going to get a ship that didn't like to wander so far. At least this last child would know me from the beginning.

'After a long fight I got my ship, but in a company in which my father-in-law had no thumb because he would not countenance this great drop in social prestige. But now I was home for nearly half the year when the sea was frozen. Not that I didn't work. Oh, I worked; there was plenty to do. But very soon I wished I wasn't at home at all, for my wife, at the age of thirty, decided she was going to have no more children. She developed a malaise; it was so bad that her mother must come and look after her. Then it was decided that this arrangement could not go on, and so it was just a matter of time before my wife takes up residence in her old home, and of course, the family go too.' Again he spread his hands. 'I am very welcome. I have two rooms set apart for me all to myself. There is a side door to them so my big feet won't dirty the hall floors which are polished every day. I talk with my children, who are always very polite to me – even my eldest, who is now nearly sixteen and thinks I am a very funny man, I make her laugh. Look, here is a picture of her.' He undid the leather case and took out a number of small thin square boards and, passing one to Katie, he said, 'That is she.'

Katie looked down at the delicate watercolour portrait of a young girl, but, strangely, she stared at it without pain. There was pain in her, but it was for him she felt the pain. She had always had an acute awareness of loneliness in people. Look how she had felt for Miss Theresa, and even for . . . Mark Bunting, but she had never sensed it in Andy until this moment. And now she saw that the loneliness in him was a big, wide, deep thing, eating at him. She looked at the portraits of the children one after the other, at the boy's face the longest; then, raising her eyes, she said, 'He looks like you.'

'Yes, he does. And I called him after me, Nils.' She screwed up her face. 'Nils? But I thought your name was Andrée.'

He laughed now. 'Andrée Fraenkel are what you call surnames and I was always called by the first one, Andrée, so I let it go. I do not like Nils anyway.'

She smiled a little and shook her head, saying, 'That's funny. It's like calling somebody here Smith or Brown or' – her smile widened a little – 'Mulholland.'

'Mulholland.' He brought her hand to his face and rubbed it down his beard. 'It is a mouthful, Mulholland.' Then, picking up a square of board, he said, 'These are my grandparents.'

'Oh, they look nice.'

'Yes, they are nice; they are good people.'

He had not shown her a portrait of his wife, nor did she ask about her, but after he had returned the squares to the leather case he looked towards the fire and said, 'Well, Kaa-tee, what do you think of me now? I have a wife and four children in Norway, and I love you. And I say I cannot live without you. What do you think of me now?'

She did not pause for a second but, thrusting out her arm, she pulled him to her as she said, 'The same as I did afore, only more so, more so. It's funny, but' – she rocked herself a little in his arms – 'I've . . . I've imagined that if you told me what you just have I would be jealous, burnt up, but I'm not. It's strange, I'm not.'

'Oh, Kaa-tee, Kaa-tee.' He went to kiss her, then stopped and, turning round and grabbing at his wallet, said, 'This thing must be settled once and for all. For days and days I have thought. I am responsible for you now; more so because it is through me your brother went. My pay on the little bucket is not as big as I used to get on the great ships – fourteen pounds a month – but I make it up with what I carry on the side.' He gave her a knowing little smile. 'From men to monkeys. But what I made hasn't really mattered up to now because my wife expects nothing from me. Because she refused to take money from me her conscience is eased, and

I leave it like that, so what I am going to do is to arrange that you have a half-pay note.'

'No, no, Andy. No.'

'Yes, yes, Kaa-tee. Yes.'

'But you won't be able to leave me anything; me not being your . . . '

'These things can be arranged; I'll see to it before I sail again.'

She gazed at him. It was as if in some magic way he had made her secure for the rest of her days. The nagging feeling of want that was never far from her mind slid away. His half-pay note, something coming in regularly. Oh, oh, she didn't deserve him, she didn't. She fell against him and they remained still, their cheeks together, their bodies joined, staring into the fire. Then, quite suddenly and for no reason that she could explain, she asked, 'Is it a beautiful house you have in Norway?' It was quite some time before he answered, 'Yes. Yes, it's a beautiful house, Kaa-tee,' and his answer saddened her.

CHAPTER FIVE

THE SIX MONTHS that followed was a period of fulfilment and was perhaps the happiest in Katie's life. Except for a nagging guilty feeling concerning Joe, and the feeling of panic she would get if Andrée's boat was late, she was at peace, and happy. Her bust developed, her hips lost their flatness, and her mind was groping and opening to knowledge as it never had done before, not even from the books Theresa had lent her, for she was seeing different places, going jaunts, as Andrée called them. She did not think it odd that it was a stranger to this land that had to show her the city of Newcastle for the first time. She saw Newcastle as a place of excitement, bustle and grandeur, with its Assembly Rooms and, of all things, a row of baths where people could go and wash. But, above all, what attracted her most in Newcastle was the wonderful theatre, and she had actually been and seen a play there. They were building a theatre in Shields but it wasn't finished yet.

All she had known about Newcastle before this visit was that it was the city that kept the rest of the towns on the Tyne poor, taxing them for the use of their own river, refusing them independence, and after her visit she could, in a way, understand the attitude of the city to the towns that crowded the river, because she saw them as servants to a master. But one servant, Shields, spat when the name of Newcastle was mentioned, for had not the vessels bound for the mouth of the Tyne to go all the way up to Newcastle to check in at the quayside so that the Newcastle Corporation could have its toll. The Shields men hated the Newcastle men. But part of that particular strife had ended in August when Shields, after a long, bitter fight, had been created a separate port, and Andrée said it was a fine step forward.

Andrée's life was linked closely with the Tyne now, for at the beginning of the winter he had left the Norwegian company and signed on, not with Palmer's who hadn't a vacancy yet, but with a firm who were running boats to Harwich and London, but by sail, which made his comings and goings still subject to wind and weather.

When next his boat docked for any considerable time he was going to take her all the way to see Alnwick Castle, and they might have to put up for the night in an inn. He loved showing her strange places. He had even said that one day he would take her to France. Oh, he was wonderful, wonderful. The thought of his kindness brought tears welling into her eyes, especially his kindness towards Lizzie. Not even her mother or father had treated Lizzie like he did. He had brought her a doll, of all things, from one of his trips. It was a clouty doll, dressed in scarlet and green. He had said he thought Lizzie would like it, but she had thought, poor Lizzie won't know it's there. But a strange thing had happened. After the doll had lain near her stomach for a day Lizzie had picked it up, and now she nursed it continuously. And another thing he had done concerning Lizzie; he had insisted that someone should be brought in to see to her when they went out. He said he didn't like the thought of her being tied up; he said he understood it was necessary sometimes but not for long stretches. Once he'd had to chain a man in the bilges because he had gone mad, and seeing Lizzie tied up reminded him of it. And so she got Meggie Proctor to come and give an eye to Lizzie, and he had made it worth her while. There had been one time when he had put off their jaunt because Meggie was bottled and incapable of even climbing the stairs.

But this period of harmony for Katie came to an end the night Meggie Proctor had visitors.

Meggie had got into the habit of popping up to the top floor whenever she was hungry, or short of a copper, and this would happen when there were few boats in the docks – at least boats with white crews, for, as Meggie openly said, she wouldn't let an Arab or a nigger within a mile of her.

At first Katie had resented Meggie's visits, and for obvious reasons, but you couldn't resent a person like Meggie for long, and now at times she even welcomed her, for Meggie was a bit of company, and she could make you laugh. Also, Meggie was tactful in her way, because she never came near the top floor when the captain was home.

The regular visits of the captain had placed Katie in a class apart, not only in the estimation of the other occupants of the house but of the whole of Crane Street, for, as they all agreed, it was a set thing, the Swede was standing by her, not here the day and gone the morrow, leaving the belly big and the heart with sorrow, like the majority of them did.

Katie was unaware in what esteem her neighbours held her; she only knew that they spoke civil to her and gave her the time of day, and no-one had poured the slops out of the window on her, as they had done on

Meggie Proctor and Jinny Wilson in the street opposite, which backed on to this one. Most of the women in that street were respectably married, with the men coming home each night from the docks; it was these and their like who never missed a chance of drenching a whore. She would have died, she told herself, if this had happened to her, for it would have put the label on her; which was why, although she welcomed Meggie into her kitchen, she would never, if she could help it, walk down the street with her.

She was, this particular evening, sitting sewing and she was being extravagant. She had two candles lit because she didn't want to strain her eyes too much and make them red. She had discovered a little shop that dealt in good-class ladies' second-hand dresses, and yesterday she had bought one and was now altering it.

She stopped sewing for a moment and lifted her moccasined feet up on to the fender and, dropping her head back, she looked at the clock, which was another present from Andrée. It was wonderful to have a clock in the house and not have to rely solely on the sun or the one o'clock time gun going off from the ballast hill across the water in North Shields. She wondered now where Andrée was, if he had reached Harwich. If the weather had held for him he would have done it in four days; that could mean he would be in at the beginning of the week, and home for Christmas. Their first Christmas together. She did not wonder if he would regret this first Christmas away from his family; she knew whom he wanted to spend his time with; there was not the smallest shred of doubt in her mind with regard to it. She only hoped he docked at Shields this trip. The last twice there hadn't been much time to see to anything, for his ship hadn't docked in the Tyne at all. It being rough weather, he had docked in Sunderland the first time, then at Hartlepool, the water being deeper in both places and not so much chance of the ship going on the Black Middens, or the hard sands, outside of Shields harbour. She was afraid even of hearing any mention of the Black Middens, for it was only a few years ago that thirty-three sailing vessels sheltering from a storm had been dashed to pieces on these sands.

But Andrée said that, with the new innovation of the dredging to clear the channels and the new piers of the North and South Towns forming a safe harbour at the mouth of the river, Shields would soon be a first-rate port. She didn't know about it becoming a first-rate port; the only thing that concerned her was that Andrée's ship should go safely in and out, and not have to go to Sunderland or Hartlepool, because that meant he could spend less time with her.

She folded up the dress and put the kettle on the fire, which was low now, and she decided not to make it up again but to go to bed. What was there to sit up for? Besides which, she never wasted coal . . . or food. Although she loved food and always had done, she kept her fare very meagre except when Andrée was home, and this had enabled her to save a few shillings each week out of the pound that she was allotted.

She took some hot thin gruel in to Lizzie and made her comfortable. Lizzie's condition was changing and puzzling Katie; she was not eating so much but her body was expanding noticeably. She wondered if she should get a doctor, but asked herself what could a doctor do? Only physic her. Anyway, she decided to leave the matter until Andrée came back. He always seemed to know the right way to tackle anything . . .

It was half an hour later, as she lay in bed on the point of sleep, that there came to her the sound of muffled laughter and footsteps on the stairs. The laughter roused her, and as she recognised Meggie's voice she thought to herself, 'She's got a load on by the sound of her. I hope she's not coming here.' But a few minutes later it was evident that Meggie was coming to visit her, as there came a knock on the door and Meggie called softly, 'Katie, Katie. Open up a minute. Katie. Come on, open up: I want a word with ye.'

This was not the first time that Meggie had paid her a visit when she was drunk, and from experience she knew it would be no use telling her to go away. She shook the sleep from her, pulled herself up out of the bed and, groping her way towards the table, picked up the candlestick, took the candle out and lit it in the dying embers of the fire; then, sticking it back into the socket, she went towards the door.

As she undid the bolt the door was pushed quickly forward, almost overbalancing her, and Meggie stumbled into the room. She was, Katie saw, very drunk, and Meggie could be very nasty when in drink, so she said to her quietly, 'Aw, Meggie, I was . . . '

Before she could say 'abed' Meggie had thrown her arm backwards and cried, 'Come on. Come on in.' Then, turning to Katie, she said, 'I've brought me friends. You're not the only bugger who's got friends with money, Katie Mulholland, you're not the only bugger. Come in. Come on in.' She now waved to the two dim figures on the landing, and one of them came forward and into the light cast by the candle which Katie still held in her hand. He was a town man, she saw instantly, by his dress; also that he was of the class. He was a man in his middle years, portly, with a red face and a little beard under his chin.

As the man's eyes swept over her she bent sideways and made a grab at her skirt lying with her clothes across a chair, and as she held it in front of her she lifted the candle higher and cried to the man, 'Get out! Get out, I tell you!'

'Now look here, Katie Mulholland, divn't get on your high horse; ye're no better than ye should be, so don't put on airs. We're all lasses together in this hoose . . . Come on you in.' She again waved towards the landing, and a man came out of the darkness and through the doorway, and when he stepped forward the light from the candle fell on to his face.

The very last time Katie had seen this man it had been in the light of a candle. In the five years that had elapsed Bernard Rosier had changed; he had become fatter, and his face redder, but there was no mistaking him. As their eyes met in recognition Katie felt the blood draining from her body. One minute, such was the shock she felt she would collapse under it; the next minute there was tearing through her a wave of rage and she heard herself screaming, 'You! You, get out! Get out of my house!'

His eyes were narrowed, his face was smiling, one corner of his clean-shaven mouth was lifted upward, but nothing of him moved except his head, and that slowly began to lower itself while his eyes still remained on her. Under his smiling gaze her rage seemed to lift her from the ground. One second she was still holding the candlestick, the next it was hurtling through the air. At some point, the candle leaving it made an arch of light, and before it fell to the ground she saw that she had not missed in her aim. There was a loud cry and the dark room became full of curses, mingled with Meggie's screeching.

When a match was struck and held aloft she saw Bernard Rosier leaning against the doorway, his face covered with blood that was running from a gash above his eye. There was another voice from the landing now which Katie dimly recognised as Mrs Robson's. She had a candle in her hand and she held it high above the three figures crowded in the doorway.

'What's all this?' she was saying. 'What's all this? It sounds like murder. What are you about? I'll get the pollis.'

'It's her! It's her!' Meggie was screaming now. 'She hit him with the candlestick. He's my friend. We just come up to see her. She's mad.'

'Trollops, the lot of you. Get down, out of here. Get down to your own place, Meggie Proctor, or I'll have the pollis called in, I'm tellin' you. Decent people can't sleep in their beds.'

'Look at his face. Look at his face. It wasn't us, it was her. My God! Look what she's done to his face.' Meggie was now pointing to Bernard Rosier, and he, with his blood-covered hand pressed against the cut over his eye, was staring across the room to where Katie, her back to the table, held in her hand the other brass candlestick, and in a position from where it could come flying at him at any moment.

'Come on, B. Come on, let's get out of here.' The older man had to pull Bernard Rosier from the room, and on the landing he said, 'Let me have that candle,' and Mrs Robson answered, 'Get out! Find your way down as you found your way up.' The man swore at her; then, pressing Bernard Rosier before him, they groped their way after Meggie, who was still screaming virulently.

Mrs Robson now stepped into the room and, coming to Katie, she took the candlestick from her hand, picked up the candle from the floor and lit it from her own, and placing it on the table she said, grimly, 'I don't blame you for this, so I won't do anything about it. I heard her bringin' them up an' yappin' on my landin'. But if I thought you had asked them up I'd tell your Swede, 'cos I like fair do's. I don't like to see a man made a monkey out of.'

On this, the woman who had always complained about Lizzie's crying turned abruptly and went out and closed the door behind her.

Katie, groping towards a chair, sat down. One hand was still holding the skirt over her breast. The feeling of rage was gone, and in its place was fear. It was the same kind of fear that she had experienced that night in his room. On that night he hadn't opened his mouth, nor had he tonight; and as on that occasion his silence had spoken louder than any words, so had his visit tonight. As she remembered the look in his eyes when the other man had pulled him around and through the doorway she began to whimper, very like Lizzie did, and then to say over and over again, 'Oh, Andy, Andy.' She said his name louder and louder, as if the incantation would ward off some evil, some evil that she knew was about to befall her.

It was three hours later when she went to bed and she was still telling herself that she was no longer a child, she was twenty-one years old; she was a woman, and she had Andrée behind her now. But it was of little use. The feeling of evil Rosier had left in the room was filling the air and she was breathing it in.

The following day every movement on the stairs brought her to a quivering standstill. She rose early before the house was astir, and, making three journeys to the backyard in the dark, brought up a good supply of water. She had got this task over early because she didn't want to come face to face with Meggie.

The day passed and no-one knocked on her door, and when at last she allowed herself to go to bed the main thought in her mind was, Whatever he's going to do he's not going to bring the pollis. But this thought didn't lessen her apprehension, and the following morning it was increased if anything.

When in the afternoon she had to go out to get in some food, she found herself tiptoeing down the stairs, and she almost ran there and back to the shop; so that, on reaching the landing, there was a stitch in her side and her breath was coming quickly. As she unlocked the door she gazed around the room amazed that she should find her furniture still intact. Dropping the bass bag on to the table, she now hurried across the room and looked in on Lizzie, where she sat with the doll on her stomach, her eyes fixed on it, and she leant against the stanchion of the door, opening her mouth wide and taking in great gulps of air.

Going back into the kitchen, she sat down before unpacking the groceries. She'd have to pull herself together; she couldn't go on like this. If only she had someone to talk to, someone to tell her fears to. If only Joe was here. She could have told Joe the whole story, whereas she'd only be able to tell Andy part of it. But there, if Joe had been here Meggie would never have brought her friends upstairs. The whole thing would never have happened. What was coming upon her? Was it the Bible retribution because, as Joe had said, she was bad . . . No! No! Whatever came upon her wouldn't be because she was bad, because she wasn't bad. If living with Andy was bad, then there was nothing good in the world. She wasn't bad. She wasn't. She wasn't like them downstairs. Yet because she lived in this house, and this quarter, and had Andy, she had their stamp on her. It wasn't fair. It wasn't . . . 'Stop it!' She had spoken aloud, and still aloud she said, 'Pull yourself together, woman.'

She got up and unpacked the groceries, but in the middle of doing this she turned and looked towards the door. She hadn't bolted it. Moving swiftly towards it she shot the bolt in, then stood for a moment biting her lip before she returned to the table to finish her unpacking.

CHAPTER SIX

IT WAS FIVE o'clock on Christmas Eve and Andy hadn't come, and he wouldn't come now because the tide was going down.

Last week she had bought one or two baubles in the market to hang around the chimney piece. There was a fancy paper doll in red and blue, there was a coloured paper chain and a paper clown dangling from a spring, but she did not hang them up. What was the use? There was no joy in her, nothing she did seemed able to move the fear that weighed on her. She had sat before the fire until it lost its heat, and she was preparing for bed when she heard the quick heavy tread on the stairs. Her hands cupping her face, she stood gazing towards the door, and when the handle turned and the voice came to her, saying 'Kaa-tee, there. Kaa-tee', she stumbled towards it, and after fumbling at the bolt opened it and fell into his arms, and to his astonishment she burst into tears.

'Kaa-tee! Kaa-tee! Oh, my Kaa-tee, what is it? Wait. Wait, wait a moment.' He pressed her from him. Then, stepping back on to the landing, he pulled in his bag and lifted another tall package gently into the room, and, hastily closing the door, went to her where she was standing now, her back to the table, her face bowed in her hands, and again she was in his arms and he was saying, 'Kaa-tee, tell me what is the matter. Why are you like this?'

She tried to speak, but her crying choked her words and he stood bewildered, stroking her hair, looking round the room the while as if searching for an answer to her distress. And then his eyes came to rest on the bedroom door and he thought he had found it, and the pressure of his arms increased as he said, 'Lizzie?' Then again, 'Lizzie?' But when her head moved against his neck he again looked about him; then, pressing her from him, he demanded sternly, 'Tell me. Listen to me, Kaa-tee. Tell me what has happened to cause this . . . Them?' He now thumbed the floor, and again she shook her head.

'What then? Come, you must tell me. Your brother?'

'No, no.' She forced the words out. 'I'm . . . I'm sorry, Andy. It . . . it was like this.' She put out her hand and, gripping his, moved towards the fireplace and the high-backed wooden chair, and when he had sat down he took her on his knee and she put her arms about him and laid her head against his neck and told him what had happened. And when she finished speaking and he made no comment she raised her face and looked at him, but he was staring into the fire and it was a second or so before he brought his gaze to hers, and then he said, 'This man's name. You have told me everything but his name.'

'I can't, Andy. No, no, I can't. I'm . . . I'm frightened. I don't want any more trouble; I've had enough, Andy, I've had enough.'

'But can't you see, Kaa-tee.' He now gripped her shoulder. 'You're having trouble all the time, and you're living in fear of more trouble. Let me put a stop to it. Tell me who it is.'

'No, Andy.' She pulled herself away from him and to her feet. 'I'll never do that, never.'

He was sitting on the edge of the chair now with his beard thrust out to her. 'I can find out; there are ways and means. I can go to the house where it all started and work back from there.'

'It won't help you. Please, Andy, please.' She turned to him, her hands joined on her breast. 'Just let it go now. But I had to tell you because . . . because I've been so worried, I thought he would send the pollis.'

'God Almighty!' He sprang to his feet. 'I can't go away and leave you and think of you worrying like this waiting for a pollis man to come through the door every minute.'

She smiled. 'Oh, Andy, you're not in the house yet and talkin' of going away. I'm sorry, I'm sorry.'

Her arms were around his neck again. 'I should have kept it to myself. Come on, nothing matters now, nothing, nothing, nothing.' She made her smile wider. 'How long have you got?'

He didn't answer for some seconds, just gazed at her face; and then he said, 'Three or four days – perhaps more, because they won't load on the holiday.'

'Oh, good. Good. So let's forget it. Let's forget about everything.'

'Yes, let's forget it, as you say, Kaa-tee, let's forget it.' He kissed her hard now, after which he cried, 'See what I've brought you,' and going across the room he picked up the large package that was standing against the wall and brought it to the table, on which he put it down gently and said, 'Guess what I have here!'

She stood close to his side and looked at the tall parcel, and she smiled as she shook her head. 'I can't. I haven't an idea.'

'Wait, wait.' Rapidly now he pulled off the string and the paper and lifted into the middle of the table a glass lamp. Then he looked at her face, at the light and pleasure spreading over the tear-stains.

'Oh, Andy, Andy, how beautiful.' She put out her hand and stroked the pale, pink-tinted oil bowl of the tall lamp, then traced her fingers down the slender blue stem to the scalloped base. 'Where . . .where did you get it?'

'Here' – his big blond head was bouncing up and down – 'in Shields.'

'Here?' She sounded incredulous.

'You should have had it two trips ago. Candles! What do people want candles for these days when there are oil lamps and gas coming in? So when I saw Orm's little lamp – Orm, he is my bo'sun – it was so tiny, like so . . . He measured about two inches between his finger and thumb. 'Like this one in every detail. It was swinging from the end of his bunk.' He wagged his forefinger. 'Swing, swing, swing. "Where did you get that?" I said to Orm. "In Shields, sir," he said. "I know a family there who all work in the glassworks. The father is very clever." "Do you think he could make a big one like yours?" I asked him, and he said "Ja", he was sure, but I would have to wait for it; just at spare times his master let him create something for himself . . . And there it is.'

'Oh, thank you, darlin', thank you, thank you.' She was enfolding him again, and when he saw the tears in her eyes once more he cried, 'But she's no good without oil and there is only a little in her. Come, we'll go out shopping. But first my bag.'

Now, bringing his sailor's bag on to the mat before the fire, he pulled out his gifts and handed them to her: coffee, butter, tea. He held the tea aloft, saying, 'You have tasted nothing like this. China . . . A-ah!' He smacked his tongue against the roof of his mouth and they both laughed as he ended, 'It's nearly as good as gin. And mocha . . . Coffee; oh, it's good, first thing in the morning after much drink.' Again they were laughing. Then he handed her up a ham, a whole ham, and candies, three boxes of them, and last, from the bottom of the bag, he tumbled a length of woollen material, and as he pushed it into her hands his face stretched into a wide grin as he said, 'For bloomers, warm bloomers.'

'Oh, Andy! Andy.' She was on her knees, half laughing, half crying as she hugged the piece of material to her breast and rocked herself back and forward, and as she gazed at him she kept repeating his name.

Lastly he put his hand into the inner pocket of his jacket and brought out a small, hard, black case and, handing it to her, said, 'Yuletide gift to my Kaa-tee.'

When she opened the box she saw lying on a bed of red velvet a fine gold chain with a heart-shaped locket on the end. She raised her mist-filled eyes towards him, unable for the moment to say anything. Then she opened the locket, and there, gazing back at her, was a miniature portrait of himself. The other side of the locket was blank and, pointing to it, he said, 'Your likeness – that is for your likeness, I will have you painted.'

The locket cupped in her two hands, she stared at him. Then her body crumpled up against him and again she was sobbing unrestrainedly, and this time it seemed as if she would never stop.

Andrée sailed the day before New Year's Eve. He went on the morning tide. It was bitterly cold and there was a light breeze blowing, and after seeing to Lizzie she had hurried along the river bank, and there in the early light she had seen his ship, guided by a little tugboat, making downriver for the opening in the piers. Long after it had passed from her sight she had stood until, the cold penetrating to her bones, she turned slowly about.

She did not make her way straight home but went towards King Street, cutting through the market place, which was thronged, even at this early hour, with shoppers storing in food for the New Year festivities. She noticed that beyond the town hall the windmill rearing high up above the houses in the corner of the square stood out starkly against the low grey sky. This was a sure sign of bad weather, and she prayed that it would hold off until Andy got well out into deep water. She made her way between a herd of sheep and horse-drawn carts laden with everything from potatoes to squealing pigs, past the women who sold their vegetables from deep wicker baskets, past the rows of stalls, taking care to avoid the women hawkers with their wares slung on their backs who almost pushed you over to make you buy, and so she came to King Street and the chemist's.

She had seen in the *Shields Gazette* last Saturday an advertisement which said that the chemist had a cure for dropsy, and that's what Andy said was wrong with Lizzie, she was swelling with water. When he was home the trip before last they had gone across to North Shields to a chemist there. This journey had been the result of another advertisement in the *Gazette*, but the medicine for which Andy had paid two shillings a bottle had no effect on Lizzie, except to make her sleep.

The chemist in King Street only charged her ninepence for the medicine and told her it might take up to three months' treatment before she saw any noticeable change in the patient.

On her return journey she skirted the market place and took a short cut home, and when she came down the steep hill of Thames Street into Lower Thames Street, which ran parallel to the river, she collided with two children, a boy of about six and a little girl of about four years old. The boy was holding the child's hand, and neither had a coat on. The child was wearing a dirty serge frock and her feet, like her brother's, were bare, and on the small heels of both children and on the backs of their hands were smears of blood from the keens and chaps that were splitting the skin.

That was one thing she'd never had to suffer from, bare feet. Joe for a time had gone barefooted, but her granda had seen that that had never happened to her, for he'd had a knack of making a rough kind of shoe out of old boot tops. He would sit and knead the leather between his tallow-coated hands for hours at a time, until it was pliable.

'Wait,' she said to the boy as they went to pass her, and opening her purse she brought out a shilling. 'You've got a ma?' she asked.

'Aye, missus.' The boy moved his head slowly.

'Your da, is he working?'

'Aye, missus; he's at sea.'

She knew what that meant; she had learned from Andy that it wasn't only miners, and shipyard men, and the farm labourers who worked for a mere pittance; the sailor's wage was not only desperately low but his food and the conditions under which he worked were horrifying. She said now, 'Have you any brothers and sisters?'

'We've got nine, missus. We had ten, but Jimmy he got buried last week. He was older than Bess here . . . next to me.'

She bent right down now until her face was on a level with his. She wanted to take her handkerchief and wipe his running nose. His hair was black, but white-streaked with nits. There, too, she had been lucky, for her mother had fought a constant war against body lice, bugs, and dickies in their heads. As she gazed pitifully at the children she realised that in an odd way her early years had been good. She said, 'I live at No. 14, Crane Street. Do you know where Crane Street is?'

'Aye, missus; along there opposite the river.'

'Well, do you think you could come every Saturday morning and I'll see what I've got for you.'

He looked at the shilling in his hand, then looked up into her face and said solemnly, 'Aye, missus. Aye, I will.'

'Take that to your mother now.'

'Aye, missus. Ta, missus.'

They moved on, their feet making no sound on the filth-strewn road.

Once in the house she slowly took off her things, looked into the room to see that Lizzie was all right, then, coming to the fire, she poked it and drew her chair close to it; and she sat for a long time staring into the flames, thinking of Andrée, wishing him clear of the sandbars. After a while she began to think of the two children and the blood running out of their hands and feet, and from thoughts of them her mind went to Sarah. It was the first time for many a long day that she had allowed herself to dwell on her child. She would be five years old now. Was she bonny? Oh yes, she would be bonny. She'd be talking too, talking differently from what she herself did, talking like Miss Ann and Miss Rose . . . like Miss Theresa. Through the years there had been, deep down, a bitterness in her and a feeling of resentment against her mother and Joe for persuading her to part with her child, but mostly against her mother; but since she had known Andrée the feeling had lessened. She would always regret having given up her child, yet in a way she was glad she had given her a chance of a new way of life. Here her lot would have been that of a child of the riverside; perhaps not like those two children she had seen a short while ago, for she would have kept her child clean, spotlessly clean, but she could not have done anything about her environment, because Lizzie would have dictated their environment. She heard a voice saying in her head, 'I would like to see her. Just for a moment, and hear her speak.' The voice brought her to her feet. No! No! She must never do that; she must never try to see her, because once she saw her she would never know peace again.

What she must do was to have another child. She was surprised that she hadn't fallen before now. She would love to have a child by Andy . . . Oh, and the company it would be when he was away. And not only one: two, three, as many as time would allow.

She couldn't have too much of anything that was Andy's. She didn't question that she had no claim on him to keep them; as long as Andy lived he would see to her and all that was hers, of this she felt sure.

On New Year's Eve it snowed heavily and the whiteness turned the drab, smoke-blackened view from her window into a pretty picture. Everything outside looked bright and lighter, but inside the house, inside her heart everything was dull and heavy. She felt more lonely today than she had done since Joe left the house. She had hoped that, it being New Year's Eve, the first New Year's Eve they had been separated since they were children, he would let bygones be bygones and pop in.

There was preparation and bustle for the New Year all about her. The house was noisy. She had heard Meggie's voice from down below shouting, and calling, a number of times. She had not seen Meggie since that awful night, nor did she want to. There had been two fights in the street today so far; she had watched one of them from the little window in Joe's room that faced the street. It was between two women. Women fighting were always more ferocious than men, she thought. Men struck out with their closed fists, but women tore with their clawed hands, kicked and bit. Before it was over she had returned to the kitchen. She heard the yelling of the second fight, but she did not go across the landing and into the room to see what it was all about. Fighting sickened her.

Then, in the early evening, she had no time to think of her loneliness because Lizzie had one of her wailing fits, and she could do nothing to quieten her.

Lizzie sat, as upright as she could, making this wailing noise, and after some time Katie became apprehensive of the effect on Mrs Robson. She kept listening for her neighbour's step on the stairs. Mrs Robson had spoken kindly to her after the business with Meggie that night, but she hadn't seen her since. She was a woman who kept herself to herself, but on New Year's Eve she wasn't likely to put up with Lizzie's wailing without making some protest. In desperation she put her arms about Lizzie and rocked her, saying, 'There, there. Give over, Lizzie. Give over.' But Lizzie, her loose mouth wide open, took no heed of Katie's plea and continued to emit this weird, penetrating, animal-sounding wail.

It was around half-past six that the thing she feared came about. It began as a sort of distant confabulation, and when it died away she thought that Mrs Robson had gone down to consult with Meggie Proctor and Jinny Wilson as to what should be done about the awful noise up above. But then she could hardly have reached the ground floor when the knock came on the door. Katie paused before going to open it, and when she did she had her hand to her throat. It was an apprehensive gesture, but her expression of apprehension changed to complete bewilderment when she was confronted by two young women whom she had never seen in her life before. From the light of the lamp she could see their faces plainly and those of the two men standing behind them. One minute, as she stared at them, there was silence; the next, the room was filled with such a hullabaloo she wondered if she had gone crazy, because this wasn't like a New Year's call of any kind. Besides, they were utter strangers. The girls had pushed her aside and dashed into the room and were racing around yelling and shouting, and the men after them. It was as if the four had been released by the same spring, and as she stood, holding her head and yelling at them, screaming at them, there came a sound of quick, hard footsteps on the stairs, and in the doorway appeared two policemen, and Katie turned to them as if to rescuers and cried, 'Get them out! Get them out!' and the two policemen got them out. They pushed them on to the stairs, where one policeman remained with them and the other came back into the room and said to her, 'Get your coat.' He nodded towards the back of the half-open door.

'What?' She swallowed deeply, bringing her head forward with the effort. Then she put her fingers to the side of her mouth and after staring at him in stupefaction for a moment she said quietly, 'But I needn't go, I've done nothing. They forced themselves.'

'Come along,' he said, 'I know all about it.' As he put his hand out to touch her she sprang back and cried angrily. 'What do you mean, you know all about it? You know about what? I've never seen those people in my life afore, not until a minute or so ago.'

He moved a slow step towards her, saying, 'Now look here, lass, I don't want to handle you, but if I have to I will. I'm givin' you a choice; get your coat or I'll take as you as are.' Again she was holding her head in her hands and, her voice almost a whimper, she said, 'But you can't, you can't, I've done nothin'.' She moved her hand in a low sweep towards the bedroom door. 'Listen. That's me sister. She's sick, very sick, I can't leave her.'

'Somebody'll see to her. Come on.'

'No.' Her voice was again loud. Then she repeated, 'No!' But even as she yelled her defiance at him and told herself it was all a mistake, it would soon be cleared up, her whole body was swamped with fear.

When he came at her, after whipping her cloak from the back of the door, she beat him off with her fists and struck at him until her arm was twisted behind her back and her body bent double, and like this she was thrust out of the door and down the stairs, and some part of her mind noticed that all the other doors in the house were closed.

She stopped crying out when she reached the street, but when she came to the end of it she clutched at a lamp-post with one hand, and in a loud voice appealed to three men standing within the range of light. 'I've done nothin',' she cried out. 'I've done nothin'. Help me. Help me. I tell you I've done nothin'.' Her arm was wrenched almost from its socket and she cried out again, but in agony from the pain this time. When they reached the police station in Chapter Row she was pushed into a room where the two young girls were sitting on a form. There was no sign of the men.

Once the policeman had released his hold on her she staggered towards the girls and, bending over them, she beseeched them, 'Tell them, will you tell them, I've done nothing? Tell them I don't know you. Do I?'

The eldest girl, who had a thin face capped by tattered fair hair, looked up at her coldly, and her answer was, 'Shut thy gob.'

Katie slowly straightened her body and stared down into the upraised faces, into the cold, narrowed eyes.

Then she swung round to where the two policemen were talking to another one behind the counter, and the policeman who had handled her was saying, 'We got the tip-off . . . procuring. That'll be the charge, procuring. The fellows got away but the lasses will testify.'

The policeman behind the counter put his head to one side and looked at Katie over the shoulder of the man who had been speaking. He looked her up and down and then he looked back at the policeman, and, bending forward, he whispered something in his ear, and to this the policeman said, 'Oh no. It's her all right. We've had our eye on her for some time. Starts by being kind to a family you know.' He nodded, then cast his eyes back to Katie. 'The old game. Saw her at it just this mornin'. Gave a shilling to a bairn. We talked to him after. She told him to go round every Satada mornin'. She had asked him how many there were in the family. Same old game.'

The man behind the counter had continued to look at Katie all the time the policeman had been talking. Then, taking his eyes from her, he wrote something in a book before saying, 'Well, we're nearly full up here, and by mornin' comes we'll be pushing out at the seams; you'd better take her along to the Cross.'

'What about the two lasses?' asked the policeman who had brought them in. 'There's nothing really on them. They said she invited them to the house for a bite and then she produced these fellows.'

'Have you got their names and addresses?'

'Aye,' said the policeman. 'And I know them.'

'Then let them go; we'll get them when we want them. Here.' He beckoned towards the two girls with a lift of his head, and when they stood at the counter he stared at them hard before saying, 'Get yourselves off home, and let this be a lesson to you.'

They nodded at him. Then, turning around, they went out without looking in Katie's direction.

'Please, please.' Now she was at the counter gripping its edge and bending towards the man behind it, imploring him to listen to her. 'Please, it's all a mistake, I tell you. I've done nothing. It's . . . it's a put-up job, it is. Will you listen to me.'

'Now! Now! You'd better be careful what you're sayin', put-up job.' The man pushed out his chest and patted each side of it with a thick, short hand. 'Put up by who? What would anybody go to that trouble for? You've been caught red-handed, so face up to it.'

'I tell you, I tell you . . . ' She stopped suddenly and, her voice dropping, she looked wildly about her and muttered, 'I must have help. I must have help.'

'Have you any relations around?'

'Only a brother in Jarrow.'

'What's his name?'

'Joseph Mulholland.'

'Address?'

She lowered her head; then shook it, saying, 'I . . . I don't rightly know. He lives with people called Hetherington, somewhere off Ormonde Street. It's, it's Mayhew Street, I think. Mayhew Street . . . Please . . . ' She put her hand out across the counter towards him.

'He'll be notified.' He now looked at the other policeman and, jerking his head, said, 'Get going.' And they got going. They stood, one on each side of her, and like that they walked her out of the room and into the crowded street and through the crowded town towards the market place, which only that morning she had crossed on her way to the chemist's. And they took her to the town hall where there were four, dark, damp cells, and in one they locked her up and she started to scream. She screamed for an hour until a woman came and slapped her hard across the mouth, and then she became quiet.

CHAPTER SEVEN

IT WAS THE third day of January 1866. The magistrate took his seat at ten o'clock in the morning and noted that the first case he had to deal with was of one Mrs Bunting, commonly known as Katie Mulholland. Her offence: procuring young females for improper purposes. He made a motion with his head to the clerk of the court, who made a motion with his head to the usher, and Katie Mulholland was brought in.

The magistrate glanced at the prisoner and his eyes were returning to the paper before him when they switched back to the woman in the box. Her face was beautiful, tragic, the eyes holding a wild stare. The clothes, although rumpled and dirty, were not of the usual quality and type associated with a . . . He looked down at the paper again . . . procuress. He looked at her long and hard, and he continued to look at her long and hard before he said, 'You are charged, Catherine Bunting, with the offence of enticing two young females to your house, there to use them for improper purposes for your own gain. Do you plead guilty or not guilty?'

'Not guilty.'

'Speak up.'

'Not guilty.'

The magistrate continued to stare at the prisoner while he sat back in his chair and let the case take its course. He listened to the policeman's evidence of how he had watched the house in No. 14 Crane Street for some time. It was frequented by foreigners, mostly from the ships.

When the prisoner was asked, she admitted to being visited by a Swedish captain. When she was asked how often, she couldn't give any definite reply. Then came the two girls, the main witnesses. The magistrate saw them as low, ignorant, slovenly types, who could be easily led into this sensual and shameful life. One of the girls said she had worked in the pipe factory since she was eight years old, the other worked in the whiting factory. She had been there since she was seven. They both said they earned enough money to keep them, and, as one said, she had no need to whore for it. She was strongly chastised for using this word in court and she begged the magistrate's pardon. They both swore that they had never solicited men. One of the girls said she often went into Saint Hilda's Church and that she was a good girl. This was the one who explained that they had met the prisoner that day in the market and she had invited them around to her house for a sup of something and a bite, it being New Year's Eve; and they'd hardly set foot in the door when she brought the two men from the bedroom, and these men had set about them. When this particular girl had begun to describe what the men had tried to do the magistrate silenced them, saying that the court understood fully what the men had intended to do.

And then the prisoner was standing before him again. She was crying and talking rapidly in a hysterical fashion, shouting about lies and the whole thing being planned. The magistrate found himself listening to her, and he knew that he would have discounted the evidence of the two girls if it hadn't been for that of the policeman and the fact that the woman herself admitted to receiving foreign sailors into her house, although she had only admitted to one man.

When the prisoner became silent and stood staring at him in a most disconcerting fashion, he leant over the bench and asked of the clerk if she had any relations, and when told she had a brother but he was not in court, nor had he been seen, the magistrate nodded his head. A man would not like to recognise a sister who had gone the way of this one.

It was noteworthy that if the case had been the last one of the day the sentence passed on Catherine Bunting would have been twelve months; as it was, she got off lightly. 'I sentence you to three months,' said the magistrate, 'in the house of correction, and during that time I hope you will come to see the error of your ways.'

It was almost a fortnight later when Andrée came up the stairs and, turning the handle of the door and finding it locked, called, 'Open up there, Kaa-tee. Open up.'

When silence greeted him he took his fist and banged on a panel, and when there was still no reply he looked towards the little table on the landing where had always stood the wooden bucket and the washbasin. It was no longer there, not the washbasin or the wooden bucket or the table.

'Kaa-tee! Kaa-tee!' After banging on the door again he looked down the stairs, and there at the foot stood Mrs Robson, and with her head well back

she called up to him, 'It's no use doing that, she's not there any more.'
He left his bag where it was on the landing and slowly went down the
stairs, and when he had almost reached the bottom he stopped and,
hanging over her, said, 'What did you say?'

Mrs Robson was a thin, tight-faced little woman and her voice had a
tight sound too, but there was a kindly note in it as she replied, 'Just what
I told you. She's not there any more; they took her away.'

Now he was standing in front of her, his hairy face close to hers, so
close that she lent back to get away from it – she didn't like hairy men.
'Look . . . ' She cast her eyes down the next flight of stairs. 'Come in a
minute.'

He followed her into the room, and the first thing his bewildered gaze
alighted on, amidst a clutter of oddments on a dresser, was the glass
lamp he had bought Katie at Christmas. His head down, his beard tight
against his breast he stared at it; then, pointing a finger towards it, he
turned to her and said, 'How did you come by that?'

'Well' – she closed her eyes while at the same time raising her eyebrows
– 'if I hadn't taken it the others would have nabbed it. I took as much as
I could 'cos I knew you'd be back. I wasn't pinching anythin'; I don't want
her stuff. You can have them any minute you like. I only hope you
manage to get the rest back as easy. They're down below; both of them
had their whack.'

'Look. Look.' His voice came from deep within his body. 'Tell me,
where is she? Kaa-tee.'

'She's in prison, doing three months.'

She watched him take off his hat and lift the hair from his brow before
she said, 'They said in the court that she was keeping a bad house.'

'A bad house?' His face was screwed up, his clear blue eyes lost behind
his narrowed lids.

'Aye, that's what they said. You were mentioned – not by name, just
as . . . well, as sort of her having foreign sailors.'

'You me . . . an . . . ' He drew the words out, then repeated, 'You
me . . . an she has gone to prison because of me?' He stuck one finger in
the middle of his blue, cloth coat.

'Well, no, not you alone . . . ' Mrs Robson folded her arms across her
chest, and before she could go on he barked at her, 'What do you mean,
not me alone? You would say Kaa-tee . . . ?'

'Now don't get all worked up, I'm not sayin' nowt. I'm just tellin' you
what they said in court. But I can give you me opinion, if you want that.'

'Your opinion?' He was staring at her, but not seeing her; at the moment he seemed only capable of listening to her words, then repeating them. They had locked his Kaa-tee up for keeping a bad house, and he was part of that bad house. But his Kaa-tee keeping a bad house? God Almighty! His Kaa-tee with the white light all about her. He never looked at her but he saw her through a white light, the white light of pure love, something which few men experienced but which he had with Kaa-tee. He heard the woman say, 'Now take your hands off me and don't get rough, 'cos it won't work.'

He shook his head and loosened his grip on Mrs Robson's shoulder; and, standing back from her, he said, 'I'm sorry; I have been shocked . . . ' Then: 'Lizzie. What about Lizzie?'

'They took her to the workhouse. An' the best place, I should say. Sit yourself down.' She pointed to a wooden chair against the scrubbed white table. Then she sat down opposite to him and, leaning across the table, whispered, 'If you want to know what I think, the whole thing was a frame-up.'

He stared at her and repeated her words, but only in his mind now, and waited for her to go on. 'You see, it was like this. I heard a bit of a kerfuffle on the stairs, an' since that night when that Meggie brought her pals up here I've had me ears skinned; besides which I was out to catch them young brats that goes round the doors knockin' at the rappers. Three months they can get if they're caught. Not that the slops don't want something better to do than go hounding bits of bairns for a bit of a game.'

When he made an uneasy movement she said, 'Aye, well, I'm comin' to it; just give me a minute. I was just sayin' about them rappin'. Well, there I was, standin' behind the door 'cos I'd heard the creepin' on the stairs, you see, and then they stood on me landin' there and started to jabber, low like, so I put me ear to the keyhole, but I couldn't hear what they were sayin', except for one thing. An' I heard this twice. The same thing. It was, "Five minutes he give us." That's what I heard. An' I heard it twice, as I said, an' it didn't make sense, not till after. Then I heard them go upstairs, quiet like at first, and then I heard her, Katie Mulholland, comin' out of the bedroom where that lass had been wailin' all the afternoon. Shockin' it was; I was for goin' up. If it hadn't been New Year's Eve an' her on her own, like, I would have gone an' played hell, but I didn't. An' I heard her comin' across the floor, and then all hell was let loose. I'm tellin' you you'd think somebody was bein' murdered. Well, I was goin' to open the door . . . well, I had it open, but I shut it right quick when I heard some more comin' up the stairs. I didn't know then they were the slops. Then I heard Katie scream. God, did she scream! The Lizzie one had nothin' on her that night. She screamed blue murder. An' then they all came downstairs, and she was screaming all the way . . . '

He put his hand out and stopped her flow, and after a moment, during which his lips were drawn in and lost behind the mass of fair hair, he asked, 'Did you know the people who went upstairs, the . . . the men?'

'No, I didn't see hilt nor hair of them, not even the day in court when she was brought up; but the lasses were there, an' I can tell you for nowt they're as much good as a six weeks' unsmoked haddock.'

'The names?' he said.

'I don't rightly know their names, except they're known as Sue and Bridget. I heard that outside the court. But I can tell you who'll know all about them. Him that runs the *Anchor*, he'll know about them or I'm very much mistaken . . . Look,' she said, 'will I make you a cup of tea? I've got some tea.'

'Thank you.' He rose slowly to his feet. 'Thank you, but no.' Then, looking around the room, his eyes picked out the chiffonier with Katie's china on it, and her books, and he said, 'The rest of the things are down below, you say?'

'Aye, atween the two of 'em. But it's not much use takin' them, is it, 'cos you can't get them in upstairs.'

He turned and faced her fully and, his eyes narrowing again, he said, and in a tone that he hadn't used before, for it held a deep threat, 'It will all go back where it belongs, Mrs Robson, or else they will answer to me. If there's a spoon missing they will answer to me.' His tone changing again, he said, 'But I thank you, I thank you for what you did. And I'll tell you this also. I'll have Kaa-tee out of that place quicker than the wind can fill a sail.' On this he turned from her and, going out of the room and up the stairs, picked up his bag, and when he came to the bottom floor he rested the bag against the outer door and, returning to the hallway, banged first on one door and then on the other, and yelled in a loud voice, 'I'm coming back for Kaa-tee's things. Do you hear me in there? I'll be back.' He waited a moment, and when the door did not open and no voice answered he picked up his bag again and marched down the street to the docks and his ship.

But Andrée was to find that he couldn't get Katie out of that place quicker than the wind would fill a sail. For two days he went round the town gathering information. He started with the police station, but found it was like beating his head against a stone wall, a stone wall of prejudice. He was a foreigner; the woman he was enquiring about was not his wife, just a woman who had been put away for keeping a bad house. At the end of the second day he returned to the back room of the *Anchor* and Jimmy Wild. It was on midnight and the bar had just closed, and Andrée sat in the dirty, low room sipping a mug of hot rum.

There wasn't much about Shields and its people that Jimmy Wild didn't know, nor yet about the inhabitants of the village of Westoe, or that of Harton. He had seen men press-ganged from this street; he had seen a man murdered just outside the door there; he had seen men knife each other, and women who had come into his bar laughing together tearing the scalps off each other when they eventually left. He knew practically everybody in his vicinity by sight, but he had never seen Katie Mulholland, and he said this again.

'One thing's certain, Captain; she wasn't in the racket. If she'd been . . . well, you know yersel she'd have made her way here; they all start from here. Whether they go up or down, this is the startin' place around these quarters. Let's face it, I know, I know. But your lass . . . well, I've never set eyes on her. An' you know somethin' else? I'd never heard her name mentioned until the case came up . . . No, a bit afore that, when Meggie Proctor took those two swells round to her place. It was the next day I heard about the rumpus, an' it was then I heard the name of Katie Mulholland for the first time. She had hit one of the blokes with a bottle, or a candlestick or somethin', and split his head open.'

Andrée now strained his neck upwards and, gripping his glass, said, 'Those men. That's it. You knew those men; those two?'

'No, Captain, no. One of them I'd seen twice afore with Meggie Proctor, the other one I've never clapped eyes on until that night, and then only for a minute when they came in and picked her up.'

'What were they like? Come on, describe them.'

'I can't, Captain. Well, what can you remember of strangers through the fug that's in here at nights . . . ? Only one thing sure I can tell you, that is they were gentry; and perhaps another, and that is there's something fishy about the whole business. It's like a put-up job from start to finish. Everybody round about says the same thing. The coppers had got a backhander from somebody, and they're not the blokes to risk their good jobs at eighteen bob a week for no small fry. It's somebody of importance that's at the back of this. That's the local opinion, an' it's never far out . . . '

It was around two o'clock when he returned to his ship, but not to sleep. At half-past ten tomorrow he'd be going out on the tide, he'd have to do something before then; find someone to carry on the probing; someone who wouldn't be afraid of . . . the gentry. Someone like an investigator or solicitor . . . a solicitor, yes; the one Katie went to, that was it. He knew the office in King Street, she had pointed it out to him. She said he had got a barrister to speak well for her father.

This decided, he trimmed the lamp afresh and wrote a letter to her: 'Oh, Kaa-tee, Kaa-tee, my darling Kaa-tee.' Then went on to tell her of his love and his faith, and his determination to clear her name and to get her out of that place as soon as possible. He addressed the letter to Her Majesty's Prison, Durham.

It was eight o'clock when he left the ship again. He posted the letter; then, going to the house in Crane Street, he went upstairs and knocked on Mrs Robson's door, and when, bleary-eyed, she opened it he said abruptly, 'I've had no luck, and I sail today. Will you go and visit her at the times they allow?' When he saw her hesitation he added quickly, 'I will pay for your travel, and there's half a sovereign for every time you visit her. What about it?'

'All right, all right, I'll go, and mind, not that I'm doing it for the money alone . . . '

'Thank you. I have written to her. But you tell her that I'm doing everything to clear her . . . You will, won't you?'

'Aye, I'll do that. But I don't see much use in raising her hopes.'

He pushed one and a half sovereigns into her hand, saying, 'One to pay the travel and you, and spend the half on food for her.'

'Aye, aye, I'll do that, 'cos it's lean fare they get in there. What about upstairs?' She jerked her head.

'I've seen to that. I've paid the rent for four weeks in advance. Here is the key.' He handed it to her. 'Tell them' – he looked downwards – 'that if everything isn't returned by the time I get back again there'll be some broken pates flying around this house. You understand?'

'Aye, I understand.'

'I must go now.' He paused. 'Thank you for your help; you will not lose by it.'

She returned his nod but gave him no farewell, and he went down the stairs, and as he passed through the hall he beat his fist once on Meggie Proctor's door; it was a warning. Then he marched out of the house.

When he reached King Street and the office of Chapel & Hewitt he saw by his watch it was five minutes past nine. Without pausing he pushed the door open, went along a dark passage and up some stairs and to a door which again read 'Chapel & Hewitt, Solicitors'. After knocking he was bidden to enter, and when he opened the door he saw sitting on a high stool, at a high desk, with a ledger before him, a tall, thin man of middle age. On the sight of him the man slid to his feet and, coming forward said, 'Yes, sir, what can I do for you, sir?'

'Are you Mr Chapel or Mr Hewitt?'

The man smiled, a soft deprecating smile, saying, 'Neither, sir. Mr Chapel is deceased. I'm Mr Hewitt's chief clerk.'

'Is he in?'

'Yes, sir. Do you wish to see him?'

'Yes, I wish to see him.'

'Will you take a seat, sir, and I will ascertain whether he is available.'

Andrée waved the seat away, and the clerk hurried now towards the door of another room, and after knocking he entered. It was perhaps three minutes before he returned and, holding the door open, said, 'Mr Hewitt will see you now, sir.'

Arnold Hewitt was a good judge of character – it was a necessary qualification of his profession; and as he looked at the big, fair-haired man, whom he dubbed, even before he had opened his mouth, as a Swede or Norwegian, he saw that his client, if he was to be so, was a man of purpose, a man who would waste no words and a man who would likely pay well for deeds.

Almost immediately Andrée confirmed the solicitor's summing up of his character by saying, 'I haven't much time to waste; I sail in just over an hour back to Norway. I want you to do some work for me.'

'Yes, if it is within my capacity, sir, and such work as I am used to undertaking, I will oblige. Kindly take a seat and tell me what your business is.'

Andrée again ignored the offer of a seat and began:

'Just this . . . ' There followed, in clipped, rapid but good English, Katie's story as Andrée knew it. He commenced at the beginning – at least at the beginning of this last affair when Meggie Proctor had brought the two men upstairs – and as he talked the solicitor listened attentively with the main part of his mind, but there was a section that was telling him that this was a strange, a very strange coincidence, for he had been in court on the day that this girl, this Katie Mulholland, had been put away for three months for importuning, and not only had he felt that the woman was innocent but also he'd had a strong suspicion that there was some jiggery-pokery going on. How had the two men, the two vital witnesses, to his mind, in the case, been allowed to escape? These men that the prisoner, it was understood, had housed, and for whom she had procured the two girls. And then there was the telling point of who those girls were. They came from a family that stank, a family whose name was a byword in the low quarters; but all that this implied had gone by the board on the evidence of the policemen . . . And this man sitting before him now was the foreign sailor who had been mentioned in the case. And there was something stranger still in his mind with regard to this woman: it was not the first time he had come across her. She had paid a tidy bill five or six years ago for the defence of her father, but the whole case was a foregone conclusion, the jury being made up of picked pit officials. They had used the Mulholland man as a scarecrow to keep the miners quiet. He remembered at the time that the girl had been befriended by the Rosiers. It was Rosier's daughter who had brought her along here, that was why he had taken on the case. And now here was this Katie Mulholland being befriended yet again, but by a burly sea captain this time and a foreigner into the bargain. It was an interesting state of affairs.

Of course he would work for him, he would do all he could. He was speaking aloud now. 'Just leave it with me, Captain Fraenkel. I will make all the enquiries I can, but you must understand I can't promise you any magic results. She has been sent to prison for three months. Magistrates don't like to think they have made mistakes, you understand?'

'But you will do something. Find out why this has happened; above all, find out who the men were who Meggie Proctor brought to the house that night, frighten it out of her, anything so that my . . . Miss Mulholland will be freed. And I know this much now, she won't be free until I learn the name of one of those men. This is the second time he has harmed her, and it's worse than the first . . . '

'Wait, wait.' The solicitor lifted his hand. 'You mean she knew who the man was whom this Proctor woman brought to the house? She had seen him before?'

'Yes.'

'And she never told you his name?'

'No. Would I be asking you now?'

'But it is strange that she did not tell you his name, after telling you so much . . . '

'Not at all. She was afraid of what I might do to him. He, this man, he gave her a child when she was but a child herself. As I understand it, he was the cause of her marrying the man, Bunting, who was killed by her father because of his treatment of her.'

'Yes, yes, I know all about that, Captain.'

Andrée drew his chin in, then, leaning forward over the desk, he said softly, 'Well now, sir, you've seen her, so you'll know she's not capable of doing what she has been imprisoned for. She's a fine woman, a wonderful woman, and she has suffered much. This last is beyond her endurance, and I am afraid of what it will do to her; so you see how important it is that you move quickly.'

'I will do all I can, Captain. Leave it to me. How long do you expect to be away?'

'Ten days, a fortnight. A fortnight at the most.'

'I may have some news for you when you return.' Andrée drew in sharp breath and repeated, 'May have? I want news!'

'Yes, of course. And I can assure you we'll do our utmost for you.' He stood up and extended his hand. Andrée took it, then made for the door, and Mr Hewitt accompanied him, and again assured him that he would give the matter his special attention.

As Mr Hewitt returned to his office he beckoned his clerk to follow him, and once he was behind his desk he looked at the tall man standing at the other side, and it was with some pride in his voice that he said, 'You remember the Mulholland woman who was put away for three months for procuring?'

'Yes, sir.'

'He wants us to work on it. He is the foreign sailor who was mentioned in the case. You remember I said I thought there was some jiggery-pokery going on in that business, for if ever a woman proclaimed her innocence from the dock she did. You remember I said that?'

'Yes, sir, I remember distinctly.'

'He seems a man of substance, Kenny. An educated man. Not all ships' captains are educated.'

'I agree with you, sir. Are you going to take the case, sir?'

'Yes, Kenny. Yes. Yes, I've promised to do what I can. Not that I can see us getting her out of Durham before her time's up, but we may be able to clear up one or two matters that are of as much interest to me from one angle as to the captain from another. Did you know that this Mulholland girl had a baby when she was very young, and that she was visited by this child's father a few weeks ago, and that she hit him with an implement, splitting his brow open. And don't you think it strange, Kenny, that the incident of procuring should follow? Who, Kenny, could bribe the police? Not a poor man.'

'No, sir. Definitely not a poor man.'

'Someone of importance. A name behind them. Money. Gentry, Kenny, don't you think?'

'Yes, sir! Gentry.'

'The captain would like to know this gentleman's name, and, Kenny, so would we.'

'Yes, sir. Yes, sir. Indeed we would like to know his name.'

'So that is what we will work on, Kenny, unearthing this very mysterious gentleman who resented so much being hit on the head with a candlestick.'

The conversation between Arnold Hewitt and his chief clerk was serious; there was no hint of humour in it. It was only that the solicitor and his clerk were in the habit of discussing cases in this fashion.

Chapter Eight

It was in the middle of March when Andrée brought his ship into the Tyne yet once again, and the usual berthing procedure was hardly finished before he stepped from her deck and on to the quay and hurried towards King Street.

Mr Hewitt was awaiting him. He had word that Captain Fraenkel's ship was in, and he wasn't looking forward to another meeting with the blond giant, whose eyes would look at him with the coldness of frozen sea water when he had to tell him how little progress he had made with his case.

He was standing on his feet to greet the captain, and he shook him warmly by the hand, and when Andrée said the one word with which he usually opened these proceedings, 'Well?' he raised his shoulder slightly and spread out his hands, then said hastily, 'I'm sorry, Captain, I'm sorry. And I'm sorry for my own sake, too, because I hate to be baffled. But I'm afraid I must admit that I've come up against a blank wall on all sides. I've heard nothing . . . Well, I won't say nothing exactly, but what I have gleaned has led us to just another blind alley, I'm afraid.'

'Well, what did you learn?' Andrée's voice had a bitter edge to it.

'That one of the men, the particular man who visited Miss Mulholland that night, was not of the town. He left it on horseback.'

'Did you find out where he stabled his horse?'

'Yes, but nothing further, except perhaps . . . that he was gentry. And that places an armour plate against the wall, if you follow what I mean.'

'I follow what you mean,' said Andrée grimly. 'About the other. Did you arrange that I could see her?'

Mr Hewitt lowered his head. 'I'm afraid not, Captain. I feel very sore about this, but they would make no concessions . . . If . . . ' Mr Hewitt now examined his fingernails, then drummed the pads of his fingers on the desk before going on, 'If you had any claim on her – I mean legal – then it would have been a different matter, but as it is . . . '

'Did you find out if her brother had been to visit her?'

'We investigated that part of it, and I'm sorry to say that he hasn't.'

'God Almighty!' Andrée leant his elbow on the desk and dropped his head to his hand.

'And I have a little further news that might add to her distress. Her sister has passed away.'

Andrée's head jerked upwards. 'Lizzie? Dead?'

'I'm afraid so, Captain. About a week ago.'

'She is buried, then?'

'Yes.'

'Where?'

Now Mr Hewitt lifted his gaze from Andrée's face and looked at his hands again before he said, 'In the common grave. You see, I had no instructions.'

Andrée lowered his head on to his hand again and said, 'No, of course not; you had no instructions.' After a moment he rose, saying abruptly, 'I will call in again before I leave. Good day to you.'

'Good day, Captain.'

Andrée now made his way to Crane Street, and going swiftly up the stairs he knocked on Mrs Robson's door. She, too, appeared to be waiting for him, for she opened the door immediately.

'It's you,' she said. 'Well, she's all right. I saw her, but she doesn't speak much; she's very quiet like.'

'How does she look?'

Mrs Robson cast her eyes downwards, then folded her arms across her stomach and moved her body back and forward two or three times before she said, 'Well, what would you expect in a place like that? She doesn't look robust. She's peaked, thin; she's lost weight. She looks all eyes. They were big afore, they're like saucers in her face now.'

It was a while before he said, 'You took her some food?'

'Yes, but I couldn't give it to her. I had to give it to one of them wardresses. It seemed a waste to me, for I don't suppose she'll ever see the skin of a sausage.'

'Did she get my letters? Did you ask her?'

'Aye, I did, but . . . but, you know, she never answered me, she just looked at me; stared like, funny like. She didn't even nod. I thought she hadn't heard me, but she could through the grid, an' so I asked her again, but she still stared. Anyway, the time's running out fast now, it's only a couple of weeks off. Sometimes if they behave themselves they let them out a day or so early, so they tell me.'

'There'll be one more time to go,' he said as he handed her the money, and as she took it from him she said, 'Aye, there'll be one more time, an'

I'll be glad when it's finished. It's no picnic to go there; it gives me the willies.'

He turned abruptly from her and went up the stairs, and outside the door he stopped and picked up the *Gazette*, then let himself into the house.

The room looked dim and it smelt damp. The furniture that had been brought back was set higgledy-piggledy around the place. He walked slowly to the bedroom, and as he looked at the wooden base of the bed he said to himself, 'Poor Lizzie. But it is better this way, much better.' His nose wrinkled slightly as he closed the door, for the human smell of Lizzie still pervaded the room.

In the kitchen again he stood looking around him. With Lizzie gone there would be no need for her to stay in this house, in this vicinity at all. Yet she would have to have some place to come back to, somewhere familiar. Would that be a good thing? Or wouldn't it be better to make a clean break altogether? But that would take arranging. He would want to consult with her as to where she wanted to live. Anyway, he would have this place whitewashed and scrubbed and papered, and everything shining for her coming back. He would leave that to Hewitt – he would engage someone – but the place must be ready for her.

He sat down on a chair that was standing in isolation on the bare wooden floor and he said aloud, 'Kaa-tee! Oh, Kaa-tee!' As he spoke he twisted the paper, that was still in his hands, until it split. What would this have done to her? He had no illusions about prisons, and he did not comfort himself with the thought that women would not be dealt with so harshly as men. The women they engaged to look after female prisoners were coarse dregs of humanity, sometimes lower than their charges, and it was clear to him that any air of refinement or difference, say beauty, such as Katie's, would be bound to bring the worst out in them, and all this, added to the rest, would leave its mark. He looked down towards his hands and smoothed the twisted paper as if he was smoothing her hair back, smoothing the beautiful skin, her face, the soft warm suppleness of her breasts and hips. As he stroked the paper into flatness over his knees he shook his head.

They'd had a great deal of amusement out of the weekly paper. He it was who had arranged that the *Gazette* be delivered to her every Saturday. Not only had he liked to read it when he came in, but the daily *Telegraph* sheet which they supplied and delivered free he considered a further source of interest for her.

She used to say to him that she got their money's worth of laughs out of the advertisements alone. Although she had read them over and over again she would laugh till the tears rolled down her face when he would read them aloud, giving a special intonation to certain words and interposing his own language here and there. 'Come to the Albert House, 11 and 12 Market Street. Patronised by THE NOBILITY and GENTRY . . . Printed pine pattern all over Barege Long Shawls reduced from 22s. 6d. to 16s. 9d.'

'South Shields Races. To be run for over South Shields Sands on Whit Monday . . . Bra! Bra! I shall enter *Orn*.'

'Sailing to Hull. Great reduction of fares. First-class steamer Neptune leaves the North shore for Hull, every Saturday, two hours before high water. Fares: Best Cabin 4s.; second ditto 2s.; Steward's fee, Best Cabin is. Do you hear? *Horer De*? Steward's fee only a shilling!' Oh, she had laughed and laughed. Would she ever laugh again?

Andrée found that he was reading the advertisements once more. 'Old established family wine and spirit vaults. Old Highlander Inn, 11 King Street, South Shields. The best and cheapest in the trade.'

Then almost below this was the advertisement that he could rhyme off without looking at it. It was printed in the shape of a wine glass and headed 'The Tree of Dissipation'.

THE
sin of
drunkenness
expels reason,
drowns memory
diminishes strength,
distempers the body,
defaces beauty, corrupts the
blood, inflames the liver, weakens
the brain, turns men into walking
hospitals, causes internal, external, and
incurable wounds, is a witch to the senses, a
devil to the soul, a thief to the pocket,
the beggar's companion, a wife's woe,
and children's sorrow – makes man
become a beast and self-murderer,
who drinks to others' good
health, and robs himself
of his own!!
The
root of
all evil is
DRUNKENNESS!!!

He had always taken a drink after reading this one. His eyes moved wearily over the paper, until the name Crane Street caught his attention, and he read:

'For sale: Nos. 12, 13 and 14 Crane Street. These desirable, three-floor houses in close proximity to the docks for sale. Apply Tollet, Estate Agents, Fowler Street.' Three times he read this before he looked around the room. What would happen when the houses were sold? What happened in England when houses were sold? Did they let the tenants stay on? He supposed so; there would be no reason for turning them out. They might raise the rent; but that didn't matter much, he would see to that. He looked at the advertisement again. Nos. 12, 13 and 14 Crane Street to be sold. If he had been at home in Norway and his wife had read these words she would have looked up immediately and said, 'I wonder how much they're asking for them.' And likely as not she would have added, 'I wonder if Father's seen it.' And he would have had to bite on his tongue to stop himself from saying, 'Aw, Kristin, don't talk foolish. It's likely one of his; are not nearly all the advertisements his?' And she would have answered, 'Why are you so bitter against my father?' To this he would have said what he had said to her before, 'I'm bitter because he has grown rich doing nothing. He buys a house, repairs it, then sells it for twice its value.'

The last time he had said words to that effect she had accused him of being jealous of her father's power. 'You,' she had said, 'are a big man, but you have no power, only over your little boat. And you and she are at the mercy of a bigger power, the sea, so you are always small inside. Whereas, my father, who is not half your size, and whom you despise, he has power; he is a great power in the town because he owns almost a third of it. You have never given him credit for what he has accomplished. You forget that when he was a young man he started with one house, just one, and now because of his industry he is a great man, a powerful one. When you have power such as he you are afraid of no-one, men large or small.'

It was on that occasion he had said, 'You should not have married; you should have stayed with your father.'

He rose to his feet but he still stared at the paper. His father-in-law had become powerful in his town because he owned property, and he had started with one house. Unless you had power of some kind you got nowhere, you were nothing, you were trampled on. And you could not have power unless you had money. He had power, of a kind, but over his ship, over men, but he was only enabled to have this power through someone else's money. He had not enough money of his own to give Katie power, which for her would mean security, freedom from the malice of – unknown men. If she had come from a family of substance none of the things that had happened to her would have happened. Katie lacked security because she lacked power; she lacked power because she lacked money. How could he make enough money to bring power and substance to a woman like Katie, a woman who was badly in need of protection? When she came out of that place she would be in need of something more than his love, something that was going to stand by her when he was far from her.

He crumpled the paper between his hands. His father-in-law had started with one house, why not Katie? Why not indeed! Why not . . . ! This much he could do for her . . .

Fifteen minutes later he was standing in the agent's office.

Oh! they said. Yes, they were very desirable houses, 12, 13 and 14 Crane Street, but they were being sold as a lot, not separately.

'How much?' he asked.

Well, they were very desirable properties and they were going very cheap, three hundred and fifty pounds, and would bring in an overall rent of thirty-five shillings a week.

'You'll be hearing from me,' he said.

As he walked towards King Street and the solicitor's office he took stock of his own capital. He had not three hundred and fifty pounds. All he possessed of his own was about two hundred, but his name was good.

Mr Hewitt was surprised to see the captain again so soon, and when he learned of what he intended to do he said he would advise caution. 'Property is at a low ebb, Captain,' he said.

'Offer them three hundred,' said Andrée.

'What!'

'I said offer them three hundred.'

'But Tollets are rather tough customers.'

'So am I, Mr Hewitt. I know all about the buying and selling of property. Have you heard the name of Petersen of Bergen? He is a Dane, but he's one of the richest, if not the richest in that city. He buys and sells property every day of his life. I happen to be connected with him; I know how these things should be done. Offer them three hundred. Tell them I am wavering between those particular houses and some, say, in . . . Find out where there are other empty ones and mention their names. I will call back this afternoon. I would like this business settled before I sail in two days' time.'

'Ah! Captain Fraenkel.'

'Never mind! Ah! Captain Fraenkel. In this at least I want to move. Do as I say, Mr Hewitt. Good day to you.'

Two days later, about an hour before Andrée sailed, he signed a temporary notice of purchase to buy Nos. 12, 13 and 14 Crane Street for the sum of three hundred and fifteen pounds, and the name he signed on the paper, after laying a deposit of thirty-five guineas, was the name of Mrs Catherine Bunting, known as Katie Mulholland. It was at his insistence that the signature was written thus. Also Mr Hewitt was given strict instructions as to what he was to do with the agreement, or a copy of the same, whether fulfilled or temporary, on the first Wednesday in April, the day when Mrs Bunting would be free.

Chapter Nine

On the morning of Katie's release the sun was shining though the air was bitterly cold, and here and there, as if they had strayed from the pack on its way farther north, a snowflake glided down.

The big woman with the huge breasts looked at Katie as if she was loth to let her go, as indeed she was. She had not found such an outlet for her sadistic tendencies for many a long day, but do what she might she couldn't rouse this one to the kind of retaliation that might lengthen her sentence. Purposely now she led her down the stone corridor and through the sacking room where Jinny Fulton and her crowd were gathered, plying their needles. She led the way between stacks of hessian and piles of sail canvas, and almost to the foot of Jinny Fulton herself, and when Jinny cried out 'Aw! Here comes Lady Go-Lightly to say goodbye to us poor creatures,' she did not reprimand her. She only slanted her gaze towards her and twisted her lips into the semblance of a smile, which smile told Jinny that she had her permission to go ahead, and she went ahead. She thrust her arm out and drove the long curved steel needle she held in her hand through Katie's skirt and into her calf. Because of her petticoats only the point penetrated, but Katie screamed out and Jinny Fulton, putting her head back, roared; then, gathering a dobble of spit into her mouth and taking direct aim, she fouled Katie's skirt. The wardress stopped and, without reprimanding the prisoner who had committed the offence, said to Katie, 'Wipe that off. You don't want to go out like that, do you?'

Katie had nothing with which to wipe off the filth from her skirt except her fingers; so, bending her knee, she rubbed the skirt against the stone floor, and this brought a howl of laughter from Jinny Fulton and those nearest to her. But all the women in the bag room didn't laugh. There were those that looked at the Mulholland girl with pity, and one here and there with admiration, for they knew that they couldn't have stood what she'd had to stand without doing murder.

'Tickle your Swede for me.' This, followed by a mouthful of obscenities, seemed to push Katie through the door and along another passage and into a room where a woman sat behind a table. This granite-faced individual turned a book towards her, and after she had signed her name, which action seemed an offence to this woman as it stood out against a line of crosses, she was waved away.

It was as she stood at the wooden door and watched the tormentor of her mind and body slowly putting the key into the lock of the small insert door that she thought that her legs would collapse beneath her, that she would never have strength to step through the little door in the gate and into the world again.

But she was almost pushed into it because the door banged so quickly on her heels that it grazed the leather of her shoe. And then she was standing on the rough pavement of Stone Street, blinking. The light and everything out here was different. Her vision seemed blurred against this new light. She started to draw in great draughts of air but seemed powerless to move one foot in front of the other. The road, with its stone houses opposite the prison, was comparatively empty except for two carriages standing on the other side, and some distance apart from each other. Her mind took in the figure of a man leaving the farthest carriage; then from the one nearest to her she saw a woman alight and come running towards her.

It was the sight of Miss Theresa that seemed to give power to her legs, and she turned and walked quickly away from the black door.

'Katie! Katie! Wait, please.' Theresa had gripped her arm and pulled her to a halt.

'Oh, Katie!' The two words were a condemnation of all sin, and to them Katie answered in a strange voice, quite unlike her own, 'Leave me alone.'

'I can't, I can't. Come back with me. I have a room ready for you. Miss Ainsley will welcome you. You must break away from this degradation; look what it has brought you to.' She cast her eyes swiftly up the high wall behind her.

'Will you leave me alone?' Still the strange way of speaking, slow, thick, quiet.

'No, no, I won't. I won't let you go back to that man. He has been the cause of your down . . . '

'Be quiet!' Now her voice changed; it was still thick but strong and harsh. 'Don't you speak a word against him. Don't you, I'm tellin' you, for he's the only good thing that has happened to me. D'you hear? D'you hear?'

'Don't say that, Katie, don't. I can't bear it. I can't bear the thought of that awful . . . '

'Will you be quiet, Miss Theresa, else I'll say something I'll be sorry for later.'

'No, I won't be quiet, Katie. I'll never rest until you give up this way of life. Look what it's brought you to. And not even a coat on your back. And just think where you'll end: filthy houses, foreign sailors.'

Katie stared into the thin white face before her, and then with a seeming effort she lifted the top part of her body upwards and, her voice now coming low and bitter, she said, 'The filthiest house, the worst sailors you could gather from any port, couldn't hold a candle to your brother, Miss Theresa.'

Theresa stared back at her. Then, her chin moving downwards but her eyes still on Katie, she said, 'What are you saying, Katie? My brother? You mean Bernard?'

'I mean Bernard, Miss Theresa.'

'You mean Bernard has had something to do with . . . ?' Theresa again raised her eyes to the high stone wall. Then, looking at Katie, she moved her head quickly, saying, 'No, no, Katie; you're mistaken.'

'Your brother put me in there, Miss Theresa.'

'No, no, Katie . . . I can't believe it. I won't believe it. How could he?'

Katie closed her eyes, then said, 'Because I split his head open with a candlestick. I'm . . . I'm no prostitute, Miss Theresa. Never have been, nor ever will be. I live with a man because I love him. One man, a sailor, a sea captain, a good man. But your brother and another man forced their way into my house with a woman who is a prostitute, and they wouldn't go out, and he would have come at me again and the same thing would have happened as before – I saw it in his face – and so I struck him with a candlestick. And from that day until New Year's Eve, when they came and took me away, I lived in dread of what he would do.'

'It can't be, it can't be, Katie. In the court, you remember, those two girls, they said . . . '

'They said what they were told to say. I had never seen them in me life before, nor the men with them, but in the court that day I saw one of your brother's henchmen, Crabtree, from the mine. He was another keeker. And then in there . . . ' She moved her head slowly backwards. 'He even had them paid in there. There were letters come for me an' I never got them. There was food sent in, but I never saw it. If purgatory and hell is anything like that' – again she moved her head backwards – 'I'm going to see that I never get there.'

'Oh, Katie, Katie, what are you saying?' Now Theresa had one hand pressed against her cheek.

'I'm saying the truth. And now you can ask why, if I knew this, I didn't say it in court. Well, without asking I'll tell you. It was because . . . because I didn't want another murder done. If my man knew the name of the one who had done this to me he would have cut him up in slices.' Katie's mouth was squared now away from her teeth, and she bent forward and repeated under her breath, 'Cut him up in slices, Miss Theresa. Before this happened he begged me for his name but I wouldn't say; Miss Theresa, you take a message to your brother and tell him, just one more move like this and I let things take their rightful course. And it won't be through a court of law, where there's no justice for God nor man. Tell him that.'

'Wait, Katie, wait.' As Katie went to move away Theresa grabbed her arm; then, turning sideways, she looked at the tall man who was standing at the other side of Katie now, and she demanded autocratically, 'What do you want?'

'I wish to speak to Mrs Bunting, ma'am.'

'Get yourself away.'

'I'm sorry, ma'am; I'm here on business. I am clerk to Mr Hewitt, solicitor, of Chapel & Hewitt. Would you read this letter, ma'am?' He was now addressing Katie, and he brought his body into a slight bow as he placed the letter in her hands.

Katie stared at the letter and at the man, then at the letter again. She knew the writing. It was Andy's, and slowly she ripped open the envelope and read, 'My Katie. My Katie. The house is ready for you; I have seen to it. But first go with the clerk, Mr Kenny, to Mr Hewitt, who will explain things to you. My heart is so full I cannot make words flow, but when we meet again I will tell you all. You are my life, my Katie, even more than ever now. Know that I live for you. Take heart. Andrée.'

Her red swollen hands were trembling so much that she couldn't fold the letter in two and return it to the envelope. She looked at the tall man with the kindly expression and she said, 'I am ready.'

'Katie, I beseech you.'

Katie, now looking straight into Theresa's distressed face, said quietly, 'Give my message to your brother, Miss Theresa. Goodbye.' Then, walking by the man's side, she crossed the road to the farther carriage. After assisting her inside, Mr Kenny spoke to the driver, then took his seat opposite her, and they set out for Shields. And all during the journey, during which Mr Kenny tried hard not to keep staring into the beautiful, sad, sad face before him, his mind was in a turmoil of excitement. Rosier, then, was the man they had been looking for all this time. Mr Bernard Rosier. Well, well. He knew quite a lot about Mr Bernard Rosier, for Mr Hewitt had handled transactions concerning his wife. She had been a Talford and very, very well connected. He had a memory for these things and knew that the now Mrs Bernard Rosier had a cousin in Parliament – on the Tory side, of course. Moreover, she had a cousin who was one of the ladies-in-waiting to Her Majesty the Queen. But he also knew other things about Mr Bernard Rosier. He remembered that he had been a bit of a rake in his early youth but had apparently settled down before his marriage and after, until his father died, when there were rumours of his wild ways coming to the fore again. He now owned racehorses and was a gambler, and from what he had heard only a few minutes ago he was also a trollop-trailer, as many of his kind were, but apparently he was less discreet than most, and vindictive – ah, yes, cruelly vindictive.

Mr Kenny had a strong desire at this point in his thinking to see Mr Bernard Rosier get his just deserts over this affair of the woman sitting opposite, but he knew that he never would, at least not legally, because the name of Rosier was too important roundabout. He knew that Mr Hewitt would confirm this, and strongly. Mr Hewitt would never act as the stick to stir the midden in front of the Rosier mansion, but it was a pity – oh, a great pity. And on this point, too, Mr Kenny thought his employer would concur with him. Mr Kenny was a reserved man, a man who could keep secrets – a necessary attribute to being a solicitor's clerk – but he was also a man who had a way with clients. It was part of his duty to put them at their ease, but now he found great difficulty in opening a conversation with the woman opposite. He felt that her past experience, her many past experiences, had put her beyond small talk and generalities. Whatever he had to say to her must have point. He said, 'Captain Fraenkel desired Mr Hewitt to have your apartments redecorated. Mr Hewitt left the matter in my hands. I have followed the captain's suggestions as near as possible; I hope the result will please you.'

Katie moved her head twice before saying, softly, 'I am sure it will.' She had the desire to finish her words on the 'huh!' of a laugh, for the transition from back there to this man with his smooth, ingratiating manner seemed unreal. Back there was real, but he wasn't. Yet he came from Andy.

Andy. She tried to recall his face, but his image went into a great pale, hairy blur. That's what happened to her lately. At night when she tried to conjure him up, willed him to be real, the result was muzziness. But

Andy was real, he was real and good. He was the only thing in her life that she could trust. She was going to ask him to take her away, as far from this area as possible, for there was nothing here to hold her any longer, only bitter memories. If she asked him he would do it . . .

When, the long drive at an end, the carriage entered the market place she could not keep her eyes turned from the Cross where they had taken her that night and the woman had slapped her in the mouth. Did she but know it then, that woman had been kind. All she had done was strike her for screaming. She was to find that there were a thousand and one other ways to terrify a human being. To have someone stand looking at you unblinking for an unendurable space of time until you ate the beetle-strewn filth that was called food; and when your stomach revolted and you were sick, to leave you with it all over your clothes and not allow you any water for hours and hours. Oh yes, the woman who had hit her in the mouth had been kind.

Mr Hewitt rose to his feet to greet her, and took her by the hand, and in a most courteous fashion he asked his clerk if it would be possible to get Mrs Bunting a cup of tea, and Mr Kenny replied, 'Surely, surely.'

Half an hour later, again in the carriage, and again in the company of Mr Kenny, Katie was driven from the solicitor's office to No. 14 Crane Street. The street was comparatively empty and there was no-one at the door when they arrived, and when they came to Mrs Robson's door it was closed. But no-one went past Mrs Robson's door without her knowing. With Mr Kenny behind her she mounted the stairs to her house. And there on the landing she saw the wooden table and bowl and bucket, but with a difference, for the table was standing on a rush mat, which covered the whole square of the landing.

Mr Kenny, now bowing slightly towards her, handed her the key and she opened the door and stepped into her home, and slowly she looked around her, and Mr Kenny also looked around him. He was very proud of his handiwork.

'Do you like it, Mrs Bunting?'

'Yes, yes. Thank you. It's lovely.' Katie looked from the whitewashed ceiling to the wallpaper which had little bunches of pink flowers all over it. She looked at the table. It was highly polished, as were the chiffonier, the chest and the chairs. And lastly she looked at the bright burning fire.

Her eyes were moist as she turned towards Mr Kenny and said, 'You've been very kind.'

'Oh, ma'am, it's nothing. It's been a pleasure.' He had his hands joined in front of him and he bowed his head several times over them as he spoke. 'I hope I can continue to be of service to you. Anything you would like to know you have only to call on us. As you know, ma'am, Mr Hewitt emphasised this.'

'Yes, yes, he was very kind to me. I . . . I can't quite take it all in yet.'

'No, no, I can understand that, but you will have grown used to your new position by the time the captain returns, which should be, we estimate, in about four days' time.'

'Yes.' For the first time the skin of her cheeks moved into what might have been the semblance of a smile.

Mr Kenny now pointed to the cupboard and said, 'The captain gave me a list of the food he thought you would need. I hope you find it adequate for the time being.'

'Thank you; I'm sure I will.' Katie followed his gaze to the cupboard. Then she looked at him again, and after a moment of silence between them he said, 'Now I must take my leave, but believe me, Mrs Bunting, we will always be at your service, any time.'

'Thank you, Mr Kenny.'

'Thank you, ma'am.' He held out his hand and she took it; then, with seeming reluctance, he made his departure.

Katie sat down in the chair near the table. She hadn't been in the bedroom yet. She would need to get her breath before she could go in there. She looked at the long envelope she still held in her hand and she muttered aloud, 'Oh, Andy! Andy!' What he had done for her should have made her grateful, but for weeks now the main thought in her mind had been that once she got out she would get Andy to take her and Lizzie away – away from this dreadful place, the Tyne, this place that her mother had loved, and Joe still loved; this place they had condemned her to because of their love . . . And now, inadvertently, Andy had condemned her to it for a further period, for he had bought her three houses. This room where she was sitting, all this house, and the other two down the street were hers. She just couldn't take that in, not as yet; it was too much. Her, an owner of property. But inside this envelope was a copy of the transaction. Andy had done this for her. Yet at the moment it was bringing no grateful response from her. She seemed dead inside; the only thing she was still alive to was fear. There was terror in the depths of her, and she felt it would always be there as long as she stayed in the vicinity of Greenwall Manor and Bernard Rosier.

And her fear must have spoken aloud from her face, for Mr Hewitt had seen it. He had said the captain was a very discerning and wise man. He believed that the surest way to climb above fear was on the back of power, and the only way to acquire power was through gold; and one of the quickest ways to get gold these days was to buy and sell property.

But would the acquisition of property obliterate Big Bess? She could almost feel the wardress standing in front of her, her great bust touching the front of her dress, saying, 'You're frightened, aren't you? What you frightened of?' then making a swift movement with her hand and digging her nails under her chin, saying the while, 'Keep your head up. Keep your head up, an' open your peepers. What you frightened of?'

She looked down at the long envelope on the table. Power! If she'd had power she would never have been subjected to Big Bess; if she'd had power somebody would have found out that those two policemen and the girls were lying. If she had been a child of people of power Bernard Rosier would never have dragged her into his bed; she would never have married Bunting; and her father would never have died . . . But if she'd had power in any form she would never have met Andy. Somewhere, somehow, there was a reason for all she had suffered . . . Perhaps it was a kind of payment for Andy. And Andy had given her power. As Mr Hewitt said, Andy was wise; he always knew what she needed. If she was to remain in this town – and it seemed that God, or whoever ruled destinies, willed that she should – then she wouldn't live like a rat . . . a mouse was a better description, a mouse in a hole, a frightened mouse.

There was a side of her that hated her fear, hated being afraid, but had never been strong enough to tackle it, but now a weapon had been put into her hands. She lifted up the envelope and ran her fingers along it, and again she said, 'Oh, Andy! Andy!' And now there came a great swelling into her chest and she knew what this meant; it meant that all the unshed tears of weeks that had dammed themselves up were striving to burst forth and drown her in a paroxysm of grief under which she might well lie for hours, even days. But it mustn't come yet; there was something she had to do first. Before she even ate anything she wanted to be clean. She would go down and get some water; she would get lots of water and heat it and wash herself. She needed to be clean as much as she did the morning after the ball.

She stood on the stairhead hesitant to pass the doors down below, hesitant to meet the curious gazes, wondering what they would say. Did it matter? No! Not any more. Mrs Robson had been kind in coming to see her and she would thank her, but she guessed that she had been thanked in a more substantial way by Andy. She guessed that without payment

Mrs Robson would never have come all the way to Durham, but nevertheless she would thank her.

She made three journeys up and down the stairs, but the doors remained closed. Later, after she had washed herself from head to toe, her hair included, she began to wonder why Mrs Robson, who she could hear moving down below, had not come out to give her a word. She just wondered, but it didn't really matter, for the dam of her emotions was breaking down.

It was some days before it was brought home to Katie why Mrs Robson had not visited her. You don't visit the landlord. The tenants of Nos. 12, 13 and 14 Crane Street had been issued with new rent books, and had been told that their landlord was now Mrs Bunting, known as Miss Mulholland. This occurrence had been a nine-days wonder in the street.

Katie Mulholland was now a landlord, she was one of . . . THEM. From someone who had done time, and was to be pitied, even scorned and shunned, she had now leaped the chasm to the other side, where lived the nobs, gentry . . . and landlords. You had to watch your p's and q's when landlords were about; you had to keep your nose clean when landlords were about. Half a word and you found yourself out on the street. That was landlords for you. But when you had one living at the top of the house – well, it wasn't playing the game. Landlords had no right to live in the same houses as their tenants. But poor people couldn't do much, could they? You couldn't do much against . . . THEM.

So it was that 'Katie Mulholland's houses' and power came into being.

CONTINUED IN VOLUME II